BY ANNA-MARIE McLEMORE

The Influencers

Flawless Girls

Venom & Vow

Self-Made Boys

Lakelore

The Mirror Season

Miss Meteor

Dark and Deepest Red

Blanca & Roja

Wild Beauty

When the Moon Was Ours

The Weight of Feathers

The
Influencers

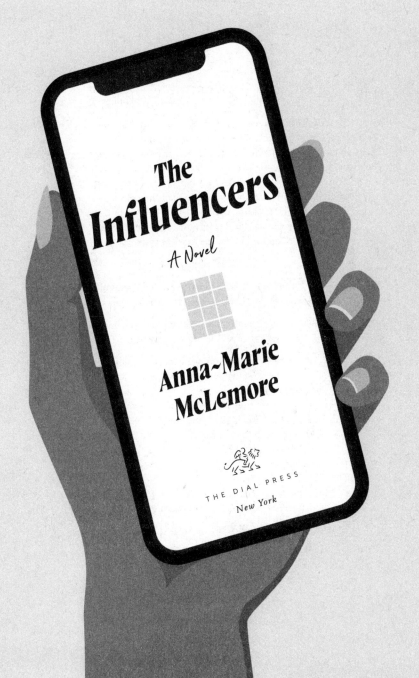

The Influencers

A Novel

Anna~Marie McLemore

THE DIAL PRESS

New York

Published in the United States by The Dial Press, an imprint of Random House, a division of Penguin Random House LLC, New York.

THE DIAL PRESS is a registered trademark and the colophon is a trademark of Penguin Random House LLC.

Library of Congress Cataloging-in-Publication Data
Names: McLemore, Anna-Marie, author.
Title: The influencers: a novel / Anna-Marie McLemore.
Description: First edition. | New York, NY: The Dial Press, 2025.
Identifiers: LCCN 2024045749 (print) | LCCN 2024045750 (ebook) |
ISBN 9780593729175 (hardcover) | ISBN 9780593729182 (ebook)
Subjects: LCGFT: Thrillers (Fiction) | Novels.
Classification: LCC PS3613.C57854 I54 2025 (print) |
LCC PS3613.C57854 (ebook) | DDC 813/.6—dc23/eng/20241004
LC record available at https://lccn.loc.gov/2024045749
LC ebook record available at https://lccn.loc.gov/2024045750

Printed in the United States of America on acid-free paper

randomhousebooks.com

1st Printing

First Edition

Book design by Debbie Glasserman

Art by AlexPhotoStock

To Cassie

Thank you for being one of my first friends
in a city where I knew no one.
We all miss you.

What an influencer is, is someone who's effectively monetized their identity. That is their work. The performance of
an attractive life.

—JIA TOLENTINO

If everything is possible, nothing is true.

—ROBERT L. FITZPATRICK

the week
after

THE FIRST 24 HOURS AFTER THE MURDER OF AUGUST INGRAHAM

we the followers of Mother May I

When the news first broke, everyone wondered: Who was May Iverson? And why did she look so familiar?

But we already knew her. We'd been watching her for years.

Mother May I's very first post had been almost twenty-five years ago, on a platform that didn't even exist anymore. She'd started with tricks for bad hair days, the fastest way to frost a cake, last-minute Halloween costumes, stunning table decor from things you probably already had around your house. May Iverson, the woman behind Mother May I, was a mom of three, and then four, and then five daughters (at the time of that first post, the eldest, April, was four, twins June and July had barely started walking, and January and March would be born over the next couple of years).

May Iverson was both maddeningly glamorous (how were her nails never chipped?) and relentlessly encouraging. She reminded us all that we were doing the best we could. She told any of us who needed to hear it, "You are a good mom. And all this is optional. Your kids' happiness doesn't depend on a wire-ribbon bow. This is all for fun. Remember, you're already a good mom." That became her reassuring catchphrase at the end of every video. *Remember, you are already a good mom.*

As her following grew, so did her ad revenue and her rate for sponsored content to show off a new planner or setting powder. Mother May I would tell us about the lipstick that stayed all day so a busy mom didn't have to reapply, as though she was sharing a secret with a friend. She'd detail the benefits of the meal-kit service that made her evenings "just so much more relaxing. This has turned my routine into a gourmet ritual." Until she was, increasingly, making her living by telling us how to live.

Cosmetic companies sent her KitchenAid stand mixers in the latest colors, ostensibly as birthday (and later, wedding shower) gifts, but more likely so she'd give their new bronzer a good review instead of saying that it skipped on application. Designers delivered free gowns and jewelry for fundraisers, hoping she'd show them off in front of the step and repeat. A fragrance line made a perfume bearing her name, pennies' worth of ester chemicals in a fancy bottle, surrounded in the ad by flowers and billowing fabric.

In two and a half decades, May Iverson had turned herself into a name that drew both sneers and aspirational sighs. She had turned her content into an empire, complete with makeup, swimsuit, and kitchenware collaborations. She had—thanks to the work of surgeons, aestheticians, coaches, and trainers—kept her fifty-three-year-old face and body looking so astonishingly young that no one could believe her eldest daughter was now twenty-nine.

A lot of us thought she'd changed in the past five, seven, maybe even ten years, and not in a good way. It didn't ring true anymore, her still giving tutorials on the flood-iced cookies she used to make for school bake sales. It wasn't just that her children were all adults, all in their twenties, long gone from the world of locker-room linoleum and PTA fundraisers. It was that the designer bag on her kitchen counter declared she could have just as easily bought immaculately frosted cookies, or made a donation.

She made stabbing tries at being relatable by talking about the puffiness under her eyes, and then showed off tricks with spoons chilled in the refrigerator, even though she could afford weekly facials and frequent microneedling. She relayed her favorite ways to mix and dilute essential oils, even though we all knew she had home fragrances blended especially for her by a famous parfumier in Lyon.

She said she never dieted—"it's more about being in harmony with your body, listening to your body, loving your body"—but then did sponsored posts for appetite-suppressing tea. The few times she cried genuinely on camera threw into harsh relief how different it looked from when she faked it, and how often she had. There was the time she complained about caterers not bringing out micro-batch cheeses early enough, so they didn't soften properly by the time her first guests arrived. Even those of us who still adored her cringed remembering her post about how so many designer boutiques didn't carry heels in a size as small as hers, that they had to special-order them. She said this shyly—"I'm not even short, I don't know how I ended up with such small feet"—though with a smile she couldn't quite contain, like a humble-bragging Cinderella.

But when it came down to it, she didn't need anyone's forgiveness for being fake. She knew what she was doing, and so did we. With every display of metallic-painted Halloween pumpkins, with every holiday ribbon adorning the banisters of her mansion, with every time she documented getting one of her daughters ready for a ballet recital, lipsticks and juice boxes spilled across her vanity, she was producing a specific version of herself. May Iverson was constructing Mother May I. And we watched because, whether we admitted it or not, we wanted to know how to do the same thing.

It wasn't so much that we all wanted to sew our children one-of-a-kind tutus, or make grocery lists so ornately decorated that they could have gone into scrapbooks. Sure, some of us did. But most of the time, it was far simpler than that.

Life requires artful lying. It just does. You have to tell your husband how much you loved catching up with his mother. On a bad morning, you put on a little extra blush to make yourself look less miserable than you are. You run into someone from the gym you haven't gone to in months and tell them you've switched to a 5 A.M. workout, that must be why you keep missing each other.

You get coffee with a friend you haven't seen since elementary school, suddenly realize you have nothing in common, that every minute together feels stilted without the mortar of jump ropes and sticker trading. But when both your cups are empty, you still have to say *We should do this again soon* or *Let's not let so much time pass next time.* And you hope she is lying just as much as you are, because if you have to do this again, you might need defibrillating levels of espresso or to snort lines of sucralose off the café table.

May Iverson was good at fake. She made fake look good. And whether we admitted it or not, we watched to learn. We wanted to learn how to lie and make it look that pretty.

June Iverson

*G*uess *he finally pissed off the wrong person.*

The words were almost out of June's mouth.

Then June read the room. Or rather, the only other person in it.

July sat on the edge of the distressed vegan leather sofa, almost crying but not crying, facing the TV but not really watching it anymore.

August was dead. And the neighbors were all sniffling on TV, pretending to be surprised. Were they fucking kidding? August had screwed a lot of people out of a lot of money, often with nothing but the twist of a contract clause. Former partners. Investors. Men who were basically loan sharks in Givenchy. What did he think was gonna happen? Seriously, white guys with eight-packs thought they could get away with anything.

But her poor mother. August had been the one making bad decisions, yet it was her mom's house that got torched. It would probably be five years and fifty thousand dollars in therapy before Mom realized this was a blessing in disguise. Whatever six-pack sorcery August had cast on her mother (Who had he been trying to fool? He'd never had an eight-pack in life or in death), it would take some concerted deprogramming to get her mom back to normal.

June decided right then that she and July would take their mom out of town. Tomorrow. That new spa in Sedona. Red rocks, turquoise pools, desert air purified by cactuses. If their poor mother was going to cry on a bathroom floor, it might as well be manganese Saltillo tile.

July was wrapping her arms around herself, palms on her goose-bumped elbows, as the sound and the light of the broadcast washed over her.

"If you're cold, put on a sweater," June said, and she knew as soon as she said it that she sounded like a bitch. So to make up for it she pulled a peacock-blue cardigan from July's sweater shelf and threw it at her.

Then June called their mother. No texts. Not right now. Nothing written down.

June was always the one calling their mother, putting the phone on speaker for both her and July. Even on the best day, July was tragically timid about bothering their mother, like she was an interruption as unwelcome as an underpaid sponsorship opportunity. Plus, July was constantly losing her phone under the five thousand pets that lived in this loft with them. The dogs flopped on it without noticing, and the cats curled up on it like it was a heating pad. Once, Buttons the rabbit had tried to chew on it but had quickly lost interest, luckily for both Buttons and the phone warranty.

Their mother didn't pick up.

June *could* have called her father. And it wasn't like there weren't situations in which she would've. If the condo HOA was adding a dado rail to the hallways—very, very loudly—her father would have said *Come work over here, I'll give you the living room to yourself* before June even finished explaining the background noise. If you needed someone to pet-sit two dogs who despised each other, that was the time to call Ernesto Iniesta; by the time you came back from vacation, the surly canines would be making flower crowns together. Her father was like a skinny, Levis-wearing Mexican Santa Claus. You called

Mexican Santa Claus when you needed help with your Christmas lights. You didn't call Mexican Santa Claus about murder.

So June tried April. This was better anyway. It was a smarter first call. Their older sister usually knew what to do even before their mother did. When she needed to be, April was a snake—efficient, cold-blooded, and chic.

But April didn't pick up either. Her cell went to voicemail so fast it must have been off. Then her office line went to voicemail so fast that either it was busy or she'd disconnected it.

By then June was frustrated enough to try January. Her little sister wouldn't have been her first choice, because January wasn't really what you'd call good in a crisis unless it had to do with an electrical short or a jammed fire extinguisher.

June stayed on the line as it rang anyway, mouthing *pick up, pick up, pick up*. At least if she got to January, she could get January to call April, or, if April's phones really were off, email her. April always answered January. April would have walked out of a contract meeting with an international hotel chain to answer January.

The call clicked over to voicemail. At the sound of her younger sister's recorded message, professional to the point of sounding robotic, June hurled the phone down. It hit the hand-tufted rug at the same moment June yelled "motherfucker!" loudly enough to echo out into the complex's tile–and–sod grass courtyard.

July startled. She raised her head with an expression so wounded she looked as though June had slapped her.

"Sorry," June said. "But you know how bad this is gonna get. We need a plan, all of us. We need to decide what we're doing about the publicity shitstorm that's about to hit us before Mom's entourage decides it for us."

June paced over the rug, practicing the breathing her energetic alignment coach had assigned her. Count four in, hold three at the top, seven out. Try not to hate her mother's incompetent team, who, just last year, had decided she should put her name on a foot massager that couldn't run off a standard outlet.

Her mother wasn't picking up, and where the hell was her mother anyway?

Her oldest sister wasn't picking up, because apparently April lived under a rock the size of her sit-stand desk and hadn't seen the news yet.

July was still swaying forward and backward on the edge of the sofa, so it didn't exactly look like she was in a headspace to strategize.

January was probably up on a scaffold adjusting some lights and ignoring her coworkers' whispers, because that was what June's little sister did; every time she had a feeling she didn't like, she bought a new crescent wrench. (Which June couldn't exactly judge, because that was how she herself ended up with a Lucite drawer tower full of vintage T-shirts.)

And it wasn't like they could call on the youngest Iverson, so that was everyone, at least everyone June could safely try right now.

Count four in, hold three at the top, seven out.

"Why don't we just go find them?" July asked.

June opened her eyes.

"January said something about tech week, so we know she's at work." July got up from the sofa. "April's doing quarterlies so she's offline but she's not leaving her desk. Let's just go find them and we'll keep trying Mom."

"If April's doing quarterlies she literally locks herself in her office with that stupid ambient noise machine," June said.

"No, she doesn't," July said. "She smashed it the last time Mom called her. Do you think we should get her a new one for her birthday?"

June felt disbelief and exasperation coalescing on her face into what was probably a very ugly, very fine-line-inducing expression. July wanted to discuss birthday presents? Now?

"Sorry," July said.

June pictured a field of pink and orange wildflowers until she could feel the muscles in her face easing.

"We wouldn't even have a way to get into April's building," June said.

"January does." July shrugged her purse strap onto her shoulder. She looked so small that June expected the strap to slip off, like there wasn't enough July to hold it up. "April gave her a key card and an access code. That's why we go get January first."

June snatched her keys off the reclaimed antique drawer pull mounted on the wall. "I knew there was a reason I keep you around."

we who were watching the Iversons

W e thought this would all be settled the day the news broke, that we'd have an easy consensus on whether any of the Iverson girls were capable of murder, and, if so, which of them was most likely to have done it.

But we didn't agree.

Within hours of the news leaking, some of us were saying it was January, the second youngest. Growing up, she'd been short and skinny and bird-boned, with skin as pale as her hair was dark, and she still was now, at age twenty-four. She was sometimes spotted in real life but practically didn't exist online, and hadn't since she'd turned eighteen and moved out of the Iverson mansion. She always was the strange one, the one who stuck out. Sure, she was nearly as pretty as her sisters, but she lacked some essential polish and glow. She lurked in the background of Mother May I's posts, like a feral cat who'd wandered in through a door absentmindedly left open. Her eyes were forever wide and serious, and whenever her mother coaxed her into smiling, she looked like a snarling animal.

To some of us, that snarl was a clear sign of something wrong with her. It hinted at a vicious streak held tight behind her teeth.

A lot us felt sorry for her, though. There was always a pleading look in her wide eyes. She was trying her desperate best to deliver the camera-worthy smile that came so naturally to her mother and older sisters, a smile that would not have to be clipped away during editing. There was a pitiable question in those rounded eyes. *Is this it, Mommy? Am I doing it?*

Some of us thought the murderer had to be April, the tall one seen in blazers and skirts that would have been boring if the blazers hadn't been bright—magenta, cobalt, lemon yellow—and the skirts in coordinating prints. Surely the oldest of the Iverson daughters was the only one with the nerve and will to do something as final as killing her stepfather.

But the rest of us stood ready to defend her. After all, there was something unrelentingly motherly about April Iverson, even back when she'd been a child herself. So often she had read to her younger sisters. She had woven ribbons into their braids. She had patiently attended their construction of cashew butter sandwiches, her face showing no resentment over the gleeful messes she would later have to clean up.

Even in childhood, she showed meticulous flair—adding an edging of decorative tape to her younger sisters' school binders—and as an adult, her business website didn't have a pixel out of place. Anyone who wrote to her through the contact form received an immediate confirmation thanking them for their inquiry, with tastefully embedded images in brand-coordinated colors.

If April Iverson, now twenty-nine, were to kill someone, she wouldn't do it so haphazardly that she had to burn down a nineteen-thousand-square-foot mansion to cover it up. The body would have been neatly buried in some national forest, so adeptly that no one would have ever found it. And if they had, they would have noticed how well she had placed it, the decomposing corpse nourishing ancient trees and fairy rings of wild mushrooms. They might have even appreciated the ecologically appropriate genus of wild violets she had planted over the gravesite.

There was a small but insistent contingent putting forth March, the youngest Iverson. We remembered March as the one who'd grown as fast as a dandelion, quickly surpassing one-year-older January before either was in kindergarten. March Iverson was as quiet as January, but in every other way her opposite. Where January had that unblinking stare, March blushed as easily as she smiled, a constellation of dimples dotting her cheeks. As a child, March had seemingly never met a set of overalls that she didn't like, which May Iverson first resisted—*Don't you want to try these pants? They have butterflies embroidered on them*—and then decided to find endearing: *You know what? If my child is willing to dress herself and get out the door on time, I don't care if she's wearing a clown costume.*

But March Iverson hadn't been seen online, or in real life, in years. When she turned eighteen, she fled both the spotlight and the known world. Now she was twenty-three, and probably living in Wyoming or Kansas, in some county where the population varied so little that they hand-painted it on the sign.

This was exactly why some of us suspected March. Could she have been waiting this entire time in shadow, reemerging to commit just such a shocking act? Could this have been her aim in disappearing all along?

Alluring as such conspiracy theories might have been, they didn't ring true for most of us. How could anyone look back at those old videos and think March Iverson was remotely capable of anything like this? All you had to do was look at her, how painfully shy she was, squirming and fidgeting under the camera's gaze in a way so sweet and disarming that you loved her even if she wouldn't meet your eye. If this wasn't evidence enough, all you had to do was look at the timeline. If March hadn't been seen in the same city or even state as the rest of the Iversons in the last five years, when would she and August have even crossed paths? August had entered the Iversons' lives only two years ago. March never had a chance to meet August Ingraham, let alone know him enough to hate him.

Among all the other conjectures was a bright confetti of theories that June had done it, or July, or—most delicious of all possibilities— both twins together, the two Iverson daughters who had become miniature versions of their mother.

Granted, only one of them had their mother's coloring; June was a California rock-song blond, with eyes that perpetually looked dreamy and slightly stoned. July, on the other hand, had dark hair and brown skin, and the whites of her eyes were as bright and sharp as winter. But the twins' contrasting beauty made them an indivisible set. Now, at age twenty-six, they had identical smiles—identical to each other's and to May's—and their mother's natural instinct for angling their faces toward a camera, talking from a script as though they were just thinking out loud, laughing in a way too polished to be real but plausible enough that if you wanted to believe it was genuine, you could.

Our first argument against June and/or July was a simple *why?* What did the two Iverson daughters who were famously close to their mother have to gain by killing their stepfather and torching the house?

Still, it was too poetic of a conjecture to give up entirely. After all, June and July made sense, in some thrilling and tragic way. They had been stars in their mother's content from infancy through adulthood. But since their mother had gotten remarried, the twins hadn't shown up as often in Mother May I's posts, so why wouldn't they resent the man sucking away their mother's time and attention?

Could July Iverson really kill someone, though? She had a notoriously soft heart, and so many pets—she couldn't turn down finding, or giving, a stray a home—that no one could tell for sure if she'd gotten another one three months ago. It was impossible to know if the fuzzy blur in the background of her posts was her puppy Meringue or yet another new member of what she called her fluff family.

June seemed more likely. She was ruthlessly protective of July. Everyone had seen Mother May I's post—almost twenty years ago now—about June pushing a school bully into the gravel, May Iverson's face reluctantly proud as she told the world the whole story. June could be just as fierce in the work of protecting her whole family, whether shoving an intrusive photographer (despite July begging her not to) or biting back against rude comments at a juice bar or a fundraising gala (despite July begging her not to).

Even among those of us who thought June had it in her to kill her stepfather, it wasn't as though we thought she had planned it out.

None of us put forth a scenario in which June charted out a murder, start to finish, alibi to cleanup.

But if her mother's new husband was pulling May Iverson away from her daughters, perhaps even insisting she spend less time with them, wasn't it possible that June might have gone over to the house, when she knew he'd be alone, to confront him? Couldn't a heated argument have resulted in her accidentally killing him? And wasn't June the most likely to make another horrible, spur-of-the-moment decision she would regret later: all the lighter fluid in the house and a thrown match?

Anyone could have killed him. Rivals. Spurned investors. Friends-turned-enemies.

But we had a feeling, right from the beginning, and this was the one thing most of us could agree on. It was probably one of the Iversons.

July Iverson

July looked over at her sister, then back at the road. "Do we know where we're going yet?"

"I'm still trying to figure out which theater." June had her feet up on the dashboard, the rest of her curled around the single focal point of the expanding universe: her phone. "Why doesn't she just post what she's doing like a normal person?"

Lacking direction from June, July kept driving straight, until June's hand flew out across the gear shift.

"What?" July startled, checking mirrors and blind spots. "What did I do?"

"Pull over," June said.

"I can't. I'm in the fast lane."

"Pull over," June said, pressing harder on the second word. "Pretend there's an ambulance coming up behind you." She took her feet off the dashboard. "You always pull over for them."

"Because it's the law," July said under her breath. But she put on her blinker and parked at a stretch of sidewalk in front of a new-construction apartment building. July was half-expecting some comment from June about how they'd really embraced the industrial-farmhouse-with-a-touch-of-glam look, and how they could, at least in part, thank their mother for that. *It's sweeping the city. What hath that woman wrought?*

Instead June shoved her phone in July's face.

There, on the screen, was their mom, at a press conference. The local news' chyron spanned the bottom of the screen. Their mother stood in a white suit, hair in a middle-parted low bun, expressing overwhelming sadness.

Whenever her mother was onscreen like this, July remembered that feeling of being a little kid, and her mother coming downstairs before a photoshoot or a brand anniversary dinner. She always looked so airbrushed, filtered, touched-up, that she seemed like someone July had never met. July and June would both watch in awe as she left, like they were watching a Barbie doll who'd come to life just in time for her 8 P.M. reservation.

The pieces of their mother were all there onscreen now. The gleaming blond of her hair. Her cheekbones highlighted with a surgeon's precision. The knife-sharp crease of her lapels. Not for the first time, July wondered what magic allowed her mother to look so perfectly feminine wearing tailored suits. Whenever July tried a similar outfit, she looked like she was unsuccessfully attempting drag.

But there was a shakiness around her mother now, like the porcelain of her skin might crack if she moved too suddenly.

All around her were fellow influencers. There was the one who'd had so many fillers and cheek implant updates she looked like a caricature drawing of herself. There was the one who called herself a prairie mom when she in fact lived on a sprawling ranch with two temperature-controlled wine cellars and a separate kitchen for her private chef. There was the redhead who pretended she didn't wear colored contacts. Each of them touched the squared-off shoulders of her mother's blazer as though they were at a healing ministry.

"Glad she's surrounded by loved ones during this difficult time." June threw down the phone. "The bitch can't even call us?" She kicked the dashboard, and the glove box rattled open. It had long ago broken after repeated smiting by June's pedicured feet.

June launched into a volley of swearing and increasingly profane insults, each tailored to and directed at their mother. To anyone else, she might have sounded enraged. But July knew her sister in a way that made her adore her, despise her, fear for her, vibrate with contempt with her, all depending on the day, the hour, and whether they were both about to get their periods.

Right now, July could feel June's hurt so much it was one set of fingers around both of their hearts. It clutched them so hard July couldn't even touch June, like it would complete a circuit and short them both out.

This was how June sounded when she was so hurt she couldn't stay still. The longer June swore, the closer she sounded to crying, and the closer she got to crying, the louder she screamed.

July felt the rattle of that scream in her own chest. That was the worst part of knowing June this well. June's screams weren't just her own. They got inside July and stayed like they'd been hers the whole time.

the guy in the sweatshirt

As soon as he saw the news about August, he thought of calling. Then he thought about how all of this had been a bad idea.

He'd known that from the beginning. It was a bad idea to get close to any Iverson, especially June and July, the two most famous Iverson daughters. That wasn't his biased opinion. It was objectively true. Their numbers backed it up.

He'd grown up watching the Iverson sisters, all of them. Which didn't especially distinguish him. A lot of people grew up watching the Iverson sisters. He liked being one among many. Being undistinguished. He liked watching, and he liked not being someone worth watching.

He wasn't even worth watching when he was right next to June and July. Even their friends couldn't remember his name. To them, he was mostly *the guy in the sweatshirt*, which he didn't even mind, even though *the sweatshirt* was their slightly disdainful code for the kind of outerwear so generic it could have been purchased anywhere from

Walmart to CVS. He was that generic on purpose, so indistinct as to be anonymous.

It was still a bad idea to get close to June and July Iverson, even anonymously. It was pretty much always a bad idea to go anywhere near the Iversons.

But he was still thinking about calling. He should call. Shouldn't he? Wasn't it weirder not to?

But which one of them?

As the eldest, April might have been the natural choice, the most respectful choice. But he was pretty sure April didn't like him very much.

Maybe June? June seemed the most likely to answer. Unless you were catching April on her office line, June was always the most likely to pick up the phone.

June also seemed the most likely to take offense if he didn't call her first. And he was just about to when her picture, the one she'd added to her contact in his phone, filled his screen. There she was, on a beach in a thin T-shirt and an aqua bikini, mouth wide open in a laugh that could have been fake but that looked real, as she played Frisbee with July's dogs. Her hair was the same color as the dunes, the wind blowing it everywhere.

For a minute, he was so confused by whether he'd actually dialed that he almost missed her picking up.

Before he could even say hello, June's decisive voice came through the line.

"Don't come over," she said.

"Okay," he said. "I won't. But what—"

"And stay inside," she went on. "If you need food, cold medicine, or a classic edition of Twister with which to entertain yourself, tell me, and I will have it delivered unto you."

"Who plays Twister by themselves?" he asked.

"I don't judge what you do when you're lonely," she said. "Just stay inside until we know more."

"June—"

The call cut out.

January Iverson

When January came down from the catwalk, the whole theater was quiet. No one was adjusting the metal flaps of barn doors. No one was slinging twofers around their necks.

Even the set designers were quiet. For two days, they'd been arguing about wall paint—*I told you not to use that weird-ass color with that weird-ass sofa*—almost without pausing for breath. And now, nothing.

Everyone was watching her. Were they really on the edge of their seats about her lighting suggestions?

"I was right," she said. "The cables can take the weight. I know it's a little unconventional, but if we lean heavy on the practicals, the audience will feel like they're in the house with the actors. We can up the luminosity, and as long as it's diffuse, it'll still seem realistic."

Now they looked at one another a little self-consciously. Something else was going on here. Had a board member visited unannounced? Was there a major donor watching from the sound booth?

"I think we should try it," Rae said. "Keep an open mind until we see how it washes onstage."

"Yeah," Kris chimed in. "If it doesn't work, we adjust it. We're gonna change the paint color anyway, right, Georgie?" He nodded at one of the set designers.

Everyone chuckled. Even Georgie. That was the weirdest part about it, that chuckle. It was high-pitched and tentative, forced instead of brutal, the way he laughed when he screwed with the other set designers during level checks.

What was going on here? These were the guys who had been ruthless about January's former life as one of Mother May I's daughters. These were the guys who, when she'd cussed out and then fired an intern for grabbing his crotch at one of the actors, had put Luna bars in her bag because *These help with PMS, right?* Even Rae, the one other woman who consistently worked lighting in this theater, had never exactly been nice to January. She gave January the same speech she gave everyone else. *You're entitled to your opinion. You're entitled to express your opinion. I'm entitled to express that your opinion is shit.*

The theater doors burst open as though someone had kicked them.

June rushed up the aisle. "Excuse me, coming through," she said, even though no one was in the aisle except July, scampering behind her.

"Perfect," January said under her breath. "Just perfect."

Having one of your gorgeous sisters barge into your place of work was horrifying enough. Two made January want to hide in the catwalk until her bones decomposed.

"So sorry." June's heels clicked on the steps up to the stage. "We just need to borrow our little sis for a minute." She grabbed January's arm.

"June," January whispered. "What have we discussed about boundaries?"

"Is she doing acting now?" June whispered in turn to July. "Because she sounds exactly like April."

July pressed her lips together, apologetic. Why did July always take on the burden of June's bad behavior? Secondhand embarrassment was going to actually kill July one day. January wondered if it would show up on July's autopsy.

Or if death by firsthand embarrassment would show up on January's. Any second, the men would throw out flaccid jokes like *Hey, you two think we just let anyone in here?* in the hope of getting June and July, and June's ass specifically, to stick around.

But the men were still quiet.

January waited for Rae's *I'm sorry, who exactly do you two think you are? We're working here.*

But Rae said, "Why don't we all take a break?"

Mumbles of *Good idea* and *Yeah, I'm hungry* and *Did they fix the soda machine?* fuzzed the air in the theater.

The stage cleared.

January's confusion knocked her guard down just enough for June to tug on her arm. Then she was leading both January and July into the crossover backstage.

"I take it you haven't heard," June said.

"Heard what?" January asked.

June looked at July. "You take this."

"Take this?" July blinked four or five times. "What do you mean take this?"

"What the hell are you two talking about?" January asked.

"June, this isn't a press conference," July said. "You can't just tell me to *take this.*"

"Well, I'm a little busy calling April for the millionth time." June shook her phone in July's face.

"Jules." January put her hands on July's shoulders. "What is going on?"

July's doleful eyes bounced between the floor and January's face.

"Jules?" January tried again.

But something had really shut July down this time.

June let out something between a grunt, a groan, and a scream of frustration, the kind of sound that usually came right before she smashed her phone into a wall. But the anger management must have been working, because then she just huffed for a few breaths.

Still huffing, June looked from the phone to July through her messed-up hair. "Where the fuck is she?"

July looked up at January. "Do you still have April's key card?"

we who were watching the Iversons

Any of us who followed the Iversons knew that August Ingraham hadn't always been August Ingraham. Born and christened Augustus, he was, prior to meeting May two years ago, reportedly known to his friends and family as Gus, though May swore he was always August, that his own mother called him August (August would dutifully agree, and his mother was no longer alive to confirm or refute). We all accepted that his place in the Mother May I brand was a little fabricated, right down to making sure he had a month name.

Neither truly hated nor particularly liked, he mostly seemed useless, and an occasional drag on May. Where she was careful with her image, he threw his around, and seemed to enjoy it, like he was playing catch with a Fabergé egg.

He was once caught on video cursing out a parking attendant for not putting the seat back where it was—"I showed you the presets, didn't I?" (As the argument escalated, it came to light that he had, in fact, shown the presets to a different parking attendant, thus proving himself unable to tell Latina women apart despite being stepfather to so many of them.)

Even after proposing to May Iverson, he came on to women by telling them about his meat-only fasts. Whenever anyone caught it on film, he said he was only spreading the word, trying to tell everyone that if we all ate like we did when we were Cro-Magnons, the world's ills would be solved. (Who could forget June's quip following one of his carnivorous sermons at a family picnic? "Well, the Cro-Magnon diet makes complete sense for you. You still are one.")

He once threatened a bouncer's job over not being on the list at a new bar-lounge. "Don't you know who I am?" "No," the bouncer had said, "I don't know who you are. I just know who you're married to." August might have punched the guy out if the man hadn't had a few inches and forty pounds of muscle on him, and if half a dozen people in line didn't already have their phones out, recording.

There were the occasional redeeming qualities. He goaded his friends into beach cleanups: "Come on, man, get off your Peloton and show our oceans a little love." He always mentioned it would offer them a good photo op, which he knew was what would get them there, at least the ones trying to build their platforms.

In Grandma Iverson's last days, August seemed to visit her more often than May did, and almost as much as April did. He brought her flowers and called her "my best girl" in a way that made the old woman bat a demure hand: "Oh, stop it, you're too much."

Every time July found another stray, August was the one she could go to. Never an eye roll or a scoffed *Really? Again?* He would just pet the dog's ears and say, "Who's this guy? Where'd you come from?" (Rumor had it he was like this even when no cameras were rolling.) Whenever July showed up, beside herself over an abandoned kitten or a traumatized pit bull mix, August would pose with them in a post, with some caption like *Meet your new best friend* or *Don't you want to give this princess her forever home?* The sight of the spray-tanned figure, swollen with muscles, flashing a bleached-white smile, holding the sleepy or purring animal, meant they were always adopted fast.

None of this made it clear who might want to kill him. Authorities were less than forthcoming, so those first twenty-four hours consisted mostly of looped interviews with neighbors. They told reporters about smelling ash and wondering if it was a wildfire from the hillsides below, seeing smoke but not flames (or both, depending on which neighbor they asked), hearing the array of emergency vehicles rushing toward the Iverson house, and realizing this was not a natural disaster but an untimely death.

An old woman shook her head in pity; the poor couple hadn't even been married a year, and now that girl (the old woman was old enough to call a fifty-three-year-old mother of five a "girl") was a widow. A forty-something man in a golf shirt said the HOA was meeting imminently to discuss neighborhood safety. A woman who looked like she was dressing up as May Iverson for Halloween, right down to the nail shape, said that yeah it was sad but what did anyone expect would happen when you put everything online and there were so many crazies out there?

Another old woman—the chyron identified her as the first old woman's roommate—said she didn't think it was a burglary but also wondered how they would even know, what with the fire. And she had a point. How *would* they know? Seventeen-thousand-dollar purses (was it up to twenty thousand dollars now?) lined a wall of May's second dressing room (or was it the third dressing room?), and how would anyone know if they were all ashes or if the killer had made off with a few on each arm?

That said, we knew enough from the neighbors to deduce that a burglary gone wrong seemed unlikely. August's body and the fire were on opposite sides of the house, so chances were low that he had walked in on someone trying to crack a safe. This was personal, clearly. And that was what was so perplexing about it. August Ingraham just didn't seem effectual enough to warrant that kind of effort.

Yes, there were rumors of disputes with partners and investors in a pH-balancing, lean-muscle-optimizing protein powder business (In-FITnitum, or, as June called it, "a name no one can pronounce for a thing no one needs"). There was even talk of arguments with the fitness celebrities hired to endorse it. But supposedly all that had been settled out of court months ago.

For the most part, August seemed like a kept husband who wanted to be a famous personal trainer, and then just wanted to look like a famous personal trainer (he never did get around to completing the certification). He was the testosterone-fueled counterweight to the sparkling-rosé-fizzy, lip-glossed world of the Iversons. And he seemed to like that, being the center of masculinity in their frilled, feminine lives.

At least that was what it looked like.

April Iverson

Finishing quarterly reports required absolute focus. No pinging of emails. No ringing of phones. No chirping of texts. April turned to the task only when the office was empty, the quiet so delicious that she almost dreaded finishing. Finishing meant turning everything back on.

Her reentry into connectivity was swift and rude. She had barely plugged her office landline back in when the name of a familiar law firm flashed across the display.

She was done. She had made it abundantly clear that the law offices of Asshat, Gabacho & Dipstick needed to call April's lawyer, not April. She had given fair warning. Clearly August Ingraham's lawyer wanted billable hours so badly he was willing to get his head ripped off in six-minute increments.

"Listen, you exasperating little toad," she said as soon as she picked up. "You tell August, and you tell him right to his uncomprehending face, not in one of your letterheaded emails that he probably doesn't read anyway, that I am not signing."

"Ms. Iverson, I think we can both agree that—"

"I think we can both agree"—she cut him off—"that my answer hasn't changed in the past ten months."

April distantly registered someone yelling somewhere in the building, or maybe in the parking lot. She thought someone might have even been calling her name, but then she was pretty sure it was the ringing in her ears.

And the growing probability of a lawyer-induced headache.

The man tried again. "Under the circumstances—"

"I'm not signing," April said. "Not now. Not if the angel Gabriel himself descends to say he's incorporating InFITnitum supplements into his fitness routine. Not ever. And I am doing you and August's worthless asses a favor by telling you this myself because when my lawyer expresses her anger, I assure you, she's much less pleasant than I am."

Just then, June burst into April's office, grabbed the phone out of her hand, and slammed it down.

April breathed out. June had always had a theatrical streak to her. The stronger April's reaction, the more gratifying June would find this intrusion. Put up a boundary, and June saw a welcome mat.

"Now what did you do that for?" April asked, as calmly as she had in her. "I was starting to enjoy myself. And why do you have an access card? I revoked yours, didn't I?"

June was flushed, her hairline sweaty. She was out of breath like she'd been sprinting.

July and January filed into the office behind June. That explained it. June had weaseled January's card out of her.

April surveyed their faces, trying to gauge what was going on by who seemed most upset. If it was June, it meant she'd posted something offensive, again, and wanted to run an apology past April. If it was January, it was the sexist assholes at work, again. If it was July, she wanted to know, again, if anyone at April's office was in the market to adopt a puppy or a turtle or a ferret.

But they all looked equally apprehensive.

And they almost never showed up at April's office at the same time.

"What's wrong?" April could practically feel her cortisol levels rising. "What happened?"

June crossed her arms and looked at the other two. "Which one of you wants to do the honors?"

When January told her, April felt nothing. Not because she had no feelings about the words January was speaking. More like everything she felt was a meteor hurtling toward a planet, and she was raising a polite finger, asking, *Could you hold off on making impact for just one second?*

All three of them were looking at her, like they were waiting for her to tell them what to do.

"Ground rules," April said. "Whatever questions you want us to ask each other, don't, okay?"

"Why not?" June asked. "Obviously none of us—"

"Stop." April cut June off. "Just stop. Trust me on this."

April knew her sisters. She'd half-raised them. She could almost hear the words behind their facial expressions. They wanted to spill everything out in the space between them, like when they mixed up their Lego sets and had to sort out who had what pieces. They wanted to know everything, and to be known.

"The police will talk to every one of us, and if we start talking to each other, we're not just witnesses," April said, pausing to meet each of their eyes, "we're witnesses against each other."

TWO DAYS AFTER THE MURDER OF AUGUST INGRAHAM

May Iverson

"**I** wish we didn't have to ask you this question," the older detective said.

His tone was so cautious that May instantly guessed two things.

First, he probably worried that she was as fragile as the day before. She cringed thinking of it now, how she'd been an utterly useless witness, so distraught that they could barely understand her or get her to understand them.

Second, she knew what question was coming next.

"Can anyone verify where in the house you were at the time?" he asked.

If there was ever a moment to transform into Mother May I, this was it. This—more than any speech, any brand meeting, any photo-shoot—was when May most needed to become that magnetic, smiling version of herself. She could use all the magnetism, all the likability she could get. Because no one could verify what they were really asking—whether or not she had killed him.

The detectives had come to her hotel. Linen-clean light flooded the suite, and the afternoon glittered off the distant ocean. This was a setting made for Mother May I, and yet May could not summon her.

"No," May said. "I was alone."

"No one else at the house saw you?"

"I didn't think anyone else was home," she said.

The detectives glanced at each other.

"Forgive my crassness," the older detective said. "But you manage a residence of that size without staff?"

"I do have people who come in to clean and to maintain the landscaping," she said. "But I don't really have full-time help at the house anymore."

They looked like they were trying to phrase a question delicately, probably some version of *Has there been a recent change in your finances?*

She decided to spare them the discomfort of asking.

"Lately I've wanted to embrace minimalism further," she said. "It's my decor aesthetic, and I've wanted it to become more of a lifestyle."

"So you thought you were alone in the house," the younger detective said.

"I didn't even know August was home," May said. "He had a meeting that he thought would go late. I always like to look"—she swallowed and recovered—"liked to look nice for him when he came home. But I thought I had a while until he got back, plenty of time to shower and wash my hair. So I was in my fitness studio practicing my Gyrokinesis exercises. I had no idea he was home until I saw his bag in the front hall."

Despite being three pounds under her goal weight, May felt leaden, her heart dragging her down toward the floor. She almost didn't care what the detectives thought of her. They couldn't think anything worse about her than she already thought about herself.

May had been in the house when her husband was murdered and she hadn't even noticed, and this somehow sounded even worse than her killing him.

"I believe you're already aware we couldn't find any security footage for the timeframe of the murder," the younger detective said. "Did you know your security system wasn't logging the camera feeds?"

May instinctively shook her head. "I'm sorry, you'll really have to ask my . . ." She felt her mouth forming the word *husband* but caught herself. Why did she keep doing that? Why would her brain not process the very thing that was taking up the whole of her thoughts? She felt the shaking of her head morph from an apology into a whirl of pain, embarrassment, grief, so thick it was sucking her down.

When she looked up, the detectives' expressions were so sympathetic that she felt instantly irritated. She wanted to spring to her feet and say, *Do you get paid to look at me like that or do you get paid to go find who killed my husband?*

May reset her posture, sitting up straighter. "Try asking Junie about it. She knows more than I do. Junie had a lot of opinions about the security system." May felt herself smile. She heard herself laugh lightly. "Junie has a lot of opinions about everything."

The hotel's signature scent, dispersed by diffusing rods in glass bottles of oil, filled the suite. She let the scent calm her as the detectives asked her about any potential enemies—none that she was aware of; about August's relationship with his living relatives—distant but not contentious as far as she knew; and about any recent out-of-the-ordinary behavior on the part of her husband—nothing she'd noticed.

The suite was thoughtfully decorated, with velvet couches in retro green, black-and-white rugs, flocked bedspreads. Louder than she would have chosen, but she could still appreciate the artistry; loud always made for a good backdrop.

Yet all she wanted was to get back into her home, with what was left of her things, the last place August had been alive. To the police, it was a crime scene, but to her, it was where she and August had been married less than a year. Their newlywed energy had infused the whole house, from the whites of the pillows to the curtains as bright as bridal veils. Even their fights had the frisson of young love, the kind she'd never had with Ernesto even when they both were young. Ernesto was a good man and a good father, but everything with him had been so calm and steady and reasonable that May had started to wonder if the thrill chronicled in love songs was some collective fiction.

"We know you're compiling a list for your insurance," the older detective said. "But is there anything in particular that you think someone might have been targeting?"

Where to begin? The largest wall of her largest dressing room had floor-to-ceiling shelves of designer bags, and the collection had over-flowed into her main closet. That was half a million dollars right there. Her best jewelry was valued at more than that, but it had all been in the safe, so hopefully that confirmed that this wasn't some premedi-tated insurance-fraud scheme. If this had been about collecting money, wouldn't she have claimed her canary diamond had gone missing? And if this had been about money, wouldn't she have taken out a life insurance policy on August? She hadn't. What would the point have been? He didn't make anything.

He just made her happy.

The memory of the smoke smell, so bitter and thick in the air she could taste it on her tongue, snapped her back to the question.

"My phone's gone," she said. "Have they found any evidence of it? In the fire?"

"Not that we know of," the younger detective said.

The pit in her stomach lurched open wider. "I won't pretend I don't have parts of my life I keep private."

From the look on the detectives' faces, they must have assumed this was a euphemism for nudes/seminudes she'd sent August.

She didn't correct them. They weren't wrong.

"We know this is going to be a painful question," the younger de-tective said.

Which ones weren't?

"Do you know where your daughter March is?"

The question landed, and she felt instantly nauseated. She hadn't eaten, hadn't felt hungry, but now her stomach buckled.

She'd expected the detectives to push her harder, like they were obligated to, about whether she might have killed August. She'd thought they were sizing her up. She was shorter and smaller, they might have decided, but her toned arms probably suggested she could have overpowered him if she'd had the element of surprise.

But March? Why were they asking about her?

"No," May said, keeping her voice crisp, tearless. "We don't have contact."

There. She'd gotten through it.

"Why?" she heard herself asking. "Do you know where she is?"

They looked so disappointed when they told her no that she believed them.

They moved on quickly to the topic of when she might return to her home, as though this would distract her from the thought of the one daughter who hadn't bothered to call. Even April had come by, with fresh fruit, overnight oats, and mother-y insistence that May *for God's sake, eat something.*

At this moment, there were more people at her house than there were before a catered party. The forensics team. Insurance adjusters. Contractors working out estimates. As soon as the police and the insurance company gave the go-ahead, she could move back in. That was the beauty of having a house so spacious: one wing could be damaged by fire and reeking of smoke, and she could still live in another without even smelling the ash.

She had to keep thinking about that, about which guest suite she'd move into during the repairs, about which ones she and August had had the best sex in. She had to keep thinking about the good parts of living in nineteen thousand square feet. If she didn't, she'd keep thinking of how nineteen thousand square feet meant you could be home when your husband was murdered and hear nothing.

we the followers of the Summer Girls

August Ingraham's body wasn't even cold before the online speculation produced its first ridiculous rumor. It infested a thousand threads, as though every hater of June Iverson now felt empowered to chime in.

The idea that June had been sleeping with August Ingraham was so predictably sordid that we wondered whether a rival had started it. Or a possible suspect. Maybe whoever had actually killed August wanted the police looking the other way, at the blondest, most radiant of the Iverson daughters.

We knew better. But in order to properly refute the rumors about June, we needed everyone to understand a few basic things about her. The work of such education fell to us, because we were the ones who really knew June Iverson, and everyone else was just tuning in.

The first lesson of June Iverson 101 was that, no matter how many people wanted it to be true, the Iverson twins were not identical. This was a great letdown to many who knew nothing about the Iversons but were now scouring the news of August's murder. They were disappointed to have to rule out theories about a plot carried out by one of two identical twenty-six-year-olds: one setting the house ablaze, counting on being mistaken for the other. Differences in appearance, style, temperament, even their gaits, meant June and July were unlikely to be mistaken for each other, in daylight or in the dark.

What they had in common was that they'd both followed their mother into the world of making money off polishing and posting their daily lives. June and July each had their own personal brands, their own posts. But anyone who knew them probably knew them best through their shared content, always under the name the Summer Girls. It was a syrup-sweet play on how their mother used to call them *my summer daughters*.

June Iverson, older than July by less than an hour, was the kind of girl who tried anything once—rock climbing, kayaking, white widow—but rarely more than once. When she went out, she wore heels; otherwise, she was barefoot, the soles of her feet graying alongside the rose-salt pink of her pedicure. She tossed her head, and the flip of her hair caught the sun like it was going to keep it.

She was an aficionado of makeup that looked like she wasn't wearing makeup, except for her extensive collection of lip glosses (first a mix of brands, then only the ones that gave her collaborations with her name in rose-gold lettering). She posed more than she lived, but she was even better at making it look offhand than her mother. Maybe because she wasn't afraid to be ugly sometimes. She filmed even with the mess of her bedroom in the background—laundry piled up on the threshold of the walk-in closet, bags of new clothes rustling together alongside the bed, a box of tampons spilling onto the nightstand, one of which July's newest kitten had ripped open. June posted without covering the occasional acne flare-up, the spots adorning her temple so gracefully it almost made her more beautiful. She chugged a can of Diet Sprite, burped loudly, and then laughed even as July rolled her eyes and walked out of frame with a prolonged *ewwwwww*.

And maybe it was June Iverson's shamelessness that made people shameless in what they said about her.

But nothing about August Ingraham suggested that June would

have been interested. All you had to do was survey her dating history. There was no particular pattern regarding height, weight, or race, but taken all together, there was a string of beautiful young women interspersed with a few beautiful young men. The girls posed in pleather skirts and cap-toe heels. The boys inclined their delicate faces to the camera, holding the lapels of their patterned blazers.

August Ingraham would have stuck out among them. For one, his hair was as blond as the sand he'd had trucked in to make a beach at one end of the family pool. June had never gone for a blonde. Almost exclusively brunettes, with an occasional redhead. And that one nonbinary model who could have been considered strawberry blond. (A later picture of them indoors showed their hair as solidly auburn. The strawberry blond had been a trick of camera sun flare.)

June just didn't seem to care for blondes, despite being one. Her naturally dark-blond hair had been so expertly bleached and dyed that it was easy to forget she hadn't been born with that curtain of honeycomb tumbling down her back.

For anyone who needed further convincing, we had additional evidence. August Ingraham was hulking in a way none of June's dates had ever been. Alongside the willowy ones, June had dated glamorous fat girls—one with dyed-black hair, pin-straight; another who always wore ice-blue eyeshadow—and cuddly-looking husky boys with well-groomed eyebrows—one who looked like he was wearing false eyelashes; another who took his cat out on walks with him, the orange tabby perched on the shoulder of his tailored jacket.

When June dated someone big, they were curvy, heavy, fat. Not the kind of big that August Ingraham was. He was the kind of sharply muscled that he claimed was from dead lifts and a scientific attention to amino acids. June had never shown evidence of liking that kind of bulk. She was on record making fun of men who admired their own bodies "like they think they just saw the image of the Virgin Mary in their abs." She'd skewered August's shirtless promotional shoots for InFITnitum, "which," she'd said with perfectly calibrated disdain, "is obviously a pyramid scheme, and not even a very good one."

(She later deleted posts containing anything disparaging about In-FITnitum, which effectively meant anything she'd ever posted about the company. This was likely at her mother's request, urging, pleading, or demand. Or possibly due to August's threat to sue. Which was good, because that meant the posts had been deleted long before the murder; if they'd still been up, they might have raised a few investigative eyebrows.)

And we weren't even done. We were prepared to squash this rumor all the way into the ground. Because if all this wasn't enough to disprove it, August Ingraham was a smirker. He emitted the shining glare of weaponized charm, as though it was best to give him what he wanted while he was still doing you the courtesy of asking for it. June had never been seen with a smirker. She dated professional smilers, but there wasn't a smirker to be found among her past romances.

That smirk was one of many reasons we were surprised that May had kept August Ingraham around as long as she had. The first time he appeared next to her—sweat perpetually glossing his booth tan, his heavy arm slung across her pale coral sweater, his voice twice the volume of May's so that he seemed to be yelling even when he was happy—it seemed unlikely to last. We assumed it wouldn't be long before the breakup and a new man, maybe some independent film actor.

Then came the engagement, which we thought would end in May facing the camera in tears, wearing a mascara that wouldn't run and that she'd list under the post, along with affiliate links.

Then came the wedding, with so many rare orchids the space looked covered in poured cream.

Then we thought it would end in a swift, quiet divorce, a request for privacy at this time.

It never came. But that had nothing to do with June. It was proof of May Iverson's questionable judgment. How could anyone lay that at the feet of her daughter?

June Iverson

"I didn't object to his existence or anything," June told the detectives. "I just didn't think he was right for my mom." There was no point in lying. Everyone knew she couldn't stand August. No reason to sniffle and break out the embroidered handkerchiefs for the benefit of the city's finest. "You have women in your life you think the world of, right? No one's ever gonna be good enough for them."

The morning light through the loft windows shone on the men's faces, and June could tell that she had them. Their sympathetic smiles were laced with a touch of distant anger, as though they were thinking of the very assholes who'd dated their sisters and nieces.

"I'm the same way with July," June said. "There've been plenty of people who want to be her friends or date her or just use her, and I can't help telling her what I think. My mom and my sister, they're my whole world."

June didn't even need to try to make herself sound sincere. She was sincere.

What June was doing was exactly the opposite of what any lawyer would have told her to do. She was just chatting, volunteering all sorts of information. But wasn't being friendly and open a sign that she had nothing to hide?

"Is there anyone who can confirm where you were at the time of the murder?" the older detective asked when they came to the inevitable *Where were you?*

"Of course," June said. "My sister."

"Which one?"

"Sorry. Whenever I say my sister, I usually mean July. We were trying out some samples for a body lotion collaboration."

Why were the detectives taking so many notes? Were they going to call the company to verify? Because they could. The shareholders were probably already counting their money from the impending bump in Iverson publicity.

"When did you last live at your mother's residence?" the older detective asked.

"July and I moved out two years ago," June said.

"And you were the last of your sisters still living there?"

June nodded. "The little ones were both out practically the day they each turned eighteen." June and July should have stayed forever. Within months of them leaving, August had moved in. If June had been there, she could have scared him off.

"Can I ask you something?" the younger detective said.

Wow, a police interview in which a detective was requesting permission to pose a question. The sample bikini June was wearing must have been working its magic.

"Of course," she said, sweet as the agua de frambuesa they were sipping.

"Why didn't anyone in your family report your sister March missing?"

June felt her own temperature rising. Why were they asking that? Were they implying that the whole family didn't care? Was this supposed to make them all look heartless enough to kill someone?

Or were they saying something else? Were they implying that there was some kind of falling-out, a possible motive? Were they looking for an easy suspect? Were they trying to pin this on the un-seen Iverson?

June took a long breath to cool herself down.

"I think when people want to be left alone, we should leave them alone," she said.

She could see the perplexed expressions coming before they fully bloomed across the detectives' faces.

"That probably sounds weird coming from me," June said. "But I choose to put everything out there. It's mine and July's art form, same as our mom. But not all of us are cut out for it. If I wanted some pri-vacy, do you think I'd want my whole family putting out an APB on me? Shouldn't we all just get to live our lives?"

"I'm sorry if we upset you," the older detective said.

"I'm not upset," June said, and she thought she did a pretty good job of sounding like she meant it. "You're just doing your jobs. I un-derstand."

More notes.

"It appears that a number of your mother's smoke alarms were disabled," the younger detective told her. "Do you know why that might have been?"

June leaned back in her chair. "She covered for him, didn't she?"

They looked at her. Neither was taking notes.

"It's kind of sweet if you think about it," June said. "Well, it would be sweet if she were covering for someone who deserved it. Heaven forbid anyone think ill of August Ingraham." June crossed her arms and then crossed one leg over the other. "August had a habit of show-ing off by inviting all his friends over for Cohibas, and he didn't want the alarms alerting May and the neighbors. If my mother tries to take the blame and tell you it was her mistake, that she did it so she could sage her workspaces to her heart's content, don't listen to her. She's protecting him even in death."

The younger detective had a look like he found her honesty re-freshing.

"How many other people would have known that?" he asked.

"His business friends with the Cohibas, for one," June said.

"What can you tell us about your mother's security system?" the older detective asked.

Rage bubbled up in June. Not at the man asking the question. At the man who'd been living in her mother's house.

"What do you want to know?" June asked.

"When did your mother make the decision to remove the interior cameras?"

"There never were interior cameras."

"Why was that?"

"Think about it," June said. "One stolen clip of Mother May I fucking a date on the kitchen island, she could kiss any family-friendly sponsorships goodbye. It's not fair, but such is the slut-shaming world we inhabit. Plus if anyone got ahold of broad interior footage, it would have been a showcase for everything worth stealing, and a blueprint of how to get in."

"What about the exterior cameras?"

"There were never a lot of them," June said. "My mom won't even sit by the pool without doing her eyebrows first. She didn't want anything recording her when she wasn't camera-ready. But there were some on the outside of the house, the garages, the pool gate, the grounds."

"Are you aware that there's no footage covering the time of the murder?" the older detective asked.

"What a shock." June immediately regretted her tone. When police were involved, sarcasm was never a flattering look.

"So this doesn't surprise you."

"Not at all," June said. "And you can thank him for that."

The detectives waited for her to say more.

"August fired the security company," June said. "He was absolutely convinced he could do a better job of running it all himself, because *Why pay them when I'm here?*" June heard her own overacted impression of August's voice. Maybe that was a little much. "Ironic, isn't it?"

"How so?" the younger detective asked.

"He thought he had it handled," June said. "Look how that went for him."

we the followers of the Summer Girls

June Iverson's indolent blond beauty took up the foreground of the Summer Girls' content. So if you weren't paying attention, you could almost miss the quietly but hauntingly beautiful girl in the background.

A style feature once said that if you took a young Elizabeth Taylor and made her Latina—brown eyes instead of purple, medium-tan skin instead of that poured-cream porcelain—and added thirty-five to forty pounds, you'd get July Iverson. As a child, she'd been thinner, like April was. Her knees were as bony as March's, her elbows as sharp as January's. Her skin had a natural blotchiness—acne scarring? Rosacea? None of us knew for sure, but under the right foundation, applied by her mother before family photos, it seemed like a flush brought on by exercise. Without concealer, the violet under her eyes made her look perpetually tired.

As she grew up, she gained weight, her breasts and hips showing up, finally, in her early twenties. She began wearing staggering amounts of makeup. But the more practice she got, the less obvious it looked, so that none of us saw anything but the pop of green eyeshadow, the black or brown-black liquid eyeliner, the perfectly chosen red lipstick.

To some, July looked like the more intimidating twin. While June's wardrobe shared a palette with early Wes Anderson, July's closet was overwhelmingly shades of black, brown, and very dark jewel tones. She had that silver-screen stare found in old photos, the just-off-camera gaze of the Golden Age Hollywood starlet, as though whoever's looking directly at her isn't interesting enough for her to look back. Past age twenty-two, we never saw July without that full face of makeup, even if she was just throwing on jeans and her favorite peplum jacket.

If you didn't know her, it would have been easy to assume that her quiet was a sign of unfriendliness, even a forbidding air she intended to give off. But it was closer to shyness. Maybe she'd been born reticent. Or maybe this pulling into herself was what happened if your other half was someone like June Iverson, someone who seemed to fill up half the world, not just half of yours.

The truth was that July Iverson was a lot nicer than she looked. A little too nice sometimes. She would stand, startle-eyed, as canvassers talked for minutes straight about the cause detailed on their clipboards. She just nodded and listened because she didn't know how to get out of the conversation without hurting anyone's feelings. If a fan stopped her in a supermarket, she was too polite to nod in acknowledgment and then keep walking. So unless June was there to intercede, July could be stuck in the produce section for half an hour listening to someone talk about how they'd love to do what she does and could she just take a look at this and see what she thinks.

July Iverson lived with the dubious blessing of having become stunning only when she got older. And because it had happened late, she moved through the world attracting other people's attention, but without the sense of privilege and bravado to tell them to fuck off. She just wasn't as fearless or volatile or impulsive as June.

Except once. And unfortunately, it had been recorded.

It was the video of July that we hoped detectives would never see. It went back seven years, to when June and July were in college, and if you didn't know July like we did, you might assume things about her that we knew weren't true.

If anything will alert future archaeologists to our society's primitive nature, it will be panty raids. And if future archeologists were to uncover what exactly happened in July Iverson's dorm during her sophomore year finals week, they'd find that the men therein were not only unevolved but lazy. Instead of the customarily disgusting tradition of taking one pair of underwear from each girl's dresser, they blew through the corridor, grabbing entire handfuls from every girl's room. They tossed them out windows, where they rained down on the quad, festooning the heritage trees.

In the video, July was still, her mouth paused open. She was wearing one of her typical uniforms. Pink-brown lipstick she'd later change out for fuchsia and then red and then plum and then burgundy. What was, at the time, her favorite pleather jacket, deep green. The medium-wash jeans that she switched to indigo after graduating. Dark ballet flats.

She stared at the trees outside, the wind moving them so that flashes of sherbet orange and white lace and pink floral print fluttered into view.

Off camera, a guy laughed.

July turned, slowly.

"Did you do this?" she asked.

The laugh turned to a few guys laughing.

July stormed over, hard enough to rattle the cheap flooring. The camera followed.

"Did you do this?" she asked.

The laughing guys were taking up both sofas. One of them spread his legs, playing it off like he was just getting comfortable but staring pointedly at July.

Fast as a snake striking, July grabbed his wrist.

She wrenched his arm. His face twisted in pain. She jerked him hard enough that he buckled off the sofa and onto his knees. The other guys jumped back with a roar of amusement.

Then the roar faded.

July was holding his arm there, putting continual pressure on his wrist. Her lips were moving, but she was speaking too quietly for the camera to pick up her words. She was in profile, her hair in front of her face, so we couldn't even read her lips.

The guy yelled, with all the breath he had, "I'm sorry!"

The sound bounced off the hallway walls. "I'm sorry!"

Hallway doors opened. The laughs heard now were markedly feminine. They crescendoed along with the third "I'm sorry!"

The clip ended there.

July's career could have ended there.

Her glare, her torquing a classmate's arm, none of it fit with the Iverson brand. And it certainly didn't fit with July as we knew her, lovely if reticent, the quiet counterpoint to June's effervescence and fury.

But anyone who assumed she was done for didn't realize how many of us had endured high school locker rooms. How many had had our own pressboard dressers plundered in service of pranks both retro and newly invented.

A shaky video of July getting that guy down on his knees made her our hero.

She couldn't have known that seven years later it might make her look like a girl capable of murdering her stepfather.

July Iverson

"You'll be fine," June had told July before the detectives knocked. "You'll be great. And we're going back-to-back, so I'll practically be right there with you."

But June wasn't right here with July. July was alone, just like June had been alone during her interview immediately before. And July wasn't going to be great. She was sweating like the glasses of agua fresca on the table.

"Can anyone confirm you were here?" the older detective asked.

"June," July said. "I'm pretty much always with June."

Despite their difference in ages, the two detectives must have worked together for a while, because right now they had identical expressions. Not suspicion, but thinly veiled pity.

"We have friends," July said. "But we're each other's best friends."

That sounded sweet, not pathetic, right?

Sure, they had friends. Friends who pulled them into frame and then posted about them to draw traffic. Friends who got close to them and then posted about July's periodic IBS flare-ups and June's recurring toenail fungus, all in the name of driving up their own views. Friends who said the twins were toxic, codependent, that June was pushy and July was a pushover. That July didn't have a mind of her own, so was always looking to June to borrow hers.

Except July couldn't look to June now. June had left a fresh pitcher on the counter and said in that same chirpy voice, *I'll just be down at the pool, so you know where I am if you have any more questions.* And then she'd waltzed out the door in her bikini the color of Chartreuse on the rocks, and the two men at the kitchen table tried to keep their jaws from hitting the salvaged wood.

Only her sister could sit through a police interview and then instantly go work on her tan.

"Do you know where March is?" the younger detective asked.

That question chilled the sweat under July's boobs. Why were they asking that? What did they know? What were they not saying?

July shook her head, and for the first time since shaking their hands looked them right in the eyes. "Do you?"

we who probably knew more about April Iverson than the detectives who were about to interview her

When the detectives showed up outside Garland & Bow, we didn't know if the location had been their decision or April's. Maybe they wanted to catch the eldest Iverson daughter by surprise. Or maybe April wanted to show she had so little to hide that she would welcome them into her place of business.

Before April Iverson's textile design firm was Garland & Bow, it had been Showers & Flowers, a nod to her name and her mother's. But as she and her mother grew apart, she changed not just the name but everything. The floral logo that spilled freesia and hydrangea in all directions became a crisp sprig of laurel tied with a neat ribbon, charcoal gray. The frilled throw pillows on the office sofas were changed out for square ones with hard-piped edges.

Since the murder, we'd been checking her pages every few hours. But her last post was still several years old, that tour of the newly rebranded Garland & Bow office, overlaid with music as airy and open as the space itself. The footage was slick and pretty but removed, a little like April herself. A mix of fabrics rippled like cool water, inter-cut with shots of her employees. The women ranged in shape, skin tone, age, from their twenties through their seventies, yet they all seemed to be wearing knee-length skirts in patterns they might have designed themselves. They gestured to computer screens, reviewed color proofs, drank from logo-adorned coffee mugs.

They smiled the smiles of stock photos that come in picture frames. It seemed not so much fake as self-conscious, the nervous energy of people who want to come off well on camera.

From all reports, April Iverson's employees loved her, and more than one had said they considered her family. April had quietly cov-ered the insurance deductibles and co-pays for one's gender-affirming surgeries. She had hired a lawyer for one whose husband had just left her, and whose in-laws had the resources to wear her down in the divorce negotiations. When her assistant's wedding venue shuttered, keeping the deposit, April anonymously paid for a new location. She seemed mildly embarrassed when the fact came to light, as though someone had pointed out her bra strap showing.

We knew all this not because April wanted anyone to know, but because her employees did. They insisted that someone needed to speak up for who the real April Iverson was, a woman whose gener-ous spirit everyone might miss if they didn't look past the chill and precision of her demeanor. They felt compelled to combat all the stories that had deemed her the Iverson bitch.

For everything April may have done for her employees, she did not call them her family. When enough people pointed this out that she was obliged to comment on it, she said it was because encouraging employees to think of work as their family was manipulative, a calcu-lated way to squeeze more out of them. She left it at that, no softened ending. But we knew what she meant, that same bitter tonic of guilt and obligation that made us cancel dates and therapy appointments to help relatives set up their printers.

People remembered her saying that, the edge she gave to the word *family*.

There were some fans of Mother May I who, two days after the murder, were already arguing that April was absolutely capable of this. Allegedly she had a husband, but no one had ever seen him, they said, so who knew? These were the same people who said she was ruthless. That she was ungrateful for all her mother had provided when she was growing up. That she was utterly incapable of taking a joke, of laughing at herself. To back up these assertions, they cited reports from the early months of her business. Anytime an employee pulled up content from April's childhood—*Wow, lime-green braces, when are you gonna bring that look back?*—she fired them. No discussion.

To anyone she'd fired, she was, forever, a bitch. To everyone who stayed, she was a goddess. The few times May Iverson had managed to barge her way into Garland & Bow with a camera, we couldn't miss the admiring way April's employees looked at her.

We may not have known who killed August Ingraham, but we could already tell you this: April Iverson couldn't have done it. April Iverson was as efficient as the filament in a lightbulb. If she ever chose to murder someone, she wouldn't be so artless as to torch a house to cover it up.

April Iverson

"**T**hank you again for having us to your office," the older detective said.

"Thank *you*," April said, emphasis on the second word, as though they were doing her the favor. She took waters out of the conference room mini-fridge, each bottle wrapped in a matte black label, printed with a green logo. "You actually made an appointment. Not even my sister does that."

"Which sister?" the younger detective asked.

"Sorry." April handed them each a bottle. "June. When I mean January or July I usually say January or July. When I just say *my sister*, I usually mean June. I don't know why."

The younger detective gave an understanding smile, as though he either did the same thing with his siblings or was trying to pretend he did for the sake of rapport.

April knew what was coming. They wanted to know where she'd been at the time of the murder. They kept the timeframe vague. They probably didn't want the Iverson sisters coordinating alibis.

"I was at home," she said.

"Can anyone confirm that?" the older detective asked.

"My husband." It sounded flimsier when she said it out loud. Too bad that night didn't involve one of June's signature unannounced visits. Invasive and boundary-ignoring as they were, one really would have been useful about then. It would have given them both more solid alibis.

"How would you characterize your relationship with August Ingraham?" the younger detective asked.

"I didn't really know him," April said. "My mother and I aren't very close, so I didn't have much occasion to run into him."

"And yet you had some strong words for his legal counsel."

Great. That primordial excuse for a lawyer had struck again.

April needed to be careful here. She had to explain calmly, without sounding defensive.

"August thought I owed my mother a share of my company because, according to him, I couldn't have built it without being May Iverson's daughter," April said.

She was going to say more, but then she didn't. The less she said, the better.

"And you didn't agree," the older detective said.

"I didn't agree," April said.

They both looked at her like they were waiting for her to go on.

"August had a habit of grasping for money that I never understood," April said. "My mother had more of it than he ever could have spent."

Had she just sounded bitter? Were they about to cast her as the scorned eldest daughter?

"You said you and your mother aren't close," the younger detective said. "Why would you say that is?"

He was good, especially for the age he was. *Why would you say that is?* rather than *Why is that?* made the question sound more like an invitation than a quiz.

"We don't have much in common," April said. "We have very different lifestyles."

Different lifestyles? Why had she put it that way? It sounded like she was calling her mother either a lesbian or a homophobe.

"Different lifestyles?" the older detective asked.

"I'm more private than my mother. I'd rather not post everything I do and everything that happens to me. It means there's a lot we don't agree on."

"Does that apply to June and July too? Do you disagree with them?"

"Well, they're not posting pictures of me as a child." April crossed one leg over the other, calming her autonomic nervous system by admiring how good this new skirt print looked in final fabric form. "So what they do is their business."

"The pictures of you as a child," the younger detective said. "That's why you initiated the lawsuit against your mother last year?"

"Not a lawsuit." April had to correct this, and fast, before they ran with the wrong idea. "It never got that far. It was never going to get that far."

She noticed one particular leaf on her skirt that would have been better placed just a little to the left. Why hadn't she caught that in samples? That was going to bother her on every bolt they'd gotten into the warehouse.

"I wanted my life off the internet," April said. "But I realized it wasn't going to happen, so I stopped burning my time and money on it."

"Your lives being on the internet," the older detective said, "is that why March left home?"

The ache came fast, sharp. But it faded quickly. April had learned to make it fade quickly. What else were you supposed to do with that kind of pain? How else did you box up and store the time you'd lost with someone you loved, someone you'd practically raised?

"I'd say that's a fair assessment of the situation," April said.

"Do you know how we can get in touch with March?"

"I'm sorry," April said, trying to strike the precise middle point between clinical and polite. "I wish I could help you."

"One of your sisters disappears and none of you file any kind of report," the younger detective said. "You can see how that might seem a little odd."

"Leaving home is not disappearing."

"Leaving home and ignoring your family? Never being in touch? Never coming home? That's not disappearing?"

"Fine," April said. Now she sounded hostile. Probably because she was feeling hostile. She pulled it back. She added a disarming laugh to dispel the tension in the room. "When you put it that way, I guess it does sound like disappearing." She opened her own water bottle, the plastic crack sharp. "But if May Iverson was your mother, you'd want to disappear too."

we who grew up watching the Iversons

O f all the Iversons, January seemed most equipped to start a fire.
That didn't mean we thought she had. We just knew she
could. She had ready access to an all-you-can-pour buffet of flammable substances, everything from paints to glues to cleaning sol-
vents. So many hazardous objects were flying around the workshop in
the theater basement that they got into people's skin. June gave off-
the-cuff reports of hugging January and getting secondhand fiberglass
bits embedded in her forearms. "And don't get me started on the
metal," June said once when she really got on a tear. "There are tiny
bits of it airborne and everything. My little sister's not even allowed
to get an MRI."

It didn't make it easy for us to defend January, and a lot of people
were zeroing in on her. They deep-dove into the flammable substances a theater technician might have on hand, but it didn't stop
there. People who didn't know her, who hadn't grown up watching
the Iversons like we had, suddenly acted as though they were forensic

psychologists. They were able to determine her guilt from how she parted her hair, they insisted, or from the unsettling way she stared out from old photos.

The chatter of such onlookers was all we had to tell us who police were interviewing, and in the late afternoon on the second day after the murder, they saw January Iverson go into the station. Police hadn't gone to her like they had with every other Iverson. They'd made her come to them, and that was even more fodder for those ready to accuse her.

What most people didn't realize was that to understand January, to understand that unsettling stare, you had to go back to May Iverson's first marriage.

Those just now learning who the Iversons were assumed that May and August had been married for years, that the beautiful Iverson daughters were a product of the two of them. But August hadn't been a father to any of them and hadn't been around as they'd grown up. Before August came into the picture two years ago, May had dated a string of rich and/or entrepreneurial men, and before that was Ernesto Iniesta.

Lily May Iverson and Ernesto Alejo Iniesta married when the bride was twenty-three. Mother May I had not yet shared her first post, so when it came to the reasons behind the match, all we could do was guess. Perhaps May Iverson imagined how beautiful their children would be, especially any of them lucky enough to inherit the bride's fountain-green eyes and the groom's pronounced cheekbones. Or perhaps it was May's love for all things monogrammed, from towels to suitcase charms. Ernesto's last name meant she wouldn't need to have her embroidered tote bags and engraved necklaces redone.

If throwback pictures of the wedding—imported roses, bespoke wineglasses, a historic Victorian mansion—weren't enough to convince everyone of May Iverson's charmed existence, there was the birth of her daughters. First came a luminous little girl born in April and named for it. April came into the world on a crisp spring night, giving her mother space to slim her body back into her favorite sundresses in time for her first Fourth of July parties as a new mother.

Three years later, the Iverson family (May liked her last name, she decided, and she liked the statement made by keeping it) welcomed the twins. The older one was born in the last few minutes of June, the younger in the first few minutes of July, each named accordingly. No one knew until years later—it was one of Mother May I's few scandals to date—that when June and July were born, May had bribed and/or coerced and/or threatened (it wasn't clear which) hospital staff to lie on paper. Just a little. Just enough to put one twin before midnight and one after, so that one birth certificate would say June 30, and the other would say July 1.

May Iverson must have timed her tries for her next child so precisely that Iverson baby #4 was almost certain to be a March baby. Iverson baby #4 would be the first born since May Iverson had started posting pieces of her life online, and she was already gaining a following. She announced her pregnancy along with the news that her baby would be christened March, in honor of her favorite book, *Little Women*, gushing that she could think of no more appropriate name than the last name of those four sisters.

Hundreds chimed in to affirm her choice, saying it was perfect, saying that they too loved *Little Women*, that May was beautiful and so was her just-started-kindergarten daughter, April, and so were her twin babies, June and July, and so would be the new little girl to be born this coming March.

Except that Iverson baby #4 didn't cooperate like April, June, and July. She was early. Even then, it seemed, she couldn't wait to get away from her mother. She forced her way into the world with a raw will she must have had even before she took her first breath.

She didn't even wait until February. She was so early, she had to be named January. May Iverson shared with heart-weary strength the news that January was five weeks premature. In the years after, whenever May spoke of this, her voice would quake delicately, highlighter giving her cheeks an angelic shine.

But if January had the will to be born early, her mother seemed to have equal will to get pregnant in exactly the month she wanted. So it was all made right the next time around. The fifth Iverson baby stayed dutifully on schedule, born early in the morning on March 16, dead center of the month, and was named accordingly. Even then, baby March seemed to know that life would go more gently if May Iverson got what she wanted.

So yes, there were those who thought January was so odd—her eyes flinty, never still—that she might have been capable of murder. But we wanted them to stop and think about how January got that way in the first place.

From the moment of her birth, January Iverson became the one winter month in that golden family, an island of cold among spring and summer children. If January felt apart from her bubbling mother and laughing sisters, could we blame her?

January Iverson

"How would you characterize your relationship with the deceased?" the older detective asked.

"Honestly?" January said. And she immediately wanted to kick herself. If she qualified one statement with *Honestly?* what would they think about the rest of them? "Nonexistent. We had pleasant but very brief interactions at the rehearsal dinner and the wedding last year. I asked about him helping July place stray animals. He asked me about the upcoming show season I was working on. It was just small talk. Beyond that, I really didn't know him."

"No enemies that you're aware of?" the older detective asked.

January hesitated, and she could feel them latching on to the dead air. She had to tell the truth here. If she didn't, they'd know.

"A lot of people didn't really understand why he and my mom got together," January said. "But I don't think anyone would kill him over that."

"And how would you describe your relationship with your mother?"

April had coached her on this. *Cordial but distant.*

"Cordial but distant," January said.

Then the rest of what April had said echoed in her head.

Except say it your own words.

"We don't have much contact, but I see her at family stuff," January said.

"Cordial even after you and April took legal action against her?" the younger detective asked.

Shit.

The younger detective sounded like he'd been waiting to ask, just holding himself back.

"We've had disagreements about how she runs her life and how she ran ours," January said. "But when it comes down to it, we really can't do anything about the footage she has online. The laws aren't with us. So we sort of gave up."

The younger detective looked a little troubled. January couldn't tell if it was fake sympathy to get her guard down.

"Is there anyone who can verify when you were at the theater the day of the murder?" the older detective asked.

So that was the dance. Sympathy. Sucker punch.

"I was there alone for a little while"—they probably already knew that—"but there were a lot of people in and out. We were loading in some equipment. I stayed late, but my key card shows entries and exits. It was expensive equipment, so they alarmed the doors to make sure they couldn't stay propped open."

She was rambling now.

"And can your employer provide us with a log of all key-card access?" the older detective asked.

"I think so," she said.

"Have you had any recent contact with your younger sister?" the older detective asked.

This, at least, January could answer completely honestly. She felt her heart rate drop so perceptibly she almost wished the change was on record.

"No," January said.

"That's a little odd, isn't it?" the younger detective asked. "You two were pretty close growing up, weren't you?"

So he'd tuned in to reruns of the Iverson show.

January's first instinct was to scramble. To say, *There wasn't a falling-out. It wasn't like that.*

But she remembered what April had told her. *Calm. Breathe. First feeling you get that they're trying to corner you, ask for a lawyer and call me.*

So January kept her answer as unadorned as possible.

"Yeah. We were."

"Do you have any idea where she is?"

"None." If January sounded calm now, if she could feel her own pulse slow, did that mean they would think she was lying about everything before? Did they account for nervousness? There had to be a name for the police interview equivalent of white coat syndrome.

"Thanks again for doing this here," January said. Rambling again. And it was quite possibly one of the stupidest things she'd ever said. As though they'd done her some mythic favor by letting her come down to the station and sit in a gray-carpeted room, complete with ceiling cameras. "I really don't want people talking at my work." Why was she still speaking? Why did she think that was going to make things better? "This isn't really the kind of publicity a production wants, you know?"

The older detective nodded in acknowledgment, as though logging her gratitude. He took a half-second pause before asking, "Do you think March could have done this?"

"Absolutely not," January said without hesitation.

"Do you think any of your sisters could have?"

"Absolutely not," January said, and hoped they didn't notice the breath of hesitation this time.

"Do you think your mother could have?"

"Absolutely not," January said, and she immediately wished she could change the phrasing. Twice was fine. Three times and she sounded like a parrot taking the witness stand.

"Do you have any idea who could?"

January shook her head. Then she remembered that head-shaking wasn't good enough for the record. "I wish I did."

She didn't realize it was a lie until she heard it coming out of her mouth.

we who were watching the Iversons

The police were barely telling us anything. So by the end of the second day, all of us were running our own investigation, parallel to theirs, one in which we could all post our theories and check one another's work.

We knew so little for sure that it seemed like anyone could have done it. Anyone could kill. Anyone could start a fire in a panic to try to hide the body. It was why we couldn't stop checking, refreshing, checking back. According to *a source close to the family*—and who even knew what that nebulous qualification meant—Ernesto Iniesta had an alibi, so there went any theories about a jealous ex-husband.

Even though we had a shared gut instinct that it was one of the Iversons, we didn't know for sure. We ruled no one out. Of course we suspected Mother May I's fellow influencers/competitors. How could we not? There would have been something predictable but perfect about one mother, famous for picture-worthy after-school snacks and homemade costumes and glamorous New Year's Eve parties, trying to literally burn down the life of another just like her.

Maybe it was the one with those terrifying cheek implants, the one who claimed she invented split-dye hair color (most recently she'd gone from white blond/stoplight red to hot pink/neon green). It wasn't even the plastic that made her frightening to look at. It was the way she was always making such ugly expressions. A sneering grin after a comment like *I guess gingham's fine if you don't mind looking like a poor person.* She was the one who posed with her baby while wearing Louis Vuitton housedresses, and claimed she did every mealtime, every bath time, every diaper change herself. This, despite her complaints that her two-inch-long nails rendered her unable to operate her water ionizer. She was living proof that no matter how pretty, how rich, how thin, how privileged, you were, ugliness inside could make you ghoulish, and this probably accounted for half her following. There was something both reassuring and horrifying in watching her.

Or maybe it was the one who created a scale gingerbread replica of a different European castle every Christmas, complete with stained sugar windows and gentle blankets of fondant snow. How many years could you make that many caramel icicles without snapping?

Then there was May Iverson's best friend, or former best friend, we couldn't really keep up. The redhead who always wore white. She was always there in the clips of the moms' manicure nights, and she always snuck in little remarks. *Sometimes it takes until they're going into kindergarten to lose the last of the baby weight. Or until they're in middle school, right, May?*

Or the one with the bright green eyes and the folk musician husband, who once allegedly stormed onto the Iverson property, livid that her own twins had just gotten rejected from St. Veronica's, sure that May had snatched those precise spots for June and July. *You must have blown every trustee who can still get it up.* (Fourteen-year-old June recorded the whole thing, gleefully posting it until someone—April; the school; her amused-but-trying-not-to-seem-amused mother—got her to take it down.)

It could have been any one of them. But we didn't hear word of any of them going into the station. Maybe the police came to them. Or maybe they were never considered. Maybe it was the simple fact that they were thin, white, rich, and had that brittle look particular to privileged, overly litigious women.

Then there was Savanna Montez. Any of us who knew anything about Mother May I knew about Savanna Montez.

Officially, she was the Iversons' housekeeper turned nanny. Unofficially, she was a housekeeper turned housekeeper/nanny (we had seen her carrying laundry baskets through the background of Mother May I's posts about the family's morning routine or the hour after school). According to May Iverson's friends, Savanna had gotten so distracted with a side business that she started forgetting to pick up June from ballet or January and March from the tutoring center. This was supposedly why May had fired her. That was more than ten years ago now, yet some brought it forth as a possible motive for revenge. They wondered why detectives weren't looking into her more.

But these were amateur questions. They were questions from people watching who'd barely heard of Mother May I before the murder hit the news. Those of us who knew the Iversons knew better.

If you were going to suspect one fired nanny, didn't you have to suspect them all? Hadn't there always been nannies passing through that house? Had any of us even managed to keep count? May Iverson cycled through them faster than she changed car services. When it came to nannies, May Iverson was mythologically demanding. She wanted women who cut sandwiches at the same angle she did (without having to be told), who were pretty enough to be in the background of videos (though not prettier than May; the kind of pretty that could easily smile and wave to the camera and then recede), who could get her daughters to skip toward their math homework as though it was a shopping trip.

May Iverson wanted Mary Poppins with a Le Creuset pan of Swiss chard in one arm and a test prep book in the other. No mere mortal could ever have lived up to that. Not Savanna Montez. Not Mary Poppins herself, who wouldn't have been able to keep up with what vegetables should be prioritized for a child's brain and DHA levels, what the format changes were to this year's standardized tests, whether juice should be proffered daily or not at all. So it wasn't exactly a surprise to learn that, back when May let Savanna go, she didn't give her a reference. It really seemed an unlikely motive for murder more than a decade later.

We should have seen it coming, who suspicion and speculation would turn to next. Everyone who had ever worked for May Iverson, especially anyone who worked in or near the Iverson mansion, became a potential suspect. Gardeners and landscapers. Pool maintenance teams. Housekeepers. Personal chefs. Personal assistants. We kept hearing rapid-fire reports of the police talking to all of them, including the ones she'd let go over the years. The ones she'd fired. The ones she'd dismissed recently.

May Iverson had once employed a household staff big enough to run a boutique hotel. But over the past months, before August's murder, she'd let half of them go. "I just want to get back to basics," she'd insisted in the face of speculation about her financial situation. "I want to simplify, pare down my life, make a conscious return to what's important."

But even before the murder, there were rumors that August had instigated the firings and switching-around of job descriptions. So the detectives started there, with everyone who had worked or did work for the woman known as Mother May I. From what little we knew, that seemed to be their first theory, a disgruntled employee, or a former employee.

Except none of us really thought that would go anywhere. It was just too easy.

If the police were going to look outside the Iverson family, they needed to bring in the guy in the gray sweatshirt. That was what we had called him most of the time, *Sweatshirt*, until someone saw him answer to the name Luke, at which point he had a first name, and therefore a full name, Luke Sweatshirt.

He'd been there before the murder. But until the news coverage spread, only a few of us paid much attention to him. We didn't know if he was June's boyfriend or July's. Anytime one of the twins was spotted, the other one was usually close, so it was hard to tell who he was most interested in. Was he playing them off each other?

Unlikely. He seemed sweet but not sharp enough to hold two beautiful girls in his thrall.

Whenever we tried to describe Luke Sweatshirt, we sounded like we were calling him ugly. But we weren't, because he wasn't. It was more like, if your best friend had gotten engaged to him, you could have been happy for her without a single trace of jealousy. He was cute in a boyish way, his edges softened by a little extra weight. The slight paunch under his sweatshirt looked higher and had a more gradual slope than a beer belly, more like he still had baby fat, like he might not really lose all his baby fat until he passed thirty.

And he always seemed to be wearing that sweatshirt. And jeans. And Converse, though not the crisp new ones the twins wore in bright pink or jet black. He wore a beat-up navy blue pair, the rubber and laces grayed, a metal grommet or two missing.

He seemed nice enough. He held the girls' flat whites as they dug in their purses (maybe he was a new assistant?). A few months before the murder, he was spotted helping July with one of the rabbits who'd gotten loose (he was eventually found down the street—the rabbit, not the boy—with a cluster of fans filming him as he nibbled the edge of a lawn).

No one knew where two surreally beautiful girls had found such an astonishingly ordinary boy. Perhaps there'd been serendipity worthy of a romantic comedy, June catching his eye in a laundromat (she'd probably never lived anywhere without her own washer and dryer, so she would've only been in there if the place was retro enough to read well in photos). Or maybe it was him and July in a coffee shop, realizing that they'd just ordered the exact same thing, one extra-large cup of hot water with two tea bags, one raspberry-blackberry and one blueberry-lavender (though everyone knew that was July's afternoon drink, so that could have just meant he'd been stalking her posts).

Had July fallen in love with this boy, not realizing or not caring how he'd look on the Iverson family platforms? Or had June been trying to provoke their mother into paying closer attention? June could have gotten him nicer clothes. She had a poker hand's worth of high-limit credit cards and could have charged a shopping trip without even feeling it. She'd done it before, shaping the more hapless of her suitors—mostly the boys; the girls usually already knew what they were doing—with a better haircut or more subtle cologne. So June not doing the same with this boy seemed pointed. Had he been intended as her boyfriend-shaped middle finger to her mother for bringing August into their lives?

But if June was trying to provoke her mother, couldn't she have done better than a chubby white boy with less personality than the foam on top of June's coffee? And if that was her aim in the first place, why was he still there now that August was dead?

He could have been another August Ingraham, drawn to the Iverson money. But he didn't seem the type. It seemed far more likely that June would be using him than that he'd be using her. And if he ever tried to use July, for anything, June would probably break her multiyear vegan streak just to eat his balls for breakfast.

Though there was nothing obviously threatening about Luke Sweatshirt, there was something off here. There was something not quite right about this boy who seemed to be getting far too comfortable between two beautiful sisters.

So why were we the only ones seeing it? Why wasn't everyone else looking at him?

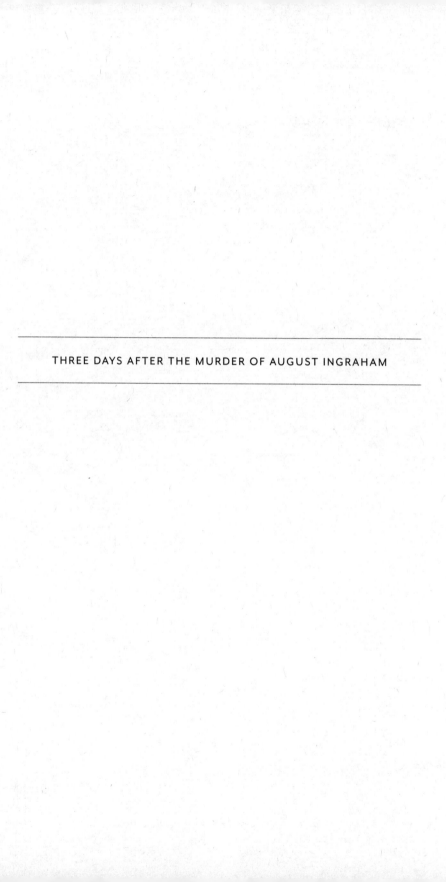

THREE DAYS AFTER THE MURDER OF AUGUST INGRAHAM

we who were watching the Iversons

"Welcome to Fine Crime, where luxury meets the law. I'm Ashley Morgan Kelly, bringing you the finer things in life and in true crime."

From what we could find, Ashley Morgan Kelly was once a very pale ash blonde, her hair so fine that even her bangs were pin straight. With a dusting of freckles across the bridge of her nose, she had the look of a classic American cheerleader.

But the woman on the screen bore little resemblance to her former self except for the gray-blue of her eyes. Her hair was now dyed black and had been curling-ironed, brushed, and back-combed to voluminosity. Her light-brown eyebrows were gone, replaced with dark-penciled arches so severe and upturned she looked perpetually inquisitive. Her face was contoured to the point of changing her skin color, and the gray and black tones of her smoky eye makeup added to the effect of her having traded in her own face for one better suited to thumbnails.

"Fine Crimers, I know you tune in for my take on some of the most shocking true crimes in history. But today we're turning to a case that's unfolding before our very eyes. August Ingraham, husband of May Iverson, known to most as Mother May I, was found murdered in the family's home just three days ago." A photo of smoke hovering above the Iverson mansion appeared in the upper right quadrant of the frame.

Ashley Morgan Kelly held a glass of white wine as though relaying a story to a friend. "On the face of it, this could be mistaken for a simple burglary, targeting a house filled with millions of dollars of valuables. But you, my Fine Crimers"—she lifted the glass toward the screen—"know better. You know that no true crime is as it seems."

She spoke about InFITnitum's financials, its investors, how the profit-and-loss statements were recently under investigation—"After all, behind many a shocking crime is the root of all evil: money." She refilled her glass from a bottle of Cheval Blanc. "But behind just as many shocking crimes"—Ashley Morgan Kelly paused for effect—"is a pretty face."

An image of May Iverson's kitchen appeared in the upper right quadrant, and then expanded to take over the screen. The photo went from static to video, showing an upload that most of us had seen years ago, and that even more of us had watched or rewatched in the past twenty-four hours. A lot of us had been going back to old content about the Iversons, and not just because they were taking up so much space in our brains and feeds. It was a little like looking at photos of dead people, searching for something in their eyes that showed any foreknowledge of what would befall them.

This particular video showed June and July at age eighteen, home from college. They had not, as everyone predicted, gone to the same college and shared a dorm room, though they did attend different schools within the same system.

Their mother was the one filming—made obvious by May's occasional comments in the background: "As you can see, my beautiful college girls are home for Christmas, and this mama couldn't be happier or prouder." The twins sat at the reclaimed barnwood kitchen table, drinking foam-topped coffee from the new machine gleaming in the corner of the kitchen.

July had kicked her shoes off and had her fuzzy-sock-covered feet tucked under her. She was wearing her favorite faux-leather jacket with pajama pants. It was the kind of incongruity we would later come to love about her, like how she would spend an hour and a half doing her makeup but forget that her nails were chipped.

June wore a chunky holiday sweater that looked like it had bits of tinsel woven in. It was one of those pieces that might have looked dowdy if she hadn't styled it perfectly, with shiny black jeans, slim cut. Things always looked different on skinny rich girls in a remodeled kitchen under dimmable recessed lighting, which was why so many of us watching made the mistake of buying that sweater ourselves. Especially when June posted where she'd gotten it, and its surprisingly affordable price tag.

June leaned over the table, a Sharpie in hand.

"Mom, you've got to see this," July said.

May brought the camera closer. "What am I seeing?"

In front of June were several sheets of paper, each covered in the same cursive words. Next to them was a printed-out copy of a Marilyn Monroe photo, black and white. The star leaned forward as though she was about to blow the camera a kiss, or maybe nod off. In the lower right corner of the photo were the looping words:

warmest regards,
Marilyn Monroe

The camera focused, showing the same four words that June had been writing over and over. When July handed the printed-out photo and a sheet of June's writing to her mother—"just look"—May, and all of us watching, could see that the writing was identical. The flourish on the M's. The rounded g in *regards*. The curlicue of the w.

May sighed. "So glad you're making such fruitful use of your education." She sounded mildly proud, impressed, but also like she was trying to seem appalled in some required motherly way.

"She can do it with anyone's." July vanished for a few seconds and then reappeared with an old box from one of the first highlight-and-contour palettes May Iverson had lent her name to.

With a few scrawls, June mimicked the signature gleaming across the palette box. The flourish on the *M*. The rounded *y*. The curlicue between the *I* and the *v* in *Iverson*. She wrote out a dozen copies of May Iverson's signature, each imitation better than the last.

May examined the writing, mouth in a serious pinch, before looking at June. "You're hired."

June cackled, throwing her head back, stamping her furry slippers on the chair next to her.

"I mean it," May said. "I like yours better. Can we put this on my neutral glam palette? It's prettier than mine."

July laughed, quieter, like the laugh left in the wake of her sister's laugh.

That laugh haunted us. It reminded us of what we already knew in the back of our minds. If June killed August, July might have helped her, or helped her cover it up. Wherever June went, July followed, maybe even toward death and fire and an act neither one of them could ever take back.

But it wasn't that laugh that Ashley Morgan Kelly noticed.

Ashley Morgan Kelly missed it entirely.

The video ended, and the screen returned to the woman with the glass of Cheval Blanc. "You may be hearing that the police have cleared the Iverson sisters, confirmed every alibi. One was at work. One was with her husband. Two were together. But we Fine Crimers know better than to believe everything we hear." She lifted the glass in a toast. "We Fine Crimers know that alibis can be fudged, or faked, or outright false. Just like a signature." She took a slow, thoughtful sip. "So I ask you, my lovers of crime and cashmere, if June Iverson was forging signatures in front of cameras at age eighteen, what might she have done in secret at age twenty-six?"

June Iverson

June had gotten a lot out of therapy, and one of the pearls was that she knew how to put aside what did not matter. It didn't matter that June hadn't liked August. It didn't even matter that the press conference had looked like a photoshoot for fine-line-reducing lip plumper. This was her mom. Her mom's husband was dead with the first tier of the wedding cake still in the freezer.

And her mom was dealing with it by employing her own chic brand of denial.

"Your usual?" Her mother crossed the hotel suite holding two champagne flutes, Clicquot in one, sugar-free Red Bull in the other. She was glowing like she'd just had a facial, and the new phone June had picked up for her to replace the incinerated one already sported a crystal-studded case.

"Why, thank you." June curtsied like she used to when she invited her mom to her and July's tea parties.

"Oh, honey." In her beige sweater and cropped white pants, and with her serene expression, her mother looked like she was about to give a seminar on a yacht. "I'm sorry we're here and not at home." Her mother handed her the Red Bull.

Was her mother really apologizing for someone trying to burn down her house? This was bad. Her mother didn't apologize—it was part of her strength as an entrepreneur—except for things that weren't her fault, and when she did, it was a warning sign of bad decisions to come. If June didn't keep an eye on her, she was going to fund a line of vitamin-infused nail polish or an independent film about reverse racism.

Her mother sat on one of the suite's three—wait, were there four?—green sofas. She arranged her legs under her, and was it a sin to hate your mother a little because she had better legs at fifty-three than you did at twenty-six?

When June sat next to her, her mother put her hand on hers. "You deserve your own full life," her mother said, "not to get wrapped up in all this."

"I want to be here for you," June said. "Do you need anything? Moisturizer? Sashimi?" June tried to tune in to her mother's energy, tilting her head down conspiratorially and asking, "A new pair of nude pumps?"

Her mother laughed, and the sound was like the light of the whole universe coming in through the hotel windows. "I have everything I need. The sponsors have been so sweet. So many of them are overnighting things to me." She gave a dry little laugh. "Thank goodness for the kindness of strangers or I'd just have my workout clothes and my black-tie gowns."

The two days' stubble on June's legs bristled.

"Your clothes," June said, registering. "Wait." The whole house hadn't gone up. When June had driven by, she couldn't even tell anything was wrong from the front. "The fire spread to your room?"

Her mother sipped her champagne, not answering.

"Mom," June said. "Did it *start* in your room?"

Her mother looked out the window in the way she did when she was trying not to let tears wear down her lower-lash-line mascara.

June's stomach whirled with so much protectiveness toward her mother, so much bloodthirst for whoever had lit that match, that she wanted to break something. The champagne bottle. The dozens of crystal vases stuffed with condolence flowers. One of those ocean-view windows.

"You need better security," June said.

Her mother turned toward her with a patient sigh. "Junie."

This wasn't just about August. Someone had set the room where her mother slept, the clothes her mother stored in her en-suite dressing room, the belongings her mother cherished enough to keep near her every night, on fire.

"Mom, I've been telling you this." Great. Now June sounded like she was about to cry.

Her mother put down her champagne glass. "My radiant girl." She put her hands to June's cheeks. "This is not your burden." Her hands smelled like her favorite hand cream, tulip-scented. "You let me handle this. You go do what you do so well. You shine. You shine like I taught you to shine."

"Someone tried to torch your house," June said. "What if they come back?"

"Hey." Her mother stroked her hair out of her face. "Who's the mom here and who's the daughter?"

June reached for the room service menu. If she could make things seem just a little bit normal, maybe her mother would talk to her. Really talk to her.

"Well, the daughter needs an infusion of carbs." June made a production of looking over the menu. "And an overly complicated cocktail. What do you want?"

"Oh, anything." Her mother was scrolling on her phone. "Surprise me."

June tried to recall her mother's latest salad kick. Was it Niçoise?

"Want to split dessert?" June asked just before calling in-room dining. "I've practically heard sonnets about the dragon-fruit sorbet here."

But the end of her sentence was drowned out by the audio coming from her mother's phone.

we who probably would've killed him too

This video of Ernesto wasn't content we recognized from Mother May I, or June or July. It showed up on the account of two brothers who were trying to drive traffic to their website, which promised a "revolutionary" approach to tournament bracketing (their online seminar was available for ninety-nine dollars). How they thought a video of May Iverson's ex-husband was going to help them was beyond us, but they made a tenuous attempt with the video title: "WE SAW THE INGRAHAM MURDER COMING JUST LIKE WE SAW THE AFC CHAMPIONSHIP MATCHUP COMING."

The camerawork was clearly amateur, but it was steady enough to show background details, and that was enough for us to place the approximate date of filming. The classes advertised on the gym's chalkboard, the convoy of food trucks in the complex across the street, the sign wishing a local baseball team good luck, they all helped us pin it down to about two weeks before August's murder.

The video began with Ernesto approaching a sweating man in a designer ripped tank, a man who was alive in this video but dead by the time we saw it.

When Ernesto spoke, his voice was low and clear.

"You fuck with any of my kids," he said, "I'll fucking kill you."

"Check the paperwork, hombre," August said.

There was an edge in that last word, a razor corner of derision. It was the knife twist of a badly pronounced Spanish word flung at this brown man.

August spread his arms in what might have looked like a conciliatory gesture if it hadn't also come with that August Ingraham smirk. "She's my wife. So now they're my kids as much as yours."

It didn't matter that August hadn't raised any of the Iverson daughters. It didn't matter that he hadn't even met May until two years ago, when the entire Iverson brood was well into adulthood. It didn't matter that he barely knew April and January and had never even met March. This was the smirk of a man who was too sure to be bothered with the facts.

His smirk flashed into a grin, like the glare off the hood of a car. "Any bets on which one's gonna start calling me Dad first?"

April Iverson

April set her forehead on her keyboard wrist rest, shaking her head, trying to clear it of what she'd just seen.

Why had her dad shown up outside August's gym? He knew better. August Ingraham was a white guy and Ernesto Iniesta was a brown man. He was never going to come out of this looking good. Even if August had bashed her dad's head into the aluminum siding, somehow this still would have ended up as her dad's fault.

And why the gym? Any gym filled with a bunch of guys like August Ingraham, they would all have had their cameras out, documenting the sculpting of their precious physiques, and her father should have known that. Half of them probably had their own home gyms, with newer equipment. August did. He'd shown it off a hundred times. Guys like him only left their personal gyms to work out because they wanted to be seen.

If her dad had to confront him, why there?

The video was climbing in views. But climbing faster was the algorithmically related video from a channel called Fine Crime, run by a woman with foundation so full coverage that her facial muscles appeared not to move.

April didn't want to add to that view count. And she knew that clicking on suggested videos just fed the algorithm and big data. Yet here April was, loading that recommended video into a new tab, toggling over to it, letting it play.

"Welcome to Fine Crime, where luxury meets the law. I'm Ashley Morgan Kelly, bringing you the finer things in true crime. Thanks to you all out there, my last video set a view count record for my little channel"—she blew a kiss at the camera—"so to show my appreciation for my Fine Crimers, I'm currently living at my desk, bringing you updates on the August Ingraham murder as fast as they come in."

Ashley Morgan Kelly ran the gym video in full, and then paused on the last frame. Ernesto Iniesta's face. The money shot. The angry brown man.

"And his alibi for the time of the murder? Supposedly, he was on an overnight hiking trip." Ashley Morgan Kelly barked out a little laugh. "An overnight hiking trip? Without posting a single photo? Fine Crimers, do we detect something a little suspect?"

By the end of the day, her father's hiking buddies had publicly released several photos that showed him in the background. In almost all, he was not looking at the camera. In some, he was backlit by a pink and orange sky. But those photos—and their related metadata— were enough to prove he'd really been where he said he was.

Ashley Morgan Kelly did not issue a correction or a retraction.

And though her father's hiking buddies meant well, they'd helped Ashley Morgan Kelly as much as they'd helped Ernesto Iniesta. By answering her commentary on the gym video, they'd proved that a question she asked demanded a response.

FOUR DAYS AFTER THE MURDER OF AUGUST INGRAHAM

we who were watching the Iversons

Even before the coroner released August Ingraham's cause of death, we already knew what it wasn't. Aerial footage showed the tarping and scaffolding over the damaged area, revealing that the fire hadn't reached the part of the house that August had been in (further confirmation that the killer couldn't have been April, who would never leave a job half done). And given the size of the mansion, where he was found, and what rooms the fire had consumed, it was unlikely that smoke had overtaken him.

So we waited to hear the cause of death, something that would reveal the nature not just of the crime but of the killer. Bludgeoned with the heavy glass of a perfume bottle or a paperweight faceted to look like a jewel. Geranium-scented cleaner in his whiskey. The teeth of a salon-quality comb to the jugular.

Which was why the coroner's statement, delivered by the police chief four days after the murder, was both disappointing and perplexing.

Death due to an apparent fall.

Within minutes, a thousand comments latched on to the dramatic image of August tumbling down one of the central staircases that led to the foyer. Those wide twin staircases, carved from marble the same pink as May Iverson's favorite private-label rosé, scrolled inward toward each other. They featured often in photos of May and the twins descending like princesses in triplicate.

How wrong such comments were. How little the commenters knew of the Iverson residence. August must have fallen down a different staircase. We realized this as emerging news stories played up the pathos of him dying in the corner of the house that had become his masculine sanctuary (without ever using the term *man cave*). That meant it was almost certainly the one that led from August's private gym and game room down to his own high-ceilinged living room. So while it would have been poetic to think of him meeting his end at the bottom of a pink staircase, there was something poetic in this too. August had hated those pink steps in the foyer, so, for his own stairs, he had a marble set crafted from Blanco Guadiana that he had likely obtained illegally, through considerable bribes, scavenged from heritage sites.

Death due to an apparent fall. No poison. No blood-spattered antiques. No platinum hair-dryer cord wrapped around his neck (Mother May I had once collaborated with a home styling tools company). No murder weapon imbued with the flair of any particular suspect. If the murderer hadn't been rash enough to set the fire to cover the crime, the police might not have even suspected a murder. They might have chalked the whole thing up to an unfortunate accident instead of employing forensic physicists to determine the path of his fall. And how amateurish the killer had been, so unaccustomed to murder that they'd run away from their own crime scene. They had been so desperate not to be in the same room with the body that they didn't even start the fire there. The only distinguishing feature of the killer seemed to be ineptitude.

But there was a different kind of signature on this crime, hidden within the fire itself. Some kind of accelerant had been used. In the police chief's statement, the word was just one of many meant to give an overall impression of the forensic science taking place at the crime scene. But we caught it.

While we didn't exactly know how each Iverson would have started a fire—it wasn't exactly the kind of tutorial that went alongside ginger-cookie Christmas trees and how to pose in a mid-century-style swimsuit—there was no stopping us from guessing.

Was it possible this wasn't a murder at all? Could August have set the fire himself and then fled from it so hastily that he'd fallen to his death? Except what motive would August have had? And why would he have been running to the other end of the house instead of out of the house entirely?

Or could the perpetrator's aim have been the fire the whole time? Was it possible that August had witnessed the arson-in-progress, and then fled from the intruder?

Before we could properly formulate any theories that would pin this all on August, we found the detailed preliminary results released by the coroner. There were no apparent traces of accelerant on his clothes or body, nor was there evidence of smoke inhalation. He had not been the one to set the fire, nor had he been near it while he was still alive.

It all led back to the same place. Someone had meant to kill him, and tried to cover it up.

May wouldn't have touched any of this with her own paraffined hands. She had ex-boyfriends who adored her enough to kill August Ingraham themselves if she were only to ask. The confirmation of Ernesto Iniesta's alibi didn't exonerate any other previous suitors.

March could have used whatever she wanted. Neighbors probably wouldn't have recognized her. She could have sent the house up with exhibition-grade fireworks and gotten away before anyone placed her.

January could have brought in paint thinners or maintenance fluids, but she wouldn't have had to. She could have taken her theater technician safety training and turned it inside out, doing the hazardous opposite of everything her instincts told her to do. A flammable scarf draped over a halogen bulb. A straightening iron left plugged in next to a set of acetone-soaked cotton balls. A Mother May I–branded dish towel next to a lit stove, or a recently Windexed glass doorknob from the Mother May I home decor line, refracting the sun onto some steel wool.

But if January knew what she knew, wouldn't she have known enough to start the fire where the dead body was? June or July or even May might have thought the whole house would go up fast enough to destroy the evidence, but January would have known better. She would have been able to guess how long it would take for the fire to spread from one end of the house to the other.

June would have grabbed nail polish remover and whatever else she could find around the house with a WARNING: FLAMMABLE label. Her panic would have lasted only until she had decided what to do, and then she would have torn through the house until she had enough to get it started. We could imagine it, June's eyes reflecting back the flames as she lit each statement throw pillow, each rug accented through with pure gold thread, each set of curtains that was replaced every six months either to follow trends or to set them.

July would have gone for the phone to call 911 the moment August hit the bottom of the staircase. It was anyone's guess whether she might have done this because she was genuinely responsible and good, or because she was afraid not to do what she'd always been told she was supposed to do. Or because, whatever else anyone could say about August Ingraham, he'd never turned away a single kitten or puppy or corn snake she'd shown up with, and if there was the slightest chance paramedics could save him, she would have taken it.

And though we had to consider every possibility, this seemed even less like April's handiwork than it did January's. April would have packaged the murder and fire together with as much consideration as she paired floral prints with contrasting lunares. Rather than such scattershot arson, she would have set the fire close enough to the corpse to turn all evidence to cinders. She might have even been able to make both look like accidents. She might have found a way to rig one of the generators—the Iversons had several, because heaven forbid their pool go unheated and their wine cellar turn tepid as the neighborhoods below weathered wildfire-season power outages. A bad enough short on a generator could kill a man and torch a house at once, couldn't it? Wasn't that why generators were so dangerous?

There was a rumor that the Iverson daughters' great-uncle, their father's uncle, had been a power company lineman and that he had once forgotten to take off his wedding ring before servicing a transformer at a central power station. He took so much amperage at once that he vaporized. Fast as lightning, there was nothing left of him. They buried his best suit empty, as though the coffin lining were a bed his clothes had been laid out on, waiting for him.

April had, according to an unnamed source close to the family, always been angry about that happening. She was angry about it even though it had happened years before she was born, and she'd never known the man who'd vanished in that moment of becoming living electricity.

Maybe she'd mostly been angry that her mother had told January about it like it was some funny story, an anecdote that added color to their family, and that January had so many nightmares about it. She'd woken up sobbing, asking if it had hurt their tío abuelo, if he'd felt it, and if he did, what did it feel like?

And there was April, telling her that it was over so fast that their tío abuelo never knew what happened, that he was an angel before he even realized he was dead or dying, even though April couldn't know that.

The Iversons never posted about any of this. We only knew because Ernesto Iniesta hadn't wanted his two youngest to be acquainted with such things before they were old enough not to make nightmares out of them. And we knew this because a maître d' on a smoke break once heard Ernesto and May arguing about it outside a restaurant grand opening, and hit the record button. Audio only. Lifting the phone might have signaled to May that he existed.

"That's my family," Ernesto was heard saying. "*My* history. I asked you not to do this."

"They'll know eventually anyway," May said.

"Then let me tell them," Ernesto pleaded. "For the love of God, let me tell them something instead of you telling them or the whole world telling them in the comments section."

"It was just a story." A laugh peppered May's words. "In a month, January won't even remember it. I just thought it was interesting.

Don't you want our daughters to know that their family's interesting?"

"Our lives are not for consumption, May." Here Ernesto's anger made the pleading fall away. "Not for your fans, your followers, your viewers. Not even for you. You can't just chop up my whole history and sprinkle the pieces over your salads like croutons."

"I never eat croutons," May said, fast as though objecting in court.

Ernesto filed for divorce four months later.

June Iverson

"**S**he let everyone go. All of them." June paced the length of the windows in July's room while July sat on her bed, knees pulled into her chest. "She let August gut her staff last year, and now that he's dead, she's doubling down?"

Animals fled from June's path, all except for one cat and the yippiest of July's dogs, both of whom kept looking at June and then at each other, as though trying to assess the situation.

"Does Mom even know how to open her wine fridge without an assistant?" June asked.

At last check, the procession of investigators, claims adjusters, architects, and GCs would soon be confined to two regions of the mansion—where the fire started, and the scene of August's death. These, and any adjacent areas that were under scrutiny by police or that needed smoke-damage restoration, would be sealed off, and her mother would be allowed to live in approved sections of the house. She'd even get her kitchen back.

This was all one big favor. This was the expedited special treatment of the rich and beautiful. And yet her mother's response hadn't been to send fruit baskets to the detectives and the insurance adjusters. It had been to fire everyone who helped her run that house. The grocery delivery guy who had a garage code. The father-son team who'd been shaping her hedges for years. The women who polished her artfully mismatched antique silverware, making sure each piece was ready to give back a gleaming reflection of its owner.

"The police cleared everyone she just let go," June went on. "They've checked their alibis, so it's not like they're suspects. And I've seen her bank statements. She has the liquidity to pay them." Her mother's analytics may not have been what they were five or ten years ago—the market for white women with moissanite-adorned nails decorating cakes had ebbed a bit—but they were still astronomically higher than most of her competitors.

"I don't get it." June stopped right next to where July was huddled in the unmade bed, the midnight-blue comforter scrunched up like bad ruching. "She didn't fire that stylist who tried to convince her she should be the one to bring back culottes. And who now, might I add, wants her to wear something to the funeral that looks like Chanel's collab with Talbot's. Nor did Mom fire anyone on her management team who, might I further add, have gotten her into some of the shittiest deals she's ever done and yet somehow are still on her payroll. But she fires the fountain maintenance team? She fires the cleaners? Do you remember when everyone had norovirus and she tried to clean her own bathroom?"

This was July's cue to laugh, to show some sign of life. They always laughed about this. Her mother had taken the toilet brush, doused it with blue fluid, sudsed up the outside of the toilet bowl, and then wondered why it didn't look the way it did when Emelia or Mary Linn cleaned it. June had laughed so hard she could barely hold the camera still and had to hand it off to July while she showed their mother where the brush actually went.

July didn't even crack a smile.

"She doesn't trust anyone right now," July said. "Would you?"

"Her life has too many moving parts for her to trust nobody," June said. "This shit started with August. She always tried to make it sound like some kind of mutual decision, but come on. He's the one who started the staff cuts, and now she's finishing this bullshit. If she goes down this road, that place is going to look like a crumbling French château. I am not participating in the making of a three-person Grey Gardens."

Getting this out was supposed to make June feel better, wasn't it? But the longer she talked, the more amped up she was getting.

"This isn't like her," June said. "You know how she is. When tragedy strikes, she deep-dives into work. When Grandma died, she did that highlighter–dusting powder collaboration. When"—June's tongue got stuck; she couldn't say the words *March left*—"you know, that was her first full-blown holiday home-decor line."

July looked up at her with those sad why-aren't-we-all-still-a-family eyes. June hated that look. What were they supposed to do about any of it except move on? Move forward.

"This should be another transformative moment for her," June said. "Companies are falling all over themselves to offer their condolences to the beautiful widow. They're sending her three-hundred-dollar eye masks for post-crying, thousand-dollar cashmere blankets for self-care nights. She's on her way to iconic. Jackie Kennedy level. This isn't the time for erratic moves."

"She's grieving," July said.

"Grieving for him?" June's laugh turned to a rough breath in the back of her throat.

That was when June noticed the faintly blue glow of July's phone.

"Really?" June asked. "I'm informing you about our mother's mental state and you're scrolling?"

"I'm not scrolling." July held up the phone, which showed a paused video. There was a woman in an appalling shrug jacket—she wasn't that old, but did anything make anyone look more ancient and outdated than wearing real fur?—who didn't look familiar. But the account name, Fine Crime, was one that had been floating around in whispers and random comments the last couple of days.

"You're not seriously watching that, are you?" June asked. "How can you even add to her view count?"

July was staring at the screen with that same unblinking look that had taken over their mother's face in the hotel suite.

"Give me that." June tried to wrench the phone away from July.

But July didn't release her grip like she usually did. She held on to it, simply lifting her eyes to June's. "You need to watch this."

"No, I don't," June said. "One frame of that lip-filler-addicted face is more than enough for a lifetime. This could not matter less."

"How do you know?" July asked.

"Look at what she was drinking." June tapped the image of a bottle on the screen. "Chopin Reserve. Now look at her view count, and how many times she's uploaded, especially in the past few days. This is as close as she has to a job, because she couldn't be uploading as often as she is if she had an actual job, or kids or an elderly mother or whoever to take care of. And we can see from her view count that she's sure as hell not paying for top-shelf vodka with ad revenue. She's a bored trophy wife or an overgrown, bored trust-fund kid."

"But June, look at this. How did she even get—"

June held up a hand and made a little zipping sound to cut July off. "Listen to me. You're giving this oxygen. If you give something oxygen, it breathes and it lives and it spreads." June set her hands on the bed and leaned down enough to look right into her sister's eyes. "So we're not giving this any more oxygen. Got it?"

we the followers of Mother May I

Ashley Morgan Kelly framed the recording as though to imply it was her exclusive content, obtained through means she could not disclose in order to protect her sources. But that was a lie. We traced it to an anonymous account that had uploaded it first, and that had uploaded nothing else except this single video.

The style didn't match any of Mother May I's content. The colors looked washed out, like faded film. That, and the uneven filming—unsteady camera, focus going in and out—made obvious how much this was not May Iverson's work.

But unlike the video in the gym parking lot, this had been filmed inside the Iverson house, in the central dining room we recognized from holiday posts.

"So I let her sign a few checks for me once and a while." May was sitting at the head of the table, reviewing what appeared to be mocked-up product labels. "So what?"

This could have been filmed by anyone. Another Iverson. A personal assistant. Any of the few employees still trusted in the mansion at that time, anyone quiet or familiar or brown enough to be invisible to May and August. And it couldn't have been that long ago, because May and August had been married less than a year, and they had only been officially dating for six months before that (*Whirlwind romance, fate, fairy tale,* said those among us who were romantics. *Rushed, impulsive, hope she got a pre-nup,* said those of us who were not).

August stood over her, declining to take any of the other slipcovered chairs. "She's a criminal," he said.

May: "It's not like that."

August moved to the dining room doorway. "It's illegal. She's defrauding you."

May: "She is not. And anyway, that's not how it started."

August: "What are you talking about?"

"Things get busy around here." May shuffled through unopened mail. "She signs for me sometimes. A delivery. A deposit. An invoice payment. Everyone does it with family sometimes."

August fumed, visibly, but also looked like he was trying to gather his rebuttal.

"She signed checks as you," August said. "Don't you get it? She's stealing your money. You gave her all the practice she needed to steal your money."

"She's embarrassed," May said. "She's living above her means. I'm not going to prosecute my own daughter for a few shopping sprees. I should have been putting aside more money for her anyway. For all of them. I always meant to. I just never got around to it."

"Why?" August said. "You don't owe them anything."

May looked at August, and it was as though a door had opened up in her, something impossible to hold in a single word. Regret. Protectiveness. Something tinged with remorse as she said, "You weren't there."

With a pensive air, Ashley Morgan Kelly offered her opinion that all this should cast suspicion on May—"Is the grieving widow really so aggrieved, or was there more conflict within this picture-perfect couple than meets the eye? Did May Iverson regret the distance that her new groom put between her and her daughters?" And on June—

"Forged signatures to fraudulent checks. If the most famous of the Iverson daughters was low on funds, apparently she was willing to break the law to round out her shoe budget. Do you want to know what I think, Fine Crimers? I think that before August Ingraham came into the picture, June knew her mother's money was as good as hers. But the presence of a new husband complicated things. Which raises the question: to what lengths might a scorned daughter go?"

But we wouldn't be taken in so easily. We saw Ashley Morgan Kelly's arguments for what they were, flimsy as the Cartier scarf bunched around her neck.

So May Iverson was loyal to her daughter. So she protected her daughter. What kind of fans would we be if we held that against her?

Luke Sweatshirt

The woman behind Mother May I was a lot of things. Stupid had never been one of them. So when a neighbor publicly came forward about loud arguments between the newlyweds, confirming that the disagreements about money went beyond a single dining room conversation, Luke was counting the hours until May Iverson made a statement. May Iverson could ignore anonymous speculation. She couldn't ignore the accusations of a real person with a name and face and mansion of her own.

"This is the completely wrong strategy," June complained over the phone. "If she starts answering every fame-whore neighbor, she might as well just give up now."

"Why?" he asked.

"Because she's giving the message that she owes them an explanation," June said. "That she owes them anything, when really they're lucky she lives in their neighborhood."

All he had to do was let June keep talking, and she told him everything. Including where the press conference would take place, and when. He silently pocketed the specifics.

He didn't tell June he was going, that he planned on staying at the back of the crowd. He was now among the worst of Mother May I's fans, showing up where he knew she'd be.

Just as carefully as May Iverson had chosen her moment, she'd chosen her outfit. She was wearing a muted purple suit, the cut familiar (a staple silhouette of one of her favorite designers, according to June; "the woman needs an update," June had said, "which she would get if she ever stopped to ask my advice"). The shade seemed carefully chosen, possibly with the help of a stylist. Not as obviously mournful or forbiddingly professional as black or navy. Not as flauntingly luxe as white. A color other than a neutral, but nothing bright or festive. After all, the funeral was tomorrow.

May Iverson had just left a fundraiser for an organization promoting STEM education for girls, one she had, according to commentators, bravely attended despite the tragedy that had just struck her family. "It's such an important cause," May had said at the step and repeat. "I couldn't let our girls down." She was still wearing the name tag she'd been given at check-in. The logo featured a stylized rendering of an Erlenmeyer flask filled with bright pink liquid, a bright pink atom model on the left side, a pink rocket ship on the right.

Leaving the name tag on looked like an absent-minded error. Luke knew it wasn't. It was a nice touch. She knew how many camera lenses would be waiting for her.

With her signature catch in her voice, May Iverson admitted, "August and I had our disagreements. I challenge you to find any couple who doesn't." Here, she looked up from her written statement, as though she was either going off script or didn't need the script for this part. "But I loved my husband."

Luke had to give her credit. No frothing herself up into sobbing. She faced the cameras, undaunted. It made her look more like April than April had ever looked like May.

"But I would never hurt him," May said. "And neither would any of my children."

She looked like she was about to turn away, a flash of gold and gemstone on the back of her blazer catching the light.

But her eyes landed on Luke. They narrowed as though she was trying to place him. Then she did, and something in her expression flared. If Luke had to put words to it, he had options. Such as, *So you're the little shit who's chasing my daughters?* Or maybe, *So you're stalking my girls and now you're stalking me?*

She recovered, softened her face, went on. "We, as a family, have experienced a terrible loss. We ask that you respect our privacy and our right to grieve."

She turned away, and that flash of gold showed again on the back collar of her blazer.

It wasn't an embellishment sewn onto the fabric. It was the necklace she had on. In front, it was just purple ribbon. In the back, gold-coated rosettes, amethyst geodes dipped in gold at the edges, raw pieces of amethyst, fluttering bits of ribbon.

Luke had to laugh, a pained, head-shaking laugh. That statement necklace was a shiny object that would distract every fashion commentator from here to next week. They'd all be talking about that gorgeous necklace, instead of talking about the words that had and hadn't come out of May Iverson's mouth.

And May Iverson knew it.

we who grew up watching the Iversons

It was hard to forget a necklace like that. Years ago, when May Iverson had first worn it, any questions about where she'd gotten it had been met with disappointing answers. It was a family piece, May said, inherited from Ernesto's mother, which Ernesto had graciously told her to keep during their unnaturally amicable divorce.

Over the years, a few different retailers had knocked it off, but it wasn't the same. Not even when Mother May I partnered with a jewelry MLM because "so many of you have been asking about this necklace, and I didn't want to keep it all to myself, because whatever I have I always want to share it with all of you. And now you can have your very own."

The necklace, called "the Lily May," sold well, then turned out to look little like the picture online, nothing like the original, and fell apart after about five wears.

FIVE DAYS AFTER THE MURDER OF AUGUST INGRAHAM

we who were watching the Iversons

At the service, May Iverson's black dress was as chic as if she were walking a red carpet. Her face was as placid as when she was doing a magnetic face mask. She broke out into occasional bursts of sobbing, as though suddenly remembering that the coffin flanked by sprays of lilies held the man she'd been married to.

None of us faulted her for this. None of us took it as evidence that she'd killed him. It was just evidence that when you'd spent so much of your life acting, posing, performing, sometimes you forgot which role you were playing, what lines you were supposed to memorize, who you were supposed to be that day.

Her children stayed close to her. All except March, who made no appearance, even now. And everyone was watching for her, so there would have no been no sneaking in and standing at the back.

January shifted in the pew. She wore the kind of sleeveless, knee-length black shift dress that had been in style for a hundred years and would likely be in style forever. Over the dress she wore the same kind of black sweater she'd probably wear with black jeans to dry tech at the theater later that night. The sweater sleeves half-covered her hands.

April looked as pressed and neat as the tasteful navy of her pencil skirt and matching blazer. She held January's hand on one side, and on the other, July's.

July was harder to see, her back up against the pew, wearing a long-sleeved lace dress that was such a deep violet it blended into the liturgical tapestries behind her.

Then there was June, in yellow as bright as the sunflowers widely known to be her favorite flower. June, looking clothed in summer itself. June, at a funeral, in canary gold, like Anne Boleyn dancing on her rival's grave.

After the service, they clustered in the narthex, ready to greet everyone they knew and everyone they didn't as though they did.

"Hey, little sister," called out one of the gossip reporters. Even those of us who hated Mother May I didn't like him. What was there to like about someone whose platform revolved around circling spots of back fat on candid bikini pictures?

And now he was heckling January.

Even on video, we could detect the shift in the air, a collective bristling of arm hairs. Security was already coming from the doors.

"Did you and your big eyes start that big fire all on your own?" this lowest form of journalistic life asked. "Yeah, it was you, wasn't it? You can tell me."

We almost paused the video to stick bags of popcorn in the microwave. We couldn't wait for June's withering reply. *Wow, jowls by age twenty-five. You must be really proud of your accomplishments.*

But the next moment happened so fast that we had to watch the footage a couple of times to understand it.

June lunged forward. The force of her was so focused, so intense, that those of us watching wondered if she might go right for the man's jugular. But January acted so fast that by the time the chaos of the moment passed, January was behind June, her arms around her, holding her back. July was standing in front of them, making a visible effort to keep her face unruffled and ready to greet guests. Security was already escorting the heckler out. It was as beautiful as a football play.

Behind July, January still held on to June. June was slowing her breathing, mouthing something that looked like a reassuring *I'm okay, I'm okay* to January. That was the oddest thing about it, their body postures. June wasn't trying to shake off January's hold. She wasn't saying *get off me* under her breath. Just in this moment, she was deferring to January like she would to April, as though some of April's oldest-sister authority had rubbed off on January.

It wasn't until January said—under her breath but we could still read her lips—"Where the fuck is April?" that we realized.

April wasn't in the narthex receiving guests.

Neither was May Iverson.

April Iverson

"Oh, hi, honey," her mother said when she noticed April come into the church choir room.

From one look, April could tell how painfully hard her mother was trying to seem like she wasn't crying. She balled up a sky-blue tissue so tight in her fist that it disappeared.

Maybe there were better places and times for this than right after the memorial service, among racks of choral robes. But June wouldn't stop texting April, and as much as April hated ever admitting that June had a point, she did.

At least the distant organ music was good cover. Good luck to anyone trying to eavesdrop outside the door.

"Mom," April said. "We're really worried about you."

Her mother turned a sniffle into a laugh. "You mean Junie's worried about me? Everything's fine. I made my statement, and everyone's even more on our side than before. She just needs to relax."

April's disbelief was so thick in her throat it made her cough. "Relax? There was just a murder in your house."

Her mother took on a well-practiced look: the chic, stoic widow. April couldn't blame her. Whatever helped her keep it together in front of the spectators who pretended to be mourners. Half of them looked like they were trying to figure out how to record on their phones without being tacky.

"August was an entrepreneur," her mother said. "He took risks in his business. He had a brave vision, and he had the courage to do something with it. Brave men make enemies."

"Enemies who came after you too," April said. "In your house."

Her mother's fingers tightened on her glossed clutch, her latest acquisition from the brand's flagship store in Paris, where the bags were so exclusive you had to be interviewed to be deemed worthy of buying one.

"So now you care?" her mother asked.

April's nerves bristled at the sharpening tone.

"You're my firstborn daughter," her mother said, "and you haven't taken my calls in months. Someone literally had to die for you to talk to me."

April sighed. "Mother."

"I wanted to put all this behind us," her mother said. "I thought we had. You stabbed me in the back, and I still wanted to put it behind us."

"I didn't stab you in the back. And I told my lawyer to drop it. Faster than she wanted me to drop it, by the way."

"I'm not even talking about that." Her mother kept her eyes on her. For once her gaze didn't twitch toward her phone, wondering what she might have missed in the last two minutes.

"The content strike?" her mother said. "I know that was you. I could have lost the income from every sponsorship in my posts. I could have lost the income from every affiliate link, every code. This is not playing around. This is not for daughters with mood swings. Strikes are meant for defamation, hate speech, graphic content, harmful misinformation."

"And infringement on copyrighted content," April said.

"Excuse me?" May asked.

"I didn't give you permission to film at my place of business," April said. "Neither did the people I work with. Nor did I, or they, give you permission to film the designs we were working on. And when you still filmed, against my stated wishes, I told you, explicitly, not to post any of what you had filmed. But you did."

"Oh, what an awful mother I am for advertising my daughter's business to millions of people," her mother said, voice rising. "Do you know what any small business would give for that kind of exposure?"

"I didn't ask for it," April said. "I didn't want it."

Her mother didn't even sound like she'd heard April. She just kept going. "I'm such a monster for being proud of my daughter."

"No." April raised her voice enough to stop her mother talking. "You're a monster for thinking nobody gets to have feelings but you. You get to feel sad, but we don't get to feel violated. You get to have boundaries, but we don't. We're forbidden to take a single picture with you unless you have your false eyelashes on, but you can strut in and film whatever you want, whenever you want, right?"

Her mother burst into tears. And April hated herself for feeling a flash of guilt.

No one ever really won an argument with their mother. Either you lost, or you won but you felt so guilty you might as well have lost.

we the followers of Mother May I

Within hours of the memorial service, Ashley Morgan Kelly had footage of June lunging at the gossip commentator.

"The fairest Iverson daughter of them all continues to show herself as volatile and unhinged. But that's not all, Fine Crimers. Take a close look at the frame. Who's missing? That's right. It seems both May Iverson and her eldest daughter April barely stayed for the closing hymn."

Was the bottle of Veuve on her side table a pointed comment about the Iverson widow, or was it a celebration of her own rising subscriber count? Fine Crime had nowhere near May Iverson's numbers, or the Summer Girls', or even June or July on their own separate accounts. But more and more people were watching.

"This is clearly a family in chaos," Ashley Morgan Kelly said. "But enough chaos to lead to murder? As we ponder this very question, we turn to a new post by one of May Iverson's closest friends."

Another video took over the screen. At first it was a little hard to see May Iverson or the women with her. The sun was setting. May and all the other women around her were reduced to silhouettes and the glowing edges of their hair.

"I can't cry anymore," May said. "I have to clear all that shitty protein powder out of my garage."

The blondes and redheads she was with raised their glasses, the wine gold against the blue of an infinity pool. (Not the one at the Iverson mansion. A different one. We could tell by the tile work.)

"He always had a smile for everyone. He was so much fun." May shook her head and shut her eyes. "So much fun. God, I miss that fun." She opened her eyes, thickened, lengthened eyelashes fluttering (not false lashes, she always made a point of saying; it was perpetually thanks to some new mascara, for which she always provided an affiliate link). "But he really was useless."

The women all laughed.

"Just useless," May said.

They laughed harder, collapsing into each other, glasses clinking more accidentally than in cheers.

When we found the original post, the fellow influencer who'd put it up was already answering the backlash. She was the one with the YSL decals on the points of her fake nails, whose high-pitched "I don't know what everyone's getting so upset about" was mimicked and mocked across the internet. (Parodies involved lip-synching and white-blond/lime-green split-dyed wigs as straight as uncooked spaghetti.)

Some condemned her for posting something so disrespectful of the deceased on the very day of his memorial service. Others condemned May Iverson for speaking that way of her late husband so soon after his death. "It's a tribute to him," the woman who'd posted it said in one of her live responses. "Did you trolls even read the caption? And can't you tell how much she loved him? Why would she have kept someone useless around if she didn't?"

Yes, May Iverson had been tactless. You would have thought that after years of practice drinking on camera and selling pieces of her life for advertising dollars, she'd have known how to hold her Viognier and her tongue.

Yes, it was bad form to speak ill of the dead. But grief did funny things. People liked to think they knew how it went, how it should have gone. *Who acts like that?* Or, *Does that look like a grieving wife? I would never do that.* Or, *How does it look, her just going on like nothing's happened? It's not normal.*

Who really knew, though? How did anyone know how they'd act in the same situation? Who was well enough acquainted with the grief of every heart in the world to make a template for it?

July Iverson

July thought she'd be able to feel it, the shift in the house after everything that had happened here. But there was no bristling of death, no bite of smoke in the air, or it was so diffused across the house that July couldn't find it. There were so many rooms and hallways and staircases that even something that massive couldn't loom.

While June got her mother settled, July checked every wet bar. She made sure each beverage refrigerator had all six of her mother's favorite bottled water brands. She'd just started a grocery list when she heard voices in the nearest living room. There were six living rooms spread throughout the mansion, each of which June referred to, unhelpfully and unspecifically, as *the* living room.

Five living rooms. July was pretty sure the one off her mother's bedroom had been destroyed.

The one where July found April and January was, like the others, primarily white. Only the accent pillows and throw blankets distinguished it, the silver and pale gray fabrics shiny enough that they would have seemed more at home on a red carpet than a sofa.

"How did someone film this without her even noticing?" April asked.

"She's always filming," January said. "How would she notice?"

In their navy and black funeral outfits, April and January stood out against the pale backdrop, and the features of the room receded. They were both looking at April's phone. A flash of the image was all July needed to know why.

Their mother and August. The conflict about June signing checks.

"And she doesn't even know who—" April noticed July in the doorway. "Have you seen this?"

July nodded.

"And why is Mom not treating this as the monumental security breach it is?" April asked.

July felt ten years old again, with April asking why she hadn't said anything when their mom forgot to sign her field trip form.

April looked past July. "Where's June?"

"Getting Mom moved into one of the guest rooms," July said.

"And has June seen this?" April asked.

How was July supposed to answer without feeling like she was telling on June?

"She didn't want to talk about it," July said.

"I didn't want to talk about what?" June entered the room in a flash of golden yellow.

"How's she holding up?" April asked.

"Saying she wants to redo that entire guest suite in palo santo." June flopped down on a sofa the way she always did, as hard as she could, like she wanted to see if she'd bounce off. "It's the grief talking. If she doesn't calm down in the next couple of hours, I'll crush up some Ambien in her La Fermière."

"And you're not even a little concerned about this?" April held up her phone.

"The bitches by the pool?" June asked. "Don't even give that brain space."

"Not the pool," April said. "I don't give a shit about the bad decisions Mom makes with her clone army. I'm talking about her and August arguing about you and those checks."

"Whatever," June asked. "Whoever filmed it is gone now. Along with everyone else who ran this place. For better or for worse."

"Do you understand how big of a problem this is?" April asked.

"Dramatics, all of you," June said. "If you want to worry about something, worry about Mom not knowing how to use her own milk frother. Don't worry about bad publicity. Have you seen what they're saying about her online, how many people are rushing to her defense? Whoever wanted to make her look bad just got everyone even more on her side."

"But where did they get it?" January asked.

"Obviously someone filmed it and then sat on it," June said.

"I don't think so," January said. "I don't think this is someone else's device. I think this is one of Mom's own cameras."

July resisted the dim understanding blooming at the back of her brain. She wanted to be wrong. She wanted the next words January said to prove her wrong.

"How do you know that?" June asked. To her credit, she sounded more curious than dismissive. It was the same way June had sounded talking to January when they were kids. *Hey, what are you building there? You're totally gonna win the blue ribbon with that. Better than the blue ribbon. They're gonna have to make a science fair gold medal for that.*

With barely a look from January, April handed her the phone.

"Look at the film quality." January sat down next to June. "The coloration. The exaggerated vignetting. The synthetic light leaks. It's all stylistic. I remember this. This was a prototype. They were trying to make a video camera look more like analog film. It's one of the only times Mom's ever called me to ask what I thought of a collaboration. So my question is"—January handed the phone back to April, but kept looking at June—"where's the camera this was taken on?"

"How would I know that?" June asked. "How would she? That thing is long gone. She doesn't keep old cameras. Especially not since we moved out. Every time her professional organizer comes over, they practically declutter every appliance in the kitchen."

"Does she wipe the internal memory from the cameras before she declutters them?" January asked.

July could tell how much it took for January to say the word *declutters* without sarcasm.

"I mean, I try my best," June said. "But you saw how far I got when I went to bat for the security system."

"So that camera could be anywhere," April said.

"Along with whatever else was on it," January said.

July didn't want to say it. Everything would be worse once she said it.

But her sisters would keep spinning if she didn't just say it.

"August." July let the name fall out of her mouth.

They all looked at her.

"Mom always wanted to get rid of the old cameras," July said.

Almost before June spoke, July felt her tuning into the same frequency July was already on.

"And August never wanted to," June said with the dread of realization.

"'Hey, what are you doing,'" July quoted August without trying to imitate his voice. The words came out flat and blank.

"'That's a perfectly good piece of electronic equipment,'" June finished the sentence, and for once, she wasn't even making fun of August as she repeated his words. She just droned them back.

June got up so fast she looked as though the sofa had thrown her off.

"Where are you going?" April asked.

She and January followed. So did July, lagging behind. She already knew where June was going: August's area of the house. It had been untouched by the fire, but because it was close to the staircase where August's body was found, it had already been scoured by crime scene technicians trained to detect so much as a stray unidentified eyelash.

These were the numerous rooms, practically a whole wing, that their mother let him saturate with sweat and testosterone and a level of clutter that she never would have stood for anywhere else. Crowded corners of workout equipment. An unnecessary number of TVs (each time he got a better one, he added it without subtracting an old one, like a new satellite dish). His shoe collection that outdid even their mother's.

And all the cameras their mother wanted to get rid of but that August always intercepted. He added each one to the collection he was amassing in those rooms.

June tore across the house until she got to the media room, an even larger expanse than August's personal living room. What wall space wasn't covered with screens was taken up by touch-latch cabinets.

"June, have they even said you can go in here?" April asked.

"This is Mom's house," June said. "Unless there's plastic or police tape, I go where I want."

June shoved a palm into a cabinet door, activating the touch-latch mechanism that was in every design magazine after their mom remodeled this room. It yawned open, empty except for a few old cameras, and the shadows of dust where many more had once been.

June opened another cabinet door, and then another, and another, stopping only when she got to the ones filled with bottles of supplements and scotch and collectible vinyl.

The cabinets were all open now, and with all of them open at once, it was impossible to miss what was missing. There was only a fraction of the old cameras their mother had once owned, and that had once filled these shelves. Stray cords and abandoned instruction manuals were the only hints to what was missing.

April and January stared into the cabinets.

"Why didn't Mom report them stolen?" April asked.

"They're artifacts," June said. "No one uses them anymore, so Mom wouldn't have missed them. It wouldn't have registered to her. Once August took them, she forgot about them the same as if she'd gotten rid of them."

"Only August would actually know what was in here," July said, like taking over the next verse of the grim song June was singing.

"And if I could barely get her to clear the memory when she was giving a camera away, she wouldn't have thought twice before handing it over to August," June said.

One by one they pulled their stares from the empty shelves and met one another's eyes. July could almost hear the math they were doing in the space between them.

Someone hadn't just killed August.

Someone hadn't just tried to burn down their mother's house.

Someone had taken pieces of all of their lives on the way out.

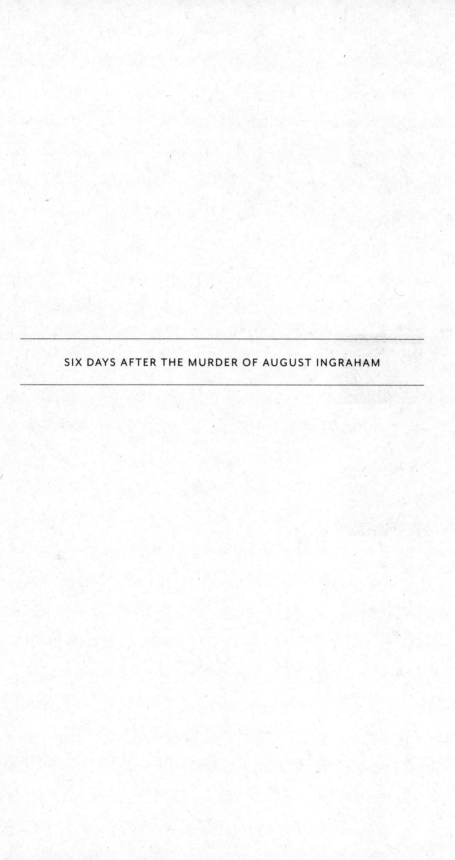

SIX DAYS AFTER THE MURDER OF AUGUST INGRAHAM

June Iverson

June and July flanked their mother as she reported the stolen items, as she had to explain that no, she didn't have an inventory. It was gone the minute August was.

The detectives explained, calmly, politely, that the information she had just told them should remain confidential. It was a piece of the investigation that they would hold back. Those electronics were a potential lead. If the thefts were publicized, the murderer might dispose of them. If they weren't, the murderer had a better chance of getting cocky.

"People get sloppy," the older detective said. "They put something up for sale online or they try to pawn it, and suddenly, we have a way in."

"Of course," her mother said. She was offering the detectives a polite, cooperative smile, but there was nothing behind it. It was like that carb-free ice cream Mother May I promoted a few years ago, a sad imitation.

Their mother may have looked like perfection right down to her lip liner, but she was unraveling. She'd even forgotten her Cartier in the safe at the hotel, their first stop after the police station. Their mother had lost enough lately. No reason to add a Baignoire watch to the list.

A hotel manager let the three of them into the room, told them to take all the time they needed, that the suite had been taken care of for as long as their mother had use of it. When June pressed, the manager discreetly mentioned a brand name, one that'd been looking to re-up its partnership with Mother May I.

As soon as the manager retreated, June whispered to July, "Let's sweep the room. She's probably left earrings and pots of La Mer all over here like acorns."

July did as she was told, but as soon as they'd checked all the drawers and shelves, July just stood there picking at her nails—hadn't she conquered that habit? Hadn't she listened to those meditations June had sent her to remove nail biting from her core identity?

The second their mother went to the bathroom, June pushed on July's shoulders to get her to sit down. She needed to relax. One unraveling Iverson was enough.

June shoved the room service menu at July. "What do you want?"

"Why are we eating here?" July asked. "You're the one who said how important it was to get her back into a familiar environment. We can pick up something when we take her to the house."

"Because"—June kept her voice low—"the HOA needs us to stall so they can get security to chase the media away. So we're having a nice, calm, leisurely farewell-to-the-hotel lunch, okay?"

When their mother came out of the bathroom, June pasted on a smile worthy of a promo shoot. But July had such a troubled, haunted look about her that June wanted to elbow her. If an abandoned carnival ride sitting in the rain had a face, it would be wearing July's expression.

Their mother crossed the room with an "Everything is going to be all right. No use worrying yourself into frown lines."

"But we don't know what's out there," July said. "We don't know what they have."

This wasn't the time. July could panic later, not in front of their mother. The two of them needed to be dauntless and cheerful for their mother. They were shepherd moons, the points of gravity keeping their mother together.

"Whoever has them has us," July said. "If they have all that, they have us. They have us in pieces."

Their mother sat on the other side of July, which meant she couldn't see June pinching July's leg.

"Can we all just disappear?" July asked. "Maybe if we disappear, they'll forget us, and they'll leave us alone."

June was about to jump in with an emphatic *no*, a speech about how nothing would prove their enemies' strength quite like cowering.

But their mother's assured voice fell over the room.

"We will get through this," their mother said. "We keep our heads up. We keep our eyes forward."

"Deny everything?" July asked. "Ignore everything?"

Their mother pushed July's hair behind her ears. Their mother's eyes looked clearer, more focused, than they had in days. "We ignore everything that doesn't matter." There she was, the version of their mother who had made millions by making millions of women want to be like her. She hadn't been at the police station, but she was here now, Mother May I, the woman staggeringly optimistic but also smart enough to build an empire.

"Remember," their mother said, "if you're hiding . . ."

July breathed out. "They'll know you have something to hide."

"That's my girl," their mother said. "We don't hide. It's not who we are."

This was the version of their mother who could weather all this.

The panic in June's chest began to uncoil. They could do this. They could survive this. They could survive anything.

May Iverson

Manifest your reality.

Concentrate your thoughts on that which you want to come true.

Shine your light on the solutions, not the problems.

Affirmations had always worked for May. And so often she had repeated them to herself by this very pool, on these very chaises where she brainstormed everything from seminars to product launches.

It had been surprisingly easy to look July in the eye and tell her what she needed to hear. Not because May wasn't worried about what was on those stolen cameras. But because there were so many things to worry about, each of them with just as much weight. There were vultures everywhere, poison everywhere.

The latest poison had come in the form of one particular argument she'd had out here with August, and just how much that vulture next door was now claiming she'd heard. She'd even run off to some commentator who called herself "Crime and Cashmere" or something like that. Everyone bored enough to glue themselves to her family's tragedy would feast on it.

Usually, May had never been stupid enough to fight with August outside. Anyone from a flower deliveryman to the car detailers could have heard. But that day, August had come blustering out of the house with "You've been cutting them checks?"

May should have gotten right up from her poolside chaise longue, said, "Not here," and ushered him back through the glass pivot doors.

Instead, she took another sip of sauvignon blanc. "It was the right thing to do."

"Without even talking to me?" August asked.

The closer he came, the more she could smell him. Ever since he'd upped his dosage of muscle-enhancement supplements, he'd started reeking like bouillon cubes. She hadn't wanted to hurt his feelings, but it was long past time to have a talk with him about it. Maybe after the next time they had sex. Make-up sex, it was looking like from August's face.

May crossed one ankle over the other. "You offered to buy the land off the farmer without even talking to me."

"It was an offer." August had deliberately blocked her sun. She could always tell when he was doing it on purpose. "I would never have gone through with it without talking to you."

"Oh?" Now she sat up. "You mean like when you didn't sink thirty grand into a pyramid scheme without talking to me?"

"InFITnitum isn't a pyramid scheme. It's a lifestyle. It's going to change the world."

May hated when he talked that way, as though it was his job to enlighten the masses, starting with his wife.

"It's a calling," he said. "People don't understand that yet, but they will. We'll see a 400 percent return by next year. I told you."

"And I told you that we have to keep it nice with our neighbors." May at least had the presence of mind to lower her voice. "We're in a fishbowl here."

"And I would have solved that problem if you'd just waited until he cracked. Any day now he would've taken my offer."

May removed her sunglasses, the prototype with the antiaging filter she was testing for her next line. "And in the meantime, I would've looked like Marie Antoinette telling him and his family and their little farm to eat cake. What was the harm in throwing some money at the problem? Actual money, not some insulting offer. For the sake of goodwill. Let everyone come away feeling like a winner."

She was just getting ready to settle back into her self-care time when August said, "It's our money."

"Our money?" May swung her legs off the chaise longue. "I'm sorry, how much do you bring into this marriage?"

"Community property state, sweetheart." He toed his sneaker at her pedicure. "Your money is our money is my money."

Their pre-nup said otherwise; a divorce might cost her, but it wouldn't cost her 50 percent. No use feeding into the negative energy, though. She summoned her most positive self, released the need to be right, and drew her legs back up onto the upholstery.

"Did that little bitch put you up to this?" August asked.

May was on her feet so fast the air around her snapped like a flag. "Call one of my kids a bitch again. Go ahead."

She had raised her voice exactly when she should have shut up.

She got right in August's face when she should have gone back in the house.

Whenever he got into one of his prickish moods, she just needed to ignore him and let him bluster it off. He always came back with apologies, a new box of Venus et Fleur, and an offer to spend the evening watching one of her favorite movies.

Instead, she poked a manicured finger into his chest. "We'll see what your little wave generator does when I shove your dick into it."

Now, May shuddered remembering her own words. Not with guilt. She didn't regret the words. August knew she loved him. He liked when she blew up at him a little. She could always see it in his eyes, the match-flare of passion.

But no one else would understand that. They'd assume they knew the inside of her marriage from one fight. She knew what they thought, that after the scent of her bespoke bridal perfume faded, after her bouquet had been freeze-dried in a display box, after her wedding dress had been preserved with all the care of a coronation gown, she regretted marrying him. Even half her fans thought that. They assumed she'd been so swept up in the idea of a glittering wedding to this man that she hadn't considered the sweat-sheened, ten-thousand-dollar-watch-wearing reality of him as a husband. They wondered if she'd seethed every time he rolled his fitness bikes across her white carpeting, every time he left her favorite car smelling of protein-style burgers, extra raw onions.

Sometimes, it was true. Sometimes, he annoyed the hell out of her. Sometimes, she wanted to brain him with the workout bag he always dropped in her beautiful foyer.

But it was fleeting and never lasted, like the top note in a fragrance. She loved him, and it was enough that she knew it and he knew it. No one could get to her by saying otherwise.

Where they could get to her was with what they said about her girls.

Her daughters had made mistakes. But May wouldn't let those mistakes map out their whole lives. Not even if they were captured by a gawking bystander tapping RECORD. Not even if they were written into the loops of a forged signature. Not even if they were logged in a missing camera's internal memory.

July Iverson

July let the video play as she wandered through the storage facility, looking for August's unit. "A breaking development in the shocking murder of August Ingraham." Ashley Morgan Kelly set her mouth in a serious line, but her eyes glinted like she was smiling. It made her face seem divided in half, like when June cracked plastic Easter eggs in two, then put an orange top with a bright green bottom.

July checked the numbers on the units to see if they were going up or down, trying to figure out if she was walking the right way. When she'd asked her mother what she could do to help, her mother had handed over the key to the unit. *Just clean it out,* she had pleaded. *The police have cleared it for evidence, so they don't care what you do with what's in it. Neither do I. If there's something you like, just keep it. Throw out everything else.*

It was the single break in her mother's otherwise cheerful composure: sorting through August's things. She could laugh about anything when she was drinking with her friends, but when she was sober, facing the clutter of her dead husband's life made her look haunted and hollow.

As July searched for the right unit number, Ashley Morgan Kelly kept talking through the phone's speaker. "We are now learning that the day of the murder, a second deceased man was apparently found on the hillside below the burning mansion."

At those words, the grief that lived in July reared up and got a little louder. A neighbor, probably June's favorite of their mother's neighbors, had died on the same day as August. But most reporting didn't even mention it. Even here, his death would be little more than a footnote, overshadowed by the murder case.

"Was this an accomplice fleeing the scene?" Ashley Morgan Kelly asked. "The culprit, acting alone?"

The grief sharpened into rage. Was she really calling their neighbor a suspect? This would destroy the old man's family.

"Or did August Ingraham's killer embark on a murderous spree?" This, voiced over silhouettes of a men's-restroom-sign-style figure running from a knife-wielding woman figure, her skirt so full she looked like she was marking a ladies' bathroom in the Victorian era. "If May Iverson was capable of killing her own husband, or if one of her daughters was capable of killing her own stepfather, could she also have killed a witness who saw too much?"

July's rage settled into a conflicted relief. Ashley Morgan Kelly was shameless in her theories about the murderous Iverson women, but if that was going to keep the old man and his family out of this, it was worth it.

July found the right unit. As she watched her own hands slipping the key into the lock, she thought of her mother facing this door. *The man just didn't know how to curate,* her mother had told her, sadly but with a fond smile, three glasses in. Her mother lived a life made for glossed heels on plush carpets, a life that would have made her completely incongruous in the unshaded glare of an outdoor storage facility. She wouldn't have known how to stand on cracking asphalt in front of a roll-up metal door.

If June and August would have ever bonded over anything, it should've been that, how little they liked to throw things out. Last year June had been sent an eye-wateringly expensive elliptical-cycling-convertible workout machine that she used intensively for a week and then abandoned, but had refused to get rid of. It now took up more space than her dresser in her bedroom, where she used it to dry her bras.

The door of the unit faced the parking lot, and recent rain had started to rust the lock shut. July fought with the key, yelling at it, kicking the door, swearing the thing into oblivion as Ashley Morgan Kelly transitioned into an interlude about imported French foundation. July didn't feel anyone watching, but even if there was, what did it matter? Let someone film her screaming at a panel of corrugated metal.

When the lock gave, her elation lasted only until she slid the door up.

Plastic jars, each one as large as a gallon milk jug, lined the unit, left wall to right, floor to ceiling. The name InFITnitum spanned each label, throwing the letters at July so many times they stopped meaning anything. Taking one from the wall and setting it on the asphalt in front of the unit had no visible effect. The one behind it seemed to advance to fill the spot.

What was she supposed to do with all of these?

"For every answer, a hundred new questions emerge in this increasingly twisted story," Ashley Morgan Kelly went on from July's purse. "But I know that I can count on you, my connoisseurs of true crime and cashmere, to bring me anything you hear."

July picked up the jar she had set down on the asphalt. She went to the edge of the parking lot, where the fraying seam of concrete gave way to a rocky slope that ran down toward the freeway. Lights were just starting to come on, peppering the orange of the haze and the deepening blue of the sky.

July unscrewed the lid. She peeled off the foil, and the fake vanilla scent hit her like a car air freshener. When the next gust of wind came, she shook the jar. The powder spooled out into the dusk like ashes and billowed out over the freeway. She shook it all out for August and for the dead man on the hill whose name no one knew.

SEVEN DAYS AFTER THE MURDER OF AUGUST INGRAHAM

we who still had a bad feeling about that guy

A lot of people thought that the way Luke Sweatshirt followed the twins around was cute. They didn't believe us when we said there was something off about him. *It's not a crime to look like a regular person,* they told us.

Maybe not, but there was something inexplicable about someone getting within ten feet of the Iverson twins while wearing plain gray New Balance sneakers. He looked like an extra in a movie from before May Iverson became Mother May I. He looked like an extra in a movie from before he was even born.

Then we got a better look at him. We saw clearer photos of his face (ones taken by observers; he was rarely in the twins' posts, and even then it was usually the back of his head). And there was something about him we couldn't ignore.

He looked a little like the Iversons, particularly June (coloring; shape of upper lip) and January (eyes; hairline). He looked almost exactly like an Iverson second cousin who'd shown up in holiday and family reunion content. If that second cousin hadn't been accounted for, we would've been sure it was him (he didn't have much of a following online, but his accounts were public, and showed photos of him, his wife, their two children, and several dogs). To many of us, the simplest explanation was that Luke Sweatshirt was related to the Iversons.

But to just as many of us, this was a disgusting theory, since he and June were so clearly dating. He followed her around not like a cousin but like a hopeful boyfriend. Sure, they looked a little alike, but there was another explanation for that, even if June's most ardent fans didn't want to hear it. June was an influencer. A certain level of narcissism was practically a job requirement. Of course she would date someone who looked a little like her. Of course she would find an ordinary-looking guy attractive because he bore some resemblance to her. We could imagine her musing as she touched up her brows. *I don't know. There's just something about him I like.* However much people want to think that opposites attract, more often than not, people date people who are similar to them. And it gave Luke Sweatshirt a distinct advantage in getting closer to the Iversons.

We reminded everyone that the police had made no arrests. No one was an official suspect, which meant everyone was still an unofficial suspect. Including the guy hovering around two girls who were way, way out of his league.

Then, a week into the investigation, came a great equalizer of suspicion. As though the universe was agreeing with us that, yes, it could have been anyone, including Luke Sweatshirt.

When we heard the truth, we were instantly drunk on it. Liquor. Wine. Imported aperitifs. All that fancy booze in the Iverson mansion. There were literal walls of it. May Iverson's champagne and rosé. August's designer whiskey, the backdrop to half his weekend posts. Apparently, after the fire, it was all gone.

At first we thought the media outlets covering the investigation were talking about theft, some very specific booze-targeted burglary. After all, some of those bottles were worth more than anything that any of us had in our own homes. But then we read on, and we realized what the reports were saying.

The bottles had still been there. It was just that they were all empty. And all the empties had still been on the property, either discarded or shattered by the fire.

At first it didn't make sense. Had someone gone on a bender before torching the mansion? Liquid courage to work up the nerve before committing a murder?

Then it came into focus, like sugar dissolving in hot water, the solution turning clear.

The liquor had been the accelerant. Whoever killed August Ingraham had poured out all the booze and then lit it. Anyone could have done it, including the guy in the gray sweatshirt. Whoever had killed August and set the house on fire hadn't brought their own supplies, so there was no accelerant to match to possible suspects. The supplies had already been in the house. That was how the murderer had done it, all that sugar on fire.

June Iverson

Usually, when June walked into a party, the decibel level shot up. She just had that effect on people. That was why she liked to show up when a party started to go flat. She was the shot of espresso that woke everyone up.

Except now. She strolled into the cathedral foyer—wow, trust-fund kids had an interesting definition of *starter home*—and a hundred conversations went silent at once.

June strolled over to the built-in bar, poured three shots, and downed each one. None of the fruit-flavored layered shit they were pouring. No signature cocktails. Three shots of Grey Goose VX, one right after the other.

She held up the rest of the bottle, faced the watching crowd, and asked, "Anyone got a match?"

Everyone roared with laughter. The tension fell away. She was still the life of the party, even if she had to make herself into a joke. And what did that matter? She'd been making herself into a joke her whole life.

Three hours later, the world was blurring, and she was sitting on a heavy wooden desk in what was, unironically, called the study. What the fuck was this room supposed to prove? The stodgy furniture didn't change what everyone knew, that the birthday boy had no profession other than spending the fortune his family had made off meal-replacement cookies.

"Show us," the birthday boy said. At least she thought it was the birthday boy. Who could tell them apart? The room wouldn't stay on its axis, and they were all in three-hundred-dollar shirts and khakis, and wearing watches worth more than most cars. "Come on, just show us how you do it." He set a few pieces of monogrammed stationery and a hotel pen down on the desk.

June slid the paper onto the blotter. "Treat antique wood with a little respect, you dick."

Everyone in the room laughed. By way of apology, the guy theatrically doffed his silk top hat. A top hat? What was the theme of this party, The Great fucking Gatsby during rush week?

"Let's do yours," June said. "Sign your name."

The birthday boy hesitated.

"What's the matter?" she asked in a film noir femme fatale voice. "Afraid I'm gonna kill you and then have lunch on your tab at the club?"

"Yeah, go on, Keough," his friends said. "What are you, scared?"

He signed his name. She imitated it, loop by scribble. This was a party trick she could do even five drinks in.

She held them both up, identical. The room broke into applause.

"Very nice," he said, as though satisfied with the opening act but ready for the main event. "Now do a celebrity."

June dreamily tilted her head, making a show of considering her options. Then, with a few flourishes, she dashed off a signature.

"Look it up," a girl said, but everything was so fuzzy at the edges that June couldn't place who'd said it. "Go look it up."

"Is it right?" Another voice June couldn't pinpoint.

"It's right!"

"She got it right!"

"Holy shit."

"How does she do that?"

Of course June had gotten it right. Everything was there. No salutations. The vertical letters. The first name sitting on top of the last. The curves of the *J* mingling with the peaks of the *M*. The double *L*, the second one larger and more looping than the first. The dagger of the *t* in the middle.

The birthday boy picked up the sheet of paper. "Who's Joni Mitchell?"

"Both sides now," June said, and grabbed a girl she'd already kissed two hours earlier. The girl wrapped her arms around June and kissed her hard enough that June could feel her vodka breath mixing with the layered-shot fruitiness of the girl's. The room filled with a distinctly masculine roar of approval, but June could block it out, because she was kissing a woman whose name she wouldn't remember tomorrow morning, and the breath between their lips was flammable enough to ignite.

"Now do your mom's," someone from out of frame yelled.

Languorously, in her own sweet time, June finished her kiss.

"No," June said, still hanging on to the girl, the girl hanging on to her. "There's no fun in that."

"Why?" the girl asked, the word laughter-carbonated. For the first time June took a good look at her outfit. Who let this poor woman out of the house wearing an extra-long camisole over capri pants?

"No challenge with my mom's signature," June said. "I invented it."

we the followers of Mother May I

Everyone knew May Iverson liked her rosé. And her chardonnay. And her champagne and prosecco. She even had a display wall of premium liqueur, the backdrop for each time she shared a cocktail recipe, a few of her "going-out glam" tutorials (like before a friend's bachelorette party), and some of her sponsorship photos (only if the brand was aiming for a younger and/or single demographic—diamond-infused mascara may have wanted to be in front of the booze; mom-focused brands usually didn't).

But the same day the news broke about the accelerant, an anonymous account posted a video in front of that wall, one that didn't look familiar to any of us. Mother May I had hosted plenty of cocktail nights, where hands manicured with sour apple green or shock blue would hold electric pink cocktails. Sugared rosemary and flash-frozen pansies would garnish glass coupes. Lace-clad fingers would lift drinks with names like Bijou, Lady Rose, French 75/Soixante Quinze.

None of them matched this one. We double- and then triple-checked.

In this one, May and a fellow influencer stood in front of the wall, dressed in bright, clingy florals that picked up the colors of the liqueurs. They had chosen the precise best time of day for photos. When the light hit the bottles, they were as colorful as stained glass. The deep blush of Lillet Rosé. The leafed teal globe of Agavero liqueur. The flame orange of Aperol and the orange-red of Campari. Fluorescent limoncello. Amber St-Germain Elderflower. A deep plum sphere of Chambord. The moss green of Chartreuse Verte and the honeyed gold of Chartreuse Jaune. Sauternes like liquid sunlight. The cherry mauve of Liqueur de Violettes. Midori that looked like the bright, poisonous green of a wicked queen's potion.

Just as they were about to take the first picture, the friend said something indecipherable in the audio. May Iverson laughed so hard she stumbled back, right into the wall of bottles. Half a row came down. With a burst of glass, the hardwood floor was covered in pink and green syrup.

The two women leaped back, saving their skirts and their pastel suede heels. They laughed so hard they had to steady themselves on a nearby bar cart, which started them laughing again when it rolled and they realized they hadn't set the brake.

Neither seemed upset. Especially not May Iverson. She looked at the mess of liqueur that cost more than the average monthly rent in the city her mansion overlooked. The money was nothing to her, and neither was the mess. She had a team ever ready to clean up after her.

All she had to do right then was laugh.

"That'll teach me to day drink," May said.

"Or drink and pose," the blond woman said.

"The fault lies not in our stars but in our selfies," May said. "Only the best for my floors." She posed like a 1940s movie siren. "No Boone's Farm for these floors."

The blonde gave a devious grin. "No Bartles & Jaymes?"

"Not since college," May said.

"No Burnett's?" the blonde asked.

"Eww," May said. "No poor-people booze allowed in this house."

They kept laughing, so hard that the bar cart, still not properly braked, rolled out of the frame, and they ran after it. Then the clip ended.

A lot of people wondered why, at this point, any of us were still watching Mother May I. How could anyone survive the on-camera words *no poor-people booze* while standing in all that bright, liquid money?

Some of us stayed just to see how bad it would get. We bowed to our queens, and then cheered at their ousting. The loftier they became—the loftier we ourselves made them—the more we caught our breaths in anticipation of their glorious fall.

Some of us were realistic, foreseeing the inevitable redemption arc. What rich, pretty, adored white woman in a renovated mansion didn't get one of those? So what was the point of joining the outrage? Everyone would be back on her side eventually, through either her own charm or the efforts of a PR firm.

Some of us were just loyal in a way that stuck, and we were the ones who knew this wasn't a coincidence. Whoever had done this had released it at just the right moment, putting a careless, unsympathetic image of May right next to the accelerant, willing us to imagine her as her husband's murderer.

We weren't having it. We would not be manipulated by whoever thought this would turn us against her, whoever had decided to kick her while she was down.

Mother May I had carbonated our spirits when our children fingerpainted on our best skirts ("It's like they know which one's your favorite, which one's really gonna break your heart if they put a big old smear of green acrylic across it").

She'd empathized with our stress-crying over the class moms' last-minute phone calls—"Don't you love those? If it's not your kid saying her science project is due tomorrow and she hasn't even started, it's Princess PTA chirping, 'Oh, I can't believe this slipped my mind, tomorrow's the day everyone brings in a recipe authentic to their family's heritage, that won't be a problem, right?' Like you can really do anything in that moment except say, 'Oh, of course not, it's no trouble at all' and start making your list for the grocery run."

When we hated the way we looked in photos, she was our older sister telling us how to pose—"Your husband's ex-girlfriend, she's really not as skinny as she looks in her Christmas card, she just knows her angles, and I'm gonna teach you all her secrets right now." She beckoned in that conspiratorial way June learned to imitate exactly.

Yes, even we, Mother May I's most loyal fans, hated her sometimes. Especially when she stood still. Her impeccably lit, meticulously styled photos could make any of us feel dowdy, like we were the girl in the front right corner of the classroom—worst seat, most attention from the teacher—wearing not only discount clothes but the frumpiest ones on the rack.

But Mother May I's videos, those were different. The videos had seen us through nights of breastfeeding, ripping seams as we tried to get into clothes that had fit a few years earlier, flapping dish towels when our culinary efforts to impress our mothers-in-law went up in literal smoke. Mother May I was there for us, telling us, *Remember, you are already a good mom.* So we would be there for her, no matter what.

And at the time, we really meant it.

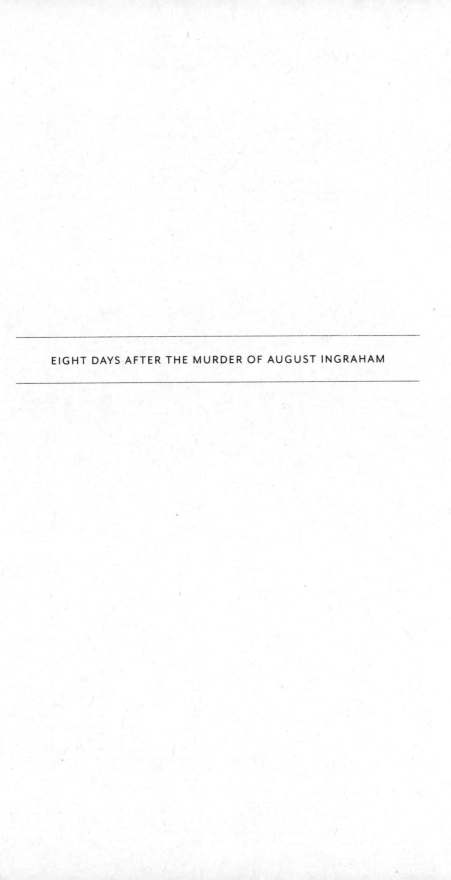

EIGHT DAYS AFTER THE MURDER OF AUGUST INGRAHAM

April Iverson

"**O**kay, Mom, slow down," April said into the phone. Her mother had been talking for a minute straight and all April had gotten was that June had left a stain on some trust-fund kid's wall during a party. "What exactly happened?"

"She committed vandalism," her mother said.

"Accidentally spilling a drink isn't vandalism, no matter how expensive the wallpaper is." A hundred inebriated guests must have done the same or worse. A rare book used as a coaster. An original Van Gogh sketch that someone was stupid enough to take out of the frame.

"This wasn't spilling a drink," her mother said. "Just look."

A few seconds later a photo came through on April's screen.

It was a shadowing of red on pale silver-blue. "What am I looking at?" But April's brain was slowly making sense of it, a silhouette pressed into a wall. It was blurry, though, a generic outline of a hundred possible hot girls.

"How do we know this was even her?" April asked.

Her mother sighed. "April."

That sigh had a point. This was exactly the kind of thing June would do, coating her naked or bikini-clad body in something deeply staining and then pressing herself against extremely expensive fabric wallpaper.

She should never have gone to that guy's party. She didn't even like him, so there was no reason for her to go except for the free obscenely expensive booze. June never tired of free things even though half her job was receiving and reviewing them. And of all free things, to be seen with expensive booze was exactly the wrong thing to do at this moment. This was a time for June to keep her image quiet and clean, not to go to the thirtieth birthday party of a guy known only for his rich family and the destruction of a historic hedge maze when he was drunkenly driving an ATV.

"The family is livid," her mother said. "She did it with the rarest bottles in the host's cellar. Château Lafite, for God's sake."

That sounded about right. The only thing her little sister loved more than free stuff was chaos. If she couldn't have gotten at the good wine, she would have gone for cherry or pomegranate juice, something to lure mosquitos into the room for days.

"Why are you calling me, Mom?" April asked. "Are they looking for a fabric restorer?"

"Talk to her. Get her to see reason. Get her to see how this looks."

June would be nothing but delighted about how this looked. The blush stain against the ice gray, the legendary image of her casually stripping off her clothes and vandalizing someone's else's house with her body, that was the June Iverson that June loved to show the world.

"This is the last thing this family needs right now," her mother said. "Make her understand."

"I can't make her do anything," April said. "I can't make anyone do anything."

"You always could when they were growing up. If you asked them to do their homework or eat their kale, they did it."

"Exactly," April said. "If I actually had the power to make anyone do anything, I wouldn't have had to do any of that, because you would have been there."

we who grew up watching the Iversons

We were all still talking about the booze fiasco when another anonymous account uploaded another video.

This one showed May and Ernesto in the kitchen of his house, a rare glimpse of Ernesto Iniesta's craftsman bungalow.

"You're not seeing the business opportunity here," May said.

"Oh, I see it," Ernesto said. "I just don't want it."

A mix of teenage and almost-teenage laughter bubbled through the background. If we'd had to guess by May's highlights and nail shape, she was about forty-one, and Ernesto was about forty-three, which gave approximate ages to the blurs of motion in the background. April would have been about seventeen, the twins age fourteen, January age twelve, March forever a year right behind her, age eleven. They were all, presumably, outside the sliding-glass doors, in the green backyard flanked by the coral-pink of drought-resistant flowers.

Except for whichever one of them had filmed this. That was what made this one different. From the level and the shakiness, it was the work of one of the younger ones, hiding in a closet or around a corner or pretending to play with one of May Iverson's innumerable cast-off cameras. Probably January or March. Maybe June or July, who were well-practiced with cameras by then but who sometimes got experimental with their cinematography.

"You don't realize what you're giving up," May said. She was in one of what she called her Earth-mother outfits, a silk dress printed with delicate archipelagos of blossoms. She tended to wear these when she visited Ernesto (the inside of Ernesto's house may have been a world unseen, but Mother May I posted often about pickup and drop-off). The quiet street practically backed up against the mountains. May seemed to dress as though a statement suit or quilted handbag would send all the residents fleeing up the slopes and into the nearest caves. Her ensembles must have been tries at seeming less conspicuous next to Ernesto's jeans and collared shirts, usually purchased from Costco.

"You're trying to monetize my name," Ernesto said.

"You say *monetizing* like it's a bad word," May said. "Don't you like money? Don't you need money?"

May surveyed the walls, covered in children's finger painting in secondhand frames, rather than pieces presciently bought when the artists' prints still went for three figures. May looked around as though staring at stalagmites of newspapers and a roach infestation. It wasn't disdain so much as concern.

May lowered her eyes to the woven rugs Ernesto had inherited from his grandmother, the colors sun-faded but still bright from being well cared for, aired out each spring.

She raised her eyes again to the water-filtration pitcher left out on the counter. A film of condensation frosted the plastic. That pitcher was evidence that Ernesto did not have a fridge door filled with three different kinds of bottled water, each from a different mythically restorative well.

The house was small. The Formica countertops hadn't been updated since the 1970s. But its weathered hardwood floors, its original fireplace, the slope of its backyard, the steady appreciation seemed to escape May Iverson's attention.

"You're not using my name for this," Ernesto said.

May brightened. "Of course not. It wouldn't just be your name. It'd be your face, your family, your history. It'd be your culture. You'd be in all the publicity."

"That is not the selling point you think it is," Ernesto said.

"Don't you want our daughters to be proud of their heritage?" May asked.

"Not by sticking my last name on your line of artisanal, pH-balanced, electrolyte-infused aguas frescas." Ernesto made a visible effort to try not to sound sarcastic. "This isn't me. This is why I couldn't take this. I couldn't take everything being out there. We could never just have dinner together. It was a date night photoshoot. We could never go to the park as a family. It was all content creation. I couldn't do it."

"Then let me do it," May said. "You won't have to do anything. You'll forget all about it except when you get the checks."

"I said no, May." Ernesto's voice was firmer now.

"Why?" May asked.

"Why are you even doing this?" Ernesto filled the pitcher from the kitchen tap. "You just want to destroy Savanna."

"What does she have to do with anything?" May asked.

"Savanna and her family are trying to start an aguas frescas business and you just happen to decide to start one yourself? You're Goliath here, and you know it." Ernesto turned off the tap. "The beverage business is brutal enough. Chances are low that she turns a profit before year five even if she does everything right. Why do you want to make it harder for her? What did she ever do to you?"

We remembered Savanna's aguas frescas, bright fuchsia from homemade pitaya syrup, deep orange with sapote, gold from mamoncillo. Their colors brightened the posts of the Iverson children in the nearly all-white decor of May's kitchen.

May watched Ernesto return the pitcher to the fridge.

"Why can't I just use your name?" May asked.

"Because I don't trust you with it." Ernesto looked surprised by the volume of his own voice, by how hard he'd just closed the fridge door.

"What's that supposed to mean?" May asked.

"You didn't even want our children to have the last name Iniesta."
Ernesto checked the fridge door, making sure the gusset sealed.

"I just wanted them to have a more relatable name," May said. "To
make things easier for them."

"And now my name could make things easier for you, right?" Ernesto said. "To help you sell something?"

"It did occur to me that it would be a nice gesture," May said. "I
was wrong not to include your name in our family more. Now I want
to make it right. I want to show you I'm proud of who you are and
who our daughters are."

"I don't know that I want your kind of pride," Ernesto said.

A knowing smile came across May's face. "Are you still upset about
my Indian princess outfit?" She draped herself and her skirt over a
stool at the breakfast counter. "Sweetie, it was a costume."

"It was wildly offensive," Ernesto said.

"It was Halloween," May said. "Besides, you have Indigenous people in your family. I thought you would recognize it as a tribute."

"A fringed suede minidress, a hair accessory made of poached
feathers, a necklace made by a company known for ripping off the
work of Indigenous artists," Ernesto said. "That's not a tribute. Neither
are your white friends wearing African jewelry on Halloween, by the
way."

"Christine has an entire collection of Africana," May said. "No one
loves Africa more than Christine."

"And she's gonna make sure everyone knows it," Ernesto said.

"What are you talking about?" May asked.

"You really haven't noticed?" Ernesto asked. "Whenever one of her
tropical vacations comes around, she calls it *going native*. She actually
says that. Out loud. On camera and in writing. Then suddenly her
thin, straight, blond hair is curly and black, her skin is six shades
darker, her lips have even more filler than usual, just when we thought
that wasn't possible."

"So women can't change their look now?" May rose from the stool.
"Does it threaten you for women to style themselves how they want?
Does that threaten your manhood?"

Ernesto looked exhausted.

"You're entitled to your opinion." May scraped a crayon smudge off the counter. "And I appreciate that you keep those opinions between us. I do want you to have someone to say them to. Because if you ever thought about sharing these opinions with anyone else, it wouldn't go well."

"Threats now?" Ernesto asked. "Really? We're doing that?"

May slowly shook her head. "Advice," she said. "You lay low. You think that protects you. But it just makes you look bad." She cleared the crayon wax from under her fingernail. "If you don't let everyone see you, you must have something to hide. The more you keep to yourself, the more everyone thinks you're keeping something from them. The more they don't know you, the more everyone's convinced you have something you don't want them to know. And that just makes them want to find out even more."

Ernesto didn't say anything. He just set a hand on the counter behind him.

"If you ever go up against me," May said, "on anything, no one will trust you. They know me. They don't know you. No one knows you."

Ernesto didn't move. None of him moved except his eyes, which drifted toward the glass sliders. Fear crossed his face. It was the fear of a man who knew Mother May I could take his children from him if he ever objected to anything.

She had more than money.

She had the currency of everyone else's opinion.

May reached for her purse. "Girls!" she called. "Time to go!"

The camera jerked and the visual went dark, like it had been stuffed in a tote bag.

But the sound kept recording. Muffled, but still audible.

"They're growing up, you know," Ernesto said.

"I know." May sounded wistful.

"No," Ernesto said. "You don't. Because they're gonna grow up and look at what you turned their lives into. They can't see it right now because they're still inside it. But they will."

"Exactly," May said. "That's why I don't fault them."

"Fault them for what?" Ernesto asked.

"That they don't thank me for everything now." May still sounded wistful, as though imagining, one day, feeling nostalgic for the time she was currently in. "They're just kids. They don't understand. But they will."

Sightings of the Iversons in the hours following this video's release found May and June with their usual brave faces. But glimpses of January and July showed them distracted by worry, expressions almost identical, as though they were each trying to figure out how those anonymous accounts were getting so deep into their lives.

Within hours of this video going up, Ashley Morgan Kelly was pouring from a bottle of wild rose gin, asking, "And just who, Fine Crimers, is Savanna?"

We already knew.

We did not tell her.

Even if we had wanted to, we didn't need to.

By the following morning, another anonymous account did it for us.

NINE DAYS AFTER THE MURDER OF AUGUST INGRAHAM

we who grew up watching the Iversons

The newest video looked like it had been recorded on one of the many cameras Mother May I had promoted, touted as perfect, the last camera she would ever need, at least until she cast it off for another with a better sponsorship deal.

From the vantage point of the video, whoever filmed it had to have been in the enormous pantry, the one in which May showed off her tinted glass containers of gluten-free pasta, dried French legumes, and peach and silver sanding sugars. But since that was where it had been filmed from, none of that was visible.

Instead, the frame showed January and March at the kitchen island alongside their nanny at the time, Savanna Montez, and Savanna Montez's daughter, Carolina, who looked a little older than March (who looked a little older than January despite being younger; we placed the time at about thirteen years ago, January at age eleven, March at age ten). They had their hands in the wet gold of masa, laughing as it squished in their palms. Savanna encouraged each of them as they formed the masa into balls and then spread it over the corn husks. "Eso es. That's beautiful."

Abruptly, they all looked up.

January and March lifted their heads, the two of them copies of each other. They were close in height, often wore the same clothing in different colors, and recently they'd gotten the same haircut. It had been drastic, each of them losing ten-plus inches so that the shortest pieces now brushed their ears, the longest chin length. Back then, we'd been surprised May had allowed it—wasn't it easier to sell Strawberry Sprinkle kids' shampoo if her kids had long hair?—but now we could see why. The shorter hair not only made them look younger, it made them look like a second set of Iverson twins, and what was more marketable than younger copies of June and July?

January and March stopped laughing. So did Savanna and Carolina.

It wasn't clear why until May entered the frame.

Savanna nodded to her, half greeting, half show of deference.

"What are we all doing in here?" May asked. The cheerful note in her voice was as sharp as the whine of a car brake in winter.

No one answered.

No one said anything.

Until March cracked, a small laugh escaping.

May took off her sunglasses, showing how little her smile had reached her eyes. "What's funny?"

"Nothing," January said, biting back a smile.

May's eyes drifted over the yellow of the masa, over the three children's small hands, then to Savanna's alongside them.

She looked at Savanna. "I think"—she drew out the word *think* into a coquettish, mock-apologetic wince—"the baseboards in the main entertainment room could use a little"—again drawing out that last word, as though she regretted having to say it—"more attention."

Savanna was the only one of the four of them who managed to stop her face from visibly falling.

"And the halls," May said. "Maybe go ahead and check those too."

Savanna nodded. She went to the apron sink. She washed the masa off her hands.

The three children stayed still. They looked down, watching their unmoving hands in the glass mixing bowl.

May watched Savanna until she blotted her palms dry and left the kitchen.

The sound of Savanna's footsteps faded to imperceptible on the recording.

"Now." May sat, her face brightening. "Why don't you teach Mommy how to do what you're doing?"

Carolina shrank away from the kitchen island.

"Oh, no, stay." May grabbed Carolina's arm.

Carolina froze, staring at the white hand on her arm.

May let go, and smiled. "Really, stay. You're part of our family. You know that." May turned to January and March. "Now, who wants to tell me where to start?"

The three children barely raised their eyes.

Then the video then cut to another clip. A different day.

Savanna was scrubbing the tile backsplash.

"Well"—May swept into the room and grabbed her purse off the kitchen island—"I'm off."

Savanna glanced over her shoulder to nod in May's direction before turning again to the backsplash. Then, as though something had just registered, she did a double take.

"Why"—Savanna took a syllable to collect herself—"are you wearing my necklace?"

May adjusted the curve of purple ribbon crossing the front of her blouson-cut suit. "I'm sorry?"

"That was in my room," Savanna said.

"I think you're mistaken."

"It was in my dresser."

"Are you really suggesting I'd steal?" May blinked three times. "From you?"

Savanna lowered her hands from the backsplash, her peach cleaning gloves looking white against her brown forearms.

"Why would I need to take anything from you?" May's smile stayed in place. She didn't sound malicious. Or taunting. She simply sounded puzzled. "What would you have that I could want?"

She turned to the doorway, the gold-dipped amethyst catching the light, purple ribbons fluttering as she left.

we who could just tell there was something wrong with that guy

Sometimes you just know things. But you know in such small ways that you don't know how to explain it to anyone else. You hear how your husband says a co-worker's name, the slight difference from the first time he mentioned her, and you suddenly wonder if he's slept with her, or wants to.

You notice the way your friend flinches, grips onto the edges of their chair, whenever someone makes a sudden movement, and you realize that something bad happened to your friend once, that they may never talk about it, that it's your job to know that without asking.

You see the way your mother looks out the window right after she opens a can of crushed tomatoes at Christmas, and you know the news from the doctor wasn't good, and she hasn't figured out how to tell you.

None of it would hold up if you tried to explain it or, worse, prove it.

That was how it was when the clip of the guy in the sweatshirt surfaced.

This wasn't like the ones filmed inside the Iverson house. This had been filmed in a public place. It had been posted not by an anonymous account, but by a rarely active channel that usually reviewed inline-skate wheels. The channel's owner labeled it with all caps and many exclamation points, declaring he'd captured June Iverson's latest boyfriend on camera in the wild, instructing all viewers to watch to the end because "YOU WON'T BELIEVE IT."

Luke Sweatshirt sat in the alley between two brick buildings, one well maintained, one crumbling. He seemingly had no clue that someone was filming him. He had his hands in his pockets and was kicking at a loose piece of asphalt, just waiting.

The side door of the theater opened, and a dark-haired woman in jeans and a black tank top and a dour expression appeared. When she went to prop the door open so it wouldn't close behind her, she saw him.

Fast as the doorstop catching, the shock on January Iverson's face turned to delight.

The smile transformed January. It lit a bubbling joy in her eyes. It turned her into a sparkling Iverson daughter never before seen. It made her, for that flash, as beautiful as her sisters.

What else could this have been except the look of January Iverson being in love? It was almost startling how luminous she became, as unexpected as lilacs from frozen ground.

A third Iverson daughter. Really? Was he going to steal April away from her husband next?

January leaped into his arms. She laughed when she realized there was an adjustable crescent wrench hanging from the black tie-line tethered to her belt loop. She still had a filmy pink-purple square of lighting gel in her back pocket.

Luke Sweatshirt laughed even though that wrench almost swung and hit him in the balls, missing only because he shifted the angle of his body. He lifted January off the ground—actually wrapped his arms around her waist and lifted her, like lovers reuniting in an airport.

First June and July. Now January. Did he think these girls were some kind of conquest? Should we have been watching for when March would materialize on his arm?

Or was it even worse than that? Was he trying to divide them? And didn't it bother anyone else that we couldn't even find his last name? Was he a self-styled manager, trying to take a percentage of their earnings? Was he some wannabe tech bro trying to get them to invest in his voice-activated mattress start-up? Was he a particularly uncharismatic cult leader convincing them that true happiness waited for them at a glampground in the Sonoran Desert?

Who was this guy? And why hadn't it occurred to anyone—not even Ashley Morgan Kelly—that he might have killed August Ingraham?

Luke Sweatshirt

"How long have you been involved with January Iverson?" they asked him on the sidewalk.

"I'm not," he said.

"Are you dating both of the twins, or just one of them?" they asked him as he was waiting for his prescription refill.

"Wait, what?" How was he supposed to answer a multiple-choice question when neither choice was accurate?

"What do you say to critics who think this is all in pursuit of increasing your own potential sponsorship base?" they asked him in parking lots.

"My what?" he asked. "They're my friends, okay? They're all just my friends."

He'd been trying to give them something by answering.

But it got worse.

With every denial, more questions came. Every time he tried to shut down some line of speculation, it deepened. He was afraid to turn down every aisle in the grocery store for fear that someone would approach with a phone ready to record. And that level of paranoia made him feel conceited. He wasn't important. He didn't matter. He was nobody.

The next time he was unloading groceries from his car, someone was waiting for him. Dread hit him square in the stomach. The woman had shown up between trips from his trunk to his apartment. She was leaning against his car, arms crossed, ankles crossed, skirt ruffled by the evening breeze.

He felt only a little relieved when he realized it was June.

She was incredibly overdressed for the sidewalk in front of a cinder-block apartment building.

"Like it?" June flicked the edge of the filmy skirt, which was already graying from the dirty asphalt.

"You didn't have to get all fancy for me," he said.

She smiled, because she'd been wearing it all day, and he knew that, and she knew he knew that. She'd been wearing it since the garden party for a friend's line of botanically infused hair-care products. The fabric flowed down in tones of pink, blue, and lavender, with appliqué embellishments that even looked like the hydrangeas in the blown-glass vase centerpieces at the event, and dear God, what was being around June and July doing to his brain? He knew all this because she'd posted about it earlier today, posing with the flower arrangements in question.

In the photo her asymmetrical dress had looked reserved and tasteful, but in person it made him feel instantly awkward. It had a slit so high that if she stepped wrong, the world was getting an eyeful.

Also in the photo had been July, trailing June like a shadow, in an almost identical dress, but heavier on the blue and purple than the pink. It had a little more coverage, the fabric pooling around her like she'd bought it a size too big. As they had in a thousand photo ops, June looked like sunrise, blond highlights like a flash of summer, and July looked like dusk, her black hair like a night river. And all this made him feel like a stalker, because what straight guy with no interest in or connection to the fashion industry randomly knew what two influencers were wearing on a given day?

June tilted her head, musing at the last of the sunset between the power lines. "What is it that the sportsball fans call it?" She straightened up, overacting the moment of suddenly remembering. "Oh, right. Rookie mistake."

"You mean that I didn't predict you were coming and buy prosecco?" He picked up the last two bags in the trunk.

"You wouldn't know this." June pressed the trunk closed. She was familiar enough with his car to do it right, to apply extra pressure in the exact spot that would make the latch engage. "Because you haven't lived like July and I have lived for oh, roughly, forever. But you don't answer those questions. You act like you didn't hear them."

"I just let them keep saying things that aren't true?" he asked.

"Yes. That's exactly what you do." June took one of the grocery bags. So this really was serious. "Because the minute you respond to a nosy stranger, you've lost."

He took the grocery bag back and handed her the other one, the lighter one. "Then I've seen you lose a lot."

"Yeah," June said. "Why do you think I know what I'm talking about?"

we the followers of Mother May I

We just couldn't get over how much that guy looked like the Iversons. And the more we looked at him, the more we realized he didn't just look like June and January. He didn't just look like a few select Iverson cousins. He looked like May Iverson. He had May Iverson's nose. He had unruly versions of May Iverson's brows. There was even a similarity to how their features were arranged on their faces.

Everyone had a theory. What if he was some secret child of May Iverson's? Or what if he had no relation to the Iversons, but planned to use his resemblance to claim that he did? What if this was all part of some elaborate grift?

Or what if he was the one Iverson none of us had seen in years? He was heavier in both weight and energy than the elfish March Iverson, but the resemblance was definitely there. What if March Iverson had transitioned?

There was just one problem with that theory. There was no way that a child of May Iverson's would have cut themself off from the family just because they were transgender. There would have been no reason to. May Iverson would have accepted a transgender son with open arms. She would have celebrated his courage, his authenticity. She would have gotten him the best care from the best doctors. She would have thrown unforgettable parties to mark the occasions of his surgeries. May Iverson had been one of the first mom influencers to show outspoken support for transgender kids. While most of her peers were still afraid to use the word *queer* in their content, she was organizing giveaways in which retailers donated shoes so that transgender girls could attend prom in their first pair of Manolos or Louboutins.

On second thought, there was more than one problem with that theory.

Luke Sweatshirt didn't have any money, and presumably if he had a way to access the fortunes of the ever-generous May Iverson, he would have. May Iverson had bought the twins matching cars for their twenty-fifth birthdays. How much more would she have given the prodigal youngest Iverson? It didn't add up. If he was an Iverson, his last known job wouldn't have been drying windows at a car wash. This guy had never been an Iverson. He not only didn't have money now, he looked like he'd never had money. He completely lacked the kind of ease that infused June and July's content. Even April had it. She may have made her own money, but would she really have been as confident, as fearless in business, if she hadn't grown up with the security her mother had provided?

Which brought us back to the uncomfortable possibility that he was a potential grifter, taking advantage of the Iversons, or his resemblance to them, or both. Maybe how much he looked like March Iverson was exactly what let him get so close to the Iverson daughters. Even if they didn't realize they were doing it, they gravitated toward someone who had similar features to the youngest Iverson.

They were looking for someone they'd lost.

we the followers of the Summer Girls

"**E**arlier in my coverage of the August Ingraham murder," Ashley Morgan Kelly said over a bottle of Rémy Martin, "we learned of a second deceased man found on the same day, compounding the tragedy of this shocking crime. Today I am blessed to share with you exclusive information provided in confidence by a source close to the man's family."

A source close to the man's family? That could have meant anything.

Ashley Morgan Kelly launched into what sounded like a forensic analysis—abrasions on the man's hands indicating speed of impact with the rocky ground, depth of impressions left by the knees suggesting the speed before falling—punctuated by the low rattle of ice cubes in her glass. The mix of these things, facts about a corpse relayed over a premium digestif, left our stomachs turning.

The position of his fallen body, Ashley Morgan Kelly said, made it clear that he had not been running away from a murder he'd just committed, or even from the real murderer. He'd been running *up* the hill, *toward* the Iverson mansion.

Where had she gotten this? Was there a coroner's report we'd missed? How did she know he was dead from cardiac arrest when we didn't? We seethed at the injustice. We were the ones who knew the Iversons, not her. But from now on whatever Ashley Morgan Kelly said would have the luster of insider information.

"All evidence points to one thing," Ashley Morgan Kelly said into the camera with solemn concern. "A case of a Good Samaritan. An old man who witnessed the ruthless acts of a killer and attempted to intervene. A man with a good heart, and that good heart gave out."

We cringed. We cringed harder at the slight uptick of one corner of Ashley Morgan Kelly's mouth, as though she could not contain her delight at her own play on words.

Ashley Morgan Kelly reined in that hint of a smile. "So today we remember this Good Samaritan, a father, a grandfather, a well-liked neighbor, a local farmer."

As soon as she said the words *local farmer*, the turn of our stomachs worsened. We knew exactly who he was. We may not have known his name, but we knew who he was better than Ashley Morgan Kelly did.

Any media coverage of August Ingraham's murder came with the standard aerial shots of the Iverson property. The mansion sat on top of an enormous hill. The hillsides running immediately down were green and lush, and though some of those slopes belonged to the Iversons, a lot of them didn't. Those were the ones with patches that were withered and dying. On a screen with high enough resolution, you could almost see where the ground was being taken over by weeds and whatever brush could survive.

It hadn't always been that way, and in fact some of the aerial shots were old enough to show everything still bright and alive. The western slope especially used to be thick with well-loved crops, thanks to a small family farm run by an old man.

He hadn't just been an old man with a ticking-down clock of a heart. He had been an old man with a love for beautiful and obscure vegetables. The red-violet of mercury and fiesole artichokes. The otherworldly fractals of Romanesco broccoli. The bright clusters of mulberry cauliflower. Rainbows of peppers set in jewel boxes of green leaves.

In the months leading up to the murder, most of those plants were already gone—either died off or so sick they had to be cleared away. Not because of blight or heat. But because August Ingraham had wanted to be able to do open-water swimming workouts without going to the beach.

August's plan for accomplishing this had been to hire a few of his friends—who were neither contractors, nor pool installation specialists, nor plumbers—to turn the enormous Iverson infinity pool into a wave pool. August plus his friends equaled a noxious combination of arrogance and incompetence, so this had the predictable result of sending tides of chlorine sloshing down toward the neighboring properties.

It wouldn't have been hard to remedy the mistake. August had the money to have the pool redone by people who actually knew what they were doing, and if he didn't, May did. If he didn't care to have it redone, he could have simply turned off the wave feature and let the pool stand as it had been before (albeit with some tiles now askew, visible in wide shots).

But he didn't. No matter how many complaints were filed, no matter how many times city fines were issued, he didn't. To August, chlorinated water splashing over the edge and down the hill only heightened the pleasing effect of the infinity pool. And swimming against waves was great for his lateral deltoids.

The increasingly concentrated chlorine ruined backyards, made the hillsides unsafe for children, pets, and wildlife, and wiped out the old man's crops.

We knew some of this from local articles, but mostly from June Iverson's late-night rants, the same way we knew that August had offered to buy the surrounding land at cut-rate prices. This was the extent of the restitution he offered the old man with the ruined farm. "Really generous, right?" June had said into her camera, her contempt so bitter we could taste it ourselves. "It's not just that shitty wave pool that's a menace to the landscape. It's my so-called stepfather. Comment below if you think my mother and the planet deserve better."

At least this was what we remembered. We couldn't find those posts now, and we hoped this was because June had had the good sense to delete them before detectives combed through her social media history.

"The Iversons," Ashley Morgan Kelly said to close her video. "A family in turmoil, taking down innocent bystanders in their wake."

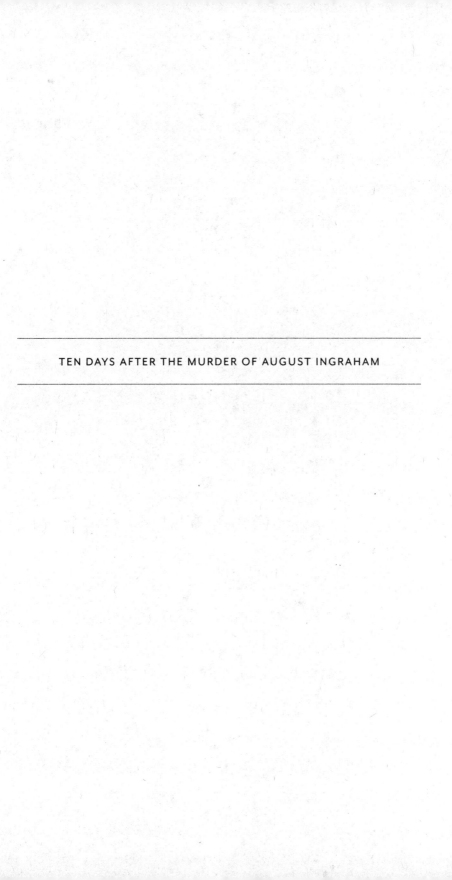

TEN DAYS AFTER THE MURDER OF AUGUST INGRAHAM

we who were watching the Iversons

In the latest anonymous video, May Iverson was sponsored-content ready, right down to the earrings that matched the buttons on her shirt. But from the first few seconds, we knew this wasn't some Mother May I outtake. She was slightly backlit, a mistake she would never make, because how could you possibly see the products if they were going in and out of shadow? And from the shakiness of the footage, we knew someone was holding the device by hand, from enough of a distance to stay inconspicuous.

The video looked about five years old. We could tell from April's blush. The way she was applying it to the apples of her cheeks was a tip-off, giving a window of a few years when all the makeup tutorials were saying to drape the color that way.

"So just to make sure I have this right," April said, "you spent not just *my* college fund on luxury cars and Botox. Not just June and July's. You spent all of it. January and March's too."

"I made an investment in our lives," May said. "Do you think this big beautiful house was free? That pool out there?"

"So Botox and overpriced sofas," April said.

"It takes money to make money the way we do," May said.

"*We? We* made money?" April crossed her arms. It was a practiced gesture, one that suggested the authority that got her younger sisters to floss. "You made money off our backs. You filmed everything so you could throw your birthday parties in Tulum."

"Yes, what a hardship," May said. "You had to be loved and adored. Constantly validated. How awful."

"You never left us alone," April said. "There was no privacy. Everything was recorded. Everything was potential material to you. Every moment of our lives was a resource for you to pick through and mine and turn into whatever you needed. You never just let us live."

Here May laughed, throwing her head back in the way she did when she laughed in posted videos. "All you ever had to do was live. You could have ignored the filming if you wanted. It would've been even better if you ignored it. I just wanted you to be yourselves."

"No, you didn't," April said. "You told us when to smile."

"Every mother who's ever taken a picture of her child has done that. See if you don't do that if you ever have kids."

Here, April flinched. It was small, but it went through her whole body.

She recovered.

"Do you know what they did to us at school?" April asked. "What they did to June and July at school? What January and March are still dealing with?"

"Of course they did," May said. "Everyone was jealous."

"You handed them all the ammunition they needed." April dropped her crossed arms. "Bra shopping. First periods. Sinus infections. They knew everything about us. The impressions they did of us. Of you."

"A little teasing builds character," May said. "How else would you have gotten it? You had everything you could ever have wanted. Every flute lesson. Every dance intensive. Every new pair of jeans."

During most of this recording—and in most photos and videos of the two of them—April and her mother barely looked related. A blond white woman in a camel sweater and white jeans. A Latina girl with a frayed denim hem skimming her thighs. You had to really look to notice the common features. April's ears were an exact replica of her mother's. She had the same hairline, a widow's peak as sharp and elegant as a slash of liquid eyeliner. The same ankles, right down to the bones. They echoed each other only in fragments.

But then they rolled their eyes, mirroring each other so precisely, so unintentionally, that it was impossible to miss the resemblance.

Once their eyes drifted from their respective points on the ceiling and down to each other's faces, the resemblance vanished again.

"Why would any of you want to go to college anyway?" May asked. "You can make so much more money doing what you've seen me do for years."

"I couldn't do that," April said.

"Oh, sweetie, don't be so modest." May's guard fell, her face softening. "Of course you could. You already know more than you think. And I can teach you the rest. You're so smart. You'd pick it up in a minute."

"I mean I won't," April said. "I don't want to do what you do. I don't want to be you. I don't want to be anything like you."

May's mouth was poised as though she was about to respond. But she didn't. She seemed to have both forgotten what she was about to say and forgotten to close her mouth.

April Iverson

"Today I have an exclusive deal for my Fine Crimers, a twenty percent discount code for SweaterChic," Ashley Morgan Kelly said, because now she had the view count to have sponsors. Her ad revenue probably wasn't paying for the Van Cleef & Arpels around her neck, but it might have covered the bottle of Armagnac she was pouring from.

April hated herself for adding to that revenue, that view count. And yet here she was, watching.

Ashley Morgan Kelly extolled the virtues of cashmere-specific detergent for a minute and a half before abruptly looking right into the camera and saying, "April Iverson. Eldest daughter of the woman known as Mother May I. Loving older sister to the four youngest Iversons."

Had April died and not realized it? Why was Ashley Morgan Kelly taking it upon herself to give a eulogy?

"But is there more to April Iverson than meets the eye?" A still from the recently released video appeared in the corner of the screen. Even that one frame made April wince, knowing someone had filmed this without her having noticed. Knowing someone had gotten the recording off a discarded camera. Knowing her mother was careless with their lives not just when she put them online but when she cast pieces of them aside on stored internal memory.

Knowing she once wore pre-distressed denim skirts, and now a nonnegligible portion of the internet had been reminded.

"Could a dispute over a piece of the Iverson fortune have escalated to violence?" Ashley Morgan Kelly asked.

April leaned back in her office chair, staring up at the ceiling.

"Could disagreements over family money have even led to murder?"

And of course, by just asking the question, Ashley Morgan Kelly had silently answered it.

we who were watching the Iversons

Within hours, another anonymously posted video appeared in which neither May nor April seemed to know they were being filmed. Again, the lighting was too bad for May to have been filming on purpose. The footage was too shaky, too handheld, for either April or May to have set it up. But we could see enough of the background to know this was one of May Iverson's home offices, the one accented in the lightest shades of sky blue the human eye could perceive.

A white Christmas tree sat in the background, lit with white bulbs so bright and cool they looked like the sparkle off snow. That didn't conclusively tell us the time of year; Mother May I filmed holiday content months in advance. But a few details confirmed it. April's red peacoat and ornament earrings. Distant holiday music. The scattered laughter of a party from other rooms.

This video looked slightly more recent than the last one. Both mother and daughter appeared a few years younger than now. Well, at least April did. Fillers kept May Iverson looking like a golden, glowing, perpetual forty-something, so she didn't appear much different in the recording than she did now. But April looked to be in her mid-twenties, an estimation backed up by the sweep of her bangs and the shade of her red lipstick.

"Don't you care about other women?" May asked.

"Of course I do," April said.

Whoever was filming stood outside the office door. May and April were too focused on their conversation to notice.

"Don't you think it's time you talked about it?" May said. "You've been trying for—what—two and a half, three years? And you're so young. That could resonate with a lot of people."

"I don't owe the world my whole life, Mom," April said.

"But don't you want to give hope to other women like you?" May asked. "Don't you want to inspire other women? You're not thinking about what kind of message of hope you could send. You could talk to them. Just like they're right here in the room with you. Talk to all the women out there who are just like you, heartbroken and barren."

The next few seconds showed April fraying faster than we had ever seen on film. She went from her usual voice—low, level, perfect enunciation, the occasional flick of her father's accent—to yelling faster than any other time on record.

"I am not barren"—these were the words she yelled the loudest.

Then she brought her tone down, just a little, like snatching herself back. The Christmas music was again audible in the background.

"Just because a woman can't bear children doesn't make her barren," April said. "I am not barren. I have life in me. I make things. I do things. I am alive. I am living. The blood in me, my heart, the air in my lungs, they are living. Every part of me is alive."

Desperation rang through her voice. As we watched we could almost feel it, the metallic tang of her grief.

"I am not barren and empty just because one organ inside me is," April said. "I grow life inside me even if I can't make one."

Whoever had posted this did not want us to believe Ashley Morgan Kelly. They didn't want us to turn April's conflicts with her mother into a motive for murder. They wanted us to feel for April. They wanted us to feel in our own bones had badly she wanted to be a mother herself. They wanted us to feel the life in her body and know she did not have death in her hands.

They wanted us to keep looking at May Iverson.

For a second, May Iverson was out of the frame, as though she'd left. But on the screen, April's expression shifted into confusion. "What are you doing?"

"That was perfect." May appeared back in frame, holding up her phone and hitting the record button. "Just say that all again, okay?"

ELEVEN DAYS AFTER THE MURDER OF AUGUST INGRAHAM

we who grew up watching the Iversons

As far as we were concerned, Ashley Morgan Kelly was flailing. Just like May Iverson was. They were simply doing it in different ways.

May Iverson was exerting obvious effort to make her life appear normal. She posted contemplative-looking photos of herself and her friends watching sunsets from resort verandas, mixed in with sponsored posts about foam pads meant to make stilettos comfortable. We didn't know whether she was trying to deflect or was in denial. It all depended on whether she'd just lost her husband or just killed him.

Ashley Morgan Kelly buried every one of her wild theories under another one, just waiting for something to stick. Ernesto Iniesta had an alibi? On to the Iverson sisters. Not getting the skyrocketing numbers she wanted when she pontificated about April? Give the people what they want and accuse January.

"You, my Fine Crimers, have been on the case, sending me your citizen journalism." Ashley Morgan Kelly presented just such a piece of citizen journalism, a video trailing January Iverson to the entrance of the theater where she worked. She was trying to hide her face in the collar of her jacket. The collar was unusually large for her, a statement collar. Was July's style rubbing off on her?

But we didn't get a good look at her or the jacket before she slipped in through the loading dock.

"Well," Ashley Morgan Kelly said while stirring up a boulevardier. "She seems awfully quick to get away from us, doesn't she?"

Ashley Morgan Kelly analyzed the Iverson family dynamics with such an air of authority that anyone might have thought she was a therapist or a family friend. She started talking over old Mother May I videos of holidays and birthday parties, but we couldn't figure out why. Nothing she showed suggested a criminal streak in January. It was all so bland. April painting January's nails gray. April putting Band-Aids on January and March after they tried pool-noodle fencing on a trampoline. What was any of this supposed to prove? There was no discernible conflict between January and anyone in the family. And all of this was before August was even in May Iverson's life, so what was this meant to suggest about the murder?

Every few videos, she would open with a for-those-of-you-just-joining-us speech, and each time, she described the Iversons as "a picture-perfect family, but sometimes a picture is worth a thousand secrets." She accompanied such introductions with an old family photo in the upper corner of the screen. It showed the entire Iverson brood—March included—as children, with May standing over them. It was from a Halloween party that any of us who knew the Iversons would have witnessed either as it was happening or in nostalgic posts by May and June.

May Iverson had dressed all of her children as characters from *Little Women*, complete with lines of buttons and skirts so full they must have been supported by internal scaffolding. April as mother Marmee—the irony completely lost on May—and the rest of them as the March sisters, twins June and July as Jo and Meg, respectively, January as Beth, little March as Amy. And hovering over all of them was May Iverson in a copper-patina-green dress and a matching spiked green crown, resplendent as a mint-body-glittered version of the

Statue of Liberty. Which had always baffled us, because was the Statue of Liberty even in place at the time *Little Women* was set?

In the photo, July looked like she wanted to crawl under one of the orange-and-purple-clothed tables. June was glaring at someone off-camera, looking like she wanted to rip them limb from limb and have the caterers serve them alongside the purple heirloom tomatoes. April looked bored and disdainful, lip curled up as though some drunken guest had just put the DJ's microphone to his ass and farted into it. March was the only one smiling widely and dutifully into the camera, thus Mother May I's posted caption: *When exactly 20% of your children understand the assignment.*

January, wide-eyed and staring, looked blank, shut down, the only one who seemed completely outside the party's chaos. She had the air both of being pulled into herself and of having exited her own body.

We really didn't believe January killed August. But the longer we looked at that photo, the more we started to wonder. And—just for the sake of argument—if she had, could we really have blamed her? How were you ever supposed to get over your own mother making you dress up as the March sister who dies partway through the book?

The photo disappeared, and Ashley Morgan Kelly looked right into the camera.

"If April Iverson would do anything for her little sister, would her little sister do the same for her?" she asked. "Could she have been talked into murder by the older sister she saw as a mother figure? Could January Iverson have borne witness to the conflict between April and their mother, and wanted to pay back her doting big sister with the ultimate act of loyalty?"

Luke Sweatshirt

"I'm gonna fucking kill her," he heard April say over June's speak-erphone.

He cringed. Cluttered as the bedrooms and bathrooms were, June and July's living room was minimalistic enough that few surfaces ab-sorbed sound. The cat trees, various pet beds, natural-fiber rabbit-friendly carpet runners, even the sofa he was sitting on did little to dampen the open-concept acoustics.

June looked right at him from across the room. She pointed a fin-ger toward him and mouthed *You didn't hear that*, before responding to April. "Can we not say things like that over the phone?"

"Like I give a shit. This is war. She can say whatever she wants about me, but when that Chanel-clad toad is accusing January—" April stopped mid-sentence and gasped like she'd had an idea. For a second, she sounded just like June. "Wait, wasn't Coco Chanel a Nazi informant? Can we get Ashley Morgan Kelly cancelled?"

"I love the spirit of this," June said, "I really do, but it takes more than that, and you know it."

Of course April knew it. Look what fans of Mother May I had seen, and yet the numbers on May Iverson's accounts had barely dipped.

"Have you seen her old videos?" April asked.

June sighed, as though gathering her reserves of patience. "No, I have not." She gave him a weary look. He did his best to look back with sympathy. "And why are you adding to her view count?"

"They're all these recaps of awful murders while she's mixing up cocktails," April said. "She's talking about people dying while she's perfecting the art of the sugar rim. Why doesn't she just make a bowl of popcorn and really be straightforward about it?"

June took April off speakerphone. Whether it was because June wanted to save him from being a witness or because she didn't trust him, he didn't know.

From the sound of it, June spent the next few minutes talking April down from suing Ashley Morgan Kelly or shoving one of her sensible-but-statement-patterned heels up her ass. How often did this happen? As far as he'd seen, this usually went the other way around.

Soon, June's side of the conversation grew so repetitive she sounded like she was pulling responses out of a bingo ball hopper. "I know." Or, "You think I don't want to do that too?" All leading back to some version of "We do the only thing we can do. We ignore her. We don't give her any more attention."

He nodded as June talked, encouraging her. Even though he was with April on this one. Even though he wanted to drive to her office right now, burst in, and say, *I know you don't know me very well, but I would be honored to help you go fuck that woman up.*

He wanted to argue with every single comment that agreed with Ashley Morgan Kelly. What they were saying was even worse than calling January a murderer. They were agreeing with the twist at the end of Ashley Morgan Kelly's commentary, that maybe January was a murderer without even having a will of her own, that she only did it to please someone else.

They thought January was weak and pliable just because she was quiet. But no one got the kind of reputation January had as a lighting designer, especially a woman lighting designer, without being tough. Determined. And as nervous as January seemed whenever anyone looked at her, when she needed to be, she could be as calm as a frozen lake.

He'd watched January do lighting hangs with one kind of wrench between her teeth and two others in her back pockets. Once, when the brake went out on the scaffold she was on and it rolled out from under her, she just held on to the lighting pipes like she was climbing a tree.

He'd seen how she watched the gels, her eyes tuned to the little translucent squares washing the lighting to amber or pink or aqua. Whenever one fell from a Source Four, she dashed across the stage as quick as a cat. The audience didn't even see her, but she was picking up that gel before a cast member slipped on it (lighting gels were the banana peels of the theater world).

When an apprentice hung a gel frame upside down, almost ensuring the metal square would fall out of the assembly and crash onto an actor's head partway through the show, January went across the catwalk so quietly that no one heard her. Even in the middle of the show, no one heard. Not even in the dramatic pauses between the actors' lines.

At the next blackout between scenes, January ripped out the frame, flipped it around, and slipped it back in, fast as cocking a gun. She never talked about any of this. He wouldn't have even known except that her awed fellow crew members couldn't help talking about it. ("I think that's when I fell in love with her," the AD said when Luke was hanging around the theater afterward, and Luke wanted to shove him out into the alley and kick his ass, and probably would've if it wouldn't have cost January her job and Luke what little anonymity he had left.)

No one could know January Iverson just from watching clips of how she dodged questions and cameras in public. If she ducked into her jacket, it was because both her temperament and her profession were about keeping her head down, avoiding trouble. Wear black, clean and sharp. Make no noise. Don't be seen. Solve the problem quickly and quietly. Whatever it is, just solve it, now.

Part of him wanted everyone to notice that, to see that, to know just how good she was at just how many things.

But he also didn't want them to. Because if they stopped underestimating her, if they knew how much she was capable of, they might twist it into her being capable of anything.

January Iverson

"Who turns down a promotion?" Rae was following January around as she cleaned up.

January spotted a cable coiled the wrong way. "I don't want it."

Rae made a series of frustrated noises.

"I don't do leadership," January said.

"And why exactly is that?"

January re-coiled the cable. "Because nobody listens to me."

Rae looked like she was gearing up to give January a pep talk.

January held out a hand to stop her. "I'm not saying that so you feel sorry for me. I'm saying that because it just is. Not everyone is a leader."

"This wouldn't by any chance be about what people on the internet with too much discretionary time are saying about you, would it?" Rae asked.

January picked up a stray gel and then looked up, studying the lights. She sighed. "Someone's making a horror show of the frame installation again. I'll give you three guesses."

Rae's face, all hard angles and silver eyeliner, usually scared people into doing what she wanted. To see such overwhelming sympathy on that face was just wrong. Like the time a pigeon flapped into the theater and onto the stage during Ophelia's big speech.

Rae took the gel from her. "Forget what everyone's saying."

Easy for her to say. Rae could walk into work without people trying to film her. January had started wearing increasingly oversize hooded sweatshirts, increasingly voluminous black scarves, things she could duck her head into, hiding as she walked.

"No one's gonna give you credit for your work if you don't even give it to yourself," Rae said. "The program's about to go to print and your name isn't even on it."

"That's the way I like it." January started climbing the scaffold.

She waited until Rae gave up, when the theater cleared out. Once all the voices faded, once all the doors had been shut, she went up to the catwalk. Whenever she went up into the catwalk, things seemed better when she came back down.

But all the words people called January followed her up.

Freak (the less inventive had called her this for years).

Psycho (this was often employed by the same people who put out the longest public service announcements about various mental health awareness months).

The weird one (the most tactful; it would have seemed kind if it weren't so pitying).

January had learned to shut it all out, even when the guys around here dug up an old post from her childhood in which she was wearing her most humiliating Halloween costume, a leotard covered in pale green balloons—*Your mom made you and your sisters dress up as fruit? How'd you get stuck being the grapes?* Or worse, when they heckled her about her mother trying to film her shopping for her first training bra, so embarrassed she tried to hide in the displays, staying still enough that her mother might mistake her for a mannequin.

Now it was all wearing fresh grooves in January's brain.

She sat in the shadows between the first and second electrics, fidg-

eting with the lengths of sash cord hanging from her belt loops, unty-
ing and tying them again.

Once she could breathe without her inhale hitching, she climbed
down.

Except that when she did, everything was worse.

And everyone was watching everything get worse.

we who grew up watching the Iversons

The latest anonymous video had just been uploaded. But it was clear from the first second how old it was.

No lead-up. No fade-in. This clip started cold, with May Iverson yelling.

"Tell me you didn't," she said.

"I didn't," a twelve- or thirteen-year-old March said.

"Go ahead," May said. "Keep lying."

"I'm not!" March said.

"Try lying one more time! See if you can make it sound convincing."

A sound like the creaking of a pipe, like the shriek of warping metal, cracked through the room. Both May and March snapped their heads toward the sound. The camera went with them.

January knelt on the shining kitchen floor. She was thirteen or fourteen, her charcoal-gray shirt and black jeans already foreshadowing the palette of her adult wardrobe.

But she did not look like an adult in that moment. She didn't even look thirteen or fourteen. She had her head in her hands, and she writhed like an overtired child.

"Stop it," January said. "Stop it," she said louder, almost yelling. "Stop fighting." She raked her hands through her hair. She screamed into her forearms. All the things she did as a little kid when she seemed overstimulated by noises or by people or by her mother trying to get her to smile or not smile or cry or not cry.

May's attention moved from her youngest child to her second youngest. She floated to the floor next to January. Her skirt settled as gently as a sunlit sheet in a detergent commercial.

"I know." May combed the knives of her nails through January's hair—that season everyone was getting their manicures filed to dagger points. "You get so overwhelmed when people get upset. My sensitive little snow child."

March sank to the floor—maybe in defeat, in guilt, in exhaustion, who could really tell?—but kept a safe distance.

"And you know what?" May gave January a gentle, encouraging laugh.

It was easy to expect stock phrases. *People get mad sometimes. It's okay to get upset sometimes.*

But then May said, "Do you know how many girls feel just like you? Do you know how many girls you can help right now just by letting them see you?"

May lifted her head. "June!" She got up from the floor. "I'll be right back, sweetie," she told January. She went toward the hall. "Junie! Can you come help me film?"

As soon as May was out of the room, January stopped crying. She straightened up. It happened fast, but it didn't seem like it was because she'd been faking being upset. It seemed more like, the moment May crossed the threshold out of the room, someone had flipped whatever switch was sending too much voltage through January. Suddenly she looked older. Closer to her real age.

January scooted over toward March. She rubbed a hand over the back of March's T-shirt.

March was curling in, shoulders rounded.

"She's going to fire Savanna," March said, eyes shut. "Because of me."

"She was going to fire her anyway," January said.

"How do you know?" March asked.

"I just know." January crossed her legs under her. Her black jeans looked identical in style to the blue ones March was wearing. They both had the same logo square stitched to the back waistbands.

January checked the kitchen doorway, watching for their mother.

"You don't have to make her hate you for me," March said.

"It doesn't matter," January said. "She hates me anyway."

The youngest Iverson didn't say anything back. How could March argue? At birth, January had ruined her mother's perfect row of months, which her mother must have seen as a first act of defiance. January could have posed for a thousand videos without complaint, and she still would have gotten May's battery-acid smile each time she threw January a pointedly snowflake-themed birthday party.

We were still trying to figure out who was posting these unauthorized videos. We wondered if it was a different person each time, either all of them colluding or each just adding on to what had come before. How many people had been through that house over the course of the Iverson girls' lives? How many people had May Iverson hired and fired? Her impossible standards were biting her in the ass, making the field of suspects impossibly wide not just for the murder but for whoever was trying to tarnish her reputation.

But this was what we did know: whoever was posting these had a strange, unnerving affection for the Iverson daughters. Every move they made seemed as designed to defend the Iverson sisters as it was to unsettle their mother. Every time certain corners of the internet called an Iverson daughter a murderer, someone registered a new anonymous account, ready with something to make us all understand why.

It was careful, obsessive, calculated. It made us uneasy even when we agreed with what they wanted the world to see. Because that kind of obsession, that kind of affection, it could turn so easily. And that sinking feeling brought us back to questions we'd asked so many times. Where was March Iverson? What had happened to her?

Only now, the shared feeling in the pit of our stomachs made us add new questions. Had anyone seen March Iverson? Was she okay? Was she alive? Did anyone know?

TWELVE DAYS AFTER THE MURDER OF AUGUST INGRAHAM

we the followers of Mother May I

We wished we could intercept everyone, jump in front of their screens before they saw this photo. To understand this photo, everyone needed to understand what we already knew. The last thing May Iverson would want was for this photo to give everyone the wrong impression. So after everything she'd done for us, we felt compelled to set the record straight wherever we could.

May Iverson had never spoken ill of her ex-husband. Even when they were divorcing, she said he was the best father in the world and that they would remain friends and that sometimes—she said this with a hitch in her voice—people simply outgrew each other.

That was the closest to venom anyone had heard her say of him, the way she leveled her eyes at the camera, the clear implication that she had been the one to outgrow him. He'd been her starter husband. She was—regretfully, with a heavy heart—leaving him behind.

We never blamed her. How could she stay with someone who remained the same size while she was becoming a greater version of herself, as though a projector was scaling her up?

Before the video of Ernesto threatening August, no one had ever seen evidence of meanness in Ernesto, no ruthlessness in the scruff of his beard, no edge hidden beneath the short black curls of his hair. Yes, he'd angled his face away from the cameras. He'd angled his children away too, gently urging them out of the frame—*Mommy's working now*—in a way meant to seem considerate but that was clearly his attempt to hide them.

It had never made him a bad man. It had simply made him unsuited to Mother May I's world.

After the divorce was finalized, May Iverson had expressed nothing but goodwill.

"The girls are with their dad this weekend. They always have the best time with him and his animals. So I know they're okay, I know they're happy, and Mom gets some me-time. And I think I'm just gonna relax and plan a little a spa day here at the house with some of my girlfriends."

Or,

"If you've been with me for a while, you all know I don't talk much about the girls' father, but you also know we're still friends, and we'll always be there for each other, which is why I have a huge favor to ask of you all: his mama's in the hospital, so if you could just send all your good thoughts and high-vibration energy and positive intentions her way, we can manifest her getting healthy."

Or,

"It's the first week of summer vacation, and the girls are off with their dad, and they're really excited for this camping trip they're all going on, which, let's be honest, he's way more qualified for than their mom."

Except for these brief mentions, Ernesto had faded into the shadows to which he was so clearly better suited. He still inhabited that same unassuming ranch house on the other side of town, shaded by old, gnarled trees, the whole property looking smaller than the mansion's infinity pool.

And it was on the doorstep of that house that a recent photo, one we were just now seeing, captured Luke Sweatshirt.

In the background of the photo, Ernesto opened his front door to this strange boy who seemed like both assistant (he'd recently been seen walking July's dogs) and suitor to the Iverson daughters.

Maybe there was a good reason. Maybe Luke was an old-fashioned kind of boy, asking a father's permission before declaring any serious intention with a girl.

It might have been believable. If it hadn't been such a good photo, so zoomed-in, so high resolution, that it showed both their faces.

The camera showed Luke glancing over his shoulder, as suspicious as a thief.

It showed Ernesto Iniesta's eyes scanning the street beyond Luke, as though searching for help. It was vigilance, but it was also shock to the point of terror, as though he was afraid of the young man about to enter his house.

Maybe Ernesto had threatened August. But that didn't make Ernesto dangerous. Didn't everyone get heated now and then, especially men facing the rivals they'd lost to?

Maybe Ernesto and May had had disagreements about business and their children, but that didn't give Ernesto motive to kill her new husband, and besides, he had a documented alibi.

This photo did not cast suspicion on Ernesto Iniesta.

This photo was yet more proof that Ernesto was more likely to be afraid than to cause fear.

The photo was proof that the guy on his front step was dangerous enough to make Ernesto afraid the second he opened the door.

Luke Sweatshirt

A woman in a light green cardigan came right up to him and called him a *two-timer*. In the middle of the post office. While brandishing a Priority Mail flat-rate envelope in his face.

Luke was too stunned and too confused—people still used the word *two-timer*? In this century?—to hear the postal clerk calling him up to the counter.

So did you kill him? some guy asked at the gas pumps.

It's him, a woman whispered to her friend when he went into the mini-mart. *That's the guy.*

It was him and the father, a voice behind him said when he was loading the coffee bean grinder at the grocery store. *The two of them, they killed him.*

In the checkout line, a woman waved a magenta-enameled finger at him, calling him a murderer. *You killed that poor woman's husband, and you killed that poor girl, didn't you? Everyone sees what you are and that's a murderer. Everyone sees, including God.*

Another woman's ears seemed to perk up, one checkout aisle over. *Holy shit, I never thought of that. Did he kill March?* She blinked false eyelashes at him, gripping her pint of açaí frozen yogurt. *Did you kill their sister too?*

Luke's stomach folded over, as stiff as the bag in his hands.

They were already saying Luke was June's boyfriend, or July's, or January's, or that he was two-timing all three of them (three-timing?).

Now they were saying he was August's murderer. And March's too?

He shouldn't have been surprised when the detectives showed up at his door. And he wished he'd been drinking because then he would have had some excuse for the stupidity of what he said next:

"Surprised it took you this long."

we who were watching the Iversons

The leaked voicemail began with one word.

"Cock?" It was half question, half exclamation.

We didn't know who'd leaked it, or how they'd gotten it. We didn't even know when it had been recorded.

But from that first word, we knew we'd probably listen to it about ten or fifteen times, that somewhere someone was already making a version on extended loop.

"Cock?" May Iverson's voice coughed out the word as though it had caught in her throat.

"Are you kidding me?" Louder now, volume distorting the recording. "Cock? Are you fucking kidding me?"

That was it.

That was the whole thing.

Even with speculation thick in the air, none of us could tear ourselves away. Nor could we make any sense of it. A sex scandal with a married politician? A secret porn tape? Ten thousand enamel alarm clocks in Mother May I's signature shade of peach, a typo turning the packaging into obscene literature?

But anyone who knew anything wasn't telling.

Luke Sweatshirt

June brought him in the complex the back way, the one the residents called the service entrance. It wasn't, not officially, but they seemed to have decided that, and to have demanded that installers of vessel sinks follow suit.

She sat him down at the kitchen island. She made them both coffee from the machine that looked so complex a NASA focus group must have written the manual. As it made its pneumatic whirring noises, he slumped onto the counter.

June pushed one cup toward him. He did not pick it up. The handle looked delicate, as if it were part of a doll's tea set, and he wasn't sure how to touch it without breaking it.

June took a painfully long sip of her drink, like she wanted to make him sweat. Then she set it down on the quartz countertop next to his.

"You fucked up," she said.

"I know," he said.

June laughed. "You really fucked up."

He sighed. "I know." He picked up the cup like a bowl, ignoring that dainty little handle.

"So how was it?" she asked.

"Oh, it was great." He leaned forward, crossing his arms on the countertop. "We swapped a couple of recipes. Discussed the latest issue of *USA Philatelic.* The lead detective's quite the stamp collector."

She sat on the stool next to his. When had she and July added this fuzzy shit to the bar stools? It was sticking to his jeans. He looked like a mint-green Muppet had attacked him.

"You okay?" she asked.

"Oh yeah, never better." He tried to make himself laugh, but it was the wrong move. It put a crack in just the right place to break him open. Then he was sobbing into his forearms, with June rubbing her hand over his back.

He hadn't meant to tell the detectives everything. But what was he supposed to do, make this worse by lying? Now they had everything they needed to wreck his whole life if they wanted to. He'd go to bed tonight knowing that. He'd wake up tomorrow knowing that. And he'd keep living with that. The only way it would end was when they decided it was time to blow his life apart.

He set his forehead on the countertop, noticing for the first time that there were pink flecks in the quartz.

"You must think I'm an enormous pussy," he said.

"Why?" June asked.

He shut his eyes. "Because I'm like this after a couple days of everyone out there looking at me, and they've been looking at you and July like this every day of your lives."

June leaned forward on the counter so she was there next to him. He could feel it even with his eyes closed.

"No, they haven't," she said. "Because they don't look at us the way they look at you. They look at us like they want what we have, even if they'll never admit it."

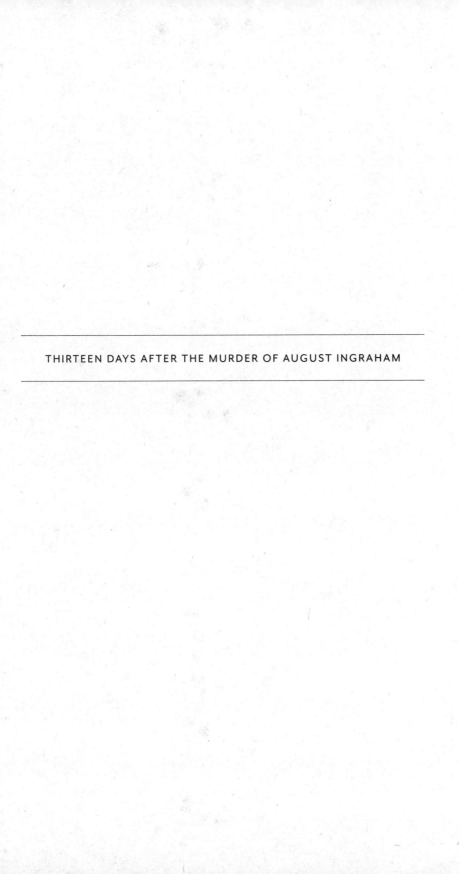

THIRTEEN DAYS AFTER THE MURDER OF AUGUST INGRAHAM

we who were watching the Iversons

It could have been a different recording. Or a continuation. All we knew for sure now was that it was a voicemail.

"Cock?" May Iverson coughed out again, the sound the same as the first audio recording. But then she went on. "You cannot put our name on this. You cannot put our name within a hundred miles of this."

Our name.

"Do you understand me?" she asked. "Call me back."

Not *my name.*

"I need you to call me back," she said. "I need to hear in your voice that you understand."

Our name.

May Iverson hadn't been talking to an extortionist with a sex tape, or a printer that had let a ruinous typo past quality control.

She had been talking to another Iverson.

May Iverson

Whenever May saw Shannon, the challenge was how to appropriately fawn over her latest four-figure dye job. This time her hair was light gray-purple—one of many colors she'd unsuccessfully tried to copyright for her channel—to the right side of her pin-sharp middle part, and silver-blond to the left.

One of the few benefits of being the grieving wife was that May was exempted from such social niceties. Bristowe had even excused her from the 10K run that raised money to send false eyelashes to older women rejoining the workforce.

"Oh, honey." Shannon leaned in for a hug, at least as far as her suit would let her. It was the new one with gold-on-black printing so thick the fabric barely bent. "How are you holding up? You look so thin." The words sounded poised between compliment and concern. "I thought you could use a little nourishment." Shannon held up a muffin basket as large as a statement centerpiece. "It's from that cute little gourmet grocer that just opened up. They have the most innovative flavors."

Poor Shannon. Half her identity was being the thinnest one in their group of friends. If May didn't fatten up, Shannon was going to have an existential crisis.

"Everything around here looks perfect." Shannon marveled at the pink marble, water-clear chandelier crystals, custom woven carpets in peach, white, and gold that all looked so much like they had before. "How have you done this? Are you a witch?"

"Believe me," May said. "You don't want to see the wings they've cordoned off."

"What I see is perfection," Shannon said as they entered the bone-white sitting room. "Even though you're too thin. And I hope you're not losing any sleep over what the vermin are saying about you. Who has a right to tell us what to do with our children if not us? We raised them. We had to decide who saw them, and when, and how."

Was Shannon about to ask for a sponsorship referral? She hadn't laid it on this thick since she was trying to get May to do a magazine shoot with her.

They sat down, and Shannon left a meaningful pause before whatever request she was gearing up for. "I was wondering if I could ask your advice about something."

"Of course," May said. If none of May's daughters were going to ask her advice, someone should benefit from all she had to give.

Shannon looked deliberately thoughtful. "I've just felt really conflicted lately."

"About what?" May asked.

Shannon drew her eyes up toward the chandelier. "Do you remember that time you had us all over for girls' night drinks?"

The pinch in May's chest came back, bristling like static. May had invited her friends over to try out new cocktail recipes so many times, and yet she knew exactly the night Shannon was talking about. Shannon had come over early to arrange the ingredients in a photo-worthy mise en place.

"I've just been thinking about what I heard," Shannon said, "and it's really been weighing on me, wondering if I should tell someone. If I have a moral obligation to say something, you know?"

May wished she could go back just far enough not to answer the door, not to answer the call from the gate so the guards wouldn't let

Shannon through in the first place, not to allow this woman she thought was her friend in this house with her threats and her calorie-bomb apricot-Brie muffins.

"What do you want?" May asked.

"I'm just having a hard time with it," Shannon said, "and I think a symbol of our friendship would really help me feel better about this ethical burden that I'm carrying for you."

"What do you want?" May asked again.

Shannon's eyes crept toward one particular door, where May had been storing the condolence gifts from brands, from local stores, from fellow influencers. They had come in faster than she could open them.

But May knew what brand Shannon was going to say before she said it.

"You know how those peasants at the store have never liked me," she said. "They're just dead set—excuse me, what a horrible phrase to use around you—they're just hell-bent on not giving me a new bag this season. And I've heard that everyone and their cousin has been sending you their limited editions from over the years to replace the ones you lost in the fire." Shannon laughed lightly. "You probably have more than you know what to do with. You probably have even more than you had before."

"Which one are you looking for?" May asked, without matching Shannon's tone, which was somehow both bubbly and strident. May kept her own voice completely flat.

"Oh, I don't want you to go to any trouble," Shannon said. "Just let me in there so I can see everything you have."

May ushered her into the room, smiling to show that none of this bothered her. But her smile was so tight she could feel it in her neck.

Shannon dug through the packages, casting aside little brown bags and little blue boxes. The truth was bitter on May's tongue. Shannon was jealous. And usually, this would have dampened May's anger—didn't she always tell the girls to ignore people who tried to tear them down because they were jealous?

But this was different. Shannon was jealous because May's husband was dead. Shannon was jealous that her own numbers had been falling for years, and she could really have used the publicity and the sympathy boost of losing her own husband. Shannon was jealous because she didn't much like her husband but she liked his money, and if he died, she could have it without having to bring him to gala events.

Shannon was jealous that May got to be the grieving widow. And May wanted to bash Shannon's head in with the crystal base of the desk lamp and scream, *Do you want a house this quiet? If you can find a way to take it with you, then take it.*

Shannon left with an indigo snakeskin that was in perfect condition but old enough to be vintage. The founder of a makeup brand geared toward pale foundation shades had sent it to May.

May seethed as she walked Shannon to the door, reminding herself over and over, like an affirmation, that she was going to the flagship store in Paris next week, that she'd get any latest release she wanted, that Shannon couldn't even get the local store to issue her a basic neutral with standard hardware. All Shannon had was flashing that bag around, living off the thrill of everyone thinking she was important just because she carried it.

It was a bargain price to make Shannon forget how unfair she thought everything was, how completely unjust that May had lost her husband and Shannon still had to live with hers.

It was a bargain price for her silence.

we who found March Iverson

We always thought it was a little surprising that March Iverson didn't turn out to be a model. She just had that look as a child. Thin. Long-limbed. Big-eyed. And even more so as a teen. She was pretty in a way that wasn't as aggressively, classically feminine as April or July, and that was more ethereal than June or January. March was all angles, softened by those big eyes. She was the kind of girl who was high-fashion androgynous enough to sell both motorcycle jackets and couture gowns.

She called to mind those really blond models who looked like they were nearly the same color all over. Near-white hair, pale skin, everything the same shade but their eyes. Except March Iverson was a browner version of that. March's hair was a light brown that nearly matched her skin, and in photos her eyes looked as true black as her eyelashes.

It was easy to imagine her as a denim model, so much so that when the ad came out less than two weeks after August's murder, it seemed like something inevitable had finally happened. We wondered why we had never thought to scour designer denim campaigns before. There she was, age twenty-three, in button-fly jeans and a boyfriend jacket. The eyes were spot on. The nose was close to the last time we saw her. Really close. So was the skin and hair color. The mouth was different, but that could be accounted for by the tilt of the model's head, the photographer's direction on how to hold the jaw or position the chin, even the shade of nude lipstick.

The model's face, her eyes, that tilt to her head, none of it showed any sign that she was capable of killing. There was no slight, involuntary lift of one corner of the mouth, no pride over having gotten away with something (or, depending on when the photo was taken, anticipating getting away with something).

None of us managed to confirm for sure the model's name. Not that it necessarily would have done any good. Even if the model's name had been found, there was no saying that March wouldn't be using a new one. One that gave her distance from the Iverson reputation. For all May Iverson's glamour and wealth, her brand might have been a little too wholesome, too approachable, for a daughter wanting to make a name as an editorial model. Mother May I's ethos was as much cupcakes and Christmas as it was brow gel and limited-run makeup bags. If March wanted her aura to be less catalog and more runway, she would have needed a new name.

This was when our questions about March picked up steam, about whether she had ever really disappeared. Maybe she'd been here the whole time, and no one, not even her mother, had noticed. Maybe she'd stayed hidden without even having to try that hard. Maybe she'd been staring back at her own family from inside a dozen magazine layouts. Maybe it wasn't just us who hadn't noticed. Maybe her mother and sisters were so used to being the subject of photographs that they didn't look too closely at ones that weren't of them.

Now we looked at this photo of her, beautiful, with a sharp enough jaw and a gaze so piercing that we wondered, just for a second, if she had it in her.

As a child, March Iverson had seemed shy and sweet, the less unnerving version of January. So if she had killed August, she would

have done it more coolly than January, with less twitching nervousness and darting of the eyes. She would have managed it as gracefully
and effortlessly as a pose, all long limbs and steps so light they were
silent. We could believe that March Iverson had grown up to be that
kind of stunning, ruthless woman. We could see it, her transforming
in the shadows during those intervening years. We could imagine her
that way, lovely, cunning, vicious, willing to let her own sisters, even
her own mother, take the fall.

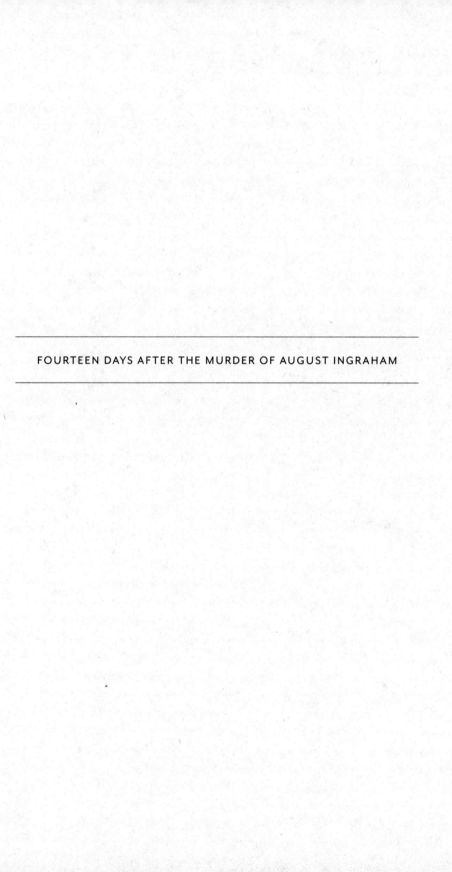

FOURTEEN DAYS AFTER THE MURDER OF AUGUST INGRAHAM

we who were watching the Iversons

Once that denim ad came out, with the model who looked so much like March Iverson aged up, we started seeing her everywhere. In the span of a single day, we saw her in an impossible number of places.

We saw her getting off a plane in Detroit, telling a fellow passenger at the baggage claim that she was determined to touch every Great Lake, and Erie was next.

We spotted her in the park near the California State Capitol in Sacramento, drifting past the redwood grown from a seed that went to the moon and back on Apollo 14.

We heard she was playing the mandolin at a bar outside Spring Hill, Florida, her hair the color of rain-soaked wheat and getting in her face as she moved in time with the music.

We heard her laughing in Brownsville, Texas, speaking Spanish to a woman who might have been a great-aunt on her father's side.

We glimpsed her at the shoe tree in Middlegate, Nevada, tying the laces of a pair of Keds she had worn through so completely that the rubber toe had pulled away from the sole. It flopped open like a mouth still considering what it might say, the same as any of us who recognized her, watched her, unsure how to ask if she was who we thought she was. And by the time we thought of a way that might not scare her off, she'd thrown the shoes up toward the blue of the desert sky. She didn't even stay to watch them land, hooking around the highest branch of the cottonwood. She just went back to her car and then she was flying down U.S. 50, going exactly seventy miles per hour, speed enforced by aircraft.

We nearly bumped into her in Montpelier, Vermont, where she was carrying a stuffed animal so gigantic it obstructed her vision. She apologized, laughing, and we were so charmed to see an adult walking down State Street holding a rainbow plush narwhal that by the time we realized why she looked a little familiar, she was gone.

We encountered her at Greyhound stations and waiting for Amtrak overnight trains to begin boarding. We wondered if that was really her at a deli counter, politely, almost apologetically, asking if a certain bread contained a particular kind of nut she was allergic to.

We saw the silhouette of her on playgrounds after dark, or in the rain, always times when kids and their families had long since gone home. March spun alone on the metal roundabouts that Mother May I had decided were too dangerous for her own children, but that her own children had secretly loved, that thrill that March Iverson missed even now at age twenty-three.

She flew around, her hair spraying drops of rain, the hammered steel merry-go-round slicked wet so that it threw back the traffic lights' yellow, then red, then green.

It was strange seeing her from that distance spinning like that. She was still thin, limbs rangy, so at some angles she still looked like a kid, fifteen maybe, and the fearless way she spun made her look even younger than that. But then she flew back around, and from another angle the streetlights showed her as the adult she was, young still, but not a kid, not anymore. And it was this strobing between March Iverson as we once knew her and March Iverson as she was now that made her impossible to approach.

There were those of us who loved Mother May I and wondered how her children, the children she gave everything to, could go so wrong.

There were those of us who hated Mother May I and loved the Summer Girls.

There were those of us who loved them all and at night grew up asking our popcorn ceilings why our families couldn't have been like their family, with no worse problems than spats over which sponsorships they should take or decline.

There were those of us who despised every Iverson and enjoyed watching them all the more for it.

There were those of us who had never heard of the Iversons before August's murder but had since been catching up with the fervor of investigative journalists.

In this moment, we all had something in common. We each thought we'd be the one who would know March Iverson when we saw her. Every one of us who spotted her was sure that our sighting was the real one, and every other one was mistaken, imagined, a hope, a lie.

We each wanted to be right. We each wanted to be the one March Iverson belonged to a little more than everyone else. So it was impossible to compare notes in any productive way, to sort any of it out. When you want something to be true that much, there's just no way to tell if it is.

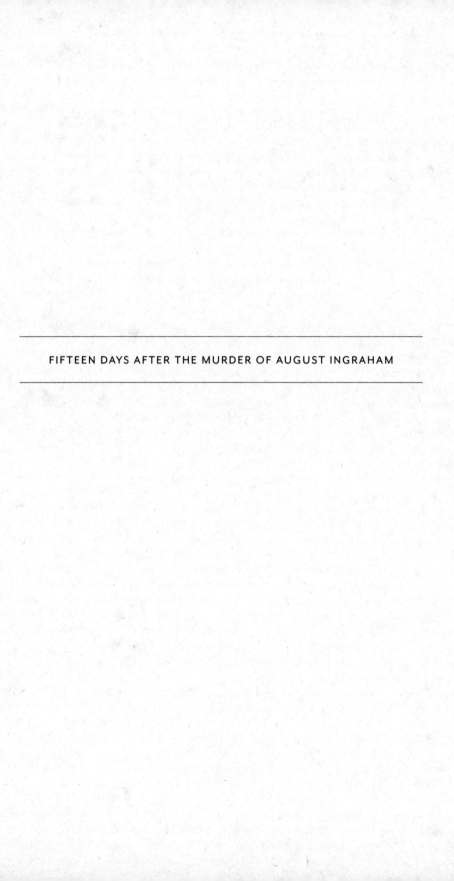

FIFTEEN DAYS AFTER THE MURDER OF AUGUST INGRAHAM

we who followed the Summer Girls

At this point, there was no excuse. It had been more than two weeks since the rest of the world had started watching the Iversons. And yet there were plenty of people still mixing up the decidedly nonidentical twins.

Photos were still getting captioned with each sister labeled with the wrong name. Self-appointed commentators who hadn't even followed the Summer Girls before the murder cited incidents in which July had shoved a heckler at a fundraiser dinner when it had actually been June. When they referenced rumors of July stomping her heel onto the asymmetrical train of a rival's ballgown (if it happened, and we weren't saying it did or didn't), it was June ripping the bias-cut charmeuse. They even brought in an old clip of June slamming her hand into a phone camera and erroneously labeled it as depicting July (and who could even blame June for doing that? The man harassing her was the same one from the funeral, that most repugnant of self-proclaimed gossip moguls—hair that looked dyed with Wite-Out, outfit like a prosperity gospel surfer dude, spare tire even as he called actresses "blobfish" for gaining five pounds).

Wasn't anyone noticing the pattern here? Anyone who knew anything about the Summer Girls knew that it was June who acted without thinking, not July. It was June we loved for having no filter, no brakes, and July we loved for her gentle way of moving through the world.

But what happened next meant that *gentle* was the last word anyone else was ever going to use for July Iverson.

It had been a long time since that clip of July sending the guy in her dorm to the floor had made the rounds, but we all remembered it. We had rewatched it many times. And not just after August Ingraham's murder, when everyone was rewatching everything. It was just one of those things we came back to over and over. Like that old lady in the talent competition whose voice came out of nowhere to bring a whole theater to a standing ovation, or a kitten and a rabbit touching noses, or a billionaire getting indicted. Every time we replayed it, it made us feel like things were a little better in the world.

Then, more than two weeks after the murder, came the uncut footage that even we didn't know existed.

As usual, it had been uploaded to a burner account, no editing, no commentary. Most of it was already familiar. July Iverson in her usual lipstick, liquid eyeliner heavy on the upper lid. The outfit we all remembered, green moto jacket and mid-wash jeans. It was a look that many of us had tried to duplicate, especially the too-nice girls among us, dreaming of forcing brutal boys to their knees.

In this, the complete footage, July spoke under her breath, almost hissing her words.

"Say you're sorry," she told him.

He grunted back.

She torqued his wrist harder. "Say it, you little bitch."

He cried out in pain.

He said he was sorry.

We didn't know who'd released this. This wasn't footage from the Iversons' archives. This wasn't a clip surreptitiously filmed inside the Iverson house. This could have been anyone in July's dorm, and we had never found out who.

Whoever released this full recording wanted everyone to see the way July stared at him, the way her dark eyes did not blink, the way her grip did not yield. They wanted everyone to see past how quiet she'd always been compared to June, how she was always the one behind June in pictures they took of themselves. They wanted everyone to see past the way her makeup made her face look doll-like—painted lips, eyeliner so precise that it looked like a thickening of her lash line, raspberry blush rounding the apples of her cheeks so that the hard angles of her cheekbones were less obvious.

July kept going on his wrist, leaning into him and saying, "Louder."

He said he was sorry, louder.

For most of her life, July's quiet manner had seemed to serve her well. It read as polite, classy, even mysterious. But after the unedited video came out, people called it unnerving. Creepy. Aggressive. Hiding something loud and violent within her.

If she'd been blond and blue-eyed, she might have gotten away with it, the Nordic winter queen. One of June's rivals had played it that way. Her white-blond hair, her glaring aqua eyes, her thin, pursed lips all made her the perfect spokeswoman for electrolyte-infused ice. In photoshoots, she was draped in gowns made of faux white fur (Mother May I's generation was still wearing calfskin boots, but June and July's contemporaries, even the ones who made ruthlessness part of their image, wouldn't touch real fur). This snow-pale blonde posed on plastic thrones meant to look carved out of glaciers, underlit with neon blue. She held handfuls of electrolyte-enhanced ice so calmly she appeared as though she didn't even feel the cold.

Someone like that could have survived this video. It might have even been good for business. But things were different for July. When it came to the Iverson daughters, and how clear it was that their father was Latino, July was second only to April. The near-black brown of her hair, the brown of her skin, the deep brown of her eyes that she inherited directly from Ernesto Iniesta, all of that would work against her. Whoever released the unedited version probably knew that.

The footage went on. It got worse.

"Scream it," July told him, her voice ripping at the back of her throat. "Scream it so every girl in this fucking dorm can hear you, you little shit."

That's when it clicked back, temporarily, to what everyone had already seen in the apparently highly edited version, him yelling, with all the air in him, that he was sorry.

But it kept going beyond what we remembered, because July kept going. She pressed him harder, until he said it over and over, until he was screaming it, half pain, half repentance.

Before we had even finished watching this, we had theories about who had released it. Maybe the influencer who had started her own swimsuit line and blamed June and July's direct competition for its failure (June and July had partnered with a major manufacturer to sell Summer Girls–inspired swimwear: bikinis in seashore pastels curated by June, high-coverage, vintage-inspired one-pieces chosen by July).

Or it might have been the one who was jealous that July had gotten the sponsorship deal with a company that made bottled water tailored to their customers (which was allegedly based on what mineral content would most effectively absorb into their cells, which was allegedly based on their body chemistry at any given moment).

Within twenty-four hours, July lost that sponsorship.

Within twenty-four hours, July lost a lot of sponsorships, up to and including various pet treat endorsements.

Whoever had released the original, edited version of this video years before had wanted us to love July Iverson.

But whoever had released this version had wanted us to turn on her.

They wanted us to see in her something new and vicious and feral.

A rival, most likely—now that so much attention was on the Iversons, could one of her college friends have been so mercenary as to sell the original?

But it was impossible not to wonder, just for a second, if June, or someone who loved June—or at least loved her more than July—had done this. June had been in open conflict with August Ingraham. And here was evidence that July, the quieter Summer Girl, was far more ruthless than her vulgar, laughing, sun-blond twin. June might have been the one throwing obscene gestures at cameras, each middle finger topped with a gleaming powder-blue nail, but here was proof that July was the one we should really suspect.

The footage kept going for a few more seconds.

July let him go.

She dropped him so fast that he collapsed. He fell back hard enough to hit his head on the wooden frame of the common-room futon and then just lay there, writhing.

If it had been June Iverson, she would have curtsied, taken a bow, strutted down the hall.

But July just walked out of there. No pride. No swagger. Eyes dead ahead.

Not like she was doing a victory lap.

Like she had just killed someone and couldn't be bothered to look back.

April Iverson

"You summoned me, my queen?" June asked as she runway-walked into April's house.

April almost never had June—and, by extension, July—over to her house. If it wasn't June's comments on her decor—"cobalt and lemon, how . . . courageous"—it was June's seeming inability not to take out her phone and take photos of herself and her surroundings.

"I know what an honor it is to be invited to the palace"—June gestured at the tile countertops, the carpeted stairs leading up to the two bedrooms, the hanging fruit basket—"and I come with a gift of gratitude."

April winced as June took out her phone, but then June prodded it to show it was off. "See? Not a chirp or flash to be had. I'm here for quality time."

April grabbed June's phone, threw it in June's purse, and shoved the purse into a closet, where her own purse and phone were already stashed. She shut the closet door.

"Wow. I guess I need to read the updated security protocols around here." June took the step down into the living room. "Where's Tim? I was gonna ask him to explain two-point conversions to me. I have this charity powderpuff thing next month."

"He's at work," April said. "I'm going to ask you this once, and I ask that you have enough respect for me to answer honestly."

"Okay, Deep Throat," June said. "What's going on?"

"It's you, isn't it?" April asked. "You're the one putting out the videos."

June's laugh was short and caustic. "You really think I did all this? Killed August, torched Mom's house, cleared out August's little media room, all as part of my dastardly plan?"

"I didn't say anything about August," April said. "But you have almost as much access to everything in the family video archives as Mom does. If all those old cameras were stolen, what an opportunity, right? You can put out anything you want and blame it on that."

"Do you have a wall with a bunch of photos around here somewhere?" June asked. "Do you use red string to connect them like on TV, or do you go for something with a little more flair, like floral-patterned ribbon?"

"You know the family archives better than anyone," April said. "You filmed half of them."

"That's a pretty big leap, Jessica Fletcher."

April gave her a look to remind June that she'd known her for her whole life, that she had clocked more time around her than their own mother.

"I might have filmed one of them," June said, overshooting a little on the faux casual. "Maybe a couple."

April kept that stare on June until the casual fell away.

"It was kind of a game for us." Now June was scrambling to explain herself. "Mom was always saying how important it was to know when a camera was on you. But it kind of worked against her. She was so used to having camera lenses on her that she didn't even notice one more. So sometimes I liked seeing how often and how long I could do it without her noticing. Then I realized I could do it so much that I taught the little ones to do it."

April knew how often they played with cameras that her mother had discarded in favor of higher-resolution models. But she didn't realize how often they were filming without anyone noticing, not even April. April had so often been too tired, too overwhelmed, too frayed, from looking after the four of them while keeping up with her classes, to think anything of those old cameras, except that she was grateful for any time they kept one or two of them occupied.

Mischief and pride gleamed in June's eyes. "Guess we were better at it than we thought." The pride apparently overwhelmed her instinct to defend herself long enough for her to say, "Of course, no one was better at it than I was."

"Of course not," April said. "You filmed everything you ever did. If you didn't have a camera out you had a phone out."

"Exactly," June said. "If Mom ever noticed anything, she just assumed I was taking videos of myself or of a perfectly decorated pan of ganache brownies or a new wall display. Phones were even easier. All I had to do was smile and adjust my hair, and she never even knew it was the rear-facing camera I had on, not the front one."

April sighed, and she could feel it in the center of her chest. June really had made their mother proud, hadn't she? Even as a child, she knew that there was no point in leading a charmed life unless everyone saw it.

The one Iverson who could capture so much invisibly was the most visible Iverson of them all.

June snapped out of being pleased with herself. "But just because I filmed some of them doesn't mean I posted them. I would never do that."

There was a flicker of something else in her eyes. Not pride. Hesitation.

She wasn't completely lying. But she wasn't telling the whole truth either.

"What about the 'cock' voice messages?" April asked.

All smugness drained from June's face, leaving behind a stricken ghost of an expression.

"Mom left those on your voicemail," April said. "Who else would have had them?"

"Okay, just let me explain." June was backing up toward the coffee table like April's accusation was a weapon. "That wasn't my fault."

"How was that not your fault?" April asked.

"This was before August died," June said. "Mom was flying off the handle. Like, at escape velocity. And it was so ridiculous and kind of funny that I played the messages at a party or two. I didn't send the files to anyone. Listen to how fuzzy the posted recordings are. They're not the original message. The background noise is cleaned up, but you can still tell. Some bitch must have been sound recording without me noticing. Ironic, right? But that was weeks ago. I had nothing to do with posting those, or any of the videos. Why would I do that?"

"I don't know. You tell me," April said. "Maybe because you have a twisted definition of *publicity stunts*. Maybe because someone is throwing our family into chaos, and who loves chaos more than you? You just love poking shit to see what happens."

June's laugh was thin with disbelief. "Have you looked around? You're saying incriminating things over the phone. January is one encounter with an overly aggressive true-crime vigilante away from never leaving her apartment for the rest of her life. There were already only four of us showing up at family holidays because one of us never wants to get within a mile of chez Iverson again. Especially now that spot March Iverson has become some kind of new national pastime. Oh, and have you heard the one about us killing our own sister? Because that one's floating around now too. Yeah, we were picking up the vintage flats July got resoled, and we were barely outside the store when some jerk asked July if she'd buried March in the backyard. If there wasn't already an active murder investigation going on around us, I would have put a leather awl through the second scrotum he clearly had in place of a brain."

June was waving her hands around, and the more frantic her gestures got, the more April could see her panic, her frustration. Those gestures were so similar to when June was small that they called up a kind of muscle memory in April. April wanted to wrap June in her favorite sky-blue blanket from when she was a kid, validate her feelings, tell her yes, June's braces really would come off one day. Yes, June was right, the school dress code was sexist. Yes, they'd see Grandpa again, death was just goodbye for a little while.

"I'm not poking shit," June said. "I don't need to. Shit has already been thoroughly poked." June's arms fell to her sides. "Even if this was what I wanted, which it isn't, I wouldn't need to do a damn thing. Our family isn't in chaos. Our family *is* chaos."

SIXTEEN DAYS AFTER THE MURDER OF AUGUST INGRAHAM

we who followed the Summer Girls

After the footage of July and the guy in her dorm surfaced—the unedited version—most companies wouldn't touch her, or the Summer Girls as a unit. It had to be June on her own. The Summer Girls stopped promoting that palo santo toner. July was no longer the face of that jewelry line's collection of reversible earrings. A nail-art company discontinued a set of July-selected jewels, previously sold alongside a June-inspired set of coastal flowers.

But among all the sponsors who dropped her, one wouldn't have let her go for a million dollars: a lipstick line that named their shades after botanically derived poisons. Foxglove (deep lilac-pink; matte finish). Hemlock (deathly white). Ivyberry (deep blue-purple). Nerium (a soft pink with a warning glint). Nightshade (true black; high-gloss shine). Wolfsbane (a particular shade of purple that collectors said they couldn't find in any other brand).

The collaboration had been in the works for months. They'd taken July on because she had the fan base, the accessible glamour, and the hint of mystery (made all the more pronounced by the contrast to June's perpetual oversharing). That was already enough to thrill them. But now, they probably couldn't believe their luck. Now, July Iverson's ethos was not just mystery but danger, and what could have been a better fit for their brand? We knew this because they were rushing the collection, moving up the drop date, putting out early promotion.

The July collection was all reds: Holly (brilliant crimson), Bittersweet (scarlet with gold shimmer), Yewberry (the color of cherry hard candy), Cyanide (deep apple red). In the publicity photos, July posed among dark green plants and forbidding-looking berries, her mouth painted in the various shades, each topped with clear gloss for extra shine. Her nails were blood red as she held the silver lipstick tubes or a waxed apple or a vial smoking with dry ice. Her hair had been conditioned, flat-ironed, and coated in enough dimethicone that when the fan blew it out of her face, it looked like slices of black glass. She stared down the camera, deep green eyeliner flicking at the corners of her eyes, heavier than she usually wore it.

Each ad for the collection had a similar caption.

Dangerously beautiful.

Venomously beautiful.

Deadly beautiful.

The company had bet on a critical mass of July's fans picking up a shade or two. But this wasn't just about us anymore. This was about everyone who couldn't look away from the Iversons. Now the company was banking on people buying the collector's box with the artistic rendering of July Iverson, drawn from one of those promotional photos. They were counting on people buying the whole set not just because they were fans but because they were fascinated. They must have known everyone would be taken with July Iverson the same way people became taken with stories of famous con women, thieves, murderesses.

And the marketing department was going to town. They showed previews of the collector's box, accented with silver and gold foil, July's features raised by sculpted embossing. They released another publicity shot with the words LIMITED EDITION in gothic lettering, and the caption *When she goes away, so do these.*

June was already filing a complaint against them for libel related to the new, unapproved marketing copy. We found this out when June ripped them apart in a fifteen-minute live rant, tearing into them for using the suspicion against her sister to sell lipsticks.

July, however, didn't fight back. She dutifully promoted the images and previews of the upcoming collection. We couldn't fault her. It was probably in her collaboration agreement, and who would have wanted a breach of contract suit with a cosmetic company?

But if there was ever a time to try to get out of a collaboration, wasn't it now? Lipsticks named for poison? A company that had never been able to keep the word *deadly* out of its ad campaigns?

She had to know it would look like she was flaunting something.

July Iverson

"**W**hat the fuck, Jules?"

June was pacing around the living room in her usual route.

July sat on the sofa, waiting for June to tire herself out.

"'Deadly beautiful'?" June stood still long enough to say, "Do you know how bad this makes you look?"

July already looked bad. They all did. If June had been paying attention to the bottom of the internet, she'd know that.

"And it doesn't exactly make me look good either, but that's not what I'm worried about." June waved her hands in a gesture that was half exasperated, half reminiscent of her star turn as Adelaide in their high school's production of *Guys and Dolls*. "Why not install runway landing lights leading the investigation directly to you? It looks like you're saying *fuck you* to the detectives."

July set her elbow on the sofa arm, but the accent fabric was so tightly woven with such fine thread that her elbow slid.

"I'm trying to get you out of this," June said. "My lawyer says you have a real chance to break your contract. Why aren't you helping me help you?"

Everything July wanted to say collected on her tongue.

So you can go for a guy's throat at a memorial service and I can't do this?

You prance around swearing and shoving people, and I'm supposed to just smile and apologize for you.

You're the blond one and I'm the brown one, so that's how it works, right? You're the fun one, and I smooth it over.

June was staring at her so hard that July worried—no, hoped—that maybe June could hear everything she was thinking.

All these things July could never say out loud, maybe if June stopped long enough to really look at her, July would get just enough of a window to say them.

"You know what?" June's face shifted and softened. "You're stressed, I'm stressed. We just need to relax. I think someone needs a little aesthetic therapy." June scrolled on her phone. "I've been working on a vision to give our space a little refresh. Maybe beachy pastels. I promise, your thoughts will feel clearer just looking at it."

June was off and running, fast enough that July couldn't stop her. So there was really no point in saying anything.

SEVENTEEN DAYS AFTER THE MURDER OF AUGUST INGRAHAM

we who followed the Summer Girls

As the poison-themed lipstick company sent their July collection boxes to press, the oddest lead yet flew around the internet: a grainy candid photo of June Iverson months ago, holding a wrapped Christmas gift.

What was that supposed to tell us? Was holiday spirit now a sign of criminality?

Our comments asking for clarification were answered with links to a video from last December, one we knew well, and that many of us had watched several times.

"Every holiday season"—here June spoke in a movie trailer voice, an *in a world where* voice. She wasn't in frame yet. Instead, the video showed inflatable lawn decor of Santas and penguins. Christmas trees. LED-lit snowflakes.

"An exceptional swath of humanity emerges from the shadows cast by icicle lights"—a woman's manicured hands unfurled what looked like a roll of wrapping paper printed with some kind of wreath pattern. The woman slid a pair of kitchen shears through the paper, smooth as a blade through water, while June's voiceover said, "the people who glide the scissor blades through the wrapping paper. The thing is"—with a classic record scratch, the film cut to June's disdainful face—"it's all bullshit. See, I always thought there were two kinds of people in this world." She uncurled one hand on the side of her face.

"People like my mother, who glide their scissors through the wrapping paper"—this against footage of her mother sweeping a pair of gold scissors through paper printed with foil dots. Faint background music played, Vivaldi's "Spring" and some kind of *Sleeping Beauty*-style stock audio of birds chirping.

June unfurled her other hand on the other side of her face. "And the rest of us sorry [expletive beeped out that was almost certainly *fuckers*]"—this against footage of June overacting trying to cut wrapping paper. The edge ripped and frayed before she even got to the other side.

"But I'm here to tell you"—June came closer to the camera—"we can all ascend to that higher plane of existence. We can all join that superhuman swath of society. We can all"—now it looked like she was nearly touching her nose to the camera—"glide the scissors. And we're gonna show you how."

The rest of the video was June and her usual student, July, waving at the camera.

"It's all about three things," June said. "One: the quality of your scissors, which don't have to be expensive, they don't have to be the diamond-bladed ones or whatever my mother and her friends use. You just have to know what you're looking for, and I'm gonna show you how to look for a good pair of scissors on a budget. Then there's two: the quality of your wrapping paper. Because guess what, the superhumans who glide the scissors are not superhuman at all, and the rest of us aren't being evolutionarily left behind. We're using cheap wrapping paper that frays if you dare to breathe on it wrong. We all need a wrapping paper upgrade and, say it with me, it doesn't have to be expensive, it just has to have good weight and a good finish. So next I'm gonna show you how to look for a good wrapping paper, and to prove you don't have to sell your favorite bag to do it, I'm taking July and we're gonna find the perfect roll."

She paused, as though listening or considering. "Of course you can come with us," she told the camera. "We thought you'd never ask." She gave a this-way sweep of her hand.

After June and July deliberated over prints and the weight of paper, after June gave tips to July and to everyone watching, after July loosened up enough to challenge June to a duel with rolls of paper printed with Christmas lights, they were at the checkout counter.

"When we get home," June said, "we're gonna talk about the third thing, which is what surface you're working on. So stay with me, because we're about to reveal"—again June came right up to the camera—"your inner gliding goddess."

That post opened up a new lane of brands wanting to partner with the Summer Girls. Office supply companies, wrapping paper manufacturers, small shops making artisan tape tinted in tasteful colors. They knew that the views on that post weren't just about the entertainment value of June's purposely bad acting, or July's weirder side coming out in the gift wrap aisle. They were because June knew something about us. She knew that whenever she obliterated one of those things that made us feel inferior, we loved her even more. Maybe Mother May I had done that once. Maybe she had done for our mothers what the Summer Girls did for us. But if she'd ever had that gift, we couldn't find it in her now. It got lost among her five-hundred-dollar face creams and first-class tickets in the 1A seat.

In the rest of the video, June taught July the perfect way to wrap a gift, starting with cutting the paper. The roll they used was distinctive, snowflakes swirling in a blizzard of holly berries and forest-green ribbons. The video never showed what the gift was. At the time, most of us assumed it was a prop paper box, with random household items shoved in to give it convincing weight.

While that months-old video featured each Summer Girl in perfect makeup and casual weekend wear, the just-released photo captured June in workout clothes, hair in a messy bun. It showed her carrying that exact box from the video—same dimensions, same paper, same apparent weight—down the hill, toward the house of the man with the chlorine-ruined farm. The higher vantage point of the photo meant it had to have been taken by someone on the Iverson property or an adjacent property. Sure enough, when we tracked down the original source, it was a neighbor who had shared it with all the self-congratulation of having cracked the murder case.

(Few stopped to ask why a neighbor had been taking random photos of the Iversons. Hindsight made it seem like common sense, as though the photographer must have known it would one day be evidence.)

It would have seemed like a small thing, a neighborly gesture, something perfectly normal, an Iverson carrying a Christmas gift to an old man and his family. But that one photo seemed to be the cue that everyone watching from their hilltop mansions needed to speak their own piece.

The HOA past president said he'd seen June going down the hill on other occasions. The first few times, June had reportedly gone right back up, presumably after the old man or one of his children slammed the door in her face, as they might have rebuffed any Iverson.

But June kept trying. She was as persistent in winning them over as she was in breaking in a recalcitrant pair of new heels. And it had, apparently, worked. Because the woman who'd won last year's front yard Christmas display contest had spotted June with the old man and his daughters. They'd been walking the ruined hillside fields sometime last spring, seemingly searching for the green flash of surviving plants.

Another neighborhood resident said that last fall she'd seen June on her knees in one of the farmer's plots, lovingly tending to a patch of carrots. Yet another had heard June by the Iverson pool the year before, yelling at August about the disastrously malfunctioning wave mechanism. "I couldn't say for sure, but it really did sound like she was threatening him. *If you don't take care of this, I'll take care of you*, that kind of thing. And I knew it was her this time, not her mother, because the language she used next"—the neighbor whistled in scandalized wonder. "May Iverson may be a lot of things, but she doesn't have a mouth like that."

We had no respect for these gossiping neighbors, bored in their

mansions. And yet all this, proof that June had had a previous friendship with the old man, gave new context to that wrapped present.
That small gesture ended up making her look like she might have
been on the old man's side, or worse: ready to avenge him and his
poisoned land.

Maybe June needed an excuse to kill August. How could she ever
have admitted what we already suspected, that she felt jealous and
sidelined by her mother's new marriage? We imagined her pushing
against that feeling, calling up everything to prove it was impossible.
After all, hadn't she welcomed, with endless shrieking and clapping
hands, the news of January's impending arrival, and then March's?
Hadn't she always shared the spotlight with July? Hadn't she always
been trying to give it to her, to get her to come forward enough that
she could shimmer?

If June didn't feel jealous of her twin sister, her beautiful twin
sister with her red lips and her bras two cup sizes above June's, then
how could June let herself feel any jealousy over August Ingraham?

All ignorance and vitriolic comments aside—and we'd seen
plenty—June did not hate men. She'd always loved her father. You
couldn't miss it in old photos or recent ones. But there was always
something gentle and quiet about Ernesto Iniesta. He wouldn't hesi-
tate to make pink confetti cake for the twins' birthday. He'd picked
up tampons at the store without flinching. When January and March
got a cat that would live at Ernesto's house, and named the cat Cotton Candy, Ernesto sustained no apparent damage to his psyche or
masculinity.

Then there was August, reeking of sports drinks and the chemical
smell of a new pair of collector's edition sneakers every week. He had
invaded May Iverson's distinctly feminine world, one of soft metallic
accents and a hundred shades of white. He had put his feet up on the
cream sofa and set a microbrew down on the restored antique table,
no coaster. He had looked around at the Iverson wealth, grinning and
slow-nodding, as though this was what he had always deserved, and
finally the world knew it.

And June had had to watch.

That didn't mean June hadn't truly cared about the old man and his family and their generations-old farm. We knew she did. If this had been all about spite against August, she wouldn't have been down in the dirt, trying to salvage what still lived, letting the chlorine in the soil eat away her manicure.

But maybe that had been the reason to go through with something she'd already wanted to do. To end the parade of sweat-soaked gym towels thrown over upholstered chairs. To rid herself of the veneer-capped smile August flashed when he showed up to lunches meant to be just for her and her mother.

Maybe she was already close to doing something drastic, and the rush of chlorine washed her over the edge.

Luke Sweatshirt

It was late, and she buzzed him in right away. Making an appointment beforehand had probably helped. *In case you haven't noticed,* June had told him, *advance planning is April's love language.*

April had her feet up on a second rolling desk chair. She'd kicked her heels off, and wore something between flats and slippers in their place. The cup on her desk let off a smell like she'd added something to her coffee, confirmed when she asked, "Can I get you anything? Water? Decaf? Grand Marnier?"

When he said no, thank you, she kicked the second desk chair across the room and said, "Here, take a seat."

He caught the rolling chair before it crashed into the two guest chairs.

He didn't know quite how to start. What could possibly be a good opening here?

Before he'd decided, April spoke.

"You know what I've always wanted to do?" April gathered her hair into a bun and pinned it in place with a matte black pencil. It took several tries to stab the pencil through, and when she let go, half her hair escaped. She did not seem to notice.

Holy hell, April Iverson was drunk.

"I've always wanted to post up in Mother May I's house when the Grande Dame is off in some eight-thousand-dollar-a-night villa in Santorini." April raised her logo-adorned coffee cup. "And just redecorate the whole place while she's gone. Magenta, shamrock green, bright blue, some rich browns, a fabulous color scheme she'd absolutely hate." April set down the cup and spread her hands out in front of her, imagining. "Not a trace of white to be seen. No peach or rose gold for miles."

He felt a laugh building behind his lips. "How about a trampoline in the middle of the foyer?"

"Perfect!" April pointed at him. "Bedspreads patterned with kittens or pumpkins."

"Or Bible verses," he said. "In big cursive lettering."

"Oh, she'd hate that!" April's voice went gravelly with glee. "She made us all dress up for Nativity plays every year, but she didn't even own a Bible until she could get one with custom white binding." She took a drink from her coffee cup. "You know, so it wouldn't clash. Because I guess your standard black Bible clashes somehow?"

"Black goes with everything," he said.

"Exactly." She raised her glass. "Just like the Bible. Just like kittens and trampolines and pumpkins. But that woman doesn't believe in saturated colors." April tilted her head back. "Everything in that house looks like overexposed film. And when I think about redecorating, it's not just a revenge fantasy, I promise." She was almost slurring now. "I want to liberate my mother from the unbearable whiteness of being Mother May I."

He laughed.

This was probably as good as things were going to get with him and April.

"Here." She produced the liquor bottle from her desk drawer. "Have a drink with me. I'm ordering you." Her smile said she was kidding. But underneath, he could see the April from all those videos, her gaze commanding not just the Iverson girls but her own mother.

So he did.

"Wait"—April unscrewed the cap and handed him the bottle, no cup—"what'd you want to talk to me about anyway?"

He took a swallow. It tasted like sweet, expensive mouthwash stuffed with flowers, but he needed it.

He'd come to ask whether April thought what strangers on the street thought, that he could have killed August, that he did kill August.

But now, when he spoke, that wasn't the question that came out.

"You don't like me," he said, "do you?"

He immediately hated how sad he sounded.

April sat up. "Oh, querido," she said. "Is that what you really think?"

His chest tightened, a buckling that warned him he was going to cry if he didn't watch it, and he'd cried more than enough this week. But April Iverson had never called him querido before. April Iverson, as far as he knew, had never called a stranger that before. And what else could he be to her except a stranger, the weird guy who was always around her little sisters? The weird guy who other strangers called a murderer.

"It's not that I don't like you," April said. "I just don't know you."

It felt like absolution, a blessing from this woman who was more the Iverson matriarch than May Iverson was. It was enough of a door opening that it gave him hope, but because he hadn't expected it, it had so much weight that he didn't know what to do with it. He didn't know how to hold it. He handed her back the bottle, afraid he couldn't hold that either, that he couldn't hold anything.

"You're in good company, though." April took the bottle. "I don't really know anyone anymore." She leaned back in her chair. "Not even my own sisters."

we who were watching the Iversons

The next video to show up online wasn't from a burner account. It was posted on a seldom-active, low-traffic channel, this one specializing in designer shoes, and it had the all-caps title "SHOULD WE HAVE SEEN IT COMING???"

This video was taken from too far away to pick up any words. Even if it had been taken closer, the rush of the intersection probably would have drowned them out. Cars flew between the camera and the two figures in frame, shown only in pieces.

The figures were outside June and July's favorite place for infrared light therapy. No July. Just August yelling at June, his hands flying through gestures that made us afraid he might strike her. Even with June in heels, August towered over her, with all his height and all the bulk of a man whose sole vocation was the perfection of his body.

We couldn't help holding our breath for June, forgetting for a moment that as we watched, August was already dead, and June was alive.

If June was afraid—and the recording didn't show her face clearly enough for us to know—her body didn't give it away. She tugged the back of her miniskirt down, as though to make a point that she didn't give a fuck what her mother's husband thought. She even seemed to adjust underwear that had ridden up on her; this was how bored she was with August's ranting. He could yell if he wanted, but she'd have to squeeze him in between the infrared sauna and scratching her own ass.

Then August said something that sent both her hands up, a posture ready for fighting. She tilted her head in that defiant way she'd been doing since she was four years old, at a birthday party, standing between her friends and the meanest boy in their class.

The tension in her hands, seen through the flashes of cars streaking between the parking lot and the camera, curled her fingers until they were fists. For a second she looked like she might be about to bash August's head into the hood of his own Tesla.

Then June seemed to take a deep breath. Her fingers uncurled. Her shoulders dropped.

She walked away. August kept yelling, but she and the honeycomb of her hair spilled into her car like she'd muted him.

Some held on to that vile theory about June and August, and were convinced that the postures between them, the yelling, could only indicate a lovers' quarrel. But we knew June well enough to know better. June and August disliked each other in a very specific way. It had never been an enemies-to-lovers kind of clashing. It didn't have that kind of heat or give to it.

This kind of dislike was mincing and brittle, marinated in disdain. June's smile at her mother's second wedding had been so ineptly fake that we sometimes wondered if she'd made it that obvious on purpose.

The way she looked at August made the possibility plain, undeniable: she hated him enough to kill him. That didn't mean she had. But she had the rage in her to do it.

If she had killed him, she was going to get caught. Yet she didn't seem to care. Two and a half weeks after August's murder, she was still posting, giving her locations for God's sake, practically issuing invitations to detectives once they scraped together enough evidence.

Some of us wished she'd decided to vanish like March.

We wanted to imagine June in Guanajuato, her hair back to its original color, learning the same embroidery her father's grandmother had stitched.

Or to picture her in a French village flea market, upselling antiques to tourists who would think she looked a little familiar but could never place her, not without her signature lip gloss and honeyed highlights.

We wanted to envision her love affair with a Viennese opera singer, velvet-gowned on the stage, and the passion in her arias would all be for June, for her eyes and her heart, both as rich and dark and elegantly bitter as unsweetened chocolate.

It wasn't that we wanted June to be gone from us. We just wanted her to get away with it. We wanted it even more than we wanted to keep watching.

July Iverson

Each of July's hands looked like they belonged to a different person. Her left hand, holding her phone, had been trembling since she ended the call. Her right hand was steady, moving only enough to pet the alopecia-stricken Pomeranian on the sofa cushion next to her. The dog's patchy fur gave off the sunshiny smell of June's organic, dye-free, paraben-free shampoo.

The light on July's phone screen turned off. She'd made the call without thinking. Her hands kept doing things that didn't make sense, matching the rest of the world's not making sense. People died when they weren't supposed to. People abandoned living creatures in the alleys behind luxury stores for no reason except that they no longer looked the way they wanted a purse dog to look.

A key clicked in the door.

The most maternal of July's cats had been sitting on the back of the sofa, watching over both July and the dog with slow blinks. Now she lifted her orange-striped head at the sound of the door opening.

"It's not that I'm not open to any of this." June's voice entered before she did. "I'm just not understanding the atmosphere you're hoping to achieve."

It usually took July a second to figure out whether June was on the phone or talking to her. June had a habit of coming into a room as though she and July were in the middle of a conversation. It always made July feel like she'd shown up late even though June was the one arriving.

June was, in fact, talking to July. This became clear when July saw the paint chips in June's hand, the dark greens, plums, and midnight blues July had offered for consideration. Not all of them at once, not in the same room. But something to break up the anemic pastels June insisted would "refresh" the loft. In other words, take it away from the retro Italian villa look they had both decided they loved when they bought this place, and more toward their mother's color scheme.

"I think we really want a cohesive—" June stopped at the edge of the bleach-dyed area rug. "Are you fucking kidding me?"

July kept petting the dog, who was now quivering at the change of energy in the room.

"I am already at my legally allowed daily limit for Zyrtec." June crossed her arms in a way that made her look as though she was protecting her sponsor-provided dress from both cat and dog hair. "We agreed. No more."

Heat built against July's sternum. "I'm not keeping her." As July ran her fingers over the dog's ears, her throat trembled. "I'm just fostering her until she finds a home." Each word came with more difficulty, like it was being crushed under a leg of the unnecessarily heavy coffee table. "Someone just left—" Her voice cut out. Her throat was too tight, and in place of her words came tears.

"Hey." June's face softened.

July's body was shaking now just like the Pomeranian's.

"Hey," June said again, sitting next to July on the sofa, this fucking sofa June had just had to have because there was something irresistible about staggered rose-gold studs. "What's wrong?"

The phone in July's hand was still warm, and something like grief was kicking her in the chest. Except it wasn't grief. It couldn't be grief.

Because if it was grief then July was a shitty person, because objectively August was a shitty person, and didn't missing a shitty person mean you were one too?

After several attempts, July ripped the words from her own throat. "I tried calling him."

"Calling who?" June's body went a little rigid, as though about to assume a defensive posture. She was probably already running through July's recent exes, making calculations about who was most likely to need a swift kick where.

"To ask if he'd post about her." July looked down at the dog. But tears were collecting along July's lower lash line, so the dog was blurry, just like everything else was blurry. "Then I remembered." She blinked. The tears fell, and her vision cleared enough to let her see June.

June's lips seemed to be forming the question *Who?* But before June said it out loud, July saw it registering on her face. The arch of June's left eyebrow sharpened. She moved back half a sofa cushion.

"You're really crying over the crown prince of Mom's loser boyfriends?" June asked.

The blow landed softer for how predictable it was, and yet it hooked into July. It bloomed across her face in the same moment it spread through her chest.

Because it hurt, because it was sharp, July wanted to be sharp back. She wanted to bite what was biting her, and if she couldn't, she just wanted to show her teeth.

July looked from the paint swatches on the blond-wood table to her sister's face. "So you don't like my colors?"

June's face slackened. She looked caught off guard. "I didn't say I didn't like them."

June was treading lightly, and July could feel herself drawing strength from her sister's hesitancy, like the sorceress villains in the movies they watched when they were little. That was always who July looked more like anyway. June was the blond princess, quick-witted, inevitably imperiled, happy in the end. July had the brown skin, black hair, and black eyes of the witch trying to steal the prince. She had a resting expression forbidding enough to scare off cartoon bluebirds.

"I just don't think they really reflect our vision," June said.

"You mean your vision," July said.

June opened her mouth, closed it, opened it again. "Inspired by both of us."

"And why exactly don't my colors reflect your vision inspired by both of us?" July asked.

"They're—" June started talking, like she always seemed to do, without considering the end of her sentence.

July looked right at her. "They're what, June?"

June's eyes darted between the swatches and July's face.

"Just say it," July said.

June did not just say it. For once, June was thinking before she spoke, a concept so foreign that it appeared to be short-circuiting her.

"They're too dark," July said. "Right?"

"I didn't say that."

"I know you didn't. That's why I said it for you." July's hands had stopped trembling. "What about me? Am I too dark to fit your vision?"

"Jules."

"Do you want to curate me out of your design plans?"

"Come on."

"This"—July pulled June's precious color selections off the side table—"is so clearly not for anyone like me." The cards fanned out on the salvaged wood. They were each allegedly a different pastel. But they were as barely distinguishable from one another as June's army of pink-peach-nude lip glosses. "It's not for anyone with any substantial amount of melanin. Because the camera either has to focus to pick up one shade of pretty-much-white against another shade of pretty-much-white, or it has to focus on us. It can't see both. It can't see that"—July pointed at the paint chips—"and me."

"It's just a design aesthetic," June said.

"Except when it's everywhere," July said, drawing her voice lower so she wouldn't startle the Pomeranian. "When the entire world is decorated for girls like you, it's just another reminder that the entire world isn't for girls like me."

The eye had to focus on the pale or the dark, just like the camera did. Only light-skinned blondes could stand against bleached-coral-on-ivory-on-blush and keep everything in focus. Everything dark about July meant that either she got lost or the decor did.

"When this shit is everywhere, we don't belong anywhere," July said.

At an uncharacteristic loss for words, June started petting the cat. It was a conciliatory gesture so feeble that it might have been funny if July was in the mood for anything to be funny.

July picked up the Pomeranian and walked out of the apartment. All the way to the parking garage, texts lit up her phone.

> Really mature
>
> Where are you even going?
>
> If you're still gone when I get hungry I'm eating both our leftovers

July put the dog on the front seat of her car. Her brain reared up with its usual reminder to lint-roll it later so June wouldn't start the whole day cranky about getting dog/cat/rabbit/hamster fur on her embroidered jean skirt.

Then July told her brain to fuck off.

Her body knew where she was driving before she did, taking the familiar route. She was in her mother's driveway before she could second-guess it. A new round of crying was building in her chest, the pressure rising up to her throat, and there was no one else she could tell why.

It looked almost normal, the construction tarps and scaffolding mostly hidden from the front. And the door chime still worked.

Her mother opened the door, face bright with alarm. "What is it? Is it Junie?" The dog in July's arms seemed to only heighten her confusion.

"She hates me," July said.

Sympathy saturated her mother's expression. It disgusted July, and it disgusted her more how badly she wanted it, how this, her mother's fluttering concern, was exactly what she'd come for.

"Why would she ever hate you?" her mother asked.

"Because I didn't hate him." More crying spilled out with the words.

Her mother pulled her into the house, into her arms, clucking out comforting, barely intelligible words. Her mother adjusted her position perfectly, making room for the Pomeranian with the skillful care of leaving space for an infant. July wanted to relax into this, being allowed to be sad, being allowed to miss the stepdad who texted back within five minutes every time July was panicking after picking up a new stray. He'd been her mother's husband, so this was the one place July could be sad without feeling guilty that she was sad.

"Everything's going to be good again." Her mother held on to her more tightly. "I promise."

July almost believed it. The boxes in the foyer proclaimed how right her mother was, how normal everything was. The house was growing an impressive array of luxury clutter. Companies were still sending samples, full collections, yet-to-be-released products, in hopes that Mother May I would post about them, show them off, wear them, have them in the background. Usually when there was scandal, the PR packages slowed to a trickle. When the scandal died down, the deliveries picked back up. July had assumed the same would happen in the wake left by those leaked videos.

But their mother just seemed to be getting more, and now from new brands, brands who'd never sponsored her before. Were these condolence gifts, simply arriving late? Had companies seen other companies send the compassionate comforts of six-hundred-dollar slippers and cooling eye masks, and realized they'd better follow suit?

Her mother had been right. If she kept her eyes forward, if she acted as though she had nothing to hide, nothing could touch her. Maybe if July believed it enough, it would be true for her too. Even if she did not look like her mother or June. Even if the lipstick company took out a billboard calling July deadly beautiful.

"We may have lost someone," her mother said, "and we may have lost our way a little, but we're still a family."

July looked over her mother's shoulder.

In these rooms, it was as though the world had no brown or black or red, as though the whole universe had never heard of any of the colors July was. There was a bleached runner made from an antique carpet. There was the supposedly pale pink marble that always looked white to July. There was the bone-pale frame around the foyer mirror.

There was no telling these colors from the ones June had arranged in her fan deck. As though by osmosis, June had absorbed the pallid tints with which their mother painted their world. They were both creating a universe with which July clashed. In their delicately toned world, July was dark and garish, the thing that stood out from everything else, the thing best removed to give the room a sense of cohesion.

Whether they loved June or reviled her, people thought of June as fearless, brazen, vulgar, shameless. But growing up, June had been the one always watching their mother, waiting for how she would respond. June's facial expressions mimicked their mother's in ways June probably didn't even realize.

June was a sunflower, forever seeking the disinfecting light of their mother's approval. July had seen it their whole lives, how something seemed to ease in June whenever their mother told her that she'd put together a particularly innovative outfit, that she'd arranged an afternoon snack in a way so perfect that their mother wanted to post it on her own page, that she'd taken a photo that made her look almost as beautiful as she was in real life. With every scrap of affirmation from their mother, June took a deeper breath.

June and July's followers loved June for not caring what others thought. But when it came to their mother, June was the most highly attuned approval seeker of them all.

July's eyes found the one bit of vibrant color in the foyer, the new staghorn ferns mounted sideways on the wall like hunting trophies. They protruded from the wooden plaques that served as their bases, fronds sticking out like antlers. They looked determined but nearly defeated, drooping under the weight of growing indoors instead of on the side of a tree, on this continent thousands of miles away from where they belonged.

Even through her mother's hug, a chill reached July. At first she thought it was how sad those ferns looked in this house, and then she thought it was how sad everything looked in this house.

Then she realized it was the air coming in from the front door her mother had not shut, and the bristling suspicion that her mother had left it wide open on purpose, hoping the neighbors would see.

we who were watching the Iversons

The next anonymous upload began with June at her mother's kitchen table, Sharpie flicking over a sketchpad, trying out version after version of the new signature that would later adorn the packaging of a May Iverson bronzing palette or food storage set.

August walked in. Even on film, the air around him seemed like it had hard edges.

It was difficult for us to pinpoint the exact month or year of this one—once adult June found her favorite shade of corn-syrup blond, she mostly stuck to it. But considering that August had only come into the Iversons' lives two years ago, it couldn't have been that old. From the sweatshirt June was wearing—an illustrated rendering of crystals from her mother's latest athleisurewear collaboration—we placed it at about a year before, June at twenty-five.

Without looking up, June said, "Did you know Ingrid Bergman once signed a note with a bunch of question marks and exclamation points?" She flicked the marker again. "We think of that kind of punctuation as modern, but I guess it wasn't."

August grabbed the page out from under the Sharpie, so quick that the felt tip left a twirling black flourish all the way to the edge.

August threw down on the table what at first appeared to be a handful of cash. But once the papers landed, the colors looked off.

"What the hell are these?" he asked.

June took her time looking up. She took her time looking at the pieces of paper.

"Cancelled checks." She went to the next page. "I didn't know they still did those anymore. Wait, is my mom still partnering with that checkbook manufacturer? I never really understood that collaboration, but I liked it. It was retro. Made me want to buy a pink rotary phone."

"Shut up," August said.

"Sorry." June widened her eyes in a look of *What's wrong with you?* "I thought you were trying to make conversation."

"I want you to tell me who these checks are for," August said.

"I never really liked quizzes," June said.

"It was you, wasn't it?" August asked.

June smoothed out the paper. "Wait, what question are we on now?"

"It was you." August slammed his hand down on the table.

The cancelled checks shivered.

June didn't flinch.

"Who are they for?" August asked.

June tipped her head toward the checks. "You can read them as well as I can."

"I fired these people," August said. "Why the hell are they still getting paid?"

"I guess you'll have to ask my mom about that," June said.

"You signed them." August picked up a handful of the checks and threw them across the table.

A few fluttered off the edge and down to the polished concrete floor.

"Do you want me to hire someone to prove it?" August asked. "You want me to get a handwriting doctor to look at these? I'll get the best."

"Oh, I'm sure," June said. "The best my mother's money can buy."

August inclined forward, like he was about to lunge, but held himself back.

June didn't flinch.

"If you're getting this upset, I really think you should talk to my mom," June said, injecting her voice with condescending concern. "Marriages don't last very long if you don't get everything out in the open, you know. It's not healthy to keep it all bottled up."

"She'll side with you," August said. "She always fucking sides with you little brats."

"Then if I were you I might take the hint."

"What are they doing for you?" August asked.

"Excuse me?" June asked.

"The people I fired," he said. "What are they doing for you?"

"Nothing," June said.

"Then why are you writing them checks?"

Maybe June felt bad for the staff who no longer had jobs once August got it into his head to do what he called *cleaning house*. Maybe she thought May and August and their now joint accounts owed it to them.

Or maybe June really meant what she said next.

"Oh, you know, just to piss you off." She flung her highlighted hair over her shoulder. "You're really not gonna be here long, so I'm gonna annoy the shit out of you while I can."

That was when we remembered the video posted a few days after the murder. August had thundered about June forging checks while May serenely shrugged him off, defending her daughter's petty thefts. Whoever was posting these almost wanted us to think better of June, to know the checks she'd been writing hadn't been for herself.

At least that was what we would have thought if it hadn't been for those words.

You're really not gonna be here long.

NINETEEN DAYS AFTER THE MURDER OF AUGUST INGRAHAM

January Iverson

January couldn't get away from her.

All January had done was look up a few instructional videos, searching for potential fixes for a loud cooling fan in the catwalk, and there she was: May Iverson in an ad before the video began.

What in the algorithm thought January was the target audience for anything Mother May I was selling?

Usually, January couldn't tell one of her mother's ad campaigns from another. They were all either severe and sophisticated or airbrushed and ethereal. This one was the latter, for a company specializing in foundations that had crushed gems and other iridescent minerals mixed in.

It started with her mother's finger coming right at the camera.

January flinched, as though the pointed nail might pierce the screen.

"Hey you," her mother said, from a vantage point a little higher than the viewer. "Yes, you. Eyes here." She knocked the camera like she was knocking every viewer in the forehead. The camera jerked as though reacting to the impact. "Trust me. You want to pay attention to this."

The option to skip the rest of the ad came up. But January didn't. The echo of that finger knocking into the camera kept her still. It kept her watching even as the ad switched over to afternoon lighting and her mother dressed like Golden Age Hollywood's idea of a Greek goddess. The voiceover introduced the new line "fit for Aphrodite herself" (crushed pearl, signaled by the image of her mother in a white gown on a giant prop clamshell). The spa-like music scored the light glancing over the high points of her mother's face.

May Iverson tipped her head back to show her wrinkle-free neck. She laughed into sunlight, walking alongside a pool flanked by white columns. The closing whisper of her voice, the line that led into an atmospheric setup showing the product packaging, encouraged all of humanity to "Beam your face to Mount Olympus."

Thanks to April, January knew the backstory behind that tag. The company had made the phrase part of their narrative, saying that May Iverson's offhand comment, uttered as a makeup artist applied her highlighter, had inspired the whole campaign. But apparently the line was a revision of her original utterance, "Beam your face to the heavens," which was changed, along with the original celestial theme, after another influencer accused their mother of ripping it directly from her content.

But that wasn't what stayed with January. It was that first moment, when her mother stood above the camera, knocking it in the forehead, making January look at her. January couldn't stop thinking about it, like a song she hated but couldn't get out of her head.

we who grew up watching the Iversons

In the latest anonymous upload—another unauthorized video—the sky outside the house's windows was dark, cut by buckling threads of light off the pool. Right in the frame was January, no older than six, seven at the most.

"I don't want to, Mommy," January said.

"We're almost done," May said. "We just need one more shot."

The camera was stationary, at a flattering height. This was a video May Iverson had set up herself, even if she had never posted it, had never meant for this part to be seen.

"You just have to focus and then we'll be all finished," she said.

January made a whining sound, but held it in the back of her throat, blunting it.

"Hey." May stood over her. "Eyes here." She poked January in the middle of her forehead. "Pay attention."

January cringed into herself, like she wanted to disappear into the gray overalls her father had given her for Christmas, the ones she seemed to wear for three months straight.

"Hey." May poked her in the forehead again. "Eyes up here, re-member why?" She pointed at the camera. "If people can't see your eyes, they can't fall in love with you."

Then March was there, throwing small elbows, shoving between the two of them, saying, "Leave her alone."

As often, January's and March's wardrobes showed significant overlap. March's overalls were identical to January's except that they were dark green instead of gray. But January and March were starting to look more and more different, January's hair straight and black, March's lighter and wavy. March was also notably taller than January despite being younger. Even more so because, as January's shoulders rounded, she shrank, while March stood up to full height, hinting at the striking figure who would one day advertise denim and sunglasses.

"She's tired," March said, voice lowered, sounding like April or even Ernesto. "She's just tired, okay?"

May lowered her lens. "Oh, so now you talk? Now you have some-thing to say?"

"You've been making her do this for like five hundred years today," March said.

"Because she won't do what I tell her," May said.

"Just let her go to bed," March said. "Please?"

January started crying.

As though summoned by a lighthouse beam, April came into the kitchen. She picked up January, gathering her against the softness of her sweatshirt. Oversize. Printed with the logo of the college she'd already decided on even though she wouldn't be old enough to apply for a while now. The campus was brick-filled, picturesquely greened with ivy, and three thousand miles from the hill where the Iverson mansion sat.

"Come on." April offered a hand to March, and March followed.

In a last sweep of her head, April glared at her mother.

May shuddered. She looked not afraid, but chilled. Warned. She looked like she knew the conversation was over.

That was the downside, May must have learned, to assigning your oldest daughter so much responsibility that she became as much of a mother to your children as you were. It wasn't as though May could claim that this was all necessary for them to survive. It wasn't as though May had been working minimum-wage jobs a bus ride apart. This had all been a choice, and April knew it. We could see in her face that she knew it.

And because it had been a choice, April became, in these moments, less May's daughter than her disdainful sister. Maybe May controlled the credit cards, but when April glared, May flinched. We'd known this for years. We'd seen it. But now the world had to see it. And we felt the vicious glee of our team scoring a point before the other team even knew the game had started.

May Iverson

By now, May could arrange a sales-worthy photo in ten minutes. This one she'd managed in five, while packing. It was a picture of her open suitcase, with the organizing compartments she'd been sent from a new sponsor. She had artfully arranged each item inside. Low-heeled sandals. Makeup bag. Mineral spritz. Filmy shawl as a river of color flowing across the lining.

What had possessed her to promote suitcase dividers in trend-specific prints? But she'd already signed the contracts, and she always kept her word to the brands that put down their money just to be close to her. Because despite all of the companies' PR-drafted condolence letters, boxes of brand-matching roses, and donations in August's name, they were here to make money. Their sympathy for her loss would last only so long. If she didn't deliver, they would turn their corporate backs and move on to the next name on their list.

When May looked up, June was in the doorway of the guest suite. "Oh, hi, sweetie." Now that May had gotten a good picture, she pulled the suitcase dividers out. They were bulky and could do with a redesign. "Did we have something today? Did I forget?"

June stood in the doorway, hands in her sweatshirt sleeves.

May posted the photo, in the timely fashion her sponsors loved, right in a peak usage window, tagging the company who made the organizing compartments.

Then she could give her daughter her full attention.

"What is it, Junie?" Poor girl. She was so out of sorts she'd gone a little overboard with the curling iron. Usually she was so good at making it look effortless, as though her hair was styled by the wind on a beach. Now she looked like a bridesmaid from Akron.

"I . . ." It wasn't like June to be at a loss for words. "I . . ." June started again without getting any further. She tried a third time. "I just don't know what's going on with anything anymore."

"A few behind-the-scenes videos aren't going to bring us down," May said. "You know us better than that."

"It's not that." June's eyes paused on the open suitcase. "It's July." June's voice quaked as she said her sister's name. "She won't even talk to me."

Understanding settled in May. Of course. July had been coming apart lately. How had May missed the possibility that July might pull June apart with her?

"It's not you." May adjusted an out-of-place piece of June's hair. "She hasn't been herself for a while. That has nothing to do with you. Sometimes when people are hurting, they take it out on the people they love the most because they don't know what else to do. That doesn't mean you've done anything wrong, and that doesn't mean there's anything wrong with you, okay?"

June lifted her face from the suitcase. She looked as timidly hopeful as when she was ten years old, wondering if she'd done a good job following one of Mother May I's eyebrow tutorials.

That face, that timid hope, caught May by the heart now, just as it had years ago. She'd always thought of June as the most resilient of her daughters, but this was a reminder of how careful May needed to be with her. June trusted her, and it was up to May to hold that trust in her hands as carefully as the butterflies she had released at her last palette launch.

"Why don't you come with me?" May subtly smoothed out some of those overdone barrel curls. "It could be just the thing for both of us. A little Parisian shopping?"

The two of them could show a united front. Especially with everything going around online, all the mother-shaming, everyone pretending that every family influencer hadn't done every single thing she'd done.

Everyone wanted to watch performances of perfect families while pretending that performance didn't take work, that it didn't take rehearsal.

"Remember London?" May asked. "It'll be just like that."

It had been one of their best brand trips, a seemingly spontaneous mother-daughter weekend that had actually been arranged months before by a flower company looking to gain traction. The documentation was a little much—May and June couldn't open a bottle of eau gazeuse without the corporate-hired photographers capturing it— but the resulting campaign was charming enough. It showed them gallivanting around London with their arms full of glass vases tightly packed with tulips, or pastel lavender boxes stuffed with roses. May even had one of the photos on an office wall, a framed print the company had sent as a thank-you gesture when affiliate sales shattered initial projections.

"I have some things I need to take care of here." June looked a little sad, then hopeful. "Next time?"

"Of course," May said. "Fiji, Florence, Ibiza, wherever you want." One mother-daughter post about antioxidant masks or cell-refreshing tea, and the trip would be as good as paid for. "Don't worry. There's always a next time."

TWENTY DAYS AFTER THE MURDER OF AUGUST INGRAHAM

June Iverson

It was just after 3 A.M., June was awake, and the silence was making her lose her mind.

She and July had never gone this long without talking. Maybe that one time after winter formal, but that was five thousand years ago. And the worst thing was that July wouldn't even give her a reaction. July didn't look at June like she missed her. She didn't glare at June like she hated her. She just passed her in the hall and in the kitchen like she wasn't there, and every single time, June wanted to scream, *Just talk to me! Yell at me, tell me to fuck off, just say something!*

But June wasn't saying anything either. Every time she was about to buckle, her pride reared up. Like hell she was going to break the silence first.

June distracted herself with online window shopping, which usually worked better than Lunesta. She scrolled through samples of a local artist's neon. Flamingoes. Crescent moons. Monstera leaves. Neon lighting spelling out affirmations was overdone, but a well-shaped statement lighting piece was timeless.

She moved on to throw pillows. Woven wall hangings. Bar cart accessories.

Without sleep, she had no energy to hold off the truth. She'd been a bitch to the person who mattered most to her in the world. And if her mouth and her pride wouldn't let her say she was sorry, then she could at least show it.

June got up and threw on leggings and a sweatshirt.

People thought of grand gestures as a mostly romantic thing. But the stakes were even higher with your twin sister. When you hurt someone who'd been your roommate even before you each took your first breath, you had to pull out all the stops. In this case, pulling out all the stops meant June had to do the thing she least wanted to do.

June made her way down the hall, keeping her steps extra quiet as she passed July's closed bedroom door. Their mother hadn't realized what she was asking when she assigned July the task of clearing out that storage unit. As much as June hated thinking about it, July had lost someone too. That was why she'd been procrastinating, why she still had the storage unit key, why she hadn't been able to just clear it out and close it out.

And June, true to her brand of being a bitch, hadn't even offered to help. She'd just sat on the couch throwing out unhelpful comments. *You're gonna go touch his stuff? Do you want a Tyvek suit? A single-person spacecraft, perhaps?*

June did not miss August. She did not mourn August. And that was what made her so well qualified for this job. Their mother should have assigned it to June in the first place. June would throw out August's shit with pleasure.

Two of July's cats were sleeping in the cat tree in the living room, and as June approached, they alerted and lifted their heads.

June affected a casual posture, as though she were getting a midnight snack.

She found July's bag slumped on the coffee table and went through it until she found the key to August's storage unit, the number scrawled on a plastic tag.

The cats were still eyeing June. She petted them until they closed their eyes and put their heads down again, and then slipped out the front door as quietly as she could. The last thing she needed was to spoil a good deed by waking up July.

June pulled out of the parking garage while the horizon was still orange and the sky was still dark blue. By the time she got to the storage facility, the sun had risen far enough to cast a glare off the metal siding, so it took June's eyes a minute to adjust when she slid up the unit's door. As soon as she could make out the rows of InFITnitum jars, she threw back her head and laughed. August's shitty pyramid-scheme inventory, as far as the eye could see.

Now she had to figure out what to do with all of it. Donating it was out of the question, unless she wanted to poison the clientele of the local food bank. There had to be a dumpster somewhere nearby— could she throw it all away? Or did she need to dispose of questionable supplements the way you had to dispose of leftover paint? She was going to have to load them all either into the trash or into her car for transport to some toxic-waste facility. At least she'd get her workout in for the day.

She picked up the closest jar, wondering how many she could carry at once.

It was lighter than she expected.

And it rattled.

She unscrewed the jar.

It was filled with fabric. Balled up T-shirts.

June couldn't figure out where the rattle was coming from until a slice of metal flashed into view.

Wrapped in the fabric was an old camera, one her mother had once let her play around with.

Rage flared in the center of June's chest, matching the rising glare of the sun off the metal doors.

She opened the next jar.

More fabric, tote bags this time, wrapped around another camera, one January had once taped different colors of plastic wrap over to see how the image changed.

June unscrewed another one. The same thing, an old camera she recognized. Another jar. Another camera. Another jar. Another camera.

The rage ignited and spread. What had August done? What the hell had he done?

In the middle of unwrapping yet another camera from another set of T-shirts, she stopped cold. She picked up a few of the shirts and tote bags she'd tossed to the ground. The sight of them in her hands seemed so impossible that she lost all sense of gravity. The shirts and bags could have floated off the ground and into space, and it would have been easier to believe than what June was now realizing.

She recognized these shirts and these bags. All of them—every single one—were promotional merchandise that brands had sent to July.

we who grew up watching the Iversons

The next videos were released in a rush, one right after the other, like asteroids pummeling a planet. They jumped across time, showing May in her mid-forties, then her thirties. They showed middle-school-aged April and March, even though they were in middle school years apart. June and July were thirteen and then minutes later they were nineteen.

First was May trying to coax March into bra shopping—"You can't keep wearing those sports bras. I know you like the colors, but you're growing up. You deserve something more sophisticated, something with a little more style, don't you think?"

March resisted, and May pushed until March burst into tears. May kept asking, "Honey, what's wrong? What's there to be so upset about? It's just bra shopping. Ask January. She didn't want to go either. But then we went, and it was over before she knew it."

"I don't care about the bra shopping," March said. "I just don't want to do it on camera."

May talked in reassuring tones, telling the camera that March was just overwhelmed, that she was taking so many accelerated classes this year, that she'd had so many practices lately, reassuring her viewers more than March.

Next was a montage, crossing various points in time. You could tell by the shifts in May's makeup and hair, the differences in video quality, the ages of her daughters. In each clip, she was trying to barge her way into a different bedroom decorated with different mixed patterns, saying some variation of *My baby's having her first period and her mama is just having so many feelings*. Each time, May got a door slammed in her face (April), or a plea of *please turn that off* from under blankets and heating pads (July), a yell of *get away from me* that sounded almost feral (January), a *please leave me alone* (March) that was so desperate it sounded like her heart was tearing down the middle, rough as a tag ripped off a new sweater.

All of them were trying to hold off their mother and her camera or phone so they could bleed and cramp in peace.

Except June.

The clip of June, we had seen before. May had posted it when June was thirteen. June wore sweatpants that cost more than a good pair of shoes, and a screen-printed T-shirt that read CONFIDENT GIRLS SPARKLE (from that year's collection by Mother May I). Her hair was falling down from a messy ponytail. Her mouth was marbled with lip gloss. Every once in a while, the shadow of a wince pulled at the corner of her mouth, hinting at her wringing cramps.

Still, June stood alongside her mother, a younger, same-jean-size clone of May Iverson. June posed and beamed into the camera as her mother threw an arm around her and talked about her "beautiful summer girl becoming a woman."

In the next clip, June and July were older, college-aged. July was crossing her arms over her breasts. She wore nothing but a lace-trimmed camisole and matching shorts, red edged in royal blue. June stood proudly, one hand on her hip, breasts jutting out, in an identical set. Guava pink edged in cantaloupe peach and honeydew green.

At the sight of those colors, our stomachs lurched in collective recognition. In an old Summer Girls post, the then-nineteen-year-olds had run barefoot across the mansion's high-pile white carpet, their half-naked bodies pale in the Sunday-brunch light.

May had taken the video in which we'd first seen these outfits. We'd always known that, even seven years ago. We'd known from her occasional editorial comments, a dramatic sigh for comic effect as they tossed decorative pillows at each other: "I'm so glad college has been such a maturing experience for you two." But June had posted the video, not May, from the account she shared with July.

The backlash had been fast, and forceful. Comments about how a mother helping her daughters film this was jaw-droppingly inappropriate. How May Iverson had objectified her own daughters and taught them to objectify themselves. Questions flew about what kind of mother would help her teenage girls film themselves in their underwear and post it for the world to see.

June had quickly fired back with defenses in the name of feminism and body positivity. The commenters were sex-shamers, June said. Slut-shamers. Body-shamers. "We're adults. These are our bodies. You don't get to decide what we do with them. Some of you will be on our side because you're the best and we love you, always. But some of you can't get used to the idea that we're grown women now."

May Iverson posted, with tearful pride, about how her girls were stronger and braver and smarter than any mother could ever ask for, that she couldn't be prouder of the fearless women they were becoming.

July didn't post anything for weeks. June blamed July's withdrawal on the predictable assholes who pointed out the little bit of tummy peeking out from between the camisole and the waistband of July's underwear.

But this new video showed us what we hadn't seen then. Just like with the video of July and the frat boy, we were seeing a longer version. We were seeing what had been cut.

"Don't you like it?" May asked as July pulled at the camisole.

"Yeah, it's fine," July said. "But I don't want to wear it on camera."

Her mother turned away—this was another one May clearly didn't film or know was being filmed.

May lifted an aggrieved hand to her mouth.

"What?" July asked, sounding worried and wearied. "What is it?"

May shook her head. The poured gold of her hair swept across the back of her diamond-white sweater. With a catch in her voice, she said, "I'm just so sad that I didn't raise you to be proud of your body. I tried so hard. I don't know where I failed you."

"I *am* proud of my body, Mom," July said. "I just don't want to post it like this. There are creeps out there."

"Creeps?" June asked. "You sound like Grandma."

"You're both adults," May said. "You can do with your body what you want."

"Yeah," July said. "Exactly. I can do what I want with my body. And I don't want to do this."

We watched, waiting for seven-years-ago June to weigh in. But she just kept smoothing her hair in the mirror, offering distractedly supportive comments like "You have a great ass, and anyone who tells you it's fat is just jealous because of their own flat ass."

"Don't you want to show other girls like you that you're confident in your body?" May asked.

"If we're such adults, why are you still calling us girls?" July asked.

"You're right," May said. "You're so right." She set a flat hand against her heart, beige manicure against that immaculate sweater. "And I am so grateful that you took the time and expended the emotional labor to point out my error. Thank you, sweetie. I am going to take that to heart going forward. You two are my girls, and you always will be, but I need to remember that in your own right, you are women."

July breathed out, relief in her whole body.

"Okay," she said. "Thank you."

"Of course, sweetie. I want to know the woman you are and the woman you're becoming." May handed her a throw pillow. "And as soon as we're done filming, we're going to sit down and talk all about that."

Then three more clips, from different years, ran together in quick succession.

In the first one, a young June, maybe seven or eight, was sitting at her desk. She stared at her homework with evident apprehension and nervousness, as though the worksheet was the meanest girl at her school, one who we imagined flicked pin-straight hair over her shoulder in that precise way that slapped June in the face as she walked away.

"Mom, please," June said, holding up a hand to block the camera lens.

May maneuvered around her. "Just scrunch up your face like you're frustrated."

"Mom, don't, not right now," June said.

"Really just scrunch up your face," May said, grimacing in demonstration, bringing the lens closer. "Really show you're angry."

"I *am* angry," June said. Except she didn't sound like it because now she was crying.

Next the video cut to a clip of January, in pajamas printed with planets and rocket ships, a pair identical to ones that March had.

May wielded the camera. "Now look sick, honey."

"I don't feel good," January said, her voice nasal and raspy enough that her cold sounded like it was in both her sinuses and her chest.

"Look at me, Jannie," May said. "Really look sick."

"Mom, no," January said, closing her eyes, grabbing the comforter. "No camera."

The last in the series of clips showed July in the front seat of May's car, the one with the milk-foam-white interior. July was sobbing into her hands. It took a minute to see that her hands were holding a collar with a paw-shaped metal charm. The collar looked purple, but it was paled by the hair of the animal that had once worn it. The sky out the car windows was dark, the back window lit with illegible neon.

"We just need to do this one thing, okay?" May said.

"Mom, I don't want to take a picture," July said, sobbing the words more than saying them.

"Make your face like this," May said, pantomiming a crying face.

"Mom, I don't want to do the video," July slurred in the soul-destroying way only ever really heard from heartbroken little kids and low-bottom alcoholics.

"Just come really close to Mommy"—May pulled July toward the center console—"and we're gonna look really sad together."

"I don't want to be sad together." July's words sounded parched dry by the salt of snot and tears.

"That's good," May said. "That's perfect. Just stay like that until I can get this."

"I don't want to," July kept saying. "I don't want to stay like this." But she was crying too hard for her words to be understood unless you'd been paying attention the first five times.

It was an increasingly sickening series of videos, and in the hours after they appeared online, we waited for a new post from Mother May I. An excuse we were already prepared to rip apart. An apology we were ready to find inadequate.

But she did what all her fellow influencers did whenever they wanted to edit some irritating sliver of truth out of their lives. She tried to wash it away with things that were prettier, more aspirational. She continued to put out photos of inspirational quotes, nail polish partnerships, her bag of first-class cabin essentials. She spilled out all these beautiful things, like an oyster lacquering over an invading particle. She coated every inconvenient revelation with a mineral gloss until it was so lovely and iridescent that no one could recognize it for what it had once been.

May Iverson

May thanked the man carrying her bags, tipped him, compli-
mented the suite. She was a little annoyed that they didn't
have her standard penthouse terrace available, but this room was
pretty nonetheless. With a few adjustments, no one would be able to
tell in the pictures.

The first rule of weathering a scandal was to carry on, business as
usual. And her fans had come to expect this trip. Twice a year, on
roughly the same weekends, May always traveled to Paris. Just off the
Champs-Élysées was the flagship store of a brand so selective about
their $25,000 bags that even an heiress couldn't just wander in off the
street, cash in hand, and buy one. Even Shannon, with all her husband's generational wealth, couldn't just walk in and buy one.

The brand wanted control of who was seen with their bags. They
wanted to make sure anyone who carried one was a worthy ambas-
sador of their luxurious essence.

Even the richest of shoppers had only two options:

1) Buy the bags secondhand, at a 300 to 400 percent markup—May didn't like to admit it, but she'd splurged on a few in her early days of success.

Or,

2) Go through the brand's onerous process for being deemed worthy.

Anyone who did the latter could expect to spend tens of thousands of dollars on scarves, belts, and coats, buying the loyalty of a sales associate who might offer the prize.

There was a third option, though, if you knew enough to know about it. Chances were better at that flagship store, where there were more bags on offer—more colors, more sizes, more hardware options—and a well-connected shopper could book an appointment for an interview.

May moisturized away the jet lag. Tomorrow she would meet with one of the associates, who were all the same type. White. Hair ash blond or medium brown. Women a little too old to seem bright-eyed and a little too young to seem wise or jaded, each of them wearing cream silk collared shirts. They wore little makeup except mascara and unmoving lipstick. Strands of pearls reflected light from underneath their carefully arranged scarves, as though their necks were glowing.

One of those associates would scrutinize everything from May's shoes to her eyebrow pencil, and May knew to tone it all down for the benefit of chic understatement. She set out every piece of makeup she'd use tomorrow. Sheer foundation. Rose-pink lipstick. These were the avenues of Paris, not runways or red carpets. No sculptural dresses or neon blazers, only navy, black, or white, in elegant silhouettes. Hair pulled back in a neat chignon. She laid out every component of her outfit, right down to the tinted tights—never nude pantyhose, not in Paris.

She set out her perfume, the most subtle she owned, and even then she would spray the mist and simply walk through. The slightest mistake was grounds for disqualification, and cloying perfume was among the common offenses. Most interviewees were turned away even if they had the credit limit to buy ten bags. Their shoes were deemed vulgar; May had brought the most classic pair in her collection. Or their contouring was too obvious; May wouldn't even use bronzer tomorrow. Or their nail art was distasteful; May had opted for her simplest manicure in months. Even at August's memorial service, her nails had been flashier (he'd always liked when she had jewels added to her ring finger nails, so it was a fitting tribute).

She added a statement scarf as a final touch. American ostentation was a typical disqualification, but a woman could also be eliminated if her ensemble was deemed excessively dull, along with its wearer. It was all an art form as delicate as writing a caption for an inspirational post. The wives of newly rich men were too deferential, too self-deprecating. The ones who'd grown up with money were too pushy. When one of the sales associates gave a regretful, "Ça risque d'être compliqué," the ones with money said, "Well, make it uncomplicated. Don't you know who my father is?" They were then politely, regretfully, shown the door.

May could only feel sorry for them. She made no such mistakes (at least not since she was too young to need night cream and too oblivious to realize that her American volume was practically shouting to Parisian women). May had embraced the challenge. She liked the vindicating thrill of getting something that she couldn't automatically have just because she was rich. And she succeeded every spring and fall, returning home with a new bag on her arm, the branding as recognizable as a face on a bill.

She reviewed a few collegial French phrases, but only to greet the associates. Too often, women who'd taken two semesters of French declined the offer of an interview in English, and then faltered in ways embarrassing to all present. May would begin the conversation by inquiring about the new colors of enamel bracelets; no need to seem too eager for the prize itself, plus she wanted to bring home a little present for June. May would comport herself with quiet confidence, blunting the fluorescent reek of her Americanness beneath a sheer cloud of Dior and Nina Ricci.

May moved around a few throw pillows and decorative items in the suite, creating a better balance for photos. She silenced her phone and continued to ignore notifications she had ignored during her flight. This was a time to get in the right headspace and focus on the single task in front of her. She visualized landing back in the States, where everyone would see the new bag on her arm. Everyone would remember that she wasn't just May Iverson. She was Mother May I. She was a brand. She was an empire.

July Iverson

June had been gone when July took the dogs out for their morning walk. She'd still been gone when July had gotten back, so July fed the animals, packed everything she'd need for the day, and left. She didn't want to cross paths with June if she didn't have to. She didn't want to see June's expression, wounded yet confrontational, full of both a sadness that said *I miss you* and a disdain that said *You better apologize because I'm never going to.*

Maybe June would be out—again or still—when July came home that night. Maybe June would go to some party or some brunch-themed bar opening and then pointedly upload pictures of herself having the best time with friends who were not July.

When July finally did come home, she didn't see June. All she saw was gigantic plastic jars. They covered the floor, the coffee table, the breakfast bar. They overwhelmed the space so completely that for a few seconds July wondered if she was in a nightmare. The jars had all marched out of the storage unit and down the freeway. Any second they were going to bounce toward her, each with a vindictive mind of its own, like that horrifying movie about sentient appliances that had made January cry every time their mother tried to put it on.

Then July saw June, lounging on the sofa in the middle of it all like she was doing a promotional shoot.

"You know, I never really did give InFITnitum a chance, did I?" June sat up. "You're lucky Mom's on her way to Charles de Gaulle. Literally the only reason I didn't unload this on her."

For a second, July's thoughts flailed for excuses, explanations, lies. But there was no explaining this. There were no excuses.

"You tell me everything, right now." June kicked over a jar. It fell to the ground with a metallic clunk—the camera inside. "Or I go to the police. And I suggest you choose me, because this sure as hell is gonna look like you killed August and torched the house, and you know it."

The rush of blood through July's heart told her to run. From her own sister. The best she could do was stay close to the door, as far from June as the space allowed.

"They were already gone," July said.

"Proper nouns"—June was almost yelling now—"longer sentences."

"The old cameras," July said. June had startled the words out of her. "I've been taking them, one at a time, for months. They were already gone."

"So you let me and Mom and everyone think they were stolen the day August died."

"Yes," July said, fast, as though that would make it easier to say and easier for June to hear.

"Oh"—June's knowing, bitter laugh broke up the syllable—"and you led me right to August's media room, didn't you? You choreographed that perfectly. You used me, and I fell for it, just like you wanted me to, right?"

June smiled, and the tendons in July's neck tightened. That smile looked ready to go for July's throat.

"Brava." June gave a slow, pointed clap. "I've got to say, I didn't know you had this level of treachery in you. And Ashley Morgan Kelly? You handed that bitch everything she needed, didn't you?"

Now protest reared up in July. "I didn't give her anything. She's had it in for you from the beginning. I was trying to deflect attention away from you."

"Video footage of me arguing with August?" June's disbelieving laugh grew harsher. "That was to help me? That was for my benefit?"

"He looks like the asshole, not you," July said. "I wanted you to look better, even if it made him look worse."

"How magnanimous of you."

July felt her shoulders rounding. She'd heard this cutting tone from June a hundred times. Just not toward her.

"And not all of them were me," July said. "The one of you and him in the parking lot, I had nothing to do with that."

"Not all of them were you. That changes everything, doesn't it?" June shoved enough InFITnitum jars out of the way to stand up. "And you kept all this shit in his old storage unit? Why? To twist the knife? To prove how stupid we all were?"

"No." July wasn't going to lie anymore, but she wasn't going to let June believe her own lies either. "They were here. In the back of my closet. And in the storage locker in the basement you don't use because you think it's creepy. But as soon as the police were done checking August's unit and Mom gave me that key, I saw the opportunity and I moved them. I wanted them far away from you. I didn't want you implicated."

"Oh, well, thank you for your kind consideration." June moved enough jars that she could cross more of the space between them. June always did know how to arrange a promotional display. But she clearly hadn't thought through how this one would stop her from storming across the room. "Why did you do this?"

"Because April and January were right." July had to stop raising her voice. The neighbors hearing was the last thing either of them needed. July had to remember that, even if June wouldn't. "We"— July faltered, corrected—"they deserved to have their lives to themselves if they wanted them. But Mom was never going to let them go. She was gonna leave pictures and videos of their whole lives up as long as the Mother May I brand went on. All I wanted was for her to think twice about that. I wanted her to move on from Mother May I,

to stop making her career off of who we used to be. She had enough
of a following. She could have taken the old stuff down and been fine.
But she wouldn't. Because we were her content. We belonged to her.
We were her products. We never got to decide our own lives because
she decided them for us."

June's eyes flashed around the room, like the words were getting
in but she was trying to stop them from getting in. There was a flash
of something like terror, as though listening to July, really hearing her,
would tear down the walls around them.

But then June shut her eyes and seemed to shake it away. When
she opened her eyes, her expression was filled with anger and a vindictive sense of triumph.

Only July could have found the streak of hurt running underneath
June's fury like a vein in the quartz countertop. That glimmer of pain
sliced into July. July was the person June had trusted most in the world.
Not the one June had most wanted to please; that was their mother.
But July was the one with whom June had been completely herself.

June had shown July all of herself, while July had hidden her own
anger in empty plastic jars.

"You know, I have to hand it to you," June said. "Doing shit that
made you look bad too? Genius. Who would have suspected you? But
here's the problem." June looked like she was savoring the venom of
what she would say next. "Your little tantrum accomplished nothing.
Mother May I is as popular as she ever was."

"You sure about that?" July asked.

"Check her front porch if you don't believe me," June said. "The
last few days, she's gotten more brand packages than ever."

"And who are they from?" July asked.

"What do you mean, who are they from?" June looked frustrated
with July's lack of comprehension. "The brands sent them. They're
PR gifts."

"Are you sure?" July didn't want to enjoy this. She didn't mean to.
But it was so clear that June was enjoying her own viciousness that
July felt herself matching her. "The crystal-soled oyster heels? The
cashmere scarves? Not sent by the designers. The protein bars? The
paraffin treatments? Check the boxes. There are no personalized

notes. No polite little cards introducing the products or underscoring the brand's message. Why do you think that is?"

"What are you even talking about?" June asked.

"These PR gifts are not from her usual brands," July said. "They're packages from those brands' rivals. Their direct competitors." July saw a thread of doubt cross June's face, and went on. "No one wants their dresses, their hair serum, their lipstick seen on or near Mother May I. Everyone who used to send her stuff, they want their products forgotten at the back of her closet, the bottom of her purse, the highest shelves of her cabinets. They want her to forget them and never mention them again, especially not publicly. And what better way to make that happen than to distract her with something new? Or many somethings new."

For once, July didn't have to fight June to be heard. For once, June stayed quiet.

"You were the one who taught me that that's something brands do," July said. "Remember? I heard you laughing about it when it happened to Kiley Whitcomb after her drunk, biphobic rant. Companies who'd partnered with her in the past suddenly started sending their competitors' merchandise as though they were personal gifts from their competitors, hoping she would wear and use them instead."

The doubt on June's face turned to recognition, then horror.

"Someone had to be visible on Kiley's kitchen and bathroom counters, in her cup holders, on her refrigerator, on her dining room table and desk, on her body and face," July said. "But it wasn't going to be her former sponsors, not if they could help it. They couldn't get themselves knocked off her vanity fast enough."

June was looking at the floor now. But her eyes were open wide, darting around as though looking for something with which she could refute everything July was saying.

"It's the same thing with Mom," July said. "If they don't want to be seen with Mother May I, the simplest solution is to give her someone else to be seen with instead."

Slowly, June lifted her eyes. "You know, if you were going to go to all the trouble of making yourself look bad, I wish I'd known so I didn't cover for you. That stain on that guy's wall?"

Guilt slid into July, hot and sharp.

July had wanted people to know it was her. She'd wanted them to witness it. But they were all too drunk to remember clearly, and no one took a close enough look at the blurred image to match up the span of the hips, the breasts, the width of her upper arms. They thought it was June going back and forth with her thin body, instead of realizing it was July's measurements, the shape of her.

And it was that curdling guilt that made July say the worst thing at this moment: "I didn't ask you to cover for me."

"Yeah, well, Mom assumed it was me," June said. "Everyone did. And I let them. Because that's who I am, right? I do stupid shit like that, right? So I helped you, just like I've always helped you."

Anger rose up in July fast enough to bury the guilt. "You mean like you helped me in college?"

June's expression flickered, the slightest break in the wall of her anger.

"The edited video of me in the dorm common room," July said. "I know that was you. I know you posted it."

"How would I"—June was stumbling now—"how would I have even gotten it?"

"You were friends with everyone," July said. "It would have been so easy for you to get that video of me fucking that guy up."

June looked caught. Not scared. Not guilty. More like she respected July the tiniest bit for pinning her.

"You know I never would have released the full version," June said.

"Why did you do it at all?" July asked.

"Because you were boring."

June yelled it. For a few seconds after, they were both quiet, the words ringing off the ceiling and the walls and the patinaed curtain rods.

"Because you were disappearing next to me," June said. "And you're not boring, and I knew that, and I wanted everyone else to know that. So when Candace recorded it, yeah, I got it from her, and I gave you a great edit, and I posted it. And you know what, you're welcome. Because after that, you had an edge. You weren't just pretty and quiet. You were interesting and mysterious."

"Well, thank you for granting me the privilege of being interesting," July said.

June looked as shocked to hear the words from July as July was that she'd said them. She imagined their faces mirroring each other's, identical expressions on opposite sides of the living room.

"You always got to be a whole person," July said. "Yeah, people are gonna be assholes about who you date and who you love, but when they look at you, you're a whole person. You get to do promo shoots for that Cock brand because it's cute when you're provocative. It's not threatening, like it would be with me."

"Listen to yourself talk," June said. "Have you ever thought that maybe this is the narrative you bring on yourself?"

Anger rushed into July. Fuck June's latest manifestation coach.

"In case you haven't noticed," June said, "we come from the same family. We grew up in the same house. We went to the same schools. We have the same mother and the same father. But you've always acted like somehow we're miles apart from each other."

The anger in July turned to rage.

"Because you're light and blond enough that you can do anything you want without making people afraid of you," July said.

"Oh yeah?" June asked. "Well, you better be afraid of me. Because if you pull anything else, if you put a single additional frame online, I will destroy you."

The light through the loft windows felt like the light through stained glass, cleansing and piercing enough to take July out of her body. July didn't need absolution. She needed out. Out of the fury simmering in her chest every time they'd been sick and their mother wanted to film them. The shame when their mother wanted July to eat on camera even as Mother May I fans were saying the darker twin was looking a little chubby, wasn't she? That blue lingerie with red trim that she'd never wanted to wear on camera.

July had needed other people to see it. She had needed other people to bear witness. She had needed to not be the only one carrying it, the only one who knew what had really happened.

June could destroy July if she wanted. July had already done what she'd done. The last video was already uploaded and scheduled to release.

we the followers of Mother May I

W e tried. We really did. What kind of fans were we if we couldn't stick with her through a scandal? Didn't we owe her that after years of her reassuring us, at the end of every video, *Remember, you are already a good mom?*

But despite our best intentions, we were already backing away, and then came the post that made staying by May's side impossible, even for us.

The video was old. Old enough that, as far as we could tell from the framing and how the quality compared to Mother May I's video history, it was filmed on a handheld digital camera meant more for family vacation candids than archival footage. (The details of the various recording devices May Iverson had shilled throughout the years for her various sponsorships took up an unnecessary amount of space in our heads, and at least now they were finally turning out to be useful.)

Recording devices didn't necessarily give us a conclusive date, because previous models of cameras and phones often stuck around the Iverson household, becoming toys for the younger ones to play with.

And any one of them could have been quietly taken by any of the Iversons, their friends, their enemies, or the people who worked for May, without anyone noticing. Any one of them could have been used to film this.

To get more specific about how old this particular clip was, we had to look at April, who was skinny enough for us to pin her age at sixteen or seventeen. Her face had matured early, looking like an exact composite of her mother's and her father's by age twelve, but her body took longer. Here, her limbs were bony enough to seem painful, as though a sudden movement might break her elbows or knees through her skin. Her hair was flat-ironed straight; as an adult, she would stop doing this. She was wearing the type of T-shirt and denim skirt she would never be seen in even a few years later. April's age could be corroborated by the lip color May was wearing and promoting around age forty-one.

We'd seen April yell before. We'd seen her seal off her expression like glazed ceramic.

But we'd never seen her like she was here, crying this hard. She was wringing her thin hands, her knees bending like her legs couldn't hold up her own weight.

"Mom," she said. "Mom, please, you're not listening to me."

May Iverson regarded the espresso machine with consternation. "It's so sweet of you to be concerned." Her silk blouse and floor-length skirt looked made for breezing through a hotel lobby. Her purse was already on her shoulder. "But it's really nothing for you to worry about. I have people to take care of all that."

"But they're not!" April's voice frayed higher. "They're not taking care of it! Mom, you have to take those videos down."

The espresso machine started. "You're getting all worked up for nothing, honey," May said.

"I have a friend at school." April moved in front of her mother, quickly enough that May looked at her by reflex. "He knows about this stuff. And he tracked it. Do you know how much traffic to your posts comes from criminal sites? From sites for—"

She broke off then, as if she couldn't say the words, not when doing so would put those words so close to June and July, to January and March.

"The world is a bad place, sweetie." May shook her head, the sun through the kitchen windows combing light through her hair. "We can't let that stop us from spreading joy."

"Do you even understand which videos get that kind of traffic?" April asked, the words wet with her sobbing. "You filming January eating a paleta. You filming July eating a lollipop. You filming June eating a candy cane. And why do you think those videos are so popular?"

"Don't be disgusting." May closed the top on her stainless steel mug. "I don't think I like your friends at school. I don't like how they're making you think."

May went toward the front hallway.

So did April.

So did whoever was filming this, far enough behind that neither noticed. This was back when there were more people working in the Iverson mansion than there were Iversons living there.

"If you're not gonna take them down, at least disable embedding on the videos." April was saying words that were as clear and logical as her later negotiations on conference calls.

But crying was wringing her words out, so if you couldn't hear the words, if you only heard the tone through a wall, she might have sounded like she was begging for something a mother would be right to refuse. A tattoo all her friends were getting. Going on an unsupervised trip for spring break.

You might have sided with May, with that voice so cool it could have chilled her espresso to room temperature.

But we could hear the words. And in that begging we could hear everything else April wasn't saying. *Please take care of them. I make sandwiches, I braid hair, I check homework. For once, do something to take care of them yourself.*

"I can't disable embedding." May was checking something on her phone. "It would interfere with the analytics."

"But it would mean there are fewer perverts watching your children!" April almost screamed this.

May glared up from her phone. "Lower your voice." Each word sounded like its own separate command.

April obeyed. Her next "Mom" was soft and fragile, like wet paper coming apart in her hands.

"If you don't believe me, you can track this yourself," April said. "I didn't make this up. My friend didn't make this up. It's traceable. You can see the numbers. You can see the traffic patterns."

"My car's here," May said.

"Please." April's voice was rising again. "If you don't believe me, hire someone. They'll show you."

"I have to go now, April," May said. "When you're older you'll understand boundaries, and I am setting a boundary with you by telling you this conversation is over."

"Mom, they're watching us!" April was trying to scream, but her voice was too raw. "They're watching them! They're watching all of us!"

"That's the whole point. They're supposed to be watching. We want them to watch." May went out the front door.

"Mom!" April screamed the word.

It was the kind of scream that could turn a heart into a hundred things at once. The spherical ice cubes Mother May I made with the two-hundred-dollar press she was paid to demonstrate and rave about. The globes of Luna marble adorning the garden. The thick-glassed perfume bottles with May Iverson's name on them (she'd posed for a photoshoot against a wall of orchids, the same kind that would later scent the air of her second wedding ceremony).

May shut the door behind her.

April collapsed against a wall. The bones of her shoulder blades showed through her shirt. It looked like she might slide to the floor, arms around her legs, sobbing into her knees.

But she stayed on her feet, leaning against that wall. The air seemed to go out of her. She stopped crying.

On the audio, you could faintly hear May greeting her driver outside. The slam of a car door. But whoever was filming stayed on April, watching her lean her chin back, trying to steady her breathing.

She pressed her hands to the wall behind the small of her back, palms flat against the metallic-accented paper, staring up into the cathedral ceilings.

She stayed there. Whoever was recording stayed with her.

TWENTY-ONE DAYS AFTER THE MURDER OF AUGUST INGRAHAM

we the unfollowers of Mother May I

The power of Mother May I had been her numbers. We could say whatever we wanted about her eyebrow tricks or her last-minute bake-sale recipes, but it was her numbers that determined which companies wanted to work with her. They determined her ad revenue. They determined how much she was paid for sponsorships and mentions and reviews.

And now they were falling.

Worse than falling.

They were plummeting. Fast enough to make a crashing sound when they hit the marble of the mansion foyer. On one platform, Mother May I set a record for losing more subscribers in a single week than anyone before her.

Some of us found a wild glee in this, the same way we might have enjoyed watching a hometown queen age quickly and badly after having called us ugly in high school.

Some of us denounced Mother May I, saying how deceived we felt, how betrayed, how disgusted.

Some of us twisted with the looming unease of realizing what we'd been doing with so much of our lives. We had been giving hours of our time and attention and admiration to a woman we now increasingly despised.

We marveled over how we'd missed all the signs, or hadn't wanted to see them. We woke up in the early morning dark, with the staticky sense of something left undone. That item forgotten on the grocery list. A child's form not signed for school. An appointment not cancelled with more than twenty-four hours' notice.

But then we remembered. It was the phantom twitch of wanting to check if Mother May I had posted, a habit repeated so many times over so many years it had become an instinct.

May Iverson

"Excuse me?" May asked.

As soon as she heard her voice echo off the gold-edged glass cases, saw the disapproving glances of the browsing Parisians, May corrected both her volume and her language.

"Excusez-moi?" She was in the flagship store, after all, and even when a clueless saleswoman made a mistake, it was up to her to keep her composure.

"Je suis vraiment désolée, madame," the woman in the gold-toile scarf, a pattern not yet released, told May Iverson. "C'est pas possible."

A shopper edged closer, eavesdropping while pretending to examine the lacquer pill cases.

"I'm here tomorrow," May said. "What time should I come in?"

"Not tomorrow, I'm afraid," the woman said. "Peut-être une autre fois."

"You do know I've bought two purses a year here for more than ten years," May reminded her.

"And we do appreciate your business, Madame."

"I'm coming back tomorrow," May said.

The saleswoman gave an elegant cringe and repeated, "C'est pas possible."

"I'm only here until tomorrow night," May said.

"And we do hope you enjoy the city," the woman said.

"I'm coming back in the morning," May said.

Here, the saleswoman dropped all pretense of regret. "C'est hors de question."

Out of the question.

It was a mistake. It had to be. There was no explaining it otherwise. But it would take a week and cashing in a favor to get ahold of a manager to set this straight.

May's waiting car took her back to the hotel. The second she was in her suite, she called her publicists to warn them. She didn't have the new bag, in a just-released embossed leather, in a just-released size, with rarely seen stitching. Just as she was about to tell them *Cancel everything, now*, especially the photographers they usually planted at the airport, she saw an email from the lead publicist on the very team she had been about to call.

> Proofs attached, preliminary, unretouched. I'm told they'll release sometime next month. Let's get on a call. To discuss this and a few other things. Have you seen my other emails?

As May waited for the photos to load, the chill left by the saleswoman's disdain boiled into rage.

May had heard that certain kinds of spiders devoured their own mothers after they were born, and she was beginning to wonder if her twins had been studying at their ruthless arachnid feet.

July was already careening off the plush-carpeted path May had set before her at birth. The extended clip of her in the dorm hall wasn't her fault—who hadn't done things they wouldn't want recorded?—but she hadn't exactly been doing damage control with those poison-themed lipsticks. July had been losing her way for months.

But the mock-ups in front of May were worse, as though June had decided to outdo July. Every one of them was reckless and raunchy. In the suite of a Parisian hotel, they were even tackier.

Here was June—*her* Junie—posing in front of a red barn, wearing a gingham dress that covered little more than lingerie would have. She held a paper quart carton, the illustrated label in vintage style, a happy-looking chicken alongside the words COCK VEGAN CHICKEN-FLAVOR BROTH.

Next, her precious second-eldest child was reveling in a pile of stuffed-animal roosters, wearing a bra covered in imitation feathers. And accompanying each photo was a possible slogan under the four-letter brand name.

Get some.

Better than the real thing.

You won't miss the real thing.

And worst of all, the one of her grinning daughter in a frilled apron that stopped mid-thigh, pouring a carton of vegan chicken-flavor broth into a red pot, accompanied by a caption.

Stick it right in.

May called. June didn't answer.

She called again. June didn't answer.

She called July, who didn't answer. Did anyone in this family respond to anything anymore?

May called June again and waited for the voice message.

"Do you know what this could do to us?" she yelled into the phone. "To our brand? Have you thought about that?"

One at a time, she'd been losing her hold on her beautiful, increasingly unpredictable daughters.

"Have you thought about anything at all?"

The messages rushed at her. From her publicity team, asking her to call them as soon as possible. From brand liaisons, asking her to call them as soon as possible. From pseudo-friends who were "just texting to check in." From numbers she didn't know telling her she was an awful excuse for a mother, that she should give all her money to her children, that she was a monster in overpriced eyelash extensions, that she'd probably killed her own husband because she didn't like how he smiled.

And in the center of this whirling mess was the same still shot over and over, the preview thumbnail of a video, sent from the few women she actually trusted as friends. All had captions like *This bitch is dead to us* and *So much for women helping women* and *By the time we're done with her, she's not going to be able to get a table at Wendy's.*

The thumbnail was small on May's phone, but she could still see the split-dyed hair, the cheek implants.

Shannon, in an exclusive interview with Ashley Morgan Kelly.

May couldn't stop herself. She was kneeling on the bon chic, bon genre rug in the middle of the hotel suite, her pulse sharp in her fingertips. She opened Fine Crime's latest video and saw Shannon. Shannon, the friend who'd been the first to stand by May's side at press conferences. Shannon, whose envy had curdled so completely that she was now telling Ashley Morgan Kelly everything about what she'd overheard: June yelling at August, *My mother told you to take care of that shitty chlorinated tidal wave. Why haven't you?* June screaming, *I'll fucking kill you!* before May got to them to break it up, separating them like they were children instead of her adult daughter and her middle-aged husband.

Everyone out there was busy hating May for nothing more than doing her job, hating June for nothing more than a temper that sometimes got the better of her, when they should have been finding August's murderer, finding whoever was trying to burn down May's life.

In the video, Shannon pressed her injection-inflated lips together, tearfully confessing what a difficult decision it was to come forward. She pulled her bag onto her lap and fished out a tissue. A peach tissue from a Mother May I product launch party, drawn out of the indigo snakeskin bag she'd been carrying as she walked out of May's house.

we who were hate-watching Mother May I

We tried different platforms. All her pages, channels, and accounts.

We restarted our browsers.

We checked our connections.

We tried on other devices. We borrowed our roommates' laptops and our family members' phones.

We couldn't tell who'd done it. The platforms themselves? Or had May shut it all down?

All we knew was that everything had disappeared. Recent posts. Archives. Even placeholder profiles.

It wasn't that May Iverson had deleted all her posts or set her accounts to private.

Mother May I was gone.

January Iverson

June never showed up at January's work unless she wanted something, and it was always at a thoroughly irritating time. Tonight, when January was working late at the theater, alone, was no exception. How had June gotten in? Had January left a door open? Had June charmed a key card out of someone?

June stood in the middle of a prop doorframe like an actor, right in January's sight line. "We need to talk."

"Can it wait?" It wasn't as though January could just walk away when she was screwing a mounted lamp in place.

"No," June said.

June told her about everything July had done. January tried to tune out what June was saying, but it rushed at her, everything July had posted, everything January had been trying to get out of her head for years.

When June was done talking, she tilted her head up at January, waiting for a reaction.

All January could summon was a flat, "Okay."

June took a step closer. She did it slowly, hands on her hips, as though playing to the back of the nonexistent audience. "What do you mean, 'okay'?"

January tested one position for the light, and then the next, casting it on June each time. If June was going to just stand there, she could at least stand in for an actor.

"I mean thank you for telling me," January said.

"That's it?" June kept moving, trying to make January look at her. "Aren't you livid?"

January put another screw in place. She should have been livid about something. That July had done this in the first place. That July had been sloppy enough to get caught. That June was trying to drag January into a fight between her and July. That their mother had blocked their every move as though she had been directing a play of the Iversons' enviable lives.

But the feeling vibrating through January, like the buzz of the electric screwdriver through her arm, wasn't anger.

It was envy. Envy toward June that she still lived in a world where they had all had happy childhoods. Envy that everyone else in their family somehow knew how to make seismically big decisions. January could only do that in the theater; otherwise she required April's opinion before even picking out a bedspread. Envy toward July that she got to be beautiful and adored and also ruthless enough to do this.

Envy that January hadn't thought to do it first.

"Aren't you even a little angry that she did all that without your permission?" June asked.

January could feel her face twisting into a look of *Really? Seriously?*

July had done something awful. Maybe, to June, even unforgivable.

But January still couldn't find the anger, and even the envy didn't last long. It burned off, leaving only grief. She'd had no idea July had been a fraction as miserable, a fraction as angry, as she herself had been all these years. January had never thought to ask. A hundred nights when July brought all her manicure supplies over to January's apartment, a hundred times when July talked January into branching out to black or navy polish instead of invisible neutrals, and January had never thought to ask.

January had always known, even when they were kids, that June was just like their mother. January had watched June boosting July into the spotlight, shoving her forward as insistently as their mother had done with all of them. As though June would do that if July didn't look the way she looked. July was the perfect accessory. Her clear brownness was an impeccable counterpart to June's lighter skin and all the ways she'd whitewashed herself. Every time January watched them pose alongside each other, she could see it. July was the sleek, receding darkness that made the sun of June Iverson glow even more brightly.

"How's the redecorating going?" January asked.

June coughed out a disbelieving laugh. "That's what you're going for? That's your subject change?"

"Have you steamrolled July into the paint color you want for the living room walls?" January erased a pencil mark. "What was it you were trying to talk her into? Barest Blush, eggshell finish?"

Confusion bloomed across June's face, with a hint of indignation, as though she thought January might have stolen her phone to look at her inspiration boards.

"July and I talk, you know," January said. Or at least, up until now, January had thought they talked.

June's face pulled in on itself in a way that made her look young and wounded. The expression did not evoke pity in January. Maybe it would have in April, but not her.

So January did have anger. It just wasn't toward July.

January aimed the screw gun, the crowning flourish to her laying it on June. "July and I are sisters too, even when you're not there."

April Iverson

April should have been pissed. She should've been enraged. She should have felt violated. But as soon as June told her, something inside her deflated.

No. It was worse than deflation.

"I appreciate you keeping me informed" was all April could get out. Her voice sounded as sterile as when she was keeping her poker face during a negotiation, but it was all she had in her.

"That's it? We're not doing anything about this?" June looked like she might kick over an end table or a living room lamp just to get April's attention. What were her sisters not capable of doing to get someone's attention?

As though sensing the hollowness inside April, Tim came in from the backyard. He read the room and promptly offered to make grilled cheeses and very strong margaritas.

June said yes to both, without looking at Tim. She was still looking at April.

"I'll go run by the store," April said.

"You don't have to," Tim called after her. "We have everything."

"Then start without me. I just have a quick errand to run."

April drove without really seeing the road. The street wasn't a street. It was the receding background of a pattern. The cars were tessellations of color. The signal lights were flashing polka dots.

Whatever business April had built, whatever name she'd made for herself, it didn't matter, because the only job that did matter was protecting her younger siblings. For years, April stretched and contracted herself into the shape that the job demanded, and she'd still failed. She hadn't protected any of them. Not even June, who'd become a little clone of their mother, just with a warmer decor palette. And definitely not July, who'd been holding all that protest inside herself for so long that it had turned into this.

As April turned in to her father's neighborhood, the blue-tinged foothills loomed over the narrow streets, and the bitter churn in her stomach refined into something she could name. Resentment. Anger kept in a box too small to contain it. And if she didn't let it out, it was going to wring the acid out of her stomach walls.

April pulled into the driveway of her father's house. She saw the slight shifting behind the blinds. Her father was home. He had heard her car.

He opened the door before she even got close enough to knock. He looked a little worried, as though she might be bringing bad news.

"You got out of this so early," April said as soon as her dad let her in and closed the door behind them. "Your alibi cleared you early on. But it's not just that. You got out of that house early."

Her father stood in the entryway, responding with nothing but a troubled expression.

"You got to be the good guy." April closed an open window, because that was the level of paranoia she was now at. July was melting down, and June was close behind. The last thing they all needed was someone overhearing or, worse, recording what they overheard. "That's how they all see you."

Her father took the cue and closed another window. "And you don't."

There was no challenge or accusation in his voice. He said it in the level way of a therapist demonstrating active listening.

The next window April shut was barely cracked, but screw it, she was hermetically sealing this place. "No," she said. "I don't see you as the good guy." The window was old, like the rest of the house, and even though she'd always loved its historic charm, right now she despised every historically charming detail, starting with this window. This was the house her father had escaped to without them. This was the house where he had made a life without them, except every other weekend and when their mother scheduled a brand trip.

"You got to leave." April jiggled the window sash harder. "And yeah, I know you're one of the only reasons that any of us are halfway normal." Now the words were spilling out of her, picking up speed. "But you left because you couldn't handle her."

The frame was warped from rainstorms and heat and how the hell did her dad do this without breaking a window? "But I couldn't handle her either," April said. If this thing didn't give she was going to kick it in. "You got to be the good guy, and the rest was up to me. Everything you weren't there for, everything Mom wouldn't do, every time the latest nanny was gone or fired, it was up to me."

Her dad walked over to the window and flipped the latch out of the locked position.

The sash gave under the pressure of April's hands, slamming shut. "I know," he said.

She wanted him to take on all the guilt she felt for what she hadn't done, or couldn't do right, or couldn't do enough. She wanted him to carry the guilt for one of them disappearing, for one of them twitching every time a phone came out of a pocket, for one of them becoming a future Mother May I, for one of them detonating in such a spectacular way that all she wanted was the utter destruction of everything she could touch.

"Why didn't you fight to get us more?" April asked. "Why didn't you push back against Mom about the custody split?"

Her father stood by the window, running his thumb over a spot of peeling paint. "I didn't want things to become rancorous between your mother and me. Amicable divorces might as well be unicorns, but your mother and I, that was as close as I've ever heard of."

"It was amicable because you gave in on everything!" April was yelling now. God bless this hermetically sealed house. "You let her have everything! Including us!"

"I thought that the more civil things stayed between us," her father said, and she hated how flat he sounded, like he was calmly explaining something to the child she had never really been, "the better everything would be for all of you, too."

"Bullshit!" April screamed. "Don't try to tell me any of this was good for me! For any of us. Why didn't you fight to keep us? Why didn't you fight harder, so that I didn't have to be their mom?"

Her father looked sad in a way that gave her, for the first time, a glimpse of the old man he'd be one day.

He didn't meet her eye as he said, "Because I knew I would have lost."

July Iverson

She wasn't sure why she went to his apartment. Was it to avoid June, or because she didn't want June to get to him first? June was probably going down her list, starting with April and January, though June wasn't sure which one she'd pick first. April because she was the oldest, in charge of them all? January, so that the two of them could go to April together? Next would probably be their father.

Maybe July just wanted this over with. To face the absolute contempt Luke would have for her once she told him, the wounded sense of betrayal.

But once she'd finished telling him what she'd done with the old recordings, he only stared past the railing of the tiny apartment balcony, toward the streetlights and the rushing traffic below the building.

"Say something." July's fingers were going to fidget this second-hand lawn chair into plastic scraps if he didn't. "Please say something."

He whistled softly. "I mean this as nothing less than a compliment: you are terrifying."

Then he looked at her, and smiled. The smile was more marveling than happy or pleased, but she'd take it.

"You've got ice in your veins," he said. "Or is it chilled rosé?"

"Fuck you." She shoved his arm.

He laughed. Then they both went quiet, nothing but the cars below.

"So why'd you do it?" he asked.

"I told you." She had told him everything she'd told June.

"I know what you told me." He took a sip from a can of discount-brand soda. Their mother would have felt faint even being in the same room with it. "And I believe you. It's all valid. But you did a lot more than release those recordings and show the world the real Mother May I. Your poison lipsticks? You didn't fight them on the advertising copy. So why not?"

July had grown to hate her own curated, affiliate-link-tagged life more every year. The need for precisely applied lipstick before even walking into a grocery store. The buzzing in her brain that didn't let her go to a park or a beach or on a hike without looking out for where to take the best pictures. How much she'd lost the ability to do anything without measuring how it might be a source of aspirational content.

But how was she supposed to tell their mom or June that? How could she explain how sick she was of turning her body and life into the most optimized, consumable versions of themselves? So she needed an escape hatch. She needed to wreck her image—one wallpaper stain, one unedited dorm hall fight, one incriminating lipstick campaign at a time—until it was beyond repair. She needed the damage to be irrevocable, because if it wasn't, the impulse to go back would always be there. It was what she'd known her whole life. Her brain had molded itself to the act of breaking existence into photogenic moments. If she left that pathway as an option, even a little, her brain would keep returning to it.

But if she lost all those sponsors, if all those companies dropped her, she wouldn't have to quit. Her influencer career would be over. If she didn't fight to save it, it would die. She'd never have to kill it herself. She'd never have to explain. She'd be an object of June's pity—*Fuck all of them, what do they know?*—instead of her bewilderment—*Why would you give all this up? I don't get it, I don't get you, are you okay, are you having some kind of breakdown?*

As July was trying to figure out how to explain all this to him, she realized how little she had to explain. She had taken all this action precisely because there were so many things she didn't know how to say. If anyone understood what that was like, it was him.

"I wanted out," July said. "And I didn't know how to tell them."

"Them?" he asked.

With that one word, June and their mother—who had felt like interchangeable, identical obstacles for so long—separated into the two distinct people they were and the two distinct challenges they presented.

July was always going to disappoint their mother at least a little. She wasn't June, so how could she not?

But disappointing June was different. July telling June she wanted out would be July revealing herself to be someone other than who June needed her to be. Being half of the Summer Girls kept July tethered to June in a way that was sometimes smothering, but it was also what kept them connected. They didn't just perform the act of being constantly together. They *were* constantly together, both by virtue of being close and because being together was intrinsic to their livelihood. If July declared herself done with the entity that was the Summer Girls, would June have taken that as July being done with them as sisters? It wouldn't have mattered how carefully July worded it. June could so easily have considered it a rejection of her and their shared lives.

Would July be a little less June's sister if she wasn't half of the Summer Girls?

Who was July if she wasn't half of the Summer Girls?

Who was July if she wasn't standing next to June?

"It was about June," July said. "I didn't know how to tell June."

TWENTY-TWO DAYS AFTER THE MURDER OF AUGUST INGRAHAM

June Iverson

June lay back on the deck chair and shut her eyes. She listened to the waterfall feature of the courtyard pool. She let the sun warm her body. And she attempted to summon patience and love for everyone in the universe, starting with her family, who had lost their collective minds.

After a check-in with her energetic alignment coach, June realized she'd been too harsh with July. What July had done was clearly a cry for help.

But not only were April and January not enraged at July, they didn't even seem concerned, and June couldn't understand why. July was not okay. What happened to August seemed to have pushed her over the edge, but whatever was going on with her had clearly predated his death. Did July need a break from making appearances at events and keeping up their sponsored-content schedules? Was she having a mental health crisis she was too ashamed to get help for? June couldn't have blamed her. Legions of shitheads on the internet threw around OCD and BPD as insults.

But an uncomfortable suspicion crept in at the edge of June's theories. Maybe it was June. Maybe June had pushed July to do too many promo campaigns, to shoot too much content. Maybe she hadn't really heard July about what sponsorships and fundraisers she did and didn't want to do. Maybe July said yes so much because she didn't think she could say no.

June would've called her mother, but she was pretty sure her mother was already on the plane back. And besides, her mother was far too fragile for this. She might crumble and not leave her house for the next month, or she might unleash on July so explosively that July would never tell anyone what was really going on. Before June told their mother anything, June needed to figure out how she was going to bring July back into her right mind.

The first step was to clear her own mind. June needed to treat herself with love, care, and compassion so that she could offer love, care, and compassion to the lying, conniving, backstabbing force of destruction previously known as her sister.

June soaked in the morning light that would signal to her brain that it was time to wake up, to be alive, to do what she needed to do next.

A shadow crossed her lounge chair. "Miss Iverson?"

the neighbors of June and July Iverson

No one in the complex had wanted the Iverson twins to buy that unit. At least none of them who knew who the Iverson twins were. The residents had imagined parties that would overturn every potted lemon tree in the communal courtyard and leave the newly replaced lounge furniture at the bottom of the pool. They envisioned the overly lip-glossed June barking, *You're ruining my shot*, as they passed through the background of her selfie, just trying to get their mail. They dreaded the transformation of their peaceful complex into a film set for the twee, aspirational movie the Summer Girls produced from the raw footage of their lives.

But it didn't happen that way. At the mailboxes, June greeted everyone with a *Hiiiii* so prolonged and chirpy it grew extra syllables. There were parties, but the parties didn't come to June and July. June and July went to them, dressed in tops that were beaded or sequined enough to catch the falling sun like handfuls of pennies. July was quiet, shy even, except when she encountered one of her neighbors walking their dogs; then she'd be on her knees on the atrium tile, telling them they were the prettiest girls and the handsomest boys.

The neighbors' biggest complaint was that June was perpetually repositioning vacant lounge chairs to get the best angle of sun, and the scraping against the stamped concrete became as grating as the beep of a dying smoke alarm.

That was where June was when the detectives came for her. When they did, she was polite and prompt. She didn't make them wait. She got up from her pool chair. She put on her shoes and her wrap dress that doubled as a beach cover-up (she had advertised it before, the rose-gold hardware reflecting the shine of the ocean during the promotional shoot).

The owner of unit 11 almost felt a little bad that she'd let the officers in, holding the door for them. She'd thought they were there to follow up on the Aston Martin that had been reported stolen by the owner of unit 73 but had really been taken out for a joyride by his son.

The residents didn't understand why the police were coming for June. Hadn't the Iverson girls been here during the time of the murder? Hadn't the wife from unit 65 and the father from unit 46 both seen the Iverson girls themselves?

Before June could go with them quietly, July must have heard the odd combination of footsteps in the courtyard, the heavy, sensible shoes alongside the click of June's heels. Because within a few seconds of the detectives' arrival, July had rushed onto the balcony of the twins' loft, stopping only when she met the scrolled railing. From above the courtyard, she stared down in terror at the aquamarine pool flanked with gracious trees and golden tiles.

That would be the neighbors' shared memory of July in that moment, her among the umbers and mustard yellows of the faux-Tuscan-villa decor. July's tan skin and black hair lent her the air of a young Italian woman who might at any moment burst into a passionate plea in that very language. Or maybe an aria.

Whole articles had ripped June and July to pieces for choosing to live in this collection of luxury lofts, decorated in a style considered increasingly passé. Warm stone, natural wood kitchen cabinets, ochre detailing, it was all the opposite of the sanitized white-on-white that was the key feature of their mother's house. When they moved in, the residents heard the twins' whispered conversations to and from the parking garage, July telling June to ignore the comments. "Well, that wouldn't be any fun, would it?" June had said back, her glee echoing through the atrium. June picked out the kind of peasant blouse and brown skirt she must have imagined on an Italian vintner's daughter. She painted her lips the color of crushed grapes. She wove leaves into her hair and took photos alongside the potted citrus trees. In one photo, she gave the camera a smile and a middle finger, and it was this one that she posted, along with:

> Fuck anyone who tries to shame you for what you like. If fanny packs make you happy, buckle one on. If everyone's wearing neon and you love neutrals, break out the brown eyeliner and wear it proudly. If the world's going matte and you like dewy, then shine like a jellyfish, because it's your face and anyone else's face can go fuck off.
>
> I love the Italian countryside look, and I have since I was a little girl, so yeah, when it was time for my sister and me to get our own place, of course I fell in love with somewhere that made me feel like I was in Umbria or Abruzzo or Pienza. I love my mom, and I think she's got spectacular style, but I'm just not a clean lines, floating staircase kind of girl. I like my pastels a little warmer, my floors a little more orange-toned, my neutrals a little beachier. I don't like glass except in windows. I don't like shiplap or apron sinks or shaker cabinets or any of that fake barn shit. But if you do, fuck anyone who tells you not to. If you love a magenta lipstick I'm trying out, try it along with me and show it off. If you hate it—and believe me, you're not catching my sister with hot-pink lips—stick with your favorite red or nude.

Upon reading this post, sharing around screenshots of it, the residents of the complex felt themselves swelling with righteous defiance.

Yeah, fuck their friends' all-white kitchens with a single decorative backsplash tile "for a pop of color." Fuck their friends who asked when they were going to cover "those god-awful textured walls" with white shiplap. The residents of the complex liked their faux villa, and anyone who didn't could go fuck themselves with an Edison bulb.

> As long as it doesn't hurt anyone—and trust me, our society will not collapse because you wear indigo jeans when everyone else is wearing medium wash—like what you like. Fuck everyone else.

It was with this same fuck-everyone-else attitude that June went with the officers. She didn't even dip her head as more residents came out of their doors or to their balconies to see what was going on. She met her neighbors' eyes, nodding as though they were simply running into each other in the fitness center.

The neighbors had been watching June so intently that they didn't even realize July wasn't on the balcony anymore until they heard her voice in the courtyard.

"What are you doing?" she asked the officers. Her bare feet and the hems of her yet-to-be-altered jeans slapped against the glazed ceramic tile stairs. "You can't take her."

The officers explained that they simply wanted to talk with June.

"But you've already talked to her," July said. "You've already talked to all of us—what else is there?"

They simply wanted to ask her a few more questions, they explained.

"You can't," July said again, this time to June. "If you tell them, then—"

"Shut up, July." June's tone sharpened so quickly that it zinged off the tile steps.

The collective nerves of the complex residents alerted, a mix of fear for these young women and fear of who might move in after them if they both went to jail, because they were good neighbors, and it was always so hard to find good neighbors.

July may have looked terrified, but she didn't cry. She didn't even look like she was about to cry. Her eyes simply widened a touch more, and then she did exactly as June said.

After June had ignored July's advice and posted that iconic photo with the middle finger, it seemed sponsors couldn't talk to her fast enough. The magenta lipstick she'd casually mentioned—she hadn't even been wearing it in that post, but in one a week earlier—saw a measurable sales bump. Her permission to everyone to like what they like had, apparently, made her fans more open to liking what she liked. Her unwillingness to tell everyone else what to do made them want to do what she was doing. And brands knew it. They weren't stupid, and neither was she.

June had ignored her sister's caution then. She wasn't about to start heeding it now.

June reconfigured her features, quick as the pool reflecting off her sunglasses.

"They're just asking me questions. Nothing to worry about." June turned a smile to the officers. "Right?"

They all nodded together, and it was impossible to know who was conspiring in the lie with whom.

So June went with them.

And July didn't stop them.

June Iverson

If there was a contest for the most depressing uses of gray and beige, this interview room would have crushed all competition. Whatever they asked her, June would keep herself calm by imagining how she might redecorate. A piece of abstract art there, a subtle patterned rug here.

Then the detectives showed her the phone records, and she couldn't even feel the metal and vinyl chair underneath her. She was back in the day of the murder, trying to keep it all from replaying in her head. If she let it replay in her head, it might replay on her face.

And the detectives, seated across the table from her, were watching her face as though it were an uploaded video. They didn't look exhilarated. They didn't even look pleased with themselves. They were just watching her in a fixed, focused way that was so much more unnerving than millions of people watching her on their screens.

The detectives had everything, right down to a printed transcript of the increasingly frantic texts June had sent, rapid-fire, to July.

Call me

Really

Mom has unleashed that squid of a lawyer on me

I'm not even kidding

It's about this fucking cock thing

Her apoplectic voice messages were funny and I didn't care but her
    lawyer?? REALLY???

Whatever you're doing, drop it and call me

Call me, or I'm gonna go punch Mom's $3000 an hour lawyer

Right in his diamond-plated sack

Then I'll break my hand

And his huevos

And it'll be your fault

Because you didn't call me

That day, June had called July eleven times, and had left four voicemails. That had to be a record for June. She rarely left voice messages. It wasn't the power play April thought it was. It was just that in the moment of hearing the prerecorded greeting, June could never figure out how to sum up everything she had flowing out of her into the tidy container of a voice message. It was just easier to call back incessantly until whoever she was calling gave in and answered.

"July Iverson," June had said in the first message that day, fast, then repeating the name stretched out, a lock of hair pulled taut in a flat iron. "July Iverson. Where are you? I know you don't post where you actually are in real time because you're worried about safety and stuff, but this is me we're talking about, not your adoring public. I should be able to find you whenever I want, which is always, at all times."

"Pick up," June had said in the second. "Pick up, pick up, pick up, pick up," she said, each iteration accelerating on her tongue. "Pick up! I need to talk with *someone* in this family who has *some* kind of tether to reality because our mother has officially unclipped from the space station."

"If you don't call me back in two minutes," June warned in the third, "I'm gonna start stalking you." She drew out the final word in a playground taunt. She had sounded like a brat and she knew it, but she had really *really* needed to talk to July, and she had really needed July to hear that. "I know you think you turned that off when you got the new phone, but I went into your settings and turned it back on, so call me now or I *will* come find you."

"What the fuck?" June had asked in the fourth message, because July never let this many calls go, and June was wavering between pissed off at her and worried that July had fallen into some scenic canyon while trying to take a selfie. "It says you're at home but you're not at home. Why did you leave your phone at home? I need to talk to you and you're the only one I can talk to about this and I need to know you're okay and that Mom hasn't buttonholed you because if she's trying to turn you against me on this I will kill her. I know you would never, but I will kill her for trying. Okay, I'm going to drive around and search every inch of this city and then the state and the solar system until I find you. So if you want to stop me from killing Mom and adding disastrous amounts of carbon emissions to the atmosphere, call me."

Now the detectives were saying they had some questions about June's original statement, the one in which she said she was with July the entire day, and had been nowhere near the Iverson mansion.

"Yeah," June said. "I imagine you do."

Fear was making her wrap dress damp, and clingy in all the wrong ways. But coming up through her fear was a slice of vindictive glee.

The record of where July's phone had been, the path of cell towers that had picked it up, didn't put her at their mother's house that day because July had left her phone at the loft. The truth was that July had been at the house too. And June could fuck her over so spectacularly. She could pay her back for the lies, for the utter havoc she'd caused.

But as June looked down at the pages of information, the contrasting data from June's phone and from July's, the white of the paper looked so bright and blaring that she could barely read what was printed on it. The white of the paper crashed into the beige and gray of this room, and they both crashed into her thoughts of redecorating this room, redecorating her and July's living room, those paint chips that must have all looked white to July. Through June's increasingly cluttered thoughts rang the memory of July's words.

You're light and blond enough that you can do anything you want without making people afraid of you.

How differently things went for a blond girl than for her darker sister. How differently things would go in these rooms, in a court-room, in Ashley Morgan Kelly's frame-by-frame commentary, in facing the world. If July had felt invisible or blurred against tones of pale peach and washed-out blue, this would make her visible in all the worst ways.

That vindictive glee turned to protectiveness, the kind that made June get her claws out.

They'd come for June, but they sure as hell weren't getting her sister.

Luke Sweatshirt

He had barely pulled into a parking spot, and July was already opening the door.

"If you try to stop me"—July got out—"you're dead to me."

"Wait, what?" He shifted into Park.

"And get out of here before anyone sees you," July said.

So that was why she'd called him. Not for moral support. She'd wanted a ride to the station in a nondescript four-door.

Apparently, her strategy was working. No one seemed to be taking note that July Iverson had just gotten out of a beat-up car. No one appeared to be raising their phones to document the sighting of a Summer Girl alongside a vehicle missing two of its hubcaps.

"July." He turned off the car and was about to get out when July whipped her head around and leveled a glare at him that stopped him in place.

"Dead to me," July said. "Got it?"

She turned back toward the front of the building.

Luke took quiet, innocuous steps after her, hands in his pockets. That was what normal guys did to look casual, wasn't it? He kept a few good strides behind her. If she turned around, he could say he was just taking a smoke break. He didn't smoke, but she didn't know him well enough to know that for sure.

July had taken only a few steps when none other than a back-from-Paris May Iverson pulled up in one of her fleet of luxury cars. This one had a finish with a sheen like a pearl, but apparently she was willing to risk having it towed, because she didn't even park in a spot. She left it crooked in a fire lane and leaped out, lunging toward her daughter.

May Iverson must have seen the news hit social media the minute she landed. Enough neighbors had seen the police come for June that it was already a mythical occurrence online, complete with diverging versions of the tale. Some accounts had June throwing an Aperol spritz in an officer's face. Others had her sobbing so pitifully that the officers looked pained, but at least her waterproof mascara was impervious to her tears, so she met her fate puffy and red-faced but with fabulous lashes.

"Jules." May caught up with her daughter before she reached the line between the asphalt and the concrete in front of the station. "Don't do this."

July turned. "She is not taking the fall for this."

Shit.

So that was what July was doing here. "Of course she's not." May took off her sunglasses. "We're going to get her the best lawyers in five zip codes." With a few clicks of her heels on the asphalt, she crossed the distance between them. "I'll talk to her. We'll all talk about this."

July drew back. "I'm not letting her go down for us."

Luke came closer as inconspicuously as he could.

"It can all be fixed." May gathered July into a hug. "I can forgive you. I've already forgiven you. We can be a family again." May shut her eyes. "There's nothing you've done that can't be fixed."

July kept her eyes open. "Are you sure about that?"

May stared at July.

"Did you think I was just going to let everything go?" July asked. "Did you think I wouldn't do it again?"

The first trace of disbelief crossed May's face. "You didn't do all this. You couldn't have."

July slipped from her mother's grasp. She didn't push her away. She did nothing sudden or violent. She just slid out of May Iverson's hold as though she'd gone liquid.

"After what you already knew I did"—July laughed lightly—"you still thought the only thing I was capable of was being your daughter and June's sister."

The disbelief on May's face twisted into anger.

"After everything that happened the first time," May said, "you brought all this outside our family? You decided to show it to the world?"

He was barely keeping up with this conversation. The first time? The first time of what?

"You looked me in the eye and you acted as scared as I was," May said. "You acted terrified about what could get out. You pretended it was your worst fear that what was on those cameras could get out."

"And you fell for it," July said, so softly that there was no arrogance or spite in the words. "Just like everyone who ever wanted to be you fell for Mother May I."

May's patterned skirt, one she had just shown off in a sponsored post last week, fluttered in time with the flags snapping over the station.

July stepped from the asphalt onto the station curb.

"You ungrateful little bitch," May called after her. "I made you."

July stopped. "Yes, Mother." She turned around. "You made me." The wind threw her hair into her face, and she unstuck it from her lip gloss.

"You made me," July said. "So if you don't like what you see, take it up with Mother May I."

"July Iverson, if you go through that door," May said.

"Check my birth certificate, Mom," July said. "My last name is Iniesta. We all started out Iniesta. We put on your name because you told us to."

"If you take one more step," May said.

Wow, these women liked threats.

"If I take one more step, what?" July turned back. "What are you gonna do?" She spread her arms, not like a saint. Like a queen threatening to burn down a kingdom. "You know what I'm capable of. You've seen it." The wind turned, blowing her hair out behind her. "You really want to try to stop me?"

July reached the door and went through.

He should have gone back to the car. But he was already this close to May Iverson, and he was inching closer, as if the wind were nudging him forward.

May was scrambling with her phone. Probably calling that legion of lawyers. For once, the Summer Girls' interests were not aligned with hers, or with each other's. It was gonna be a hell of a bill.

He hadn't exactly decided to speak when he heard himself say, "You have to let her go."

May looked at him as skeptically as if she was about to tag different parts of him with affiliate links. Baby fat he was too old to have. Jeans and sweatshirt. Hands in his pockets.

"I'm sorry," May said. "Who exactly are you?"

He opened his mouth for a second. He felt his mouth making the start of an *M* sound. But he didn't get to make it before May Iverson interrupted him, so he wasn't even completely sure what he'd been about to say. May? Mother May I? Ms. Iverson? How was he supposed to address this woman to whom he was a stranger?

"Oh," May said, and a laugh carbonated the syllable. "Right. You're the chubby boy who's fucking, what, one of them, both of them?"

He stood there. The wind blew his hair into his face and then out of it, the cloud cover passing over and away from the sun. He stared at her, surprised that he could.

He'd wanted to believe he had no pull toward this woman, that she was no one to him. But he had been about to say the word *Mom*, and he knew it. It was the single word meant to tell her who he was. It was a single syllable of *Don't you know me?*

He had been trying to say the name he had once called her so maybe she would wonder why he looked a little familiar.

He had meant to remind her that he had once been hers, even if she didn't know him now.

Maybe she couldn't fathom that someone so unremarkable had once been among her styled, photogenic children. Maybe that was why she had missed the resemblance—because, to her, there was none.

But now she was looking at him, really considering him instead of demonstrating her disdain that he was in her field of vision. He didn't know what did it. Maybe it was that his eyes were the same light brown they'd always been. Or that the shape of his browbone was mostly unchanged even if testosterone had made the brows themselves thicker. Or maybe it was the scar on his chin from when he and January had tried to ride accent pillows down a staircase, the scar she'd always covered with concealer before she photographed or filmed content but that was visible now when he lifted his chin. Whatever it was that did it, it hit her so quickly that she dropped her phone. The cold shock of her face told him. She knew. She'd gotten it just then.

He wanted to be cold-blooded about it, to look right at her and ask, *Do you know me now?*

But the second the possibility entered the air, he knew he wasn't ready. To be ready, he'd have to be ready for any reaction. Her revulsion. Her rejection. Or perhaps worse, her embracing him publicly, right here in the open, taking a picture of them both that would be accompanied by a long post about her brave son and his journey. The last five years would be explained away as nothing but transgender shyness. She would tell him that the world was ready to see him instead of asking him if he was ready to be seen.

So he walked away.

For a second May Iverson seemed to waver between coming after him and picking up her phone.

The phone won.

July Iverson

The officers were polite. Overly polite, even. They asked if she wanted a soda. July didn't know if this was deference to the Iverson name or if this was strategy, the lower-ranked officers knowing that there would be hell to pay if they scared her off when she had come here of her own accord.

They apologized for the wait, apologized that the detectives were not available when she arrived, as though they were out at dentist appointments and not questioning her sister. The officers told her she could wait here, in this generic gray upholstered chair, in this generic gray upholstered room where people denied or admitted the biggest things they ever had or hadn't done.

There were a lot of things June and July had promised never to speak of.

The fastidious, compulsive way June emptied the bathroom trash during her period, as though the volume of blood was something so obscene even July shouldn't witness it.

The weekend their mother chose a brand trip to Fiji over seeing June and July as the sheep in the school Nativity play. July managed to get the Roomba to pick up the end of a roll of toilet paper. The robot ran away with it, spooling the roll out over the house and then running over it in circular patterns. The result was a hundred thousand pieces of shredded bathroom tissue welded to the luxury carpets, and June rolling around on them, laughing so hard her side cramped. They both maintained, at the time and to this day, that it had been an accident, that they had no idea how it had happened.

And then there was the day August died, their shared promise of silence.

When the detectives came into the room, they made no mention of the room they'd just come from. The younger one carried himself with a what-can-I-do-for-you openness, like a manager at a hotel. The older one had a welcoming stillness that he had probably cultivated to be inviting, the look of a priest who not only was willing to hear your confession but assured you that you would feel better afterward.

On the way here in her brother's car, July had tried to plan out how she was going to play this. But what little she'd figured out evaporated in the face of the detectives. She was left making this up as she went, how to tell the truth, or as much of it as she could while leaving June blameless.

"I was there," July said. "The day it happened."

"You were there at the house?" they asked her.

"Yes," July said.

July had waived her right to a lawyer. They likely thought this was the hubris of the pretty and rich, or the resignation of the guilty. July didn't bother to clear it up for them. She let them think what they wanted.

"Why did you go over to the house?" they asked her.

July breathed out. "Because August asked me to."

"Why?" they asked her.

"He wanted me to delete something from a security camera," July said.

"We were under the impression that the security system didn't record. That there was no security footage from that day."

Shit. If she was going to clear June of any blame, this was the part where July had to pretend to know more, not less, than she knew.

"My mother thought that," July said. "I let her think that. But the feeds did save to the computer's hard drive itself, at least temporarily. When the computer's hard drive would get full, it would start writing over the older security footage."

She was impressed with herself. She almost sounded like she knew what she was talking about.

"There was no recorded footage found on the computer," the older detective said. "At all. So what happened to it?"

The weight of what she was about to do landed on her. This was it. This was worse than taking the old cameras and pretending the murderer had taken them. This was worse than admitting that she had let her mother file a false police report about stolen items. This was about the murder. This was obstruction of justice. This was destruction of evidence. This was admitting that they might never find out who killed August, and it was her fault.

Even if she hadn't done it by herself, it was her fault.

Because she'd been the one to ask June to do it.

"I erased it," July said. "August had called me earlier that day and asked me to."

The detectives looked curious, interested. Not angry. Probably an act, but a convincing one.

"Help us understand something," the younger one said in his best Columbo just-one-more-thing voice. "Why were you willing to delete your own mother's security footage for August?"

July hesitated. "I know he wasn't the best guy in the world. But he was always nice to me. And he was always nice to the strays I brought him."

"Your sister didn't want any more at your place, huh?" This came with a slight laugh, a bid for camaraderie. They were trying to find a crack between the Summer Girls.

"Any time I got panicked because I didn't know what to do with a stray," July said, "August was always really calm about it. He always said we'd figure it out. He always found them homes. And usually with friends who liked posting pictures of their pets, so I got to see them too. I got to see they were okay and taken care of."

"What did August want you to delete?" they asked her.

"I don't know," she said, and wondered if they could tell from her irises or the tiny muscles in her temples that she was lying. "I didn't watch it. He asked me not to. He begged me not to. He said he wanted to explain everything himself."

"Did August tell you what was on it?" they asked her.

"No," July said. "But he did promise me it wasn't about my mom. He promised it had nothing to do with her. And I could hear in his voice that he meant it."

"When you went to the house, did you see anyone with August?" they asked July.

"I didn't see him at all," July said. "The first thing I did was go to clear the security footage." She was changing the sequence of events here, and she knew it. And she couldn't think fast enough to figure out if they'd be able to figure it out. "Then I went to go find him."

"Did you?" they asked her.

"No," July said.

And it was true. She hadn't found August.

She'd found her mother.

June Iverson

When they left the room, they were gone for a while, which she assumed was either urgent business—she tried not to take personally someone else being more urgent than her—or some technique to make her sweat.

"We can appreciate you wanting to protect your sister" was the first thing they said when they came back.

Blood rushed into June's head.

"But she's already admitted that she was there that day," they told her.

They didn't overplay their hand. They didn't make it vague and threatening with something like *She admitted to everything*. They didn't mention the murder or the fire. That was how June gauged that they weren't bluffing.

"You have a chance to tell us the truth here," the younger detective said. "And you know this will all be easier for you both if you do."

we who followed the Summer Girls

However much we loathed Mother May I, we still watched June and July. We still wanted to know what boots July was wearing. We still wanted to know what hair product June was using in the ever-evolving art of imitating the saltwater waves she got naturally at the beach.

Yes, some people resented June and July for being rich and beautiful. But we didn't love them because they were rich or beautiful. We loved them because of what they were not.

So many influencers made their image and their living off proving that they were better than you. Their just-woke-up photos looked as flawless as full-coverage foundation. They flaunted parties and after-parties that mere mortals would never be invited to. They advertised products that were already sold out. They were like stores that tried to build a sense of exclusivity by treating customers badly, who told their employees not to help shoppers, to glare at them, to snap at them not to touch the T-shirts marked up 5,000 percent.

The Summer Girls had always represented the opposite of all that. Instead of claiming that they "never worked out," they shared footage of them trying every device and routine, and they were just as likely to skewer one as recommend it. June was open about everything from her upper lip hair to uncontrollably farting during her period (which led to sponsorships for creme bleaches and wellness-branded digestive enzymes). July never hedged about her dry hands, which looked twice the age of the rest of her (that led to a hand treatment sponsorship), or about using a lip brush to get her perfectly glossed red lips ("It doesn't look like this when I just throw it on right out of the tube, and I'm not gonna pretend it does"). If one of their collaborations with a brand sold out, they told their fans that they were lobbying them to restock, and then the brand did, and everyone made more money.

June and July were not like their mother's friends, standing on the balconies of their mansions, laughing and yelling *Hello, peasants!* down toward the freeways as the smog-laced sun glanced off their cocktail glasses. The Summer Girls were like May Iverson used to be. Their currency was not *You can't have this,* or *You're not good enough for this,* or *You'll miss out on this.* It was *We're trying this out, come try it out with us.*

That was their magic.

But that magic would do nothing for June now.

We had no doubt that June would be breathtakingly foolish from the moment the officers came for her. She'd either waive her right to a lawyer, or grudgingly tolerate one and then repeatedly ignore him. The more forcefully a lawyer told her to keep quiet, the louder she'd probably get.

We loved June Iverson because she was beautiful and shameless, and for these same reasons, we knew it was all but over for her. And yet, instead of feeling inevitable, it felt wrong. It was the opposite of a false start. A false ending, a false landing. It was unsteady under our feet, like stepping on old concrete cracked over and over by the shrugging and flinching of the fault lines under California.

June Iverson

"What really happened that day, June?" the detectives asked her, with all the sympathy in the world, as though they themselves could feel how it must weigh on her. She hated the sound of that sympathy. She wasn't some pitiable girl who'd gotten herself wrapped up in some mess. Her mistakes were hers. What she'd done that day was hers.

But there was something about how they asked the question. It was how quietly they spoke the words, the space they left after. She was in that day, living it again, how everything started.

After June had found July's phone at the loft, she'd gone out looking for July, which the detectives probably knew from the location of her own phone. She'd started with the pool and the courtyard. Then their favorite coffee spot. Then the donut place with an owner so enamored of July that he had named a green-frosted cruller after her. Everywhere they got their nails done, their infrared energy recalibrated, their heel-shortened tendons stretched.

When June finally found July at the Iverson mansion, it was with a flourish of taking off her sunglasses and a hearty "Where the fuck have you been?" She grabbed July by the shoulders and physically turned July in the cardinal direction of the driveway. "This is the last place any of us should be. Mom is in orbit. She's mythologically pissed off at me, when I'm the one who should be pissed off at her."

"June," July said.

"I swear, if I see her—" June looked around, half-wary, half-hopeful. "She sent her lawyer after me. Over vegan broth! Some legal garbage about me degrading the brand of the family name? Have you ever heard such regal bullshit in your life?"

"June," July said.

"She thinks she knows everything." June raised her voice a little; so what if their mother overheard. "Remember she told me never to talk about sex because it's bad for my career? Well, everyone loved that interview when I talked about anal play. There were no letters from her lawyer when I said the words *butt plug* on a podcast with a million listeners, but now that I might actually make some money that has nothing to do with her she has a problem with it." June took the deep breath in of a sudden revelation. "Maybe I could do a line of sex toys. Picture it." She spread out her hands as though telling a hopeful starlet she was about to make her famous. "The prettiest, most elegant butt plug set you can imagine, with my smiling face on the box. I'll have every single one engraved with the word *Iverson* in beautiful, *very* legible script so I can stick her Hallmark-wholesome name right up my—"

"June." Now July had grabbed June's shoulders, interrupting the thrill of her product-launch fantasies. "I need a favor. No questions asked."

"No questions asked means you're gonna owe me, you know that, right?" June said.

"Yeah," July said. "I know."

"Fine. Lead the way, and then let's leave. Because if I don't get some prebiotics and a lunar light bath before I have to see Mom, I'm going to take her favorite eyelash curler and curl her head off with it."

When July led June to the enormous closet that served as a security room, June couldn't help doing an August impression. "'Baby, we don't need to pay that security company, I can set it all up.'" She rolled her eyes. "I was the one cleaning all this up from the spaghetti bowl it became when he"—June did very pointed air quotes, a perfect imitation of how their mother did them—"'worked his magic.'"

"Do you know how to delete something from it?" July asked.

"Of course I do." June started messing with the keyboard. "When am I looking for?"

"I don't know," July said. "Earlier today?"

"Earlier today?" June asked. "Want to be a little more general?" But when June saw the pinch of worry above July's right eyebrow, she said. "Okay, how about this, which camera?"

The pinch deepened.

"Garage area?" June asked. "Front? Backyard? Any hint at all?"

July looked at the floor.

"How do you not know?" June asked. "What is this even about?"

June drove her questioning stare into July until July confessed.

August had called her.

"August?" June made a sudden movement, and her arm almost pulled out two cords. "You're doing this for August?"

"I don't know why he called me," July said. "He's supposed to be the one running this, right?"

"Sure, but I'm the one who fixed it," June said, "and now that it works, he can't get his asshole head around the system."

"Then why would he call me?" July asked.

"Because he knows I don't like him," June said. "Plus he probably thinks everything you know, I know. Or maybe he can't even tell us apart. And why the hell should I ever do anything for that lower life form?"

"He said he had an argument with one of his business partners," July said.

"Yeah, sure he did," June said. "That's worth calling you to wipe a security drive."

"He told me he doesn't want it to end up on the news," July said. "And he told me he doesn't want Mom to see it before he gets to explain everything."

"How considerate of him," June said.

"Our loft would be Noah's ark without him," July said. "You know that."

"Oh, he likes adorable animals," June said. "Call the Nobel Committee. No one else on Earth likes puppies and kittens." But she turned back to the monitors. This was going to be fun. June at least had to admit that. "Let's see what he wanted to hide." She lit up with anticipation. Maybe the footage was of August ushering another woman toward the pool house, which June would immediately send to her mother. Or maybe it was a business partner beating him over the head with a plastic tub of muscle enhancer.

"June," July said.

"What?" June asked. "I didn't say I wouldn't watch it."

July stood by, quiet. If she wanted June's help, all she could do was let her review the recordings, and July knew it.

June pulled up a file and played the video. On one of the exterior driveway cameras, there was August, shoving an old man.

The satisfaction went out of June. Rushing into its place was a shock of recognition: it was their neighbor from down the hill.

And August pushing him so hard that he lost his balance.

The man fell in that painful way that suggested old bones, the lost weight of aging. Both June and July cringed, wondering if the man would get up, wondering if he'd broken something. Was he still out there?

But on the footage, the man did get up. With a searing dignity he stood, and walked away from August and the Iverson house.

Containing her rage made her hands tremble so much that June accidentally closed the recording. July was dry-heaving over a trash can. June had known who August was since the day she saw him park his Tesla in an ADA spot. But to July, the sight of August shoving an old man to the ground must have been a blow.

Good. Sure, it hurt July, but July needed to see him for what he really was.

June took a deep breath to steady herself. She opened a series of files in different tabs, all the day's footage from every security camera. Scrolling ahead a couple hours, scanning for anything of note, she saw

July arrive, then herself, but stopped and let it play when she saw the old man from down the hill appear again, on a different camera's feed. In contrast to his composed exit off the Iverson property earlier that day, he was running away as though it was him who had done something wrong.

June checked the time stamp. She confirmed it against the time on her phone.

Now. This was happening now. This was feeding from the exterior cameras and being recorded to the hard drive as June watched it. The old man had come back, and now he was fleeing, and whatever he'd just done, June cheered him on. Maybe he'd decided he'd had it, and it was time for a little revenge. Maybe he'd gotten into August's private garage. Poured sugar in the gas tank of his Panamera. Or shoved a potato in the tailpipe of the Zimmer. Or he'd gone for the gold, August's prized vintage Firebird, and keyed the Screaming Chicken.

Whatever it was, June would make sure the old man got away with it.

June guided July to a chair, advised her to close her eyes and put her head between her knees.

While July did, June wiped the logged recordings from the last hour. She deleted them from the trash, erasing all evidence of the old man coming back up the hill for revenge.

"Keep your eyes closed," June said. "Focus on your breathing." And while July was keeping her eyes closed and focusing on her breathing, June went into the system settings. She stopped the camera feeds from writing to the hard drive. This would all look like one big system malfunction. Even better if their mother blamed August.

June just needed one more thing before they left: a copy of August shoving the old man. She pulled her own flash drive out of her purse and connected it to the computer.

But when she went to grab the file, it was gone.

All the files were gone.

June had accidentally deleted everything, including the one section of footage she wanted.

"No," she said under her breath, her skin cold while the center of her flared hot. "No." She checked the trash, but she'd already cleared it. "No." She checked where else the system might have been saving backups. Nothing. She'd cleared it all.

Not only were the security camera feeds now saving to nowhere, the hard drive was empty of all previous recordings.

Another "No" slipped out of June, louder this time.

July sat back upright. "What? What's wrong?"

"Nothing." June grabbed hold of July's arm. "Come on. Mom's already livid, let's not let her see us messing with stuff in here."

June rushed July out of the house and toward their cars. The cameras did not catch them. The cameras no longer caught anything. They had nothing to tell.

"It's my fault," June now told the detectives. Her voice was the opposite of her Summer Girls voice. It was weak, trembling, hopeless. It wouldn't have sold a single sponsored product. "It's my fault I can't prove anything I'm telling you. Because I messed it up, and now everything's gone."

She wanted to go back to that day, to stop her own hasty, impulsive hands from doing what they always did, acting too quickly, too carelessly.

"July had no idea what I'd done," June told the detectives. "She didn't see what I did with the computer. She never even saw that our neighbor came back to the house. She was too busy heaving into a trash can."

When they had pulled away from the mansion, June drove slowly, slower than usual. She wanted July to follow right behind her, and she knew that July was shaky enough that she would not speed. On her most reckless days, July went three miles above the posted limit. Any traffic cameras that caught the Iverson twins only showed two cars following all rules of motor vehicle operation, along streets they'd driven hundreds of times.

Luke Sweatshirt

April wasn't answering calls or texts.

He drove to her office anyway. He passed the streets and parking lots he'd first gotten to know as a child, the words on the storefront awnings different, the metal of the street signs faded, the stucco of the buildings covered with different coats of paint.

Once, his mother had thought he was one of the Iverson girls. But the truth was he could watch the Iverson girls in the careful way he did only because he had never really been one of them.

Then he had left them for a while. He had avoided their inquiries when he could (a restrained *Are you okay? I'm worried* from April). He had responded vaguely when one of them—really, when June—got loud enough that he couldn't ignore her (a shouting all-caps UM HELLO ARE YOU DEAD OR SOMETHING??? CALL, TEXT, SKYWRITE, YOUR MEDIUM OF CHOICE).

After a while, he started to miss them. It came on slowly, then built until it was impossible to ignore, this ache of not only being their brother but wanting them to know it.

So one by one, he told them. One by one, he asked them not to tell anyone, especially their mother, where he was and who he was.

First he asked January to meet him outside of town, over the county line, at a diner next to a truck wash. Neither the diner nor the truck wash was anywhere their mother would ever be seen, and neither was retro or kitschy enough to attract influencers like June. With his head down and a jean jacket over his usual sweatshirt, no one looked at him twice. He was utterly forgettable.

January seemed as unsurprised as he'd hoped.

So after that, he asked July to the same place, where no one had looked twice at him. July had responded with a comprehending, wonder-tinged "Oh," as though this explained everything, absolutely everything, from his absence to the astrophysics of the Milky Way's impending collision with the Andromeda Galaxy.

June, on the other hand, sneered in a way that made his surgery scars burn until she said, "You have the entire world of men's fashion open to you and *that's* what you choose to attire yourself in?" and he realized she was sneering not at his body but at his sweatshirt.

April, he saved for last. Not because he thought she was the least likely to keep the secret from their mother. That was definitely June, who might say it impulsively and then try to play it off—*So what if I told her? What's the big deal? It's not like you're a flat-earther or a jorts enthusiast.* Followed closely by July, who would probably buckle under the matching inquisitive stares of June and their mother.

No, he told April last because she had been his mother in ways neither of them could say out loud, and not telling her who he really was, staying away so long that neither of them knew each other anymore, felt like the worst kind of ingratitude. April had been turned into a mother since she was old enough to use the stove. In the act of becoming Mother May I, May Iverson had left such a vacuum in their family that April had only had two choices: leave her siblings with no steady maternal presence except nannies their mother fired at her whim or spend her own childhood trying to fill that void.

Whenever their mother let a nanny go, she'd turn to her eldest daughter and, with a huff of being a put-upon mother of five, offer a grateful *What would I do without you?* During those interims, April was the one who mediated fights between the twins (usually about the cresting wave of stuff encroaching from June's side of the room to July's). April was the one who coaxed January out from under the kitchen table because January had heard a billionaire on TV saying that in the future everyone would have to move to Mars, and January got motion sick so wouldn't that mean everyone would get on the spaceship and leave her behind? April was the one who spent hours looking for the stuffed stegosaurus that he, the youngest Iverson, could not sleep without. All while trying to figure out what all four of them could agree to eat for lunch. (She never seemed to consider what she herself wanted for lunch. Probably because no one was asking her.)

And after all that, he'd just left her, and he'd taken almost five years to tell her why.

April had been right. She didn't know him. And not because of who he had become and what his body now was. But because he had been silent. He had been gone from her life.

For months after he'd told each sister, he braced for the phone call from their mother or, worse, an expansively supportive public post that was ostensibly meant to call him home but also had the benefit of being good for platform engagement.

But nothing happened. No calls. No posts. His sisters kept his secret. To her credit, July hadn't even told June. To June's credit, she hadn't held that against July. (He'd had awful visions of June's reaction, a revenge bender of melting July's lipsticks in a saucepan while yelling *How dare you keep this from me?* across the breakfast bar.)

Now everyone knew, even his father. He could've been more delicate about that one. He'd just shown up at his father's house with a pathetic "Hi, remember me?" And whoever had taken and posted that picture in which his father looked terrified of him had only captured his father's initial shock. They had either missed or omitted his father's joy in the moments after, his father pulling him inside, his father asking why the hell he had stayed away so long.

Marc had come back. He had told his sisters and his father who he was. And ever since, he'd been tuning out the chatter saturating the name that had never really been his. If everyone found out, they would break their brains trying to reconcile who he was now with what they remembered from years ago. *That's March Iverson? Really? Are we sure?*

He drove by billboards, including one of the denim model that so many people were convinced was March Iverson.

He did not look like a denim model. He didn't even look like an Iverson. He looked like a painfully ordinary young man who hadn't yet lost his baby fat, when he had once been a child and teen so wispy he barely had any.

The story of Marc Iniesta was the story of a boy who had once been called a girl, a son mistaken for a daughter. This was the story of a boy who hid inside the girl known as March Iverson, all the while becoming more sure about the boy he was and the man he would become.

Marc's was the story of a boy who didn't want his transition to become content for his influencer mother. The testosterone injections, the binders, the surgeries. These were things he needed. But they were also things he could not let become fodder. He could not let them be curated and styled until they fit comfortably into the narrative and brand that was Mother May I.

He could not let Mother May I push her way into his doctor's appointments and the post-op room. He could not let her wear him down until he relented and she documented his injections. He could not smile when she threw her arm around him, pulling him into a frame he did not want to be in, telling the camera how much she loved her son, how brave he was, what a proud mom she was. He couldn't let her pin him in place like that, for take after take, adjusting her emphasis on certain words, then others, as she told the world it was a mother's calling to be there for her children no matter what.

This was what Marc knew, from an age so young he couldn't pinpoint it: in the process of becoming Mother May I, May Iverson had turned each of her children into more consumable versions of themselves. And Marc could not let that happen to the boy he knew he was. So he held Marc inside himself, protecting him inside the shell of his own heart. He fell asleep thinking of him, with the wonder and affection of a lover.

One day, he had told himself growing up, he would leave. In the meantime, he would let Mother May I, and the world, have March Iverson. *That's March Iverson? Really?* No, it wasn't. March Iverson had never really been him anyway.

April still hadn't responded by the time he got to the building. Calling first to make an appointment was the only way he'd ever gotten into April's office, her clearing him to come up. So he found himself in front of a desk, the kind that demanded he explain himself.

He said he was there to see April Iverson.

"Who should I say is here?" the receptionist at the desk asked without looking up.

Some stranger behind a screen had decided that his name was Luke, claimed they knew on good authority, and then it had spread and stuck. So he'd let it happen. He'd taken it on. He'd even started thinking of himself as Luke Sweatshirt. In public, his own sisters had even started calling him Luke, a code name furnished by the very people he was hiding from.

But now he wanted to shrug it off. He wanted there to be room for the name he'd chosen for himself. If he didn't do it now, if he didn't decide that he belonged with his own name and that he belonged with the Iverson sisters even though he was not one of them, he might lose his nerve forever, or at least for another five years.

"Marc Iniesta," he said.

The woman looked up, phone handset paused in her grip.

He had always watched the Iverson girls, just like everyone else. The difference was that he had watched them even more closely. He knew them better than everyone else watching.

He begged his heart rate to come down; otherwise he was going to run out of this building.

He breathed out. "I'm April Iverson's brother."

January Iverson

She knew that look, the one she was seeing right now. January had seen it on April their whole lives.

She'd seen it on April when June reminded their mother about a dance recital where she and July would play twin peppermint fairies, and their mother had sucked in air between her teeth and said she had a really important brand trip, and June understood, didn't she? Just as June nodded, her face tight against crying, April swept into the space as fast as their mother had left it. "Dad'll come. Abuela'll come. And I'll be there to see all the other mothers seething because you two are the prettiest bailarinas on earth."

She'd seen it on April's face when doctors scheduled January's tonsillectomy on a date that inconveniently coincided with the launch of a holiday clutch collaboration. "How could he do this to me?" their mother had fumed after hanging up with the scheduler, as though the surgeon had conspired to thwart the product line. And in the end, it was, of course, April who was there with the thermometer and the Pedialyte, while May posed among ice sculptures of the newly released products.

January had even seen it on April's face the weekend their mother married August. May had decided on a cake designer so exclusive that he wouldn't even take calls for dessert budgets under five figures. His booking rate was more cutthroat than Ivy League admission statistics. But as it turned out, there was a reason he booked so few jobs. He didn't need them. He had family money, and his confectionary work was more to appear self-made than born out of any culinary ambition. So when he didn't feel like doing a job, he didn't. And it was far easier to flake on a momfluencer than an Oscar winner, so he did. He met May Iverson's screaming voicemail messages with nothing but silence and implied indifference. So April called in several favors, an elaborate, sugar-flowered wedding cake materialized, and May threw her arms around April with sobbing declarations that *this is the best gift a daughter could ever give a mother.*

For years, January had watched April learn that when there was awkward silence, when there was a hesitating beat, when no one stepped up or stepped in, it was her job to. It always came with a tensing under her eyes and around the bridge of her nose. And it was this expression that January noticed first when she told April that detectives had brought June in and July had followed after.

January could see the current in April's body as she reached for her purse and went for her office door. April was going to fix this. January didn't know how—Would she manage to get June to shut up for once? Would she try to confess herself?—but she knew that's what this look was.

A mirroring current shot through January. Before she could name it, she was following April. She was right behind her before April reached the door.

January threw her arms around her.

"No," January said, the word low and quiet.

April stopped, surprised by the impact. But then she was patting one of January's hands. "It'll be okay," she said, as though January was clinging to her like a little kid, not half-tackling her from behind. "We'll figure this out."

"No." January held tighter, her face pressed into the back of April's sweater. "I mean you're not going."

April may have been taller. She may have had a core strengthened by five-times-a-week classes, but January spent her days hauling lights on her shoulders. April was not going to win this one.

April's spine went rigid.

"Let go," she said, the words halfway to warning.

January shut her eyes, her cheek against the fine weave of April's sweater. "Let *us* go."

A shudder, small as a flinch, went through April.

"You have to let us go," January said. "You cannot fix this. It's not your job to fix things for us anymore."

April was quiet for a long time. When she spoke, her voice was coiled tight.

"But if I can't," April said, "then it was all for nothing. If you're not okay and they're not okay, I lost all that time for nothing."

The words rattled against January's ribs, her back teeth. There was nothing she could say, no refuting it. All she could do was stop April from going through that door. Or maybe just hold her the way each of them owed her, the way April had done so many times for each of them.

Then Marc was in the room, and without January telling him, he just knew. He had his arms around both of them by the time the door had fallen shut behind him. He knew January needed help holding April, and holding April here, to this point on the Earth.

January had no reference point for the sound that came out of April in the next moment. She had never heard anyone make it, and she couldn't pin it to any one thing. It wasn't crying. It was so many other things at once. It was a bear bellowing to get a predator away from her cubs. It was a mother waking up from a dream where her babies slipped from her hands like water. It was the teeth-cracking echo of a woman who was just now realizing that she was empty, that she'd spilled out the contents of herself so completely that there were no seeds, no green shoots, no topsoil, to grow it back.

People outside the office door could hear. People outside the windows could probably hear. Half the parking lot. But January didn't care. And April screamed like she didn't care. And Marc held them both like the sound didn't even touch him.

June Iverson

"I don't think our neighbor killed him," June told the detectives. "I really don't. I know you're probably thinking that, but there's just no way."

When June had first learned that August was dead, she couldn't, wouldn't, accept that the old man had murdered him. She knew he'd been there. She'd seen him on the monitor. She had seen her own hands delete all evidence of him. But she knew there had to be another explanation. From the moment she heard August was dead, she had been working on her theory, as meticulously as she'd painted pride flags on her eyelids or reviewed tag proofs for a new bikini.

She needed the detectives to know the truth about the old man. She needed them to imagine some possibility other than him meaning to kill August.

"August kept offering to buy the land on the hillsides," June said. "Like he was doing some kind of favor, even though he was the one that wrecked them with all the spilled chlorine."

She told them what they probably already knew but that she wanted to corroborate: that the prices August offered varied between insulting and ruinous. But she also told the detectives what they perhaps did not know: that the offers varied both due to August's whim and mood and out of strategy, the same way that airlines varied their ticket prices. Book your itinerary to Albany now, or the price could go up, who knows how much. Accept your neighbor's offer now, or the price could fall, there's no telling how low.

June didn't want the hillside farmer to sell. "I didn't want him to lose," she told the detectives. "And I didn't want August to win." She had thought that slipping the old man and his family money from those forged checks would be enough that he would hold fast, at least until August exasperated her mother enough for her to kick him out of the mansion.

This, June had assumed, was inevitable, at which point her mother would toss out his extensive collection of athletic shoes—some for cycling, some for running, some for lifting, some for InFITnitum ads—and June would turn off his wave pool once and for all.

But as insulting as August's offers were, the old man's indignation could not hold. June saw it all wearing him down. The corroding salts. The chemical odor. His plants rotting in the ground before they even broke through to find the light. His granddaughter told June that he'd started waking up in the middle of the night, sure he smelled chlorine, the mineral-salted pool water spilling into his dreams.

And then, finally, all that resentment seemed to have culminated in the argument, the one in which August had shoved him to the ground. The one after which the old man knew his body and his being could not withstand the fight anymore.

"That's the only reason I can think of that he would have gone to see August," June said. "To settle everything. To accept August's last offer."

The old man would have steeled himself for August's beaming face, the sense of triumph, August's slap on the old man's back. *I knew you'd see it my way. At your age, that's all too much anyway, isn't it? You don't want to work that hard, old man. Come on, let's have a drink to celebrate your retirement. What'll you have?*

But it must not have gone that way. If it had gone that way, August would still be alive and, probably, so would the old man.

June could picture how it must have gone instead. She could watch it in her head as though she'd been there. August would have been in his second-floor entertainment room, feet up on a driftwood coffee table, watching the TV that was nearly the size of the opposite wall. When the old man said he was ready, that he was giving in, August might not have said anything at first. He might have held up a hand to indicate that the old man should be quiet until the play was over or until the man on the screen with the gun finished shooting.

"I don't think August had the brains or decency to even feel ashamed of what he'd done earlier, shoving an old man down on the driveway," June said. She didn't try to stop herself from sounding bitter. Some things were worth being bitter about, and how much men like August got away with was one of them.

August might have pursed his lips, tilting his head from side to side, considering. And then, with the slow reveal of a magician turning a trick mirror, he might have said he thought the last price he offered was maybe just a little too high. It didn't seem quite right to pay that much for ruined land, did it? Then he might have offered half as much.

"Or a third," June told the detectives. "Or a quarter."

And that, June thought, would have been when the fight came back into the old man. That hillside had been cared for by his hands and his family's hands, and August was pulling at the edges, looking for flaws that could get him a markdown.

It was all speculation, and probably the detectives couldn't use any of it, but she was going to tell them her theory, all of it. She was going to draw them into it the same way she drew her subscribers in with a video intro.

She could imagine the argument, one in which both men were on their feet, August going from room to room, room to hall, the old man following. August would have turned on him, coming toward him, sudden and startling, as he had so many times with June. The old man—rattled and worn out from tamping down the rage, from carrying it back up the hill as though it weighed nothing—would have shoved August.

"He only would have done that because he felt threatened by August," June said.

He would have only shoved August the way August had shoved him earlier, a settling of the gravity between the two men. He would have only wanted August to step back, to get out of his face the way June had wanted August out of her face so many times.

And it wouldn't have been until he shoved August that he realized how close they were to the floating staircase, with all its glass edges and sharp cables.

This was where June's imagination met up with the coroner's report. August was either dead on impact, or dead by the time the old man navigated those floating stairs.

June figured it probably took the old man a while to get down them, the delay made worse by panic. Those stairs, those nearly invisible stairs, how could anyone go up and down them when they couldn't even see them, all that glass and marble against all that white decor. Even June, with her young, floor-barre-toned body, hated those stairs. She couldn't imagine the old man finding his footing with the steps always swaying like they were in some kind of continual earthquake.

The old man had then run away from the Iverson mansion. He had run from August Ingraham's dead body, afraid of what would happen to him and his family when the Iversons, with their name and their money, sent the police for him.

June, with her chin dipped low, spoke of her heart shattering on impact as she thought of him fleeing down the hill. She imagined him wondering where he'd go, where he'd hide not just from the police but from the Iversons and all who adored them. And, in the end, after all this, he was losing his farm anyway.

Maybe the detectives let her keep talking, keep speculating, because they thought she might confess something new. Or because she was pretty and young and rich and blond. Or because they remembered how she looked in a chartreuse bikini. Or simply because she was June Iverson.

Throughout June's speculation, certainty weighted her words. But when she came to the part about the fire, guilt weakened the sound of her voice, like paper crumpling at the edges. She imagined the old man, having just returned from the Iverson house for the second time that day, looking back up the hill and seeing the flames on one side of the mansion. Through a picture window he might have seen the faint silhouette of a woman, a girl, maybe two. He wouldn't have quite been able to tell from that distance. The smoke would have made her, or them, look like ghosts or illusions.

He might have wondered if one of them was June, the girl who had once irritated him so thoroughly but was now like another granddaughter. Sure, one who was still thoroughly irritating. The kind who, even as a grown woman, interrupted his chess game to ask if he'd ever thought of shaping his eyebrows, because that really wasn't just for women. Or who snuck up on him with a *Hey, what's that?* just as he was unfurling a ship in a bottle.

But he had grown to love that annoying extra granddaughter he'd found himself with. June knew that. And she knew that the thought of her caught in that house, that enormous maze of a house, with all that smoke, every dead end filling with flames, would have been enough to make him forget that he should be fleeing the scene. It would have been enough to make him run back up the hill.

"You were still in the house when the fire started?" the detectives asked.

"I don't think so," June said. "Either I missed it because I was too busy trying to get the deleted security footage back, so I wasn't looking at the feeds from the other cameras, or July and I were already gone by the time the fire started. So if he came back because he thought I might be there, that makes everything even worse, doesn't it?"

This was why they found him there, running up the hill instead of down, running back in the direction of the man he'd just accidentally killed, and toward the fire he had not set.

"He died because of me," June said, and it was only when the wet heat struck her cheekbone that she realized she'd been crying. "That's what I think. He died because he thought I was in there."

Adrenaline would have driven the old man on, hard and fast enough that he perhaps did not feel the strain on his own heart until it gave out. He might not have even felt the electrical currents in his own body shorting out until he collapsed. He might not have even realized he was dying until he was dead.

June was quiet now. She had told them everything. She'd admitted to purposely deleting data knowing she might be destroying evidence, knowing she might be helping to conceal a crime. Vandalism. Destruction of property. Whatever she thought or hoped the old man had done to one of August's cars, or to the wave pool, or to any other of August's prized possessions.

And she'd admitted to accidentally deleting the very evidence she wished she still had, proof that the only person in or near that house capable of murder was August Ingraham himself.

July Iverson

"Did you try to burn down your mother's house?" they asked her.
"No," she said. "I didn't."

"Did you have anything to do with what happened at the house that day?" they asked.

"No," July said. "Yes." The words were getting jumbled in her mouth. "No. Sort of."

"Sort of?"

They didn't sound as confrontational as July would have expected. She was frustrating them and she knew it. But maybe they felt obligated to be patient. Maybe this was standard practice if you came in wearing shoes that cost more than the asphalt they were walking on.

Or it could have been that no one wanted to push her so hard that she startled and asked for a lawyer.

Or maybe they could sense what July wanted them to pick up on, that she wasn't trying to be difficult. She was genuinely confused about how to answer this.

"I didn't set the fire," July said. "I made her do it."

"You made your sister June do it." This was not quite a question, so July figured it was confirmation for the transcript.

"No," July said. "Not June. My mother. I made my mother do it."

we who were back at square one

Within hours, the rumor picked up enough momentum that we wondered if it was true. The strange thing was not that Luke Sweatshirt had been assigned female at birth. It happened. Plenty of us grew up—partway or all the way—and figured out that the life and name we'd been born into had been wrong the whole time, like an ill-fitting sweater.

The strange thing was that the youngest Iverson had been here the whole time, and we hadn't really believed it.

If that was possible, an Iverson we'd been looking for being right in front of us, that made anything seem possible.

The four Iverson sisters had acted together; April had directed them with as much precision as when she had to get them all out the door to see their father.

They'd colluded with their mother; August Ingraham's murder was a joint effort as thoughtfully coordinated as an eyeshadow palette collaboration.

They'd all made their murderous exasperation with August known to Ernesto and Marc, and the Iniesta men had done the rest.

Or maybe it really was the investors August had screwed over, and they'd been counting on detectives to blame a family member or a friend.

Maybe they should have looked harder at competing influencers. If May Iverson had stolen recipes, what else had she stolen, and what were her rivals willing to do out of vengeance?

Anything seemed possible, which made it impossible to know anything.

July Iverson

"The weird part about all this," July told the detectives, "is that it all started with August. He collected all that old equipment because he thought it was ridiculous that my mom wanted to declutter that stuff. It wasn't even about what he could sell it for. He just didn't want her to toss out stuff that could be worth something down the line, because it was vintage, or limited edition, or whatever. One day he just handed me one and said, 'This is a good one, and look, it's even that green you always wear. You should take it with you. It still works.'"

So July had. It was a novelty, a chance for a throwback post she'd do with June, maybe. As she was about to clear out the camera's internal memory, she reviewed the photos and videos. June as an awkward little kid practicing her grin for picture day. The little ones wearing fake beards and velvet robes for a Christmas pageant, looking more like wizards than wise men.

But among those was her mother screaming at the two youngest Iversons, prodding them to react on film.

Seeing that pried something loose in July's brain. It dragged back everything she and her sisters and brother had lived, everything July had forgotten through time or force of will.

"So I asked for another one," July told the detectives. "And another one. And I was sure that he'd tell me, *No, this is my stuff*. But anything I wanted, he gave it to me."

Sure, take it, August had said. Always some variation on *It's a perfectly good camera. Take any of them you want. I'm glad you're using them. I don't know why she ever wants to throw this stuff out.*

So July kept reviewing old videos of their lives. She saw years of Halloween costumes. June and July as 1950s-style waitresses on roller skates. June as a pink-chiffon-clad princess with a tiny Marc roaring in a dragon costume. June as a giant strawberry alongside July dressed as a giant red delicious apple, with their younger siblings as bunches of grapes.

She saw the video of her mother kicking Savanna Montez out of the kitchen because Savanna could make them all laugh and May couldn't.

She watched her mother telling her to look sad, look sadder, no, sadder than that, you need to look sadder, we need to see it, show me, show them.

The dam July had built up cracked and buckled. All the anger she had never known was there rushed out, for April, for January, for Marc. For herself. Even for June, who was still too far inside it to see anything wrong.

July explained to the detectives that, over the past year, she had planted copies of everything in the Iverson mansion. God knew that May Iverson was as sloppy about her flash drives as she was about her old cameras, so July knew that if she didn't do something to grab her mother's attention, her mother would just add them to the junk drawers in her various desks. So July had labeled every one with something that would catch her mother's eye.

No one knows the real Iversons, do they?

What a beautiful family. What an ugly history.

What would Mother May I's sponsors think of this?

A picture is worth a thousand lies.

July planted each one somewhere her mother would find it. In the pocket of a new jacket, tags still on, was a flash drive showing an exchange between their mother and April. Another went in with her mother's paper clips—silver and gold wire in the shape of glass flutes—the evidence of her screaming at Marc. And hidden in her mother's studio-apartment-sized en-suite closet, in a drawer of the customized island, was another, showing her mother jabbing her finger into a small January's forehead.

July wanted to leave her mother terrified of what she might find next. She wanted her mother so frantic at trying to figure out who had done this, who was doing this, that she'd panic. And if she was panicking, she might be more susceptible to April and January's requests to take their childhoods off the internet.

"That was my plan, at least," July told the detectives. "But I never meant for what happened that day to happen. If I'd known she was going to"—July had to swallow, clear her throat, catch her breath, try again—"if I ever thought even for a second she'd try to burn it down, I wouldn't have left. I would never have left her there if I'd known what she'd do."

"What happened that day, July?"

That day, when she'd first gotten to the house, July found her mother tearing her bedroom and the surrounding rooms apart, from drawers of sunglasses and scarves to shelves of silk-infused moisturizers. She was ripping every garment down from every closet bar, looking for every last drive and duplicate recording. In her hurry, she knocked bottles of perfume to the marble floor. They shattered. She left them, the air filling with luxury scent.

The broken glass, the torn-down hangers, they drew something sharp out of July. The viciousness broke out of her like it was splintering open a locked drawer.

"Show me, Mom."

Her mother, hair tousled from cascades of cashmere sweaters, looked up.

July stood in the doorway of her mother's en suite closet.

"Show me how upset you are," July said. "Show them."

Her mother clutched the hangers in her hands. "You did this?"

"Show them how sad you are." July came closer. "Make sure they really see it."

"Do you know what I've been going through?" Her mother dropped the hangers. "Did you think this was funny? Was this your idea of a joke? How could you do this?"

"How could you do what you did?" July asked.

"What did I do?" Now her mother had a challenge in her voice. "What did I ever do except give you everything that any girl could ever want?"

"You altered our realities!" July was yelling. She could hear it even if she didn't feel it in her own chest. "We had to perform feelings instead of having them!"

Something like strategizing crossed her mother's face. July knew that look. She was creating content in her head. She was considering what response wouldn't throw fuel on the spark blazing inside her middle child.

"Why are you doing this now?" May asked. "Why are you so upset about all this now?"

"I saw it from the outside. I watched it back." July paced, fingers pressed to her forehead and temples, working it out like problems on their old math worksheets. "And I saw everything I didn't see when I was living it. You didn't fire our nannies because no one was good enough. You fired them as soon as we got attached. So we wouldn't love them more than you."

"That's not true," her mother said.

"You could've stayed with us," July said. "If you really wanted us to like you better than we liked anyone else. You could have made a living off posting a picture a day. You had the option to take care of us. You could have been with us instead of hiring someone else to love us and then hating us for loving her back."

"When did I ever do that?" her mother asked.

"Savanna," July said. "You fired her, and then you destroyed her in every reference."

"Who told you that?" her mother asked. "Who are you listening to?"

"You hated that we loved Savanna," July said. "You hated that we liked Carolina playing with us. And you hated, more than anything, that one of us loved Carolina."

Her mother's only tell was the tightening of her mouth, a slight pursing.

"Did you really think I didn't know?" July asked. "We all knew."

"It was completely inappropriate," her mother said. "March and Carolina, who knows what they were doing together."

"They were kids, Mom," July said. "They were holding hands and kissing each other on the cheek. Just say it. You didn't like one of your precious children feeling that way about the nanny's daughter."

At this point, July could sense her mother changing tack. No more defensiveness. She lifted a lily-perfumed hand to her face and began to cry.

"That's right, Mom," July said. "Pretend like you're sad, Mom. Oh, and good luck with all this."

Her mother blinked at her.

"You can't have anyone cleaning your house anymore," July said. "Not unless you're standing over them the entire time. They could find something. And we all know you're not gonna clean this place yourself. You've never done anything by yourself. And what a shock, it looks like August's not here to help. He's too busy signing up more people who are gonna lose money so he can make money. So what are you gonna do? You don't know how much I've hidden, because you don't know how much I have."

July hadn't sauntered out. There had been no feeling of victory. A knot had stuck in her chest, and she knew it would turn to a sob if she didn't keep it there. So she stared ahead, walking straight out, like she'd walked out of that dorm common room.

She had no idea that in the minutes that followed, her mother was preparing to burn everything down.

May Iverson

May drove home from the police station, her thoughts pulled back and forth between two of her children as steadily as the signal lights changed colors. When she got home, she looked at the beautiful things she owned; their thoughtful curation and the aesthetically inspiring way she'd organized them had calmed her so many times.

There was the cabinet that held her collection of more than a hundred sustainable reusable water bottles, each one in a different color to coordinate with a different outfit or bag or shoe. There was each guest bathroom, stocked with Italian face soap and French shampoo, every product displayed in plastic drawer dividers. Even her refrigerators were tranquil oases, with beverages in neat rows and condiments decanted into glass jars instead of their loud, labeled grocery store bottles.

May knew these rooms. They were artwork she'd created from the act of living her own life. But the thoughts pressing in on her made it all seem unfamiliar. This wasn't her house, not really. This was the set for a Mother May I promotional shoot, plush with embellished throw blankets, billowing with clean white curtains.

Two truths closed in, one on each side of her, like shadows flanking her steps.

The first was July, and just how much destruction she was capable of. May had known she was angry. July had made that abundantly clear. But May had never considered July capable of this level of deception. She had acted with more skill than June had when she was pushing through cramps to film a sponsored video.

When they'd all found the cameras missing, July had made herself seem truly shaken, like the alarm of a child who had tipped a vase back and forth and then been shocked when it fell and broke. Sure, July had wanted to make a point to May, but that had been between mother and daughter. May had never thought July would take it outside their family. Whatever July's grievances, May was sure July had put it all aside as they mourned August and as detectives tried to figure out who would want to tear their family down.

This was what May had thought. But May didn't know her daughter at all.

And she didn't know her son. This was the other truth pressing in on her. She hadn't even known she had a son until he'd looked at her with the open, searching stare May remembered.

That was the only thing about him that resembled her youngest daughter. May verified her own memory as she walked down the hall with the yearly family photos of her children growing up. Ones with just April, then April and the twins, then, in quick succession, all of them. Ones at their old house, where both her family and her business had quickly outgrown the seven bedrooms. Ones here, in front of the Christmas tree, at the long dining room table, in front of the pool. Ones on vacation, where they squeezed in formal portrait sessions in the snow or on the shoreline.

The young man outside the police station looked like a different person than the youngest child in these pictures. Except for the eyes, he bore little resemblance to the skinny, sharp-cheekboned girl in these photos.

May had often wondered if she should have looked harder for her youngest daughter. If she should have filed police reports, hired private detectives.

But April had convinced her not to. *Sometimes people need space,* she had told May.

And January had convinced her not to. *It was hard not being as good at everything as you and June and July.* Before May could refute January's words, tell her that she could be every bit as scintillating in front of a wide audience if she wanted to be, January had stopped her. *I didn't want it like they wanted it, and it was hard telling you that.* January had spoken with a measured wisdom so beyond her nineteen years that it set down deep roots in May. *If I hadn't known how to tell everyone that,* January said, *maybe I would have taken some time away from everyone too.*

And July had, so gently, with such sympathy, convinced her not to. *You focus on us so much. Did you ever think it's not healthy?*

And June had convinced her not to. *Sometimes eighteen-year-olds go on these weird journeys,* June had said, as though she were sixty instead of twenty-one. *Then they show back up at Christmas one year with all their stories about seeing the world or getting all the way to Bakersfield. It's just something people need to get out of their system sometimes.*

So May hadn't gone after her youngest child.

Maybe that was the only thing she had ever done right for her son: leaving him alone.

How little she'd known her children. All this time, without even knowing it, she'd had a son. All this time, without even knowing it, she'd had a daughter who could slide knife after knife into May's back without May even realizing.

May's heels clicked faintly on the marble stairs. The diffusing rods scented the air. The minimalist chandeliers cast clean, cool light that perfectly mimicked the late-morning sun.

As she walked through these rooms, she remembered the day August died. She remembered the minutes after July had left so coldly, so spitefully, without even looking back. May had kept pulling everything out of the drawers and off the hangers. She'd kept turning pockets inside out, emptying files in the satellite office just off her bedroom.

May had gone through the house, yelling August's name, as though he could help her fix this, as though he was even half as useful as he pretended to be. She'd called his name, but he didn't answer. The high ceilings and vertebrae staircases only threw her voice back.

Then she remembered that he wasn't home that day. That was the day he'd gone on and on about, a meeting that he was convinced was going to clinch getting InFITnitum into Whole Foods. That was the inconvenience of each of them having their own personal interior garages. With their cars stored separately, whenever one of them came home, they didn't have the immediate visual reminder of a vehicle missing to tell them whether the other was home or still out.

With her next step, May slipped on a spill of perfume. Swore. Caught herself. Then she saw the shine of the perfume on the floor and had an idea.

She emptied every remaining bottle of perfume over the strewn sweaters, the overturned files, the emptied drawers. When that wasn't enough, she went to the liqueurs. She spilled out the deep blush of Lillet Rosé. The bright Midori. The plum of Chambord. Chartreuse Verte et Jaune. The highlighter orange of Aperol.

She took every bottle of wine from the temperature-controlled stone cellar and poured each one out onto the carpets and upholstery. When she'd emptied them all, she went to a hallway window to check the part of the long driveway where July usually parked. Her car was gone. The driveway was empty. July had left. There was no one else in this house, no one else to worry about.

May could burn down every mistake along with these rooms.

May had taken a peach-tipped match from a wooden box. It had been from last year's homeware line, the stick twice the length of the usual match, the long-stemmed rose of matches.

Then she had lit up all that perfume, all that liqueur, all that foaming pink and amber, all that sugar and gold. She offered those flames up to appease her rage-filled daughter. She'd even left her phone behind for the fire to consume. What more compelling sacrifice could July need than that? May hadn't even backed up her most recent photos.

She had been sure this would be enough. She would burn down the house that July's memories lived in. July would be placated. May would rebuild, remodel, redecorate. They could move on.

But then, on her way out, she had seen August's gym bag. The same one she'd asked him a hundred times not to leave in the foyer. The same one he always had with him, that went with him every day into whatever car he was driving, *because you never know when you'll feel like getting in a good workout.* The same one that would only be here in the house because he was.

May had run, no longer yelling his name but screaming it. Where was he? Why was he home? Why wasn't he answering?

Then she'd found him at the bottom of those stairs. And she'd screamed so loudly that all her neighbors would have heard if it hadn't been for the roar of the fire on one side of the house and the engine sirens splitting the air as they raced up the hill.

That day, her daughter had broken her heart by hating her, and her husband had broken her heart by leaving her alone with all this.

May had thought that day would be the worst day of her life. Yet here she was, barely more than three weeks later, and everything had tumbled even further. Now she not only had a dead husband and a daughter who resented her with frightening violence. She also had a son she did not know. She had a fanbase who had once adored her but who now treated hating her like a blood sport.

May hated everyone who hated her. But not because they hated her. She hated them because of the threads they pulled at inside her. Everything she had done, she had done for her children. So why did she feel this strange, prickling guilt? Why did the thought of her children's faces make these thousands of square feet contract in on her?

Why did the faces in those family portraits look more startled, more apprehensive, than they'd ever seemed before? How had their expressions changed in still photographs? How could they possibly look so different when she'd been walking by them every day for years?

Her daughter's vengeance hadn't been sated. Everyone's collective outrage hadn't been sated. And those eyes staring out from those portraits followed her even when she left the room.

Light gleamed off a bottle of sparkling rosé, compliments of a major winery that had never courted her before, and she knew.

There was a way forward.

She could release her children from those images of themselves, trapped in double-matted frames.

She could destroy this world Mother May I had created, and then she could rebuild. She could become someone else, keeping only the parts of herself that made everyone want what she had.

She could do it right this time. There would be no leaving the task incomplete because of the shock of August's gym bag, the realization that he was home. There was no one else here. May could reduce this house, the set where she played Mother May I, to nothing. She could offer her life in flames, not just to one daughter but to all her daughters, to her son, to everyone watching.

This time, May did not bother with accelerants. She began on the second floor, going from bedroom to bedroom. She went straight for the white curtains, sheer as breezes, hanging from each tall window. Then she did the same in the halls, and downstairs. The flames were such brilliant flashes of color against the white that she wondered if a splash of yellow or gold could have really served the space.

By the time May reached the foyer again, the fire engines were screaming up the hill, just as they had the day August died. But August wasn't here. No one was here. And she had done it right this time. She had finished the work.

She could already feel it, a new version of herself emerging from the ruins of Mother May I, just as Mother May I had once emerged from her.

"Mrs. Iverson!" the voices outside yelled.

May took slow steps toward the one-of-a-kind reinforced front doors, ready to greet her guests. The moment she stepped out of this burning house, she would be someone else.

When she heard her own voice, she wasn't sure if she was speaking or if the heat was drawing echoes from the walls.

"You've been watching Mother May I." This version of her voice was thin and whispered, as though turning to smoke. "Thank you so much for joining me. And remember, you are already a good mom."

TWENTY-THREE DAYS AFTER THE DEATH OF AUGUST INGRAHAM

June Iverson

Her lawyers descended upon her with the news, like prophesying angels from heaven who charged per hour plus travel time. And lo, they delivered their message thusly: that any attempt to charge her with anything worse, anything related to the involuntary manslaughter that might have ended August's life, was too flimsy to hold up. June Iverson hadn't known she was deleting evidence about August's death. She hadn't even known he was still in the house, dead or alive, when she and July were there.

"They're still coming for your blood," the lead attorney told her. "They can't get much of it, but they're going to get as much as they can. They're trying to squeeze the highest fine they can out of you because they think you'll just roll over and pay it. But that's not going to work. I can tell you that. You're not your sister."

A surge of anger lit up June's nerve endings. *Not your sister,* as though that were some kind of compliment.

July had cooperated in getting all this over with, in taking whatever fines they threw at her.

For once, June would show half the grace July had.

"I'm paying it," June said.

"Don't be stupid," he said. "You don't want to get stuck with this. You let me handle this, and they'll be apologizing to you by the time I'm done. You'll get a Hallmark card and a dozen roses from the commissioner, you watch."

He was right. June knew that. This was a city where the rich and the beautiful got away with anything, and those who were both got away with everything.

This was also a city where, occasionally, everyone wanted examples made of the rich and the beautiful, even as they adored them. The lawyers may have forgotten that, but June hadn't. The harder she fought, the more spectacular an example they could make of her.

"I'm paying it," June said.

"This is about more than money," the lead attorney said. "This is about the record attached to it. This is about your name."

June shrugged. "I'm paying it." She sat back in this thing that was as comfortable as a recliner but as sleek as an office chair, complete with wheels. The glass-walled conference room had twelve or thirteen of them. June hadn't expected it to be just like on TV, all that glass. How did they know visiting opposing council couldn't lip-read?

By the time June had re-counted the chairs in the conference room, guessed how much the art on the walls had run the firm, figured out whether the plant in the corner was real, the lead attorney was still lecturing her about what a mistake she was making.

"Can you curse my stupidity on your own time and not in billable increments?" June took out her phone. "Because my answer's not gonna change."

First she texted July.

> You pick the paint colors

Then she texted April.

> So I had this idea.

June hoped her rare addition of a period at the end of a text would get her big sister's attention.

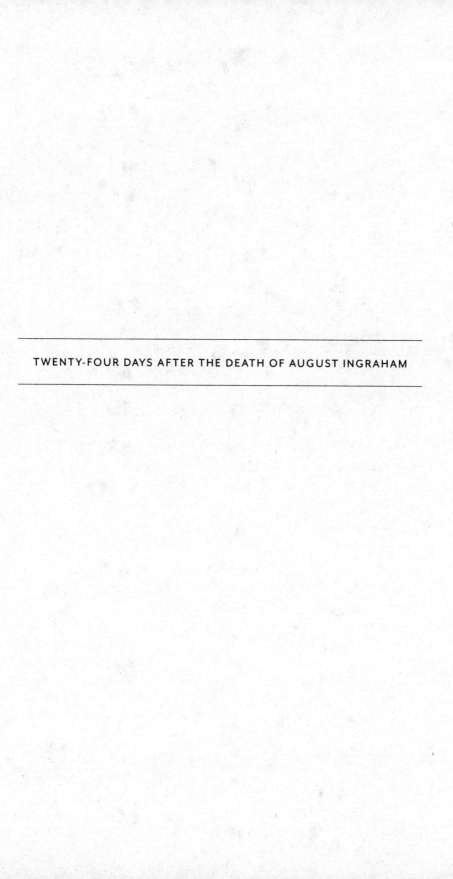

TWENTY-FOUR DAYS AFTER THE DEATH OF AUGUST INGRAHAM

Marc Iniesta

Word was getting around. He knew it would. He'd wanted it to. After he gave his real name to the receptionist who let him into April's office, he started giving it to anyone who asked.

At least no one at the taquería seemed to know who he was. He was only memorable insofar as he was güero, lighter than almost everyone else. His features sometimes did and sometimes didn't announce he was Latino, depending on how much of his hair was in his face.

As he waited for January, he looked over the laminated menu.

In his life as March Iverson, Marc Iniesta was nervous, anxious, thin, rarely hungry. Or, if he was hungry, he rarely felt it. On the Fourth of July, his mother tried to herd him toward picnic tables to eat strawberry shortcakes on camera with everyone else. When June and July offered him his pick of their Halloween candy, he didn't want any, but took lollipops in what he knew were their least favorite flavors, afraid that taking nothing might disappoint them.

When they spent weekends with their father, Marc's stomach relaxed enough for grilled cheese, roasted corn, halved oranges. Back at the mansion, April left small plates on the desk in his room, never too much at once. Squash and pepitas. Carrot and celery sticks with ranch dressing. Peanut butter and nopal jelly sandwiches (the jelly was April's own recipe; May Iverson had passed it off as hers when April declined to do a mother-daughter tutorial together). April seemed to know that he would eat a little more when he was alone and knew no one was watching, or filming.

But at the mansion there usually was someone watching, and filming, so he'd stayed skinny, big-eyed, staring out in that way that Mother May I fans identified as so particular to the youngest Iverson.

Then, when he was eighteen, he'd left. He'd taken any job he could, everything from washing gutters to barbacking to cleaning bird shit off salvaged windows. He sent postcards to his father and sisters every time he was leaving a place. He wanted them to know he was okay without knowing anything else about his life, not even where he'd been until he was already gone. He'd signed each one with *M*. Not March. Not Marc.

To everyone but his father and sisters, he seemed to have vanished entirely. And finally, he opened the door inside him, nearly rusted shut on its hinges, where he had been guarding the boy named Marc.

The clinics, the injections, the appointments to clear him for surgery, all of it together made him feel like he had just come up, gasping, from underwater. And once he did, he realized he was starving.

So he ate. Acorn squash. Paletas the colors of sunsets over water. Lime-salted pecans. April's nopal jelly recipe he learned to make himself.

He ate, realizing how long he'd been hungry.

He gained weight and lifted it. It showed whenever he took off his sweatshirt, so he usually didn't. After the surgeries, the testosterone, the weight gain, the new muscle, he wasn't quite used to his body. He didn't know it enough to want to let other people see it. He didn't like the feeling that they might, just by looking, understand it better than he did.

But today it was hot, from both the weather outside and the ta-

quería kitchen. So he took off his sweatshirt. He did it without thinking, and only realized it when January sat down across from him and
said, "I didn't think you could physically remove that thing."

He felt his forearms sticking to the vinyl-coated tablecloth. He
was sitting there in a gray T-shirt and jeans, elbows on the edge of the
table.

His first instinct was to throw the sweatshirt back on, but instead
he settled into what he understood about his body. He had both the
muscle of the man he was and the baby fat of the boy he'd never truly
gotten to be, like he was now living two lives at once.

As January looked at the menu, she eyed the sweatshirt draped
over an extra chair. "Do you just have a closet full of those things, like
a cartoon character?"

"Three of them," he said. "I've got to wear something on laundry
day."

She smiled at him, and he remembered making her laugh when
they were kids by wearing a black licorice mustache at Halloween, or
by launching her from the shallow end of the pool into the deep end.

All four of them owed April everything, but he owed January everything too. She'd let him hide. Instead of having to be himself or
having to be March Iverson all the time, he'd been able to be half of
January-and-March, the almost-twins. One of them not wearing
dresses would've been conspicuous, but when the two of them wore
matching overalls, it was cute. One of them wanting a short haircut
would have raised their mother's microbladed eyebrows, but when
the two youngest Iversons wanted it together, Mother May I couldn't
resist.

Whenever he'd tried to thank January for going along with all of
it, January had waved it away. *Mom stopped coming after me with the
curling iron and barrettes. I should be thanking you.*

January had covered for him in ways he could never repay. Then
he'd left, and January had given him the unfathomable benefit of the
doubt, assuming he had a good reason even before she knew for sure
what it was. And when he finally came back, January understood,
even without him explaining it, the sharp line he'd had to draw between March Iverson and Marc Iniesta. March Iverson had to stay in

the past, and the past had to stay with March Iverson so that Marc Iniesta could exist now.

"You know I couldn't have lived in that house without you, right?" he asked.

January pressed her lips together. She kept her eyes on the menu as she said, "Me neither."

He and January ate pipián verde, the heat of the peppers bright within the earth of the pumpkin seeds. They ate huitlacoche, the blooms like puffy gray clouds.

It was hard to say why January started crying. Or when. She was a quiet crier and could eat while doing it. She'd done it before, as though she considered crying on its own a waste of time.

Marc reached across the table.

"Hey." He set a hand on January's arm. "It's okay."

January ran the back of her hand across her eyes. "Are you?"

"Yeah, I'm okay." Marc nodded, a little too vigorously. He'd overshot. "Yeah. I'm okay. We all turned out okay." He looked away, probably for a split second too long, before looking back. "Right?"

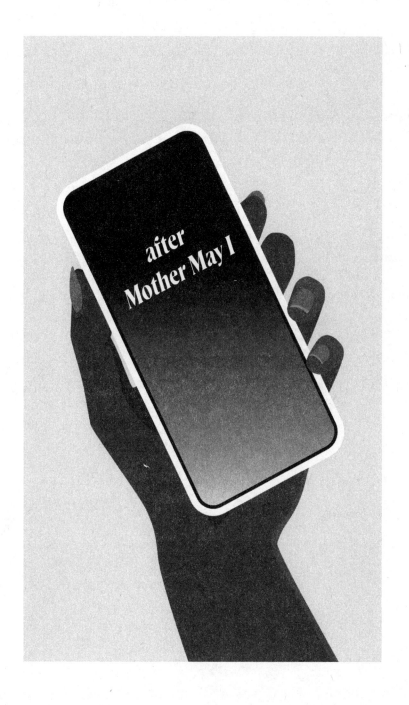

January Iniesta

January went into the theater early. She wanted to check a few levels that had kept her up the night before. Sometimes that happened. She'd wake up at 3 A.M., realizing that a preset would look more like a real suburban sidewalk or a midsummer night's forest or a seedy bar if she just adjusted these lights up and those other ones down.

While she was up on the scaffold, she heard her brother's voice.

"I don't know," Marc said as he strolled up the left aisle. "That one looks a little fuzzy."

"Oh, fuck you," January said, laughter breaking up the words as she skittered down the scaffold, quick as a spider. "What's that in your hand? Constructive feedback on my light plot?"

Her brother shook his head. "Program proof." He tapped a folded piece of paper against his palm. "And what do you know? Your name's actually on it." He opened it and made a show of studying one particular line.

ASSOCIATE LIGHTING DESIGNER . . . . JANUARY INIESTA

"Nice," he said.

"Yeah, well, Rae wouldn't let it go," January said. "It was easier to cave."

The way Marc smiled at her, not like a little brother but like a proud big brother, made her want to hide in the shadows of the catwalk even as she wanted to soak it up.

January had her own name, and it meant something. Not just what everyone else made it mean or what they decided it meant, but what she made it mean. And maybe no one could understand that better than a man who'd named himself.

After that day, Marc kept coming back. He hung around the theater, held cables and PAR cans for January, enough that even January wasn't sure when he'd officially been hired. Her only clue was that instead of his usual jeans and gray or blue sweatshirt, he started showing up in all black (still jeans and a sweatshirt).

Like her, he wore a crescent wrench hanging on his belt loop from tie line, a multi-tool on the back of his pants. He deferred to her, asking what she wanted him to do next, but the rest of the crew figured out pretty quickly that he knew what he was doing. He knew how not to overload the dimmers. He knew what to yell when someone dropped something from the scaffold or when he had to kill the lights to check a captured channel.

Marc hadn't told January everything about the years he'd been gone, so she didn't know for sure how long he'd been in this line of work. But it was obvious that it had been awhile.

She wondered how long they'd been like that, both of them doing the work of staying in the dark. They threw bright washes onto people who wanted to be seen, staying behind the sources of light where no one, not even each other, would ever know they were there.

January could sometimes feel the rest of the crew watching them, how the two of them worked, orbiting around each other like binary planets. They handed each other the right wrench without having to ask. Without comment, they took the fiberglass twofers off each other's shoulders. When Marc was up on the catwalk, January was the one to go up with the alternate gel options before Marc even knew that the color might be a little off.

They shared a subtle language that might have made anyone watching think of twins, if the idea of Iverson twins didn't already make them think of June and July. June and July's shared language was a universe away from January and Marc's. June and July's was broad gestures, laughing, color, shimmer. It was aqua and red against January and Marc's sleek black and gray.

One holiday weekend, it was just them in the theater. January and Marc had volunteered to finish striking the lights after a show run, so everyone else didn't have to come in. Marc was above her, pulling the old gels out of the electrics. He let those pieces of translucent color waft down over her.

There was weight and gravity to it being just the two of them. Just the two of them meant that everyone in that theater at that moment knew who they'd been when they'd been the Iversons. They could be quiet. They could not smile. They could sink into the stillness of being unwatched.

January held out her arms, letting the little squares of amber and pink and blue rain down on her. They took a long time to fall, swirling on their way down. When Marc climbed to stage level, they were still falling.

Later, January would swear he had started it, them spinning through the drifting color. They grabbed gels off the stage floor and threw them, laughing as they ran at and away from each other.

When all the gels had fallen, they lay down on their backs on the marley. They fanned their arms and legs through the gels, the polycarbonate whispering like leaves or snow. They looked up, like the electrics above them were the sky.

we the unfollowers of Mother May I

Over the next months, it became clear that, downfall of Mother May I or not, May Iverson would be fine. A roster of lawyers and psychologists stood ready to fend off prosecutors and insurance company legal departments. She had done nothing wrong, they argued, and if she had done anything wrong, she could not, in good conscience, be held accountable.

The poor woman had been overworked, and plagued by an ungrateful daughter who'd been hell-bent on ruining the very mother who'd made her career possible. Amid all that had come the tragic shock of finding her dead husband.

May Iverson, they said, had not been in her right mind. The woman needed intense psychological help, for which, the lawyers emphasized, she would pay every penny. She would never dream of burdening the court or the taxpayers.

They were successful enough that instead of ending up in jail or with an ankle monitor, May Iverson ended up at a private center outside Tucson. The private villas featured light therapy chandeliers and individual plunge pools to clear the mind. As far as we could tell, it was a resort, just with four-figures-an-hour daily therapy. Their staff list showed more concierges, masseuses, and aestheticians than mental health professionals.

Whatever charges were brought against May Iverson, her lawyers buried them beneath massive quantities of paperwork and money. May Iverson sold the mansion quickly, despite it being a smoke-damaged husk. Infamy and runaway lot appreciation combined to net her a hefty profit. Whatever fines or restitution she paid didn't put a dent in her lifestyle. Within weeks of moving out of the mansion, she'd bought a villa in the Santa Ynez wine country.

The ad revenue from Mother May I was gone. But money gushed toward May Iverson as one of the quiet early investors in a multilevel marketing company that sold reversible skirts and dresses (neutral one side, loud print on the other, "great for packing, you get two whole outfits for the price—and space!—of one"). Every time a sales representative lost money on pieces she wouldn't be able to sell, May Iverson made a profit.

After her stay at the wellness center, May Iverson started dating an actor with enough cachet that it didn't matter who was on his arm as long as she was pretty. He came with enough scandals of his own that May Iverson's receded into the background. He'd once been so intoxicated he didn't realize he'd driven off the highway and over a sand dune until the surf splashed against his windshield. When he made his first million, he sent custom sculptures of his dick to the casting directors who'd passed on him (they were supposedly to scale, but we were pretty sure they involved generous artistic license). He'd been fined many times for illegally landing his private helicopter in a public park, scaring Little League teams, groups gathered for tai chi, and picnic table birthday parties.

We saw pictures of May alongside him at a red-carpet event, wearing a gown that streamed around her in a way that was almost Grecian, a moneyed Aphrodite look. Style commentators raved as though she'd invented classical revival. Not long after that, the actor proposed to her with a purebred golden retriever puppy, which she would pose with, inexplicably, while promoting rescue adoptions.

That was later, though. The first time May Iverson posted after deleting Mother May I, she came back as someone else. She not only wasn't Mother May I, she wasn't even May Iverson. She'd stuck her middle name, May, in a drawer, reverted to her given first name, Lily, and taken a new married name from her new actor husband.

Mother May I had fallen spectacularly, and the woman now known as Lily Kennedy stepped out of Mother May I as easily as molting a last-season evening gown. The blond of her hair was now a few shades darker. Her contouring looked geared toward making her face appear more angular. Clothing with harder edges and darker colors crept into her wardrobe; a close-fitting leather jacket paired with white pants. She was still glowing and tan in two-hundred-dollar T-shirts. She was still living in a house large enough that we would have needed a map to find the kitchen.

When we stopped watching, we hadn't really left Mother May I. But in one motion, smooth as the flick of a blending brush, May Iverson left behind not only us, but herself.

we who followed the Summer Girls

After everything came out about August and the house and the fire, July left us for a while. Or maybe left us is the wrong way to put it. She receded. She drew back, as though trying to get out of range of a camera's depth of field.

July sometimes appeared in one of June's posts, but the Summer Girls account mostly showed June now. July was a ghost in their joint business ventures. The seeming lack of ill will—they were still spotted fencing with wrapping-paper rolls at the local Target—suggested either that June liked running it on her own, or that July was doing whatever back-end work June found to be a tedious waste of her talents.

Even June took time away, saying she "wouldn't be posting for a little bit, but don't worry, I'll be back really soon." When she did come back, it was with what looked suspiciously like a baby bump. At first it was slight, showing only under tight T-shirts and when she wore swimsuits. Then it grew, bringing along sponsorships for maternity dresses and nipple moisturizer ("no one tells you you're gonna need this").

June said nothing about the father, or a boyfriend, or any kind of partner. She didn't seem to be dating anyone. But every article had a different theory. The father was this influencer, that entrepreneur, this singer, that actor, that reality-TV regular who really wanted to be an actor.

June offered recommendations for morning-sickness-reducing tea and shoes that were both flattering and adjustable ("If my boobs had grown in middle school as fast as my feet are growing now, I would've been homecoming queen"). Still nothing about the father. So the speculation went on. It was that surprise Oscar nominee with the cute dimples. It was a studio executive who was producing a feature film starring June. It was that weird rich guy who thought sending people to Mars would age them backward. It was that other weird rich guy who wanted to put in a racetrack specifically for luxury cars between Chicago O'Hare and the Magnificent Mile.

A couple of weeks before she delivered, the first and only time that she spoke directly about the life growing inside her, we found out why she wasn't revealing the father: the baby wasn't hers. "This is my body, and these are my choices, but this is not my baby, so I'm not gonna talk about the parents on here. You can ask me how I'm dealing with my swollen ankles and how I'm covering my delightful pregnancy acne, but please don't ask me about the parents."

It was only later, after the baby was born, that June referred to the baby as her nephew. "My big sister, she's gonna be the best mother ever. Those of you who watched us growing up, you know I'm right." After that, it was easy to put it together: June had been surrogating for April and her husband.

Months later, June made casual references to babysitting her nephew so her sister and her brother-in-law could have a date night— "Adorable, aren't they? That's what I want if I ever get married, a spouse who still wants me to dress up so they can take me out." But we never saw the baby on camera.

There was little doubt that June wanted to respect April's privacy. In all likelihood, though, she probably didn't mind the flurry of speculation during her pregnancy, how it drove her numbers. How she started to become known for a different mystery than whether she had murdered her stepfather. Her smile during those nine months blew past glowing. It was a mischievous crescent moon, as though she enjoyed the way we stirred ourselves up trying to guess what she wouldn't say.

we who hoped they'd all end up okay

No one could confirm this part. No one even knew for sure how anyone would have seen it. The prevailing explanation was that two roommates had been smoking in their street-parked car so they wouldn't be in violation of their lease.

On one of the streets up against the foothills, a boy in a gray sweatshirt and jeans walked up to a small house. He knocked on the door, holding two bouquets of flowers. Gerbera daisies the color of orange sherbet, wrapped in amethyst-blue paper. Tulips the purple of violet candy, sorrel-yellow paper.

He handed one to the older woman who answered the door. Her smile quirked as though she'd been expecting him.

He held out the second to a younger woman standing just inside the house.

There was no telling how anyone could have seen through the open door clearly enough to recognize the women, not from a car parked across the street. So if anyone did actually see, they got a lot closer than they were willing to admit.

But rumor had it that the older woman was Savanna, who had once made her living looking after the Iverson children. And the younger woman was her daughter, the one who had once fallen in love with the youngest Iverson, and, to her misfortune, the youngest Iverson had loved her back, enough that his mother had noticed.

We heard that the daughter stared at the young man in the doorway. She forgot to take the flowers, a reaction we read as shock. We believed someone could have seen that. Maybe even from across the street, if the light was right, the door still open. It would have been easier to follow a bouquet of bright flowers than to recognize a face for sure.

When she did take them—any witness would have had to be observing from the bushes at this point; people had done worse to watch the Iversons—the boy apparently returned his hands to the pockets of his jeans. The girl continued to stare at this boy, handsome in a way that looked familiar, husky in a way that didn't.

No one could confirm any of this. The closest we could get was someone who swore they knew someone who knew one of the roommates.

But we wanted to believe it.

We saw them together later. Not just Marc and Carolina. But Carolina and Savanna and the Iverson children, all of them this time. On a hiking trail in the foothills. In Ernesto Iniesta's driveway with handfuls of crepe-paper streamers. Watching the lotuses bloom in the park pond.

What happened with the necklace May had stolen from Savanna was up for debate. Some of us thought April gave it back to Savanna. Some of us heard that Marc had been spotted slipping it around Carolina's neck while kissing her. Some of us thought June had stolen it out of spite months ago, or that July had passed it into Savanna's palm like a secret.

The next time we saw it, it was not at May Iverson's throat. It rested in the curve of Carolina Montez's collarbone. When the sun hit it, a vein of bright blue flashed through the amethyst like a wink, like it knew we were watching.

we who grew up like the Iverson children

An entire front of influencers spoke out about Mother May I. Loudest among her critics were mothers just like her, ones with crystal-encrusted stiletto nails and the insistence that when it came to their children, they did everything. And fathers who turned their oldest daughters into substitute mothers so that their wives would be free for private-jet vacations. Parents who herded their own babies in front of the camera to model their personal lines of toddler attire, or to demonstrate their line of child-specific mirrors meant to instill self-confidence. Even Ashley Morgan Kelly eventually branched off from Fine Crime to promote her collection of diamond jewelry designed specifically with baby in mind.

What people sometimes forgot about May Iverson was that she was one of the first to turn her life, her family, her chronicled motherhood, into millions. And because of this, her children were some of the first to grow up with their lives documented, monetized, measured by click-through rates and engagement numbers.

But there were so many of us who came after them. There were so many of us whose parents saw Mother May I and thought *I could do that. I'm just as pretty as that woman. My children are just as cute as hers. My life is just as worthy of sponsorships and embedded ads.* So many of us ended up with our lives cut up into optimized posts.

There were hundreds—thousands—of parents waiting to push their children out in front of the world. We knew because they were our mothers and fathers, and we were too small to shrug them off. They were our parents, telling us that if we didn't smile, Mom and Dad wouldn't be able to keep the pendant lighting on in the new house.

A lot of us were watching when everything happened with August and the investigation. We had been watching this whole time, alongside the people we hated because they were so often also watching us.

Some of us, with rage and guilt curdling our insides, secretly wished our parents would fall as Mother May I had fallen.

Some of us watched May Iverson's children as though they would show us our own futures.

Some of us watched in solidarity, wanting to tell the Iverson children that they were not alone. We were here too. We lived with them in the middle space between existing as ourselves and existing as the products our own parents packaged us into. We did not realize we were reaching out toward them until our fingers brushed our screens, blue light filling our hands.

We had been like April, made into small parents because our own parents decided that such work was best delegated, that their time was better spent on brand meetings. We became small parents for small children even though we were still children ourselves. We grew into adults who did not know what colors or what kind of peanut butter we liked because there were too many other needs and wants to take into account. We grew into adults who did not know if we were okay because it was our job to make sure our younger siblings and our parents were okay.

We had been like June, performing with all the effervescent determination we had in us, because the look on our mothers' faces when we got it right made the whole world seem softer around the edges and made our whole beings seem worthy of a place in the universe.

We had been like July, our hearts crackling with bursts of protest, lightning arcs of *No, I don't want this* that then fizzled under the damp weight of what our parents expected of us. We grew compliant, and then hated ourselves for our own compliance, and the only thing we could do to dull that hatred was to make sure we looked pretty.

We had been like January, hiding from the lens, but then realizing that, without the chill of a camera on us, we weren't sure if we were really there. We weren't sure if we existed without someone seeing us, and it scared us how alluring we found that possibility, that if we could only hide, we could disappear.

We had been like Marc. We pulled in on ourselves because there were things about us that were so soft and fragile they might fall apart if anyone looked at them too closely.

Right now, some of us are too young to do anything but seethe, and wait. Right now, our fathers don't understand why we don't want our clumsiest soccer drills or toddler dance recitals posted online. Right now, our mothers call us *spoilsport* or *stick-in-the-mud* when we hold our open palms toward the cameras, as though our hands can shield not just our faces but everything we are.

Some of us are not quite sure why our skin crawls when we see the familiar finger flick of our parents opening their camera apps, their faces illuminated as they receive a prophetic vision of engagement numbers. We know the raw facts of what they're doing, spinning the straw of our bodies and beings into algorithmic gold. We just don't quite know how to explain it to everyone else. It's hard to show someone else the spinning wheel for what it is when it's going so fast that to everyone else it's nothing but motion blur.

Right now some of us are too small to say anything. Or too scared. We don't know how to work up the nerve to jam our hands into the wheel hard enough to stop it, to break it all apart, to send the splinters flying everywhere.

But we will.

disclaimer

The preceding has been a work of speculation.

All information, including that pertaining to the Iversons, their friends, relatives, neighbors, acquaintances, associates, enemies, rivals, peers, fans, sponsors, partners, and detractors, is presented as conjecture or opinion.

Any resemblance to other events, incidents, locations, or persons, living or dead, is entirely coincidental.

None of the foregoing is meant to be taken as assertion, accusation, or statement of fact.

We did the best we could with what we had. We made what we could of the Iversons.

It took months to lose the impulse to check what Mother May I had posted. While getting ready for a date, there was no rewatching her tutorial on "soft glam makeup for the rest of us." Her recipe for rosemary-mint simple syrup was still floating around out there, but we could no longer replay her making it in real time and follow along.

So many of us who had watched her now drifted through the feeling that our lives were a little less real without hers playing in the background. So many of us who had watched her had been shadow versions of her, trying the same craft projects, flicking the mascara wand like she did, following her recipe for homemade French-fried onions.

It was impossible not to encounter her sometimes, like finding a forgotten sweatshirt, a lost pair of socks, or a nearly empty bottle of aftershave left by a past boyfriend. When an indoor plant looked ready to give up on life, it was impossible not to remember that she'd had a series on how to revive them. When an ill-fated shopping trip resulted in the purchase of a skirt so loudly patterned it could have been spotted from the International Space Station, there was the memory of her advice on mixing neutral classics with trend pieces.

Mother May I now lived only in screenshots, reposted content, articles, commentary. She did not exist on her own anymore. When May Iverson deleted Mother May I, she hadn't realized she was leaving her to us. We would make her out of what we remembered.

All that would be left of Mother May I was everything we would say.

Acknowledgments

There are many people who supported the process of writing this story and who transformed it into the book you're reading. Here, I'll name a few.

Whitney Frick and Avideh Bashirrad, for welcoming this story to Dial. My editor, Katy Nishimoto, for her enthusiasm for the heart of this book and her vision for what it could become. JP Woodham for the fantastic notes (and whose Lady Macbeth insights made a whole scene click). Donna Cheng and Cassie Gonzales for giving this book a cover that's both stunning and an invitation into the story. Debbie Glasserman and Simon Sullivan for the gorgeous interior design. Meghan O'Leary and Robert Siek for the thousand moving parts that are the book production process. Julie Ehlers for the copyediting. JoAnne Kremer and Chuck Thompson for the proofreading. Lauren Klein for the audiobook production. Debbie Aroff, Jordan Hill Forney, and Vanessa DeJesus, thank you for helping readers find this book and helping this book find its readers. To the entire team at Dial/Random House, thank you for turning stories into beautiful books.

Michael Bourret, who not only championed this story but helped me work through the narrative puzzles of those early drafts. Mike Whatnall, Lauren Abramo, Nataly Gruender, Andrew Dugan, Gracie Freeman-Lifschutz, and the entire DGB team. Mary Pender, Olivia Fanaro, Celia Albers, Daniel Beracha, and the team at UTA.

Parrish Turner, whose rock-solid guidance I've relied on before and relied on again for this novel.

Heather Thomas and Melissa Wiese, for your friendship, and for the conversations that started it all.

My mom, for sharing my vice of reality TV. My dad, for putting up with it from both of us.

Readers, both those reading my work for the first time, and those who've read my YA and who've come with me to this book. It's with you that stories come to life.

ABOUT THE AUTHOR

ANNA-MARIE MCLEMORE (they/them) is the author of eleven novels for young adults, including William C. Morris YA Debut Award finalist *The Weight of Feathers,* Stonewall Honor Book *When the Moon Was Ours, New York Times* Editors' Choice *Blanca & Roja,* Lambda Literary Award finalist *Lakelore,* and National Book Award nominees *The Mirror Season* and *Self-Made Boys. The Influencers* is their adult debut.

annamariemclemore.com
X: @LaAnnaMarie

ABOUT THE TYPE

This book was set in Berling. Designed in 1951 by Karl-Erik Forsberg (1914–95) for the type foundry Berlingska Stilgjuteri AB in Lund, Sweden, it was released the same year in foundry type by H. Berthold AG. A classic old-face design, its generous proportions and inclined serifs make it highly legible.